The Childhood of Sherlock Holmes

The Childhood
of
Sherlock Holmes

Mona Morstein

2000
Galde Press, Inc.
Lakeville, Minnesota, U.S.A.

First Edition
First Printing, 2000

Cover by Jason Beam

Library of Congress Cataloging-in-Publication Data
Morstein, Mona, 1961–
    The childhood of Sherlock Holmes : the butler's tale / Mona Morstein. —
1st ed.
        p.   cm.
    Includes bibliographical references.
    ISBN 1–880090–079–1
        I. Title.
    PS3563.O8815 C47 1999
    813'.54 21—dc21   99–041708

Galde Press, Inc.
PO Box 460
Lakeville, Minnesota 55044–0460

I would like to dedicate this book to the three men who had the greatest impact in my creation of it:

My father, for being a wonderful parent, and telling me he loved my spirit and had confidence that I would make him proud by succeeding at whatever I attempted;

Jeremy Brett, for his excellent portrayal of Sherlock Holmes, which caused me to develop my total obsession with the Master Detective;

Patrick Macnee, who is one of the few actors who has played both Holmes and Watson (as has Jeremy Brett), but who is best known for being John Steed in *The Avengers* television show. With consummate flair, Mr. Macnee created such a complex and evolving character that I became enamored of, and fascinated by, Steed. Spending innumerable enjoyable years imagining the entire life story of that fictional secret agent nurtured and promoted my creativity (and still does), and prepared me to create the childhood of Sherlock Holmes, once he, like Steed, took pleasant hold in my mind.

Contents

A Simple Gift

How did I come by this manuscript? I know it's Sherlockian tradition to explain to one's readers how a story like this was given to the supposed author. My explanation is lacking in melodrama and intrigue, so I feel there is no need to go into minute detail with it. Suffice it to say, I received the handwritten tale from a friend as a gift, the friend being a great granddaughter of Mr. Cobbett. Her grandmother had inherited a certain briefcase, with a certain package in it, which when unwrapped was found to be the story of the childhood of Sherlock and Mycroft Holmes. Uninterested family members played hot potato with the manuscript for generations, until it reached the home and closet of my friend. She, quite honestly, gave it to me for my birthday once we reconnected after having fallen out of contact for years, and I shared with her my newly found Sherlockian passion. I did not undervalue what had fallen into my astonished hands, and decided to publish the tale under my name.

That's it. I'm sorry I cannot dazzle you with a more involved etiology, but that is the way it happened. Enjoy!

Chapter One
Wiggins

This is both an account of my search to uncover the hidden history of Sherlock Holmes and a biography of the detective's singular childhood. It has taken me some little time to discover the participants who were able help me uncover the story of his past, but the investigative labour was indeed worth it, for the tale they told is extraordinary.

My interest with Mr. Holmes began long before most of the general public's. As an eleven-year crime reporter with *The Guardian,* I was a familiar face and trusted acquaintance at Scotland Yard by 1875. The first time I remember hearing Mr. Holmes' name was in the spring of 1879 when I was talking to young Inspector Lestrade about a series of unsolved robberies north of Kensington Gardens. Lestrade was man of middle height and a slight build, with a face that somewhat resembled a rat, narrow, thin, and pointed. He mentioned casually he had to leave for an appointment with a young man named Holmes. When I inquired who this Mr. Holmes was, Lestrade pursed his lips, put his hands in his waistcoat pockets, made me guarantee none of this would see the printed page, and assumed the rocking pose of an instructor teaching a college course.

"This chap Holmes walked into the Yard a couple of years ago during the investigation of the theft of Mrs. Farintosh's opal tiara. You probably didn't hear about the case as Mr. Farintosh requested it be kept in the strictest confidence. I had been assigned that case—one of my first as an inspector, mind you—and I must say it was coming along quite well, if a little slowly. We had narrowed the suspects down to either her husband's valet or the exterminator who had been hired to rid the house of an unfortunate amount of mice. Well, this Mr. Holmes, and a thinner chap I've never seen outside a hospital, walks into the Yard three days after the crime, is shown to my office, and says he's been asked by Mrs. Farintosh to look into the affair himself. I asked in what capacity has he been acting and he says 'as a private consulting detective.' Hmmf! A private consulting detective, whatever that is! He then goes on to state he can positively identify the thief as being the daughter's fiancee, and relates to me his findings and his explanation of the events of the crime to the very moment when the criminal stopped to put his shoes back on! Well, I decided to play along, so as not to upset Mrs. Farintosh you see, and I must say that luck was certainly with Mr. Holmes that day, for the tiara was found hidden in a hollowed-out book in the middle of the fiancee's drawing room bookshelf. This Mr. Holmes has some very fanciful and peculiar ideas about crime-solving that have occasionally been of some little aid in several minor cases. You couldn't really call him friendly, and his digs are a mess, but I think I'll go and see how he's been getting on lately and have a brief chat with him."

It was surely more than a coincidence that Lestrade arrested the long-sought robbers the next time they struck two days later, although if one had perused all the city daily newspapers' accounts of the successful ending of that crime spree, one would not have seen any mention of Mr. Sherlock Holmes.

Here and there from different inspectors and constables I kept hearing about Mr. Holmes and his "peculiar" ideas, and once in the autumn of 1880 I passed him as he left the Yard. A noticeably tall and extremely lean young man came barging through the door, clearly angry and mumbling to himself (I made out the word "idiots"), and took off walking as fast as I ever thought a man could move.

Of course, once Dr. Watson's stories came out years later, the general public immediately became enamoured with this brilliant private consulting detective. It was after the publication of "The Final Problem" in *The Memoirs of Sherlock Holmes* in December 1893 that I decided I should like to uncover more about Mr. Holmes—do a series of biographical articles on him, and especially try to uncover his secretive childhood. I am not ashamed to state that I was fascinated with the powers and the enigma of Sherlock Holmes, and felt the public would eagerly purchase papers that carried discoveries of his past. My editors agreed on my views although they stated they thought it was a hopeless cause—Holmes was dead, and his youthful years a mystery seemingly even shrouded from his best friend, Dr. John Watson, as he related several months earlier in "The Greek Interpreter." Still, to my pleasure, they allowed me to attempt an investigation.

Holmes' disdain for reporters had been renowned, and all writers who had approached him had met with the strongest, and often rudest, rebuffs. Still, some reporters continued to endeavour to interview Mr. Holmes, until an infamous incident with Edward Miller of the *Evening Standard News* quickly made the rounds of the city's news gatherers.

In that brief exchange in 1890, Miller accosted Holmes on the street as Holmes was returning home and was relentless in his questioning of Holmes about aspects of the recently published "The Sign of Four." Holmes studiously ignored the man as he strode towards 221B. Miller, a large, muscular man, had the audacity to stand right in front of Holmes, charging him to answer his questions.

By this time a small crowd had gathered out of curiosity. Holmes came to a stop, and looked Miller directly in the eyes. In one long breath and a voice loud enough to project down the entire street stated, "Mr. Miller, I fail to see why I should be bothered and harassed by the likes of a man who spent the whole of last night imbibing until very drunk while losing what little money he had to his other addiction of gambling as his poor wife lay on her deathbed."

They say Miller shrank like a poorly washed shirt, slid off into the crowd, and didn't show up at work for a week. Holmes had, of course, been right on target on all accounts, although even Miller's friends had not been aware of his excessive gambling and his mortally ill wife. Normally, such a public dressing down would have been fuel for hours of unremittent joking among reporters at the pubs we frequented. However, no reporter teased Miller; we all had our own problems and secrets we hid from sight. Holmes' uncanny and shaming exposure of Miller's concealed life chilled us rather than stimulated our usual ebullient camaraderie. All reporters left Mr. Holmes very much alone after that. It is therefore understandable that I have never sought Mr. Sherlock Holmes' help with this biography, although I was still engaged in the work of it after he returned from his three-year hiatus (for we reporters and the police knew about his reappearance right away). Confronting the man in person was frightening to me, and, although I had little to conceal from the world at large, I never had the desire to have him look me directly in the eyes.

I have since come to realise that my very first move along the lines of charting Holmes' biography was to become my exposé's final, fatal downfall. Since Holmes was supposedly dead, I reasoned his brother Mycroft would be a valid beginning point. There was a tiny chance that this terribly unsocial, incredibly private man might just want to help immortalise further his younger brother's name now that he had valiantly died protecting the innocent of Great Britain.

With nothing to lose, I presented myself to the doorman of the Diogenes Club with a note for Mycroft Holmes. To my great surprise, actually (and no doubt to the even greater surprise of the doorman), Mycroft Holmes allowed me to be led up to see him in his office in the Diogenes Club.

I noticed immediately that Dr. Watson had been correct—it was only the depth and brilliancy of the eyes that unmistakably connected Sherlock and the remarkably corpulent Mycroft as brothers. Otherwise, from Mycroft's girth; large, fleshy hands; and his slow and phlegmatic nature one would never have considered the two men were siblings. Mycroft Holmes sat me down in a plush leather chair, served me a drink, and patiently let me explain my ideas in regard to the posthumous biography I was planning.

He was fully attentive and not unpleasant, even though he himself politely begged off from being of assistance. Although he respected my desire to learn more of his brother, he certainly could not break a confidence Sherlock had evidently decided to establish for whatever reasons he had chosen. He did try to dissuade me from my biography, saying that all their relatives were unfortunately deceased, Sherlock had never been that interested in making friends even as a lad, and so forth. He strongly suggested I had chosen an impossible task to perform before which I was no doubt inevitably destined to fail.

"Why, even I don't know all the details of his life!" Mycroft Holmes exclaimed, as he reached for another sweet from the large silver dish of them sitting on his cherry-wood desk.

When I shrugged my shoulders and said I'd learned some ways to uncover information as a reporter of twenty-six years, he stood, led me to the great paneled mahogany door of his office, and wished me well in my inquiries.

It took a lot of time. But, as a widower with children grown and married, and with the support of the newspaper's editors, I had innumerable hours to put into the research. As you can imagine, I was starting from the ground floor—I didn't even know where in England Holmes had been born.

My brief visit with Dr. Watson at his Kensington home availed me nothing. Since the recent and tragic death of his sweet and gentle wife, Dr. Watson had become as asocial to reporters as Holmes had been. He was a portly man with a thick mustache and a genial, friendly face that was overshadowed with heavy lines and a darkness that betrayed his heartfelt sorrow. However, when I honestly stated my aims were solely to further lionise Holmes, not to castigate him, some of Watson's natural and unending decency surfaced, and amid a brief chat over cigars, he admitted that sadly he really didn't know about Holmes' childhood at all. He really had no leads for me to go on, assured me Mrs. Hudson knew even less about Holmes than he did, and didn't know anyone to refer me to for an interview. I had no wish to overstay my visit, for it seemed that the double burden of death he had experienced over the last few years had aged and tired him. His lost and saddened look into the fireplace was the last image I had of him as his servant girl led me to his front door, whereupon I descended the steps and re-entered the foggy January air.

Weeks spent with the shopkeepers in the Baker Street environs proved fruitless. I was met with frosty stares by Capital and Cox bank executives (Dr. Watson had told me Holmes' bank), and all inspectors or constables I conferred with were clueless. I almost suffered the indignity of getting a door slammed in my face by Mrs. Hudson (the good Dr. Watson aside, I had to try; she didn't even tell me that his rooms were still being paid for). And to my consternation, Cambridge, Oxford, and London Universities, and Bartholomew's Hospital, denied ever having had a Sherlock Holmes on their student lists. Neither did they show a Reginald Musgrave nor a Victor Trevor, and another brief visit to Dr. Watson garnered me the knowledge that those were the names that Holmes had mentioned to him, though he was absolutely unsurprised to learn they were aliases. Telegraphs to Conan Doyle at Davos, Switzterland, were fruitless as Doyle assured me Holmes' childhood days were a solid mystery to him; he just rewrote the stories that Dr. Watson sent him. The weeks continued to pass and I had not obtained one iota of useful information about Holmes.

It was because of a mere whim I finally obtained my first major lead at the end of January 1892. I had taken the underground back once again to Baker Street and had spent a few hours walking around the neighbourhood. It was a windy day, with flurries of light snow falling, but still I stood for a moment by 221B lost in thought when I saw four young boys running and skirmishing in the wintry weather. That was when I realised I had left out tracking down the only known associates I knew Holmes had possessed, his Baker Street Irregulars.

It took me two weeks of asking every young boy I met, in an ever-increasing circle from Holmes' digs, to finally find one dirty, scruffy eight-year-old, who for a shilling, told me he knew a lad that had helped Mr. Holmes on a number of occasions. For another shilling he'd take me to him.

I eagerly paid, and was led to the Underground, where my two purchased tickets took us to Aldgate. A short walk from the station and we were on Gravel Lane. On the second floor of a dark and dirty apartment building, the lad Tommy knocked on an unnumbered door.

It was opened by a woman, still remarkably youthful in appearance, her brown hair piled high on her head, her cheeks smooth and rosy-hued, a few extra pounds and a scattering of lines at her eyes the only indications of her true age. Her dress was old but not ragged, and there was deportment to her, a straightness of spine and firmness of lips, that illustrated a certain pride in herself that belied the misery of her poverty.

Tommy took off his cloth cap. "Mrs. Wiggins, ma'am, is Jimmy here? This gen'lman is wantin' to see him."

Mrs. Wiggins regarded me through suddenly narrowed eyes. "Why do you want to see him, sir?" she asked.

"I assure you, madam, I mean no harm to your boy. I am interested solely in talking to him about his previous work with Mr. Sherlock Holmes, about whom I am writing a story for my newspaper." I showed her my credentials as a reporter. "I am willing to be generous in my payment for such information."

Although my heart was beating fiercely in anticipation, I somehow managed to maintain my composure and uttered the words with a careless ease. I did not want them to know how important this was to me—I remembered Holmes' similar words of advice to Watson after he garnered vital information from the poor Mrs. Mordecai Smith in "The Sign of the Four."

A voice from behind Mrs. Wiggins rang out, "Lemme talk to him, ma." Glancing around her, I was able to glimpse five children. An unwashed lad of about fifteen, brown-haired and cheery-faced, and too long for his clothes had spoken those earnest words. Mrs. Wiggins continued to look straight at me.

" 'Ow much ya willin' ta pay?" she asked.

"Oh, a guinea to get started, and more depending on the value of the information." I took out my pocket watch and looked at the time. "But I have other people to talk to, madam, and appointments to be met, so I need to know now if you'll allow him to come speak with me."

"A guinea!" Jimmy shouted.

I heard the other children in the background whisper their delight and disbelief. Mrs. Wiggins smiled and looked demurely at her feet. "Well, that is very generous, sir. Jimmy'll tell you all he can, I'm sure."

At that Jimmy burst around his mother's side and into the hallway, pulling his tattered coat on over his thin shoulders. "Let's go, sir."

I explained to Mrs. Wiggins that I'd be taking Jimmy to my home, and that he'd be back in several hours. I paid her the one guinea as stated and gave Tommy a few bob to take the Underground back to where I'd found him.

I was almost giddy with excitement. You see, I do not feel it is too fantastic to say that as soon as I had thought of tracking down the Irregulars, my reporter's instincts, which I will not be unjustly describing as well-developed and finely honed, erupted like a volcano. I somehow knew in my bones that Jimmy held the key to get me started on my investigation.

I took Jimmy back to my home in Bayswater, not to my office, for I did not want his mind distracted by the hubbub and chaos of a busy newspaper organization. Mrs. Darrick, my housekeeper, greeted us at the door and took our coats. I saw a glow in Jimmy's eyes as I requested tea, milk, sandwiches, and sweets. I led Jimmy into my study at the back of the ground floor, and we sat in facing chairs before an unlit fireplace. Moira, my only other servant, quickly came in and with her usual efficiency soon had the fire blazing. After Mrs. Darrick and the tray arrived, I dismissed her and poured tea for myself and milk for Jimmy.

"Help yourself. Don't be shy," I said, motioning to the food as I handed him a plate.

He paused for a second, as if to ensure I wasn't going to immediately renounce my offering, and then with the gusto and lack of inhibition of a fifteen-year-old lad soon had his plate overladen with some of the meat sandwiches, and much of the sweets.

I let him eat heartily for a few minutes, smiling each time he glanced at me in between focusing on his food and twisting his body to observe the surroundings of my study with an intensity that amazed me.

"Oy, you've boxed some like Mr. Holmes, yerself," he said, with surprising clarity through his mouthful of food. "But yer weren't too good, were you?"

I was blatantly surprised and blinked several times. "How...?"

"The gloves and yer nose," he explained, shrugging his shoulders and tossing his head off in the direction to where a battered old pair of boxing gloves, tied together, hung from a nail under some bookshelves. He then pointed a finger at my face. "How many times was it broken?"

Like a child trying to cover up some disobedient act from his parents, my hand rose to my nose and felt the slight bump deforming it. "Not that many," I laughed. I leaned forward with my hands on my knees. "What else do you see?"

"Oh, not much," said the lad, placing the empty plate back on the tray and finishing up his milk. "It's not like I'm Mr. Holmes, you know. But..." Here he paused to look right and left, as if he wanted to ensure there were no spies in the room with us. "But, I'd also say, yer right-handed, and wrote an 'urried letter this morning. Yer a widower, two children, and you still grieve over yer wife's death some years ago. Yer not very social, like, and spend a lot o' time home reading." The lad snorted in glee and sat back in self-satisfied triumph, grinning from ear to ear, and slapping his hands on his thighs. Then he raised his eyebrows and with an endearing innocence asked, "Am I right Mr. Cobbett, am I right about any o' it? Mr. Holmes said I was a good student, he said I was. Not like in math or book stuff, I ain't had much study of 'em, but in observin' and deducin'. I try to do just like he taught me, but I don't have a bit o' the brains he did, so I sometimes have to guess. But, I'd never tell him I was guessin'; Lord, he hated that."

I was frankly astounded, and much to the boy's discomfort I sat staring at him for some moments as I attempted to rally my stunned faculties. Edward Miller illuminated my disjointed mentation. So this is what it feels like, I ruminated, to be laid so bare before a stranger. While truly fascinated at the veracity of the lad's comments, I felt starkly naked, like someone had discovered and plundered my innermost thoughts. I endeavoured to compose myself by my old habits of checking my cravat, pulling down firmly on my waistcoat, and sitting up straighter in my chair.

"Yes, well, um...actually, Jimmy, all of what you said is, well, true." I cleared my throat, which was actually very dry, and assumed an outward relaxed affectation by leaning casually back into the chair and crossing my legs. Inwardly, I felt as if there was a hive of excited bees buzzing around under my skin.

"Ha! That's great! That's just great, sir," Jimmy exclaimed.

"Yes, it is quite wonderful, son," I concurred. "Now, if you wouldn't mind, I should be very interested to learn how you…deduced, or guessed, such things about me."

"Well," Jimmy said, beaming all the while, "It's really quite simple."

I smiled. "Yes, I'm sure it is. But, still, I'd like to know."

The lad stood up and began to walk across the room. Suddenly he felt the impropriety of his action and turned to me. "If you don't mind, sir?"

"Not at all. Please continue."

Jimmy strode over to my desk in the corner, by the edge of the window. "I first looked at yer desk and saw the ink jar on the right side o' the writin' pad. Then I saw the pen lyin' on the pad, with the nib, here, pointin' to the jar. Well, only a right-handed man would lay a pen down, nib toward the right, see?" Here he imagined holding a pen, writing, and then putting it down with his right hand. "See, a left-handed chap would put it down towards the left. Then I thought, why this guv'nor's a reporter and so would take good care o' his writin' instruments, so as to make 'em last and all, seein' as how his livelihood and all depended on it. Also, the rest o' yer study here is pretty tidy, like. So, when I saw the pen lyin' down next to its holder, not in it, I figured you'd probably written off a letter in a rush earlier today, and without thinkin' had just laid the pen down, instead o' placin' it back in its holder, like I figure you prob'ly usually do, bein' a professional, as it were."

He paused. "Am I right so far?"

"So far you are." Generally I am most assiduous in the care I give my printing utensils. However, I had been about to leave the house that morning to cover the accidental death of an earl's son, when I remembered I needed to cancel a lunch date arranged with a reporter friend over a month ago. I hastily composed the most courteous last-minute cancellation I could think of, handed the letter to Mrs. Darrick to be posted immediately, and ran out the door. The pen never got replaced in my careless rush.

Jimmy nodded his head a few times, and drifted off into his own thoughts momentarily. Catching himself, he snapped back to attention and pointed at the mantel.

"That photograph o' you with three little ones shows you was married once, assumin' they're yer children, which yer look o' affection towards 'em clearly shows to be true and assumin' that, uh, well, that…" He flushed a little and thrust his hands into his pockets.

"Assuming I did not have the children out of wedlock," I finished for him.

He grinned. "Right. See, in the picture, yer left hand is restin' on yer lad's shoulder and so hides a view o' a weddin' ring."

"It is a safe assumption that the children are not illegitimate."

Jimmy took a deep breath and continued with renewed fervour. "All right, so the photograph shows you with three little ones. So you were married at one time, but yer wife died young, I figure, 'cause otherwise she would've been in the photograph with you and yer kids. Then the other photo down the mantel shows yer kids are about ten years older, and that photo is several years old by the looks o' it, bein' yellowed. So you've been a widower for a long time now, it seems to me. Now, I don't see no photograph o' your wife at all in the room, though I see you do wear a weddin' band. I don't think you remarried 'cause when we came into the house, you didn't ask yer housekeeper about no, uh, new Mrs. Cobbett." Jimmy stood straight up and put his hands behind his back. "So, I runs all that through me head, and deduces that you don't want no picture o' yer wife abouts 'cause it's too painful to look at her, 'cause you still miss her deeply. And you keep on wearin' the ring to avoid the attentions o' other women. 'Cause yer not interested in courtin' no one else."

I have to give this to the lad: he spoke it all most quietly and gently.

I broke the silence finally. "Quite so, lad. Quite so." After a few more bittersweet memories left my head, I asked, "And what about the reading?"

The lad shrugged. "Oh, that's easy." He pointed to the armchair I sat in. "That chair yer in looks almost brand new, but when we came into the room I noticed the cushion is already squashed down where you sit in it, night after night. There's a book on the little table next to the chair, and a bunch o' magazines in that rack right there on the floor. So I…guessed you stayed at home mostly and read a lot."

Jimmy sat back down in his chair. He assumed that faraway look again he had had by the desk. I waited patiently for him to speak further. Suddenly he began pouring out his heart to me in a river of words, his eyes growing moist.

"I can't believe he's dead. I can't believe it. I've seen him in disguises so perfect I don't even think he knew who he was sometimes. I've seen him fight three toughs who were pickin' on Susie and her sister. He was a lot stronger than he looked, ya know, and could do these funny moves so that it was really hard to hit him. Boy, though, when he hit one of 'em, they were stunned, like." He made fists with his hands and pantomimed throwing several punches, "Bam! Bam!" then let his arms fall to his sides. "It was amazin' to see. Them hooligans left the lasses alone after that, by God."

He paused, legs twitching with excess energy, crossed his arms, and leaned against the back of the chair. "I've heard him talk in about every differ'nt accent there is, I suppose. Sometimes he would let me follow him around when he was just kind o' walkin' and checkin' out the streets. My ma knew I was safe with him. He would tutor me, like, in learnin' how to observe things and deduce—as he called it—from 'em. He said he thought I was pretty good at times. Once he showed me how I could pick out sailors and solicitors, and people with heart problems, which is none too easy with that last group 'cause it can show up in several differ'nt ways, you know."

"Way back in early April 1891, just before he died, Mr. Holmes came to me one last time, and said he might not see me and the Irregulars again, 'cause he had to take care o' the gang o' criminals he'd been watchin' for a few years, and it was goin' to be dangerous as could be. He told me to keep observin' and thinkin', that I had some talent in doin' 'em. He asked me to keep quiet about him, if he didn't come back, warnin' me that some blokes might come sniffin' around askin' questions 'bout him, until I was sure he was dead. If'n I knew for sure he was dead he said I could talk if I had to if someone I trusted found me out. Then he thanked me for helpin' him out all those times and he shook me hand. He shook me hand just like that. I've been quiet for three years, now, just waitin' for him to come lookin' for us Irregulars. Just to keep me eyes sharp, I follow a chap every now and then. My sister reads better than me and it was her who read me 'The Final Problem.' Now I can talk. But I wish I couldn't. I just can't believe he's dead."

Jimmy's tears were falling steadily by the time his tender monologue was over. Call it callous, or call it being a reporter, but throughout all his sincere and plaintive outburst I had been writing as fast as I could to keep up with his reminiscing. One sign of a veteran reporter is an outward show of neutrality even during the most extreme of statements; this is often incorrectly interpreted as coldness or lack of concern. Jimmy saw me in my notebook, scribbling away evenly, apparently not affected by his sorrow.

"What exactly do yer want to know about him from me?" he asked warily, as he wiped the tears of his face. "I won't talk bad about him at all, if yer want to stain his name. I've turned others away these last three years, nosy folk I wouldn't give a broken bottle to, and I can turn you away, too."

I finished writing and said softly, "I assure, you, Jimmy, that I am just trying to find out about his childhood years because I think people would be interested. I also had great respect for the man, and only want to honour his name, not smear it. I'm hoping that you might have some clue to get me started in my investigation, but any information you can share about him may be helpful. I promise you can believe me when I say I have no intention of besmirching Mr. Holmes' reputation at all."

Jimmy took a couple of deep breaths as he thought over my words. "All right, you seem a decent sort, so I'll trust you. But, I don't know if I've got the information you want. Mr. Holmes was never a very talkative gent. Off the top o' me head, I can't think o' anything 'bout his childhood he might've said." I'm sure Jimmy could see my disappointment as I could not help but frown at his statement. He quickly continued, "But, I think I'll remember things easier and more completely, like, if I can keep it all in order in me mind, and tell it like it happened."

That made complete sense as we were talking about events at least three years in the past. Perhaps once he began recollecting those times some hint or clue would naturally slip out and become my biography's cornerstone. "That'll be fine," I agreed.

Jimmy leaned back in his chair and tented his fingers together. "Well, it's funny, but me cousin, me older brother, and meself have all worked for Mr. Holmes. It started with me cousin Jacky, who worked for Mr. Holmes when he first started up the Irregulars back in '79. Jacky was twelve then. He was the chief fellow durin' that 'Study in Scarlet' case, the first story o' Mr. Holmes what got published. Me older brother Bob joined the Irregulars three years later, and took over when Jacky joined the Navy the next year. I first joined the Irregulars in '86, when I was seven. Me brother was still the leader o' the Irregulars, then, and he's the Wiggins what Dr. Watson wrote about in 'The Sign o' the Four,' but I was in the group o' lads searchin' for the boat, too. We sure swelled out like risin' bread from seein' ourselves in print, you can bet. Well, when me poor brother died o' the diphtheria in '88, I took over as boss, 'cause though I was only nine Mr. Holmes said I had a good eye and, and..." Jimmy scrunched his face up as he searched for the correct word. "Potential. That's it, he said I got potential, the most o' any Irregular he ever worked with. Some o' the other lads, older lads, was a little put out by me bein' boss, but Mr. Holmes' word was the law. So I was the boss from then on."

The pride shone from the lad's eyes like twin suns. "See, I had the most potential," he restated, more to himself, it seemed, than for my benefit.

Suddenly he pointed at my writing pad. "You gettin' all this?"

"Yes," I assured him.

He appeared dubious and stretched his neck out to observe my scribblings. I turned the notepad around and showed the sentences to him for assurance. "I write very quickly, Jimmy. In shorthand. Please continue."

"Well, it's not like we worked for him all the time, you know. He would hire us mainly as lookouts when he had the need, and if it wasn't too dangerous. Like with 'The Crooked Man.' He also had us follow a lot o' fellows around. He taught us how to do it without bein' seen. Sometimes he'd play tricks on us to test our 'bilities. Like, the first time he did, he said at six o'clock a Lascar in a red scarf would leave a certain lodgin' house, and that we was to follow him wherever he went until 9:00 P.M., when we was to meet back at a pub we often used as a meetin' place. That Lascar was a right mean-lookin' tough, with a knife scar half 'cross his chin. He fair walked halfway 'round the East End, meetin' with several ruffians what looked scarier than him. He went into one pawn shop and stayed there until we had to get to the pub. So then we went to meet Mr. Holmes at the back o'

O'Reilly's—it's over there on Bell Lane in Spitalfields—to report in, and there was the Lascar snarlin' and drinkin' by himself! When he saw me, he waved me over, gruff-like, and I just stood there frozen in fear for me very life, I do admit. I was worried about Mr. Holmes, and had frightful thoughts that the Lascar had done him in somehow there in the pawn shop, where he'd been for so long. Then the Lascar waved me over again! I took a few steps nearer; the other lads stayed back, ready to run for the coppers if need be. When I got to the Lascar, he leaned forward and whispered, 'It's me, Wiggins.' It was Mr. Holmes! I jumped back like a frog, my cap flyin' from me 'ead. He fooled us a number o' times, I tell you, in differ'nt ways; half for us to build our skills, he said, and half, I think for himself, 'cause I think he enjoyed gettin' all dressed up, and playin' tricks on us. But then once I caught him at it."

At that I stopped writing in my notepad and looked at him askance. Jimmy immediately noted my curious skepticism and clapped his hands together. "Ha! I got yer interest now, don't I?" I found myself liking this lad immensely—his openness, his own gift for deduction, his intelligence, his friendliness, all combined in conferring upon him my highest regard. He had a voice that was smooth and easy to listen to, unlike the rough-toned and derogatory-laden vernacular so often unfortunately encountered in the poor and uneducated. He seemed to choose his words carefully; if Holmes had no doubt also instructed him on the art of reporting concisely and clearly, he had learned that lesson impressively. And it seemed that he was grateful for an audience, hungry for one, almost, for what he shared about Holmes was plainly dear to him.

"Yes, I am definitely interested. How did you catch him?"

"Well, it was June 12, 1890"—here the lad flushed a little at the recital of the exact date—"I was just ten and me and the lads had been mudlarkin' all day. I was walkin' home alone with a few pence in me pocket from a couple bits o' coal and wood I was lucky enough to find and sell. In the alley close to home I nears this old drunk, all filthy and in rags, sittin' on a box, drinkin' gin out o' a bottle in one hand and smokin' a pipe out o' the other. He coughs and spits some gin up all over himself. As I walk passed him he growls, "I know you. Yer young Wiggins, and yer cousin sails the Indie seas."

"Well, that makes me stop and look at him. I take a step closer to him, and give him a good once over. I don't recognise him. "Who are you?" I ask.

"Just an old man, trying to hold back the chill," he answers, slurrin' his words, and wavin' the bottle around, spillin' some more gin onto himself. But I felt in me bones there was something both familiar and wrong with him. And how did he know who I was?

"It hit me in the gut so hard I almost had to sit down. 'Mr. Holmes!' I fairly yelled at him.

"He stood up so smoothly and quickly I leapt two steps back and felt my heart skip a beat. 'Excellent, Wiggins,' he says, pullin' off his wig and beard. The beard must've itched fiercely, for he spent some moments scratchin' his face. Then he looked down at me and said, "Really, that was most excellent. You're coming along quite well. Tell me, how did you figure it out so quickly?"

"He began walkin' down the alley and I had to run to catch up to him. 'Well, it was a couple o' things, sir,' I says. He just keeps walkin' so I go on. 'I recognised yer pipe and the smell o' yer tobacco. But I still thought you were just an acquaintance o' Jacky's who knew me family somehow—almost every navvie smokes a pipe, and that briar is a common one. And most all navvie's got the drinkin' bad. You know Jacky got the gin habit himself. But then I got closer and didn't smell no gin on you.' He kept on walkin', sayin' nothin'. 'I mean,' I added, 'it must have been water in the bottle if you coughed it up on yerself, and spilled it on yerself, and you didn't smell like gin. So you must've have been just foolin' at bein' a drunk. And yer the only one who knows Jacky and would try to fool me like that, so I...deduces it had to be you.'

"He didn't say anything for a few more steps, until we had reached my apartment buildin'. Then he looked at me and gave me one o' his quick little smiles. 'Decidedly well done, Wiggins. You have risen to the heights tonight. Now, I shall be in need of you and two other Irregulars tomorrow evening. Will it be possible for you to accommodate me along the lines of seven o'clock, at the back of O'Reilly's pub? Same rate of pay.'

"I stayed up all night repeatin' in my mind 'Decidedly well done, Wiggins. Decidedly well done.' And at seven o'clock next evenin', on the dot, we was there at the pub."

He continued on in the same vein for over an hour, keeping me spellbound with stories of him and Holmes, and of Holmes lurking among the criminals and villains of London. Eventually, Jimmy stopped talking and turned to the fireplace in a revery. He rubbed his throat and glanced at me. "I ain't used to talkin' so much. Can I have some more milk?"

"Of course," I said, closing up my notepad. As he drank I stood and turned on the gas lamps, as the room had darkened during his tales. I picked up my pen from the pad and replaced it properly back in its stand. Although I would have liked him to continue his incredible monologue all through the night, I had promised his mother I wouldn't keep him too long. Reporter instincts aside, how could I have known just how rich a vein I had struck in this informant; this lad who had so idolised Sherlock Holmes, and who had seen him in situations no one else had? I was, I must admit, somewhat frustrated that so far he had not recalled any remark of Holmes referring to his childhood. But even if he couldn't help me with my biography of his early years, his remarkable accounts of his interactions with Holmes in themselves could be published. I moved the curtains aside and stared out the window into my small garden plot, and there was a sadness that claimed my bones that Holmes was no longer out there in London protecting all of us against crime. What a remarkable man!

I turned back to the lad, who had decided that some more sweets were necessary to wash down the milk. "Jimmy, it's time for you to return home, but I should like to see you again tomorrow afternoon. I'd like to continue recording your amazing experiences with Mr. Holmes. Would you give me the pleasure of more stories at, say, two o'clock?"

Jimmy stood up and wiped his face with his shirt sleeve. "You bet, Mr. Cobbett. Two o'clock it is."

"On the dot," I said, wagging a finger at him.

"On the dot," he grinned.

I saw him out the door and flagged down and paid a cab to take him home. His eyes bulged at that, but then he leapt into the hansom lightly and closed the door. He quickly assumed a pose of ease and comfort, looking like a young lord who has spent his life travelling in style. I handed him money to pay for his return trip tomorrow—by underground, he insisted. We exchanged waves as the horse began trotting down the street, and then I re-entered my house. Mrs. Darrick told me dinner would be ready in fifteen minutes. I went into the study and, sitting in my armchair, spent the time staring at the photographs on the mantlepiece, especially at the one that wasn't there.

I was awakened prematurely the next morning by the good Mrs. Darrick gripping me firmly yet gently on the shoulder.

"I'm terribly sorry to awaken you so early, sir," she stated, as I turned over in bed to get a blurry look at my tormentor, "but the lad walked here from his home and has been outside waiting for an hour. I brought him in and gave him some tea to warm his chilled bones, but he's so anxious to speak with you he spilled the whole cup on the Tokay rug and then knocked over and, I'm sorry to report, broke your mother's old green vase when he jumped back in shame of the spill. I fear if you don't see him immediately, the house will be destroyed before you can read your morning paper."

I sat up in bed rubbing my eyes to free them of sleep. "Who are you talking about? What time is it?"

"It's only 6:30 A.M. And the lad is the boy from yesterday, the Wiggins lad."

Now I was wide awake. "Wiggins? Tell him I'll be down in a minute." And without waiting for Mrs. Darrick to completely leave the room, I shot out of bed and quickly donned my dressing gown. My mind was fluttering with excitement, and it took me two or three tries to get into my slippers. A cursory brush of my hair and a throw of cold water on my face and I was heading downstairs.

Wiggins was back in the study, in the same chair he had sat in yesterday, but it was placed much closer to the fire and he was hunched over toward the flames covered by a heavy brown-and-yellow blanket.

He heard me enter and immediately stood facing me. "I'm right sorry about the cup and the vase, sir," he said, studying his shoelaces while speaking. "I'll figure out some way to pay you back for 'em."

I waved my hand away. "Don't worry about it. It's not important." I walked to my armchair and slid it closer to the fire as well. "Have a seat and tell me what brought you to my house at five in the morning."

The lad sat back down. Moira came in with a tray of hot tea and a couple of cups. She poured them out for us, checked that the fire was flaring, and left the room. I handed a cup to Wiggins, nodding my head to assure him it was all right.

"So," I repeated, "what brought you here?"

Wiggins put the cup down and began speaking. "Well, I'll tell you, sir. It was the most amazin' thing that ever happened to me. I got home all right and told me mum all about our talk and that you wanted to see me again today. Then everyone went to bed, but me nerves was janglin' like a thousand bells so and I knew I'd never get to sleep, so I just sat on the floor by the little fireplace we have. I sat there thinkin' 'bout Mr. Holmes and all the times I had seen him or worked with him. After a while I must've dozed off and suddenly, like in a dream, I remembered one particular time I was helpin' Mr. Holmes follow a group of criminals who'd been coinin' something fierce around the Chapel."

Wiggins' eyes were mesmerizing as the words poured out from him like water from a burst dam. "It was February 1890, and he had me stationed outside a pub in Shoreditch. He wasn't on a case, like, but he thought these criminals were workin' for some…mastermind he called it. Probably that Moriarty arsehole, now that I think of it. Uh, pardon me, sir. Anyway, it was late night and cold like a miser's heart. After a couple o' hours at the pub Mr. Holmes scared me by appearin' suddenly at me side like a ghost, but I settled down quickly because I didn't want him to know I was on the nervous side bein' out alone in the dark like that. I think he figured it out because he sat down with me on a box in the alley, poured me some hot tea from a container he had in a sack he carried, and asked me how I was doin'.

"'Fine, sir,' I said, though I had trouble holdin' the cup in my stiff hands.

"'That big fellow didn't leave the pub yet?'

"Mr. Holmes had pointed out the coiner I was to follow when we had spied on a group of 'em leavin' a lodgin' house earlier that evenin'. I'd had Davey with me, but when I got to the pub and it seemed like the coiner was goin' to be there awhile, I had Davey go and tell Mr. Holmes. Mr. Holmes had said to leave any messages in a pub on Pedley Street he often used as his center of operations in Shoreditch. See, he had helped the landlord with some big problem once and the landlord let him use a room in the back where he wouldn't be disturbed and where all us Irregulars and other helpers knew they could find him or leave messages for him. Kind o' like O'Reilly's. Anyway, I sent Davey there and a couple o' hours later there's Mr. Holmes at me side."

Wiggins paused a moment to catch his breath and to allow, I think, that particular image to sit in his mind one minute more. He took a sip of his now cooling tea, but didn't seem to notice.

"I told him that the fellow hadn't come out, and in fact, when I had snuck closer to the pub and had peeked in I had seen him drinkin' away at a table with a tall man with a bushy mustache who wasn't part o' the earlier coinin' group.

"'Very good, Wiggins,' Holmes said. We sat there in silence for a little bit and I felt ashamed that I couldn't stop my shiverin'.

"'You can go home, now, Wiggins,' Mr. Holmes said. 'I don't want to be responsible for you catchin' pneumonia. I have ended my watch of the others and will maintain the watch here.'

"I must admit I was happy to be able to return home. Mr. Holmes, though, for all his thinness, sat in the cold as usual like it was the middle o' summer. 'Aren't you cold, Mr. Holmes?' I asked. 'How come you never seem to mind the cold so much?'"

Here Wiggins leaned close to me and slowed and lowered his voice, almost sounding like an entirely different person with his new intonation.

"This is the point to what I suddenly remembered last night. It struck me like lightnin', and it took all I had to not come over to yer home earlier than I did, but even still the underground wasn't runnin' yet. 'Course, once I got here I didn't have the nerve to wake you up so I had to wait 'til I saw through yer front door window yer housekeeper up and about; and then I knocked for all I was worth. And good thing, too, she was up finally, for I was almost frozen like an icicle by then."

I interrupted this most undesired digression with unintentional asperity. "For goodness sakes, lad, what on earth did you remember?"

Wiggins blinked and flushed. "Oh, o' course. Sorry. So Mr. Holmes says, he says, 'The northern climes of Yorkshire are good training for the cold. Your problem, Wiggins, is that you've been born and bred in London.'"

With that Wiggins sat back with a look of complete triumph on his face, his smile so shining and eyes so wide one would have thought he had just found one thousand pounds, and I had to think that maybe he had.

The room became a tomb of hushed pensiveness, as I sat considering Wiggins' words and he perched on the edge of his chair like a statue of eagerness carved of marble. Suddenly he burst into animation again and said, "And then before I could ask him anything else he said, 'Go home, now,' and I did."

My head nodded repeatedly. "That is really most excellent, Wiggins. Most excellent indeed. So, he was from the North Riding."

"Right, I think so, sir. I mean he never lied. And he hardly ever talked about himself. He didn't like us Irregulars to be too talkative around him, so I just got used to bein' quiet like him and not askin' too many questions. 'In silence there is observation,' he once told me. But the question 'bout the cold just came out and there it was, northern Yorkshire. I tried to think of anything else he said about his childhood you would be interested in when I was outside walkin' up and down the street, but nothin' else at all came to mind. I think that's it."

I stood up and reached out to shake Wiggins by the hand. He looked shocked for a second and then arose and clasped his palm in mine. "Really, Wiggins, I am most indebted to you," I said sincerely. "Your fantastic association and clear memory of Mr. Holmes has indeed opened up for me a pathway I had thought was totally walled against my passage. You have done much to enable me to possibly immortalise Mr. Holmes, even more so than Dr. Watson's accounts."

I crossed to my desk and took out my wallet from the center drawer. I pulled a five-pound note from it and returned to Wiggins holding the money out for him.

"Lord, sir, I couldn't accept such a gift as that," he said.

"It's no gift, Wiggins. It's well-earned payment for probing your memory, walking and standing in the early morning cold, and giving me valuable information to assist me in my research. Take it. I insist." He still remained motionless, so I stuck the note in his coat pocket.

"There," I smiled. I wrapped one arm around his shoulder, and led him to the hallway, handing him a handkerchief from my pocket with the other. "Let's go have some breakfast, shall we?" He nodded and wiped the tears from his face as we walked.

Chapter Two
The Timms

wo days later I went to London's St. Pancras station and took the rail up to York. It was a sunny though chilly day and the countryside scenery of wide empty spaces dotted with flora still sleeping through the winter was glorious in its clean sharpness and a welcome diversion from the grime of London. One could feel the chaos and rapid pace of the city dissipate as the train clacked along the rails heading northwards, and when I alighted at York station I felt more relaxed than I had in months even though the cold was sharper and had a deeper bite than in the south. I checked into the Grand Hotel in Petergate and went up to my clean and spacious hotel room to wash up from my travels. I had telegrammed a dear old friend, Edgar Timms, that I would be arriving in York and desired to meet with him. I had known Edgar since University (where my parents had hoped I would pursue a banking career), and I had kept in, if not close, then at least consistent touch with him all these years. He had invited me to stay with him and his wife in their home, but I deferred, stating the freedom of a hotel would suit me to enhance my investigations. However, I heartily agreed to dine with them the night I arrived.

Edgar Timms came from a long line of wealthy relatives that had lived in York for three hundred years—and had family that had spread throughout the whole of Yorkshire. That was a very lucky connexion for me, I knew, and I was beginning to feel as if Providence itself might be favoring my research.

I unpacked, washed, changed clothes, and then descended to the lobby. The doorman flagged down a cab, and twenty-five minutes later, on the other side of the Ouse, I arrived at a stately manor, large, squarish, three stories, surrounded by a tall, cast-iron fence and a forest of scrubs and trees that would be its own botanical gardens come the warmth of spring. Soon I was gladly shaking the hand of a trim and clean-shaven Edgar, his hair almost completely grey though his body still fit and trim in his middle-age. I was delighted to reacquaint myself with his beautiful wife Camille as well, who though short in stature garnered respect by the clear intelligence of her eyes and the amiability which framed her oval face. We had drinks, and a very pleasant dinner of roast beef, spending the time discussing our University years, our lives since then, and our children. It was only after the table was cleared and we three retired to the drawing room for some sherry that I brought up the subject uppermost on my mind.

"Edgar, I have a most unusual question for you," I began. "It is the principle reason I have come to York."

Edgar finished off his second sherry and put his glass down on the small side table beside his chair. "Well, then old man, out with it and let's hear the singular inquiry that drags a man from his cozy London hearth to be chilled by our frigid northern air."

"Yes, I'm certainly curious myself," Camille added.

I paused for a moment thinking how I should approach the topic. I had rehearsed this while travelling, but now that I was actually to articulate my research topic I was somewhat hesitant to continue. It was not that I feared they would ridicule my interest, for they were far too kind-hearted and decent to respond in that way. It was more that I feared they would be of no help and that for all my hope and fate's guidance so far, my investigation would nonetheless die here in Yorkshire before it ever had a chance to live. I suppose I could have travelled to every town and tiny village in a quest for knowledge of Holmes, if Edgar and Camille had no clue to aid me, but the thought of such an undertaking made my soul feel as heavy as I knew my legs would become.

However, the silence my hesitancy engendered became quite awkward for us and so I began. "I am here on the quest of discovering the childhood home of Sherlock Holmes," I stated. "I have learned that he was from the North Riding, and I was hoping that maybe you—or perhaps someone you knew—might have an idea where in this area I should focus my research."

The Timms had given me their full attention, and now they sat back in their armchairs and looked at each other, their eyebrows raised high. Camille turned back to me first.

"Sherlock Holmes?" she asked. "The detective?"

"Yes. I want to do a biography on him, on his childhood. My editors and I think the public would be quite interested in it. Especially now that there's such an uproar over his death. The public are craving anything about Holmes, and I must admit that I'm fascinated by him. I had been quite unsuccessful in my investigations into Holmes' past until I discovered one of his Irregulars. You know, the young lads that helped him out at times. This lad—a remarkable lad, too, who had worked for Mr. Holmes and seemed to be held in high regard by him—remembered that Holmes had once mentioned he was from north Yorkshire. So here I am, probably on a wild goose chase."

"How very singular," Camille commented, a gleam in her eye. "You reporters do get onto some extraordinary lines. Well, Edgar, can you help Josiah? After all, I am the newcomer to Yorkshire." Camille was from Dover; they had met during the season in London at a coming-out ball for Camille's cousin twenty-two years ago. Although she had lived in York for twenty-one years, that was still a new-comer to the ancient family lines like Edgar's.

Edgar sat in thought for a moment. "I've read some of those stories of Dr. Watson's in the *Strand*. Holmes seemed to be a truly remarkable man, yet so very secretive. Why, he didn't even speak of his past to his friend and colleague Dr. Watson, did he?"

"No, not at all. Dr. Watson confirmed that to me in person. I've also tried Mycroft Holmes—his elder brother, who, according to Dr. Watson, exhibits even a higher ability of observation and deduction than did Sherlock—but he also was of no help. And I've tried Mrs. Hudson, Conan Doyle, local shopkeepers, bankers, and even several of the Yard inspectors. Not one bit of help among the lot of them. If not for this Irregular lad, you see, I'd be out of all possible avenues to explore and would've had to give up the idea. As it is, if you can't help me narrow the North Riding down even further, I may still not be able to capitalise on the lad's fortuitous reminiscence."

"Well," said Edgar, standing and crossing the room to a desk by the full length windows that opened out into the garden. He took a cigar box from the desk and returned to the chairs we had grouped into an informal circle, holding the box open to me.

"Cigar?" he asked.

"No, thanks," I held up a hand.

As I declined, he placed the box on the table next to his chair, took one out, and leisurely sat back down in his armchair. He undid the ribbon, cut the end off with his teeth, and put it in the ash tray. Then he lit it, inhaled several times, and leaned back in his chair, as if he were the most satisfied man in the world. Mean-while, it was all I could do to prevent myself from leaping from the chair, grab-bing him by the collar, and demanding his aid. Instead, I rechecked my cravat and straightened my waistcoat.

"Hmm," Edgar said.

Camille, seeing my distress, playfully tapped Edgar's arm. "Edgar, don't tor-ture poor Josiah so. Do you or do you not know anything that may be of service to him in his quest?"

Edgar grinned at Camille and then at me. "Sorry old boy, I didn't mean to be so melodramatic. It's just that I..." His eyes glazed over and unfocused for a moment. "Ah, yes, I remember it now."

"You remember...?" I asked as nonchalantly as possible as he took a couple of puffs of his cigar.

"I remember that when I read 'The Greek Interpreter,' I had a sudden flash of inspiration." Edgar lifted his hand and tightened it into a fist. "There was some-thing in that story that imprinted itself forcefully upon my psyche, and now it rings like a brazen bell inside me. As I read the tale, something about the extremely singular name of 'Mycroft' stabbed at my mind like a knife. More sherry?"

As Edgar had been speaking, I felt my body getting lighter and lighter until it seemed to me that I was almost floating gently above the chair cushion. I numbly held out my glass and, as he paused to refresh my sherry, the "Thanks" I murmured seemed to come from far below me. I could feel my heart racing and hoped that he would speak again before I suffered an apoplexy. Camille came to my mercy.

"Edgar, you beast. See what you're doing to poor Josiah. Honestly, you are a most unrepentant teaser."

Edgar laughed loudly. "I'm so terribly sorry, Josiah. Dear me, you don't look very well. I had better continue post haste before you suffer the horrors of a stroke and me a lifetime of guilt."

My sentiments exactly, I thought.

"Very well. Here is the tale. I shall try to be concise and succinct, but I am rarely either, isn't that true, Camille? Anyway, about twelve years ago, my sister-in-law's brother's son, Peter Bradley, who was a stalwart though not overly scholarly boy, took it upon himself to relieve the pressure of boarding school by travelling on horseback into the dales of the North Riding when he returned home for the holidays. He was aided in these sojourns by the estate gamekeeper. The family estate is right outside Richmond, and Peter debarked from there and spread his journeys in all directions. The lad began his travels in 1882, and the next year we held a large Christmas party for as many of the family as could come, and that brother's family attended as well. I took a liking to the lad, who was shy in socializing, yet had an intelligent and sensitive nature. Peter and I took to walking in the garden and talking between ourselves. It was during one of our talks during those days that he relayed to me the information I shall now convey to you." He drank his second sherry.

"Peter told me of several of his trips, all of which were, really, quite uneventful; just happy days exploring the Dales from the Pennines to Ripon, and Skipton to Muker; in other words, the entire area. He spoke of tiny villages and towns, waterfalls, hiking on the mountains, and described the poor people and the wealthy farmers and squires he saw, chatted with, and even took meals with. He described the houses he saw, both dreadfully poor cottages and large country homes with well-tended gardens." Edgar paused and leaned forward in his chair, clasping his hands between his knees.

"Once during his discussion of the homes, he told me of the area of Wensleydale, quite lovely country, really, and not near as full of mines as Swaledale above it. It was in the town of Carperby that he saw the ruins of many houses that had been burned to the ground, he learned, in 1810. He spoke to the local innkeeper about the tragedy and was told that a fellow had lit his fireplace and then fallen asleep as the chimney caught fire and set the thatch roof ablaze. Before anyone could do a thing, neighbouring cottages were on fire, and then the wind took the conflagration across the street. Twelve houses burned that night but, by the grace of God, no one died.

"Now, Peter said he had seen a country estate burned out, too, on his approach to the village proper, and asked if somehow that had been gutted in the fire of the horrible night. Although improbable, had the unfriendly wind carried an ember that far to wreak destruction on another local abode?

"Peter said the innkeeper with whom he had been sharing such pleasant conversation suddenly grew silent and pensive. After a moment or two, a fellow next to Peter, a blacksmith by trade, told Peter that that house had been burned down much more recently. And that was all either would say. There was such an instant and singular change in the men that it impressed young Peter to some depth. Only by frankly badgering the blacksmith as he followed him back to the smithy and offering the outrageous rate of a guinea—no lower amount would budge the man—was he able to learn the name of the house, but he could learn no more from any of them. The name of the estate was Hillcroft House, and it was inhabited by a reclusive family named Holmes that had two, as the blacksmith said, 'peculiar' sons."

Edgar sat back and raised the sherry bottle and poured some of the sweet red liquor into first my glass and then his. As he lifted the rim of the glass to his lips, I repeated, "Hillcroft House?"

Edgar nodded. "Outside of Carperby, which is a small town in Aysgarth Parish, in Wensleydale. Askrigg, about four miles southwest of Carperby, is the largest village in the area. Peter asked if I knew of the people who dwelled in that locality, but I had never even been to Carperby nor knew of anyone who had. So the matter was ended and I hadn't thought of it at all until I read that installment of Holmes' adventures in the *Strand*. Perhaps it's totally coincidental that there's Mycroft Holmes and a house called Hillcroft House inhabited by a reclusive Holmes family with two peculiar sons; perhaps they're totally unrelated. And, yet, I feel otherwise in my bones now that you have brought this new information to us."

Camille sat primly in her chair, her hands clasped in her lap. She stared at me with her hazel green eyes, her look never wavering. "Do you really think that knowledge of Hillcroft House is of a propitious nature, Josiah?"

"Well, I don't know, but it feels like a solid lead. After all, Edgar, Mycroft is hardly a commonplace name—Hillcroft sounds close, and no doubt the Pennines were the hills referred to. It would not be so hard to suppose that the name Mycroft also refers to the original house as a joyous acknowledgement by the first landowner—it could very well be a family tradition to pass on the singular

appellation through each generation. And that a family named Holmes lived there..."
I let that thought trail off.

Camille finished it for me. "That could, we must agree, be a possibility. How
very exciting."

"Well," Edgar said, standing up and stretching, "let's not be too premature in
our expectations for fear of their being dashed. It is the best I can do, but still all
the evidence is most circumstantial—in fact, there is no evidence at all, only conjecture. Josiah still has a goodly amount of both work to do and luck to find until
his editors raise champagne glasses to his success."

I stood as well and shook Edgar's hand. "I very much appreciate all the help,
old friend."

Camille now stood as well and we three began walking to the entrance par-
lor. "You both have been more than wonderful in accommodating me," I said.

"Nonsense," Camille said. "But you must promise to keep us informed as to
any progress you make."

"Oh, certainly. But, please, I must request you to not share with anyone my
plans or what you've told me tonight."

"Dear me, we should never do that. Your story is quite safe with us." Camille
winked at me conspiratorily. "Isn't it, Edgar?"

He held a finger up to his lips. "Mum's the word, my dear."

Good-byes were earnest and sincere, and I returned to my hotel in an extraordinarily good mood, which I passed on to the cabby by way of an extremely
overgenerous tip. I fell asleep quickly without needing the nightcap of the previous evenings, mumbling a rare prayer of gratitude for helpful memories and the
beneficent fate which had seemingly adopted my cause.

Chapter Three
Carperby

I arose the next morning, ate breakfast, and planned my next move. It seemed to me that the logical place to begin would be the parish church in Askrigg to check birth, marriage, and death records for the Holmes family, and perhaps do some discreet questioning of the officials and locals of the area. Askrigg was almost three times larger than Carperby or Aysgarth, I learned from the hotel manager, a treasure trove of knowledge, and held the most records for the area.

I checked with the hotel manager about transportation to Askrigg and was told that I'd first have to travel north to Richmond and then switch to a train heading west into the dales; one left Richmond very early in the morning, and one in early afternoon. As Wensleydale had developed somewhat of a name among travellers due to its recently discovered scenic splendours, particularly several spectacular waterfalls and a long massive rocky chasm, the manager explained there were now a few pubs that put people up for the night. These might be filled by tourists in the beauty of a delightful summer day, he explained; in the winter season, however, there would be no problem finding suitable accommodations upon arrival.

The weather turned even more frigid in the hours travelling from York to Richmond and then westwards into Wensleydale. Upon arrival in Askrigg, I and my stiff knees sought the warmth of the roaring fire in the cozy establishment, the George and Dragon, an inn which the station master highly recommended. It was run by the squat and red-faced Samuel Thompson, whose visage seemed to be affixed with a perpetual smile that did more than the fireplace to readily dispel the chill from my bones.

I spent a quiet evening, eating an early dinner and retiring soon after to my bedroom. I had decided not to engage the effusive Mr. Thompson, or any of the numerous villagers in the pub—who sat noisily imbibing the fine ale of the local brewer—on the subject of Hillcroft House, or of the Holmes family in general, until I had investigated the few avenues I had at my disposal. I did not want those channels possibly tainted by any adverse reaction such as Peter Bradley had experienced in Carperby. So begging off the multiple questions the sociable men naturally inquired of me as a city man visiting their country at so unfavourable a time of year, I professed a genuine fatigue from my travels and removed myself from their agreeable, yet slightly wary, company and climbed upstairs to my temporary quarters. I was glad for the extra blankets, for the weather worsened even further during the night. Only the beauty created by a light sprinkling of snow and frost, which appeared as whitened lace on the moonlit tree limbs I could see from my bedroom window, lifted my depression at the winter cold.

After a sound night's sleep and a hearty breakfast, and bearing in mind directions from Mr. Thompson, I put on my coat to set off for the town church, where the officiating vicar and registrar, Father John Brougham, maintained the birth, marriage, and death registers of Askrigg and several surrounding communities, including Carperby. I slipped out the door and, walking quickly to keep warm, I soon found myself upon the quite ancient church's doorstep. Pausing for a minute, I took several deep breaths of the chilly air, mentally adjusting my cravat and pulling down on my waistcoat, both of which were unavailable to actual touch by the thickness of my greatcoat. I then entered the church, and stepping to the back in search of the vicar, I glanced into the vestry and was amazed to see an old ash tree growing in the middle of it. I wondered at its existence. But I was immediately drawn back to the reason for my presence there and I gently coughed to attract the notice of the vicar, who was seated in the vestry writing a letter. He turned and stood upon seeing me, rather grateful for the interruption it seemed to me. I was growing a bit warm and so unswirled my scarf from around my neck, removed my gloves, and unbuttoned my greatcoat.

As it was Wednesday morning, the vicar, Father Brougham—a red-faced, squat man with a full though manicured reddish-brown beard that he stroked constantly—was not yet overly engaged. His manner was effusive and pleasantly curious. I explained I wanted to see the register to aid me in accurately writing the last several hundred years' history of the region for possible publication in a city paper. My words seemed to satisfy his guileless nature, and he led me to the small room in a corner of the church that housed the registers. I felt slightly guilty not being honest with the helpful and obviously kindly young man, who seemed sincerely flattered that anyone would lavish such attention upon the humble folk of his parish.

The registers were large books that were dated from 1600; Father Brougham, being new to the area since the preceding vicar had, unfortunately, passed away from a fever only last spring, did not know where any earlier registers might be found, and his curate was off visiting a relative and would be out of town for two more weeks.

Considerately bringing me a pot of steaming hot tea, the vicar then left me alone with the books. So it was I began a task that was to prove enlightening in a most singular manner. I spent many, many hours poring over and examining those books. Families from Carperby were listed, I soon noticed, but to my disappointment I did not see a Holmes line from there. I did find a Holmes family in Askrigg, and the vicar later informed me that the patriarch of that family had been a dealer in hardware. However, that family line was clearly illustrated in the registers and no Mycroft or Sherlock existed among the numerous birth entries of that decidedly prolific clan. Also, those Holmeses lived in town, and had never owned land or an estate. Of course, the surname Holmes is by no means uncommon, and I had expected to encounter other families with the similar appellation. The most striking aspect of the registers, however, and what set the hairs on the nape of my neck to prickling, were the pages that were strangely missing! Here and there throughout all three of the books, pages had been sliced clean as with a knife and removed. The last year in which such a mysterious excision had occurred was in the death register in a page from 1872. When I brought this unprecedented tampering to the vicar's attention, he expressed considerable stupefaction at the missing pages, repeating "Dear me, dear me," endlessly as he stroked his beard repeatedly—he had not noticed the missing pages in the few times since his arrival that he had used the books to record entries. It became clear the man was sincerely ignorant of the perpetrator and was too good-natured and naive to be suspicious of criminal wrongdoing.

Immediately after lunch that day I hired a dogcart to Aysgarth and, with the help of the senior parish clerk Michael Claygill, an elderly man with a pince nez, repeated my search in the same three registers of that town. Another Holmes family was discovered, the line of Timothy Holmes, whom Mr. Claygill informed me was the publican of the inn named the George and Dragon. I thought it judicious not to inquire between the Thompsons of Askrigg and the Holmes of Aysgarth as to which was the originator and which the unimaginative mimic of the shared name of their pubs. The stiff and formal Mr. Claygill was a long-term resident of Aysgarth, "although, of course, not a frequenter of sinful houses of ale." Nonetheless, since local talk flies into even upright ears, Mr. Claygill knew that this line of Holmes had been in the inn business for over a hundred years, and had no relations who had been landed. "And for all their doing the devil's work by serving that evil ale, otherwise they are respectable Christian folk, who attend service regularly, and cannot be said to have a blemish on their reputation." In several weary hours of deliberately turning every single page of the registers, I did not find a single one removed.

I returned to the Askrigg George and Dragon in the little wagon. With the sun setting, not even a considerable covering of heavy blankets kept me from feeling almost entirely numbed by the cold, even though it was only a four-mile ride. The young man driving the horses seemed impervious to the chilly air, however, and Holmes' words to Wiggins about the northern climate being "good training" for comfortably following criminals in the chilly city came to mind. But the inn was warm, the fire ablaze, Mr. Thompson's smile once again present, the tea hot, and within half an hour I was pleasantly thawed and drowsy. I leaned back in my chair, stretched my legs to the fire, and allowed my heavy lids to close in thought.

My affectation no doubt interpreted as napping, I was left alone to cogitate in silence. The pages missing from the register nagged at me like an ache in my side. Who had cut them out so methodically, and why? Since it was obviously not the random act of a trespassing delinquent, irresponsible vicar or clerk, it seemed most likely that it had been the premeditated action of someone who wanted to hide what those pages demonstrated. Such a purposeful theft strongly paralleled the other apparently missing information that may have been similarly excised from the public record—the lack of Sherlock Holmes' name (or his friends') on any university list, or on Bartholomew's list. The registrars of the respective schools had so emphatically informed me there was no record of Holmes' attendance at any of those places, which directly contradicted Dr. Watson's accounts of Holmes' past in the "The Musgrave Ritual," "The Gloria Scott," and Dr. Watson's original meeting with the detective in a room at Bart's in "A Study in Scarlet." It was obvious that Holmes would have entered a university with the level of scholarship his brilliant mind would require, hence Cambridge, Oxford, and London; the lower-level colleges seemed superfluous to consider. And since Bart's doesn't favour anyone walking in off the street to beat upon a cadaver and make free use of chemicals and retorts, the only possible conclusion was that Holmes had also been enrolled in some capacity at Bart's. But now, with the discovery of the missing register pages, the fascinating and exciting probability of deliberately orchestrated covert actions designed to remove all vestiges of Holmes' early life grew into an intuitive theory I realised that I wholly supported.

As my reasoning clarified, I sat up with a spry suddenness and grunted loudly; the heavily bearded fellow sharing the fire with me was startled enough to spill some beer on his pants. He accepted my apology for my rash move. "Lor', you almost killed me poor heart," he said, and I bought him a refresher. I then ordered and ate my dinner and spent some time playing darts with the locals, losing a nice few pounds doing so, until true fatigue claimed my bones and I was again climbing the inn stairs to my neatly made-up room. I soon fell asleep under two heavy quilts, hoping that tomorrow brought with it continued progress in my research.

The next day I went to Carperby. I borrowed Mr. Thompson's dogcart and mare, assuring him I had some little expertise in their handling on unpaved snowy country roads, which is not an untruth, though I had not driven one thusly in about twenty years. The four-mile drive to Carperby was enjoyable, as the weather had broken warmer and the sun shone with brilliance. To my disappointment I did not see the burnt ruin of Hillcroft House on the road from Askrigg to Carperby. The town itself was simply situated—there was one main road upon which the majority of businesses and most cottages abutted. Several streets ran parallel to the main avenue and also contained some tradesmen and homes. The principle road continued further east, though two smaller roads branched from it on the outskirts of town, one dropping down to join the main road on which Aysgarth lay and one turning north to form a loop to Castle Bolton.

I left a little late due to setting up the arrangements with Mr. Thompson, but still drove at a leisurely pace in my desire to appreciate the rural barrenness of the wintry northern land. My mind was able to bring the sleeping hedges and plants and frosted ground to life and imagine the beauty of the multicoloured vegetation at the height of summer blossoming.

It was a little past midmorning by the time I arrived in Carperby. Although slightly early for my afternoon repast, I thought that the warming fire of the local inn would be a welcome sight. I pulled to a stop at the Fox and Hound and called to a local lad to take the dogcart to a stable, giving him some pence for the favour. I was watching the lad lead the horse off as I opened the door to the inn and entered. This was a mistake, as there was an unexpected step down to the floor of the estab- lishment of which I was not mindful, and as a result, to my embarrassment, I landed heavily on the side of my left foot, twisting it painfully in the process. I tumbled to the floor and grabbed my ankle with both hands, as if with firm pressure I could staunch the flow of pain to my senses, which did not, unfortunately, prove to be the case. Suddenly two men appeared at my side, bending down to appraise my situation.

"Another victim claimed by that bloody step," one of them said. "It'll kill someone for sure someday, I tell you."

"No doubt a stranger such as this gentleman," the other said. I glanced up and discerned him to be the landlord of the inn by his apron and concerned expres- sion. He was tall and thin, bald but for a row of hair that ran around the sides of his head, and had watery, gentle eyes.

"Are you hurt badly?" he asked. "We have no doctor in Carperby, but Mrs. Handley knows something of medicine and herbs. And there's Mr. Piltering, a physician in Askrigg, if you think the bone is broke."

"Ah, he's a man to be avoided unless Death himself holds your hand," the first man said, a smithy by the looks of his clothes and well-muscled physique. His brown beard and hands were dirtied soot, and though he appeared to be but barely middle-aged from his head of thick brown hair devoid of any grey, his face contained a wealth of wrinkles from living a life by the drying heat of a large fire.

"Hush, William. You know it's foul to talk poorly of a man when he's not present to defend himself." The landlord grabbed my arm and motioned for William to do the same with my other. "Can you stand, do you think?" he asked me.

"Yes, yes. Thank you," I blushed. This was hardly the entrance I had antici- pated, and hardly the method by which I had intended to acquaint myself with the local folk. "I don't think it's badly injured, just twisted."

At that they lifted me up, my middle-height and medium-weight figure no more effort than a child's form to them, and with their assistance I hobbled to a chair. As the two men stood watching I untied my shoe and then removed my sock. The ankle was only minimally swollen and was not discoloured.

"It looks like I'll live," I said wryly, endeavouring to reduce the tension in the room.

"Well, I wouldn't walk on it for a day or two. That's what me Mary always says, a day or two of rest gives a limb some time to heal." The landlord lightly elbowed the smithy in the ribs. "Remember Peter Gant?" he asked William before turning back to direct his conversation to me. "Last year got his shoulder yanked by a horse and kept working all summer with the pain. Now he can't even lift his arm."

"Well," I said, "I should hope that my injury does not portend such dire consequences. However, as I have had a sprain to this ankle in the past, your recommendation to rest the joint for one or two days makes good sense. Allow me to introduce myself—I am Josiah Cobbett of London. May I board for a couple of days at your fine and friendly inn, Mr…?"

Here the landlord flushed and wiped his hands on his apron before shaking my hand. "Caulfield, sir. Adam Caulfield. And this is William Grant, the town smithy. I apologise for the lack of courtesy in not offering proper introductions myself."

I waved away his contrition. "Certainly my awkward entrance of a moment ago was the cause, not any lack of respectable propriety from you, Mr. Caulfield."

That seemed to please the landlord greatly, and his chest swelled. "Thank you, sir. And yes, we have a room upstairs for you to rest in, and, I may be so bold to say, sir, my wife makes the best kidney pies in the North Riding."

The smithy went to the door and put on his coat, scarf, and gloves. "Well, if an amputation won't be done, there's no interest for me to avoid work further. Adam, we'll talk again about our concerns later." He turned to me and nodded his head once. "Good day to you, Mr. Cobbett," and left the inn.

Mr. Caulfield and his wife proved to be more than accommodating in their assistance to my needs. With their support, I hobbled upstairs and was made comfortable in a lovely and immaculately neat bedroom at the back of the inn. A fire was started after I was arranged on the bed, and as noon arrived food and ale was brought to me that was every bit as gustatorily impressive as Mr. Caulfield had boasted. A messenger was dispatched to Mr. Thompson in Askrigg informing him of my circumstances, but he somehow forgot to return with my luggage, so a sleeping and dressing gown were procured from Mr. Caulfield's bureau, and the short, rotund, friendly, yet loquacious Mrs. Handley came and wrapped my ankle in a poultice of comfrey, speaking in a nonstop monologue about the step, ankles, knees, herbs, her irresponsible husband, and anything else that seemed to pop into her head at the moment. Due to all this good will and attention I found it impossible to sink into the realms of frustration and contrariness I had imagined from previous experience I would have succumbed to. Thus that day and the next passed with me alternating between chatting with whomever stopped in my room, reading my pocket Petrarch, and dozing slothfully.

On the second night I overheard a very singular argument, of the most vitriolic character. I had been drifting in and out of sleep since about ten o'clock, when I woke to a thirst of such noticeable proportion that the quenching of it seemed a necessity. There was no water in my room, however, which had been the first neglect of duty of which the Caulfields had been guilty. Gingerly putting some weight on my ankle, I found to my delight that there was no pain. Putting on the borrowed dressing gown and my socks and shoes, I grabbed the water jug from the little sideboard, lit the little candle, and quietly left the room. From talk I had heard earlier between Mrs. Handley and one of Mr. Caulfield's sons, I knew there was a water barrel in the kitchen. To avoid disturbing my hosts, I tiptoed down the hall with no discomfort, which had me silently praising my aging body for its youthful expression of healing potential. Alert for the sound of a creaking board, I passed the only room with a closed door, which I supposed were the quarters inhabited by the landlord and his almost as equally tall, cheery-faced, and helpful wife.

I turned the corner and stood for a moment at the top of the winding stairs. I could hear but not quite discern several voices downstairs in heated debate. Feeling somewhat ashamed, but—due to the nature of my career and interests—more curious, I began gently descending to the ground floor, straining to eavesdrop and discover the content of the argument. As I reached the bottom of the stairs, the vitriolic nature of the quarreling was made evident by the volume and acrid tones employed by the men. My thirst forgotten, I blew out my candle and slowly moved to the main inn area, guided by the light of the multiple candles placed on the table around which the men stood. I hid myself behind a large oak post that enabled me to see the illuminated men some fifteen feet away, but hopefully prevented their espying me in the dark. The vehemence of the voices was of such a vituperative quality, that even though it was not directed at me, I could not help but feel frightened by its intensity.

The discussion was between three men. The landlord of the inn, and the blacksmith who had helped me limp to a chair the previous day, by all appearances seemed to be endeavouring to calm down and appease the third man, who was about fifty years old, with a full silver mustache that completely covered his upper lip; thick, silver, wavy hair; his dark eyes beaded into pure anger; and his arm movements wildly punctuating his words to emphasise his ire.

Suddenly the third man picked up a pint glass from the table that the three surrounded and threw it against a far wall. It burst into pieces and splattered the room with shards.

"Bloody hell! It's all very well for you both to say so! You've got the inn, you've got your smithy," he yelled pointing at each of them. "You both get your money. If that's all you want in life, fine! Maybe some of us want something more! Maybe some of us deserve something more. Who are those city men to prevent it?"

"For goodness sakes, Harry, calm down!" Mr. Caulfield implored, removing another empty glass from the table. "I'll not have the inn myself if you destroy it all."

"We're only trying to keep you, and ourselves, from gaol, confound it, and have us all do the right thing," the smithy said. "You don't want what happened to that fool Cotter to happen to you, do you? He was sinful and was punished. The same could happen to any of us."

"The hell with Cotter. That was ten years ago! Things are different now, with him being dead. We can say what we want to, now."

"You're as big a fool as Cotter, if you think that," Grant said. "His brother still lives. The money still arrives regularly—no one has come to declare the pact over. And I'll not have you bringing trouble to the village like Cotter did. By God, I'll not allow it!"

"Allow it? You bloody bastard, you have no say in the matter. I'll decide what I do, and no other man! I'll make my own decisions with or without your help!" At this, Harry waved his fist in front of the landlord. He then slammed it down on the table. "A pact of nonsense! It sickens me, what's been done."

"It stuck in the craw of several of us all, Harry, 'til we grew used to it," Caulfield said, tucking his hands deep into his trouser pockets. "But, anyway, there's nothing we can do, and nothing we should. Like you say, most of us are happy with things and don't want trouble. And, even if the pact is a fraud somehow, as you feel…"

"But can't prove…" the smithy interjected.

"Even if it is," the landlord continued after a cautioning look at Mr. Grant, "we've been well paid to do and say nothing. And considering the consequences of any protest…well, we all aim to keep things as they are. I know you came late into all this, but your uncle agrees with us."

"Maybe he does, and maybe he doesn't," Harry challenged. Then he closed his eyes and brought his hands up to his temples and rubbed them. It seemed like all the fire in him was abruptly extinguished as he sat down heavily in a chair. "My uncle," he said softly. "My uncle is old and weak, and never held a sour thought in his entire life. He's still got a clarity of mind, but for how long? It's for him I'm wanting to do this."

The landlord and smithy exchanged compassionate glances. Harry took a large swallow of ale from the remaining glass on the table. "He could make a thousand pounds telling what he knows. A thousand pounds, I tell you. We could all get a lot of money, for what we know. Since those stories in the *Strand,* everybody wonders, but only Uncle Percy knows it all." Harry thrust his hands in his pockets and crossed his short legs. "It isn't fair what's been done. I've still a mind to fight it. If we all spoke together, they couldn't arrest us all."

Caulfield pulled a chair close to Harry and sat down. "You can't fight alone, and none of us will join you. I know you've travelled some and been in politics and like a good fight, but we're just simple village folk like you said, who don't want any trouble. We're happy with the money we get, and what happened to Cotter makes us very wary. Just let your uncle collect his money like the rest of us and let it go. Maybe one day we'll tell, but not now."

Caulfield paused, shrugged, and then went on. "Maybe his father did work for the government, or maybe, like you think, it's just another sordid tale of rich folks not wanting their good name to be publicly raked over the coals. It isn't for us to say." He paused again, and glanced at the smithy, who stood like a statue of granite with his arms crossed and his face grim. "Your uncle needs you, Harry; he depends on you. If you went to gaol, he'd be lost. No one to play chess with that's as bad as you."

The landlord's wink was lost on Harry, who sat there morosely. After a minute the landlord stood up and began whispering earnestly to Mr. Grant. The blacksmith was obviously agitated, however, and although he whispered back in return, his tone was curt and harsh. He pointed at Harry several times, and gradually as his temper seemed to grow, so did the volume of his voice.

Finally he erupted. "I don't care about who thinks what's fair! An honourable pact was made with each of us, the money's delivered, and no one has been harmed by our silence. They've lived up to their side and we are obligated to live up to ours. As a Christian and an Englishman I say a man's word is his solid bond, no matter how much time passes or what circumstances arise that we might benefit from. Cotter got what he deserved, I say. The devil take him! Brewster agreed like the rest of us. His story is one that won't be told if I have a breath left in my body to stop it!"

During this outburst the landlord had tried to settle Grant down and defuse the situation by raising and lowering his hands as if simultaneously and repeatedly patting two children on the head, while murmuring "Now, now." The attempt proved useless, as Grant was unstoppable in his tirade, and as the recipient of such a provocation, Harry reanimated himself. He stood—which immediately silenced the two others, though Grant's glare spoke volumes—guzzled down the last of the ale, wiped his mouth on his sleeve, put the glass down on the table, and took three deliberate steps until he was face to face with the blacksmith.

"As an Englishman myself, you can take your bloody Christian ethics and…" I shall spare the gentle reader the shocking ending to Harry's response. With that, Harry strode to the door of the inn, hurriedly put on his outer garments, and then left, not bothering to bid good night to either of the remaining men.

When the door slammed shut, the landlord put his hand on Grant's arm and said, "William, you shouldn't be so rough. He's not afraid of you, and it only makes matters worse."

The smithy brusquely shrugged off Caulfield's arm. "He's got no righteous grievance. The problem is the man has not a shred of Christian morals and has a taste for the evil of avarice. Perhaps if he spent more time praying in church, the devil wouldn't find his ear so large a receptacle for muttering sins for that fool to consider." Grant crossed over to the bar where his coat and hat were lying and put them on. Pulling gloves out of his pockets he continued, "We made a pact and get our money; everyone else is satisfied with that. Harry Brewster is the trouble, not the pact. I'll not let the town suffer for him, who's not even worth the dirt we walk on."

"Good night to you, Adam," he said as he left the inn. The landlord gave a flimsy wave in response. His mien was one of sadness, and I watched as he listlessly locked the door. He went behind the bar and picked up a broom that rested against the wall; he then began sweeping up the glass pieces that littered the floor with a laggardly pace as if it took all his energy just to stand upright.

Disavowing my thirst, I took that moment to slink back to the stairs and tiptoe back to my room. Once inside, I relit the candle, although my shaking hand needed five or six efforts to kindle the vesta. I sat down on the bed, wrapping myself in the warmth of the heavy blanket, breathing hard, my heart pounding. It took me several minutes to calm myself from the fear of discovery and the excitement of the amazing discourse I had surreptitiously made myself privy to. Then I endeavoured to order my thoughts and deduce what I could from what I had heard.

My original plan for being in Carperby had been to leisurely perambulate the village and find Hillcroft House. I had had designs to approach the smithy Peter Bradley had bribed, hoping it was the same man of twelve years ago—I wondered now if it was that man Grant—and learn if perhaps numerous guineas slipped into his palm might loosen up his previously reticent mouth. However, if Grant was the smithy of years past, it was utterly delusional to expect any valuable information from him. That mystifying pact which had been mentioned several times combined with his fervent religiosity seemed an iron impediment to him now sharing the details I wished him to impart.

That pact!—it filled me with an inexplicable dread. What was it? What exactly did it pertain to? What did it protect? Who had made it with the townspeople? Who was "that fool Cotter" and what had happened to him? What knowledge of Harry's uncle was worth a thousand pounds and why couldn't he share it? And most importantly—was the dead man referred to Sherlock Holmes? Had his father worked for the government in some unknown capacity? It had to be! But how was the government protecting itself with a pact with these village folk? What did Harry want them all to talk about? It was indisputable that there was a common thread, but I could not seem to pull clarity from the murkiness.

All those questions burned in my brain and it was clear that I was to spend a sleepless night in fitful frettings searching for answers. Thus I spent the rest of the hours of Morpheus, ignoring his noble claims upon me. As morning dawned grey and overcast, I reviewed the conclusions I had drawn. If I was right in my reasoning, certain members of this village had been coerced into well-paid silence about the Holmes family, under the dubious pretense that the government required their secrecy. One man, Cotter, had apparently broken whatever agreement had been made and suffered some unknown penalty. Had the elder Brewster worked for the Holmes family, or had he had business relations with them and therefore intimately knew the "sordid tale" of their downfall more completely than others in the village? Was Harry Brewster, Percy's nephew, now questioning the veracity of the pact's intent? Did he desire to have his uncle, at least, break with the agreement and sell what he knew of the Holmes family to an interested publisher?

Although unproven, my assumptions seemed to hold together firmly, and every drop of blood in my body flowed with the desperate desire to confirm their validity. It was now imperative that I find and speak to Harry Brewster in private. As I began my morning toilet and dressed for breakfast, I wondered how I should be able to discover and interview Mr. Brewster confidentially. I still wanted my investigation to be secretive in nature. I did not want the townspeople to disdain my presence and inhibit my movements, as I now feared they would if they knew my true line of inquiry, since the secretive pact seemed sacrosanct and Harry Brewster—the only man who seemed to be willing to break it—was considered to be an annoying troublemaker. My optimism in finding Harry Brewster was elevated by the fact that he lived in Carperby, for he had left the inn by foot scant hours ago and I had heard no horse or carriage upon his departure. As Carperby was a small town, I had every intention of nonchalantly sauntering through it house by house and store by store in the guise of a history writer of Yorkshire. I would find Harry Brewster, if it took resoling my boots to do so.

Chapter Four
Harry Brewster

o it went. Greeted happily by the Caulfields as I appeared for breakfast, I had bangers and hash for breakfast and a pot of strong black coffee. Mr. Caulfield's melancholy mood of the previous night seemed to have been completely replaced by an effusiveness no doubt inspired by the contagious amicability of his delightful wife. Reassuring them of my ankle's complete recovery, I donned my coat and left the inn. The temperature not being overly frigid, I set about my perambulations with a light heart and an eagle eye. I carried a pencil and a pad of paper in my pocket and occasionally withdrew them at particularly ancient buildings to reinforce my role of history author. I strode aimlessly with no apparent purpose other than simple interest, and in this way wound my way through the town, making frequent stops to chat with any locals I happened to meet. They were overall friendly and hearty folk, and had no compunction in allowing me to take some time from their day inquiring about their family lineage in the area.

After lunch I continued my peripatetic investigation, and it was about three o'clock in the afternoon when I was gratifyingly rewarded by the sight of Harry Brewster entering a home at the end of a side street. Although I felt a surge of elation, I nonetheless maintained my steady pace. When I came upon the medium-sized, neat, two-story stone house, with a slate roof, I paused and looked around in a lost manner, simultaneously slapping my greatcoat pockets several times, trying to convey to any observers an attitude of confusion and hesitation. Hoping I was not being overly ostentatious, I removed my pocket watch and pretended to study the time. Turning my head and happening to chance upon the Brewster's home, I slowly advanced up their walk until I was at the front door.

It took me the entire walk to replace my pocket watch in my waistcoat, as my by now unfortunately commonplace shaking had returned in my excitement. I paused at the door with eyes closed, and said a silent prayer to whatever angels might be listening to the longings of an errant reporter. I then inhaled down to my feet and knocked on the door. When no one came after a minute, I knocked again, and a few seconds later the door opened. I had decided that a direct approach would be best to gain me entrance into the house as quickly as possible, and out of the sight of prying eyes.

"Good afternoon, Mr. Brewster," I said. "My name is Josiah Cobbett, and I am a reporter from the *Guardian* in London. If you would be so kind as to allow me entrance into your home, I feel we may be of mutual support to each other." I leaned over and spoke close to his ear. "What I have to discuss is really of a most private nature to the both of us."

Throughout my short, cryptic introduction, Brewster had stared at me through narrowed lids, half his body hid behind the partially opened door. His countenance otherwise reflected no emotion and I only thwarted his abrupt endeavour to close the door by the painful expedient of sticking my left foot in the doorway.

"Wait!" I whispered emphatically. "I heard you last night in the inn with Caulfield and Grant. I can help you, I think." I grunted in discomfort at the pressure on my foot as I fumbled to remove my credentials from my trouser pocket. Finally I had them and thrust them in Harry's face. "At least hear me out," I implored. "I'm on your side."

The release of the door on my foot was wonderful. His eyes darting left and right, Brewster growled, "Come in," adding "Hurry up" as I slowly tested my ankle's integrity once again. It did not seem re-injured and I hastily entered the house.

"Who is it, Harry?" I heard a friendly and spirited voice ring out. I glanced into the left front sitting room and saw an elderly man in a chair by the fireplace, covered with a heavy quilt, and holding a book. A cane hung from one arm of the chair. The man, Harry's uncle, I presumed, had wispy white hair covering his head, a face mapped with wrinkles, and was sparely built, but even across the room I could see that his pupils sparkled with intellect and alertness. His carriage was stiff and slightly formal, not I thought from some rheumatic complaint, but rather from a dignity and properness that complimented his deportment and did not detract from his amiable presentation.

Harry stepped around me into view of the gentleman. "A Mr. Josiah Cobbett from London, Uncle. He's just visiting the area. Thought we'd do a little talking."

I removed my hat. "Good day, Mr. Brewster. I hope I am not interrupting your afternoon leisure."

"Mr. Cobbett, my whole life is 'afternoon leisure,'" he laughed in a high squeaky voice. "Your appearance is most welcome, I assure you." He held up the book. "Not much call for brushing up on French in Carperby, anyway."

I liked the man immediately. "I should enjoy very much talking with you, sir, but first, if you would be so gracious, your nephew and I would benefit from a private discourse."

"Oh, well, that's fine, young man. I understand confidentiality better than most men," he said. "Although I cannot but admit to my curiosity. Neither Harry nor I attract many visitors. However, at my age, a pot of tea at tea time is enough bribery to ensure I won't be bothersome to your secrecy."

"I'll get it right away, Uncle," Harry said, ushering me along with him to the back kitchen area. I managed a brief wave to Mr. Brewster before Harry's not-so-gentle pushes had me halfway down the hallway.

"We've no use for servants," he told me as he put a heavy iron kettle on the stove to boil. "It's just the two of us and I take care of all his needs. He's the finest man you'll ever meet and he's been nothing but good and generous to me."

I stood silently out of Harry's way as he prepared a tray with tea, cup, and a few sweets. "Wait here, I'll be back momentarily," he said as he left to serve his uncle. When he returned he directed me up the narrow central staircase to a small study at the top of the landing. Two other doors, one on each side, no doubt led into their bedchambers.

"We'll talk in here," he said, guiding me into the room. "Sorry about the chill. No fireplace." I sat down in one of the wooden chairs decorating the sparsely furnished study, an old desk needing varnish the only other furniture. Harry followed in a minute wearing an extra sweater he had procured from his bedroom next door. He sat down in the other chair and without any more delay asked, "So, what is this all about?"

My analysis of Harry's personality clearly judged that a forthright presentation of myself and my investigation would be the most judicious. I therefore spent some little time detailing from the beginning my desire to publish Sherlock Holmes' biography and related to him how my inquiries had brought me here to Carperby. I apologised for eavesdropping on him last night, told him what I had deduced from their conversation, and revealed my decision to track him down.

Harry sat quietly looking out the window of the room during the majority of my explanation. Only when I told of my deductions did he turn his head slightly to make eye contact, although his face was still unreadable. I finished my monologue and sat waiting for his reaction.

After a moment, he grinned. "Well, a reporter are you? Seems you've a gift for detecting yourself."

I was surprised by the amiable response. "I've a gift for luck, for it seems that that has been my investigation's cornerstone. The lad Wiggins, my friend's memory, my injured ankle—all led me to you more than any brilliant cerebration of my own."

"Perhaps. But you put together a feasible connexion between scrambled lines of dialogue spoken late at night with more ire than common sense in them. That was your own sleepless brain and no luck at all."

Though pleased by the unexpected compliment, his words troubled me. I hesitated before asking softly, "A feasible connexion? Was it no more than that?" My arms and legs began to feel like they were full of lead shot.

Harry stood and strode to the closed door, which he leaned against facing me. He took out a pipe and tobacco bag from his sweater pockets and soon was puffing away, emitting blue, mild-smelling smoke. I was relieved at the fumes' pleasantness for, as a lifelong nonsmoker, I find many tobacco scents dreadfully disagreeable. As if he were a mind reader, he removed the pipe stem from his mouth and pointed at the smoke with it. "No foul-odoured shag for me. Nasty stuff, that."

He pulled a few more times on his pipe, watching me all the while. "You're right about all of it," he suddenly declared, and the weight in my limbs vanished. "It's all about the Holmes family. Sherlock Holmes' family."

It seemed that he leapt across the room to sit back down. There was a sudden glow to his features like the lighting of a bonfire. "I'm not a religious fanatic like that odious Grant, but I will say that you being here in my house seems a gift from the heavens above." He reached over and grabbed my forearm. "I want to apologise for shutting the door on your foot. Especially since you had so recently injured it. But of late I've not been receptive to visitors, and I was in a foul mood from dwelling on last night's fracas and because Mrs. Handley still can't figure out what's ailing my dog. I was returning from her house when you saw me. I don't know if things will work out, but you've brought my hope up from the depths just by being here." Harry sat back up and laughed. "Ha! listen to me, rambling like Mrs. Handley."

The change in his behavior from five minutes ago was astounding and, I must say, took me aback. Although I still wore my greatcoat, in my tremulous excitement my hands habitually made the movements of pulling down my waistcoat and straightening my cravat several times. Harry raised his eyebrows at my silly routine and it was my turn to chuckle.

"I'm sorry," I said. "Just nervous. I was somewhat flustered by your rapid change of character."

"You should smoke a pipe," he replied. "Calming, and useful for redirecting the mind into purposeful action. As for the change of character, that is solely of your doing. You are the first good news I've had in years. Can you really get the story published?"

I held up both hands. "First things first. We need to proceed slowly and from the very beginning. I want to understand the situation perfectly before I make grand promises I cannot then keep. I am quite obviously in the dark about all the details surrounding the intriguing statements I have thus far heard. First, tell me what you know. Then I'll want to record your uncle's story. Are you sure he'll cooperate— what about the pact?"

Harry glowered at the mention of the pact, but then assumed a thoughtful pose. "I think he'll talk, if we use the correct approach." His eyes refocused. "I've been working on him lately, telling him that now's the time to share what he knows, before he's gone and it's all lost forever. He's rather the keeper of the guard passing down the torch; that sort of thing. And I know he's been reminiscing a lot lately; that's what 'brushing up on French' is about. But he's so noble and good hearted, he'll have to be convinced it would be for the good of all and to the detriment of no one."

"That is what I have in mind myself," I fully agreed. Inside, though, I was not so sure; my honourable resolve seemed to have developed a small yet noticeable crack. Although this whole idea had begun as a way to further extol Holmes, it was now dawning on me that this biography was likely to do anything but that to his family name. There seemed to be a dark hint of trouble lurking about Holmes' past.

Harry's candid response briefly caused an uncharacteristic sense of guilt to flare in me. "If it can be done. I'm not so sure, myself." He looked out the window again. "I am very much an admirer of Sherlock Holmes, you know. We all are here in Carperby. My uncle had a bookseller in York mail him the *Strand* each month and he's read each story probably twenty times. And I would like to think of myself as a decent fellow as well. I certainly don't mean to bring trouble to the village or to denigrate the fine name of Holmes that Dr. Watson's stories have so far extolled. But, then again..." He turned back with open eyes and raised, anxious eyebrows. "Is it so sinful to want to profit from events that happened thirty years ago? Is relating the truth about a dead man's troubled family a terrible thing to do? I really don't want to be seen as heartlessly greedy." His eyes lowered into a line of thick eyebrows and his lips thinned. "But then I think, what about the importance of publicising a fraudulent governmental 'pact' solely devised to protect the Holmes reputation? True, I cannot at this time prove that any official or unofficial malfeasance has been contrived and carried out, but I have ruminated upon that pact ever since learning of it after my arrival in Carperby, and it has sat like rotten meat in my stomach since then. The issues around that pact are causing me to lose whatever esteem Caulfield and Grant had for me, and possibly are preventing my uncle from acquiring a small fortune and achieving a worldwide fame I feel is righteously his. And I wonder if this type of 'official' pact has been made before with other villagers for other mysterious purposes."

He sat back and held both hands palms up. "You can see I'm of two minds about the whole situation. If nothing else, I would appreciate your views on the matter as a third party. But I forget my courtesies as host. Would you like some tea before we begin?"

I shook my head curtly, and removed my writing pad and pen from my pockets. "No, no. I should just like you to elucidate the entire circumstances regarding all that I overheard and all that you now allude to."

Harry stood and began pacing the room. "All right. I shall try to relate the fact as pertinently as did the entire cadre of Sherlock Holmes' clients." He cleared his throat dramatically, loud enough for the neighbours to hear, I thought, let alone his uncle.

"I myself had no personal connexion to the Holmes family, as I have been in Carperby only these last ten years. Previously I had spent thirty years in Canada, in the flatlands of central Alberta, as my father moved us from Bridlington to Alberta for business reasons when I was twelve. Uncle Percy, my father's only surviving and elder brother, a bachelor, had endeared himself to me by his frequent letters and gifts whilst we lived in Bridlington. As he was at that time the butler of a country estate in the western dales, by the name of Hillcroft House in Carperby, I only saw him very rarely when we lived in England and not at all during my thirty years in Canada, yet so strong was my impression of his gentle and peaceful nature that I considered him a dear relation from my first connexions with him. Even during all those years in Canada, we maintained the most consistent and intimate of correspondences.

"It was only when my wife died in February of 1882 that I decided to return to England and Yorkshire. I had no children to keep me in Canada. By that time, my uncle had been fully retired for a year and was living alone in this house. He, of course, invited me to live with him here; implored me, really. I knew that I could not refuse that dear old man his request, although I had always wanted to live by the sea. However, my uncle is a mild man of simple habits. Having lived in the area so long, and being afraid of large crowds and cities, and suspicious of change, for us to live together entailed a natural consideration of me accommodating his needs and not the reverse. So it was that the humble town of Carperby, and the gracious home of Uncle Percy, was made the destination for my celebratory homeward journey in August of 1882. Unfortunately, the business I left in the hand of my brother-in-law in Alberta failed under his mismanagement, and therefore I have come to depend fully on my uncle's finances, his small savings and investments, and the additional money he receives twice a year as payment for the pact."

Harry came to a standstill again by the door. "That is the pertinent history of my fondness for my uncle and my arrival in Carperby. Do you have any questions so far?"

I continued furiously penning my shorthand for a minute until I had his monologue completed. Pausing from the effort, I rolled my right wrist to keep it from cramping. "Well, a few, maybe, but I'll hold onto them until you are finished communicating your information to me. I do not want to send you off on a digression at this point. And you may well answer them anyway as the narrative expands."

"Very well," Harry said, resuming his steady pacing. "Then I'll continue."

"My uncle's greeting was effusive and I soon had settled into a comfortable, if dull, routine. I was never a very outgoing person, and a newly purchased dog satisfied my need for companionship on the walks I took into the countryside. Not infrequently I would also take my uncle's horse for longer excursions to other towns. In Carperby, my uncle and I amused ourselves with reading, chess, and card playing. We engaged in congenial conversation about politics, religion, and many other topics from the newspapers and books we perused. Twice in these ten years old acquaintances from Bridlington wrote invitations to visit and I convinced him to travel with me to the coast to enjoy the refreshing salt air, and the glorious vista from the Bempton Cliffs. Since his friends have now died, we have been happy in our mutual company here.

"Although we were generally open and free in our discussions, I quickly noticed that any inquiries into my uncle's past as butler for the country estate, a position he held for some thirty-three years, were always politely, though adamantly, left unanswered, as he would deviate onto other subjects. He also refused to clarify for me the events surrounding the ruined country home I came across on one of my rustic treks and assumed had been Hillcroft House, his employer's domicile. The landlord at the local pub was strangely ignorant of the estate's history as well, for all village news finds its asylum in the quaint village inn, and the landlord knows as much of the town people as does any fly on the wall. I thought this all greatly suspect, and due to the special nature of our dear kinship, one night after supper I begged his pardon and then asked my uncle pointedly about his avoidance of the topics. He hemmed and hawed a good deal, mind you, before he gave in to my persistency, and with quiet reserve, enacting upon me an oath to secrecy, he related to me the most astonishing event."

At this point Harry stopped and refilled his pipe with tobacco. After a few hardy puffs rose from the bowl, he lit the lamp on the desk, thus illuminating the now darkening interior, and sat down in the chair. A few more puffs and he continued.

"A little over a year before I arrived, in 1881, two men showed up unannounced at Uncle Percy's doorstep. They were well dressed and carried themselves with an official and serious, though not forceful, deportment. My uncle courteously invited them in as they requested to speak about matters affecting him and the British government. They first showed him a paper signed by the Prime Minister himself. That paper petitioned the reader of the document—'for the protection and continuance of this noble nation Great Britain'—to listen to these governmental emissaries and obey their words. Well, knowing him and his overt patriotic tenets, it was probably all my uncle could do not to break out in a heartfelt and stirring rendition of 'God Save the Queen.' I'm sure they had Uncle Percy's full attention.

"These men then began a discourse of the most shocking and astonishing content. It would have been considered absolutely ludicrous—even by a man as naturally unassuming as my uncle—if he wasn't holding a paper signed by the Prime Minister affirming his veracity.

"The men explained that, due to the extremely secretive work David Holmes, Sherlock's father, had done for the government, they were required by the ministry to establish 'as usual'—those were their very words, 'as usual'—a pact with the village folk where the special agent had lived. What ministry they were from was never imparted. They related that only by the most unforgivable oversight of a junior-level clerk had this pact not already been established in Carperby. The pact entailed each pertinent villager being listed on the official registrar as never to divulge anything about Holmes himself, his family, or his activities to anyone. This was to guarantee that no villager would inadvertently share what may have appeared trivial tidbits to them but what was actually vital knowledge to an enemy agent, should one come prying about in disguise.

"You see, they continued, the work that David Holmes had initiated was still progressing quite satisfactorily to the benefit of the country, and the government desired my uncle's aid to ensure that the enemies of Britain did not use him as an innocent yet clandestine source of information. They acknowledged that my uncle might have had no idea of Holmes' special role in the government aside from the fact that he had travelled a good deal on business. Still, they requested that Uncle Percy sign a legal document stating he would never speak or write in a detailed manner of Holmes, for which he would receive a biannual pension from the government in grateful acknowledgement. If he was found to have broken this pact, the penalties could be severe, as the government would immediately be suspicious of an act of treason. He was not even allowed to discuss anything with others in the village."

Harry puffed a few more times. "As you can imagine, Uncle Harry signed the paper. He did not receive a copy, but, two months later, received his first installment in an unmarked envelope with a London postmark. I do not know exactly who else the two men confronted and persuaded to sign the pact; I imagine only those who had close contact with Holmes and his family in some way were approached. Over the years I discovered that at least the landlord and the smithy were similarly coerced. If others signed—and the landlord's surprising reference to 'several of us' that you heard last night surely points to that assumption—they have maintained a muteness so complete regarding their involvement I feel as if this village is inhabited by monks under a holy vow of silence. Perhaps that usage of 'several' was just a calculated ruse from Williams and Grant designed to obfuscate and falsely enhance what is only their opinions. I don't really know. It may have been just the three I know who signed, or it may have been twenty more. Oh, there was a fourth man, Noah Cotter, a poor lad from a poor family who nevertheless had apparently played with Sherlock Holmes as a child.

At the mention of Cotter my head shot up.

"Ah, you're interested in Noah Cotter, aren't you?" Harry smiled.

"His name was mentioned several times last night, usually after the descriptive qualifier of 'that fool.'"

Harry snorted then grew somber. "Well, fool or not, here's what happened to him. He's the reason I am held at arm's length lately by the others; he's the example of dissension punished. This occurred in 1887 after 'A Study in Scarlet' was published; as I was in Carperby, I witnessed the affair myself.

"Cotter was a bit of a miscreant; apparently he had some potential as a lad to better himself, but once he got the early habit of drinking gin as if it were water, he turned mean and bitter. He was married with children, and did odd bits of work when sober, but nothing that elevated his family the least inch above pure and sorry poverty. Now, one day a man visited Carperby—a well-liked carpenter by the name of Silas Harker. Harker had been born in these parts, but had moved to Hertfordshire in '71 with his family when invited to do so by a distant relation who had returned to England from India a richer though lonely man. This was Harker's first journey back to his birthing town, and he brought with him a magazine called *Beeton's Christmas Annual*. None of us had heard of the story 'A Study in Scarlet' beforehand. Since, unfortunately, a good amount of the village people are rather illiterate, Harker read the story for all to hear in the pub—Cotter was among the listeners. Harker seemed ignorant of any pact. Like many in the village, he had known that the Holmes lived in Hillcroft House, but had little or no interaction with the family. However, knowing Sherlock was a native son, he correctly surmised that the villagers would be interested to hear the story.

"We all thought it to be a cracking good tale. Immediately after the reading the landlord organised an impromptu tournament of darts—no doubt, I believe upon reflection, to prevent much anecdotal sharing about the Holmeses that 'A Study in Scarlet' might well encourage. After Harker left, no one gave much thought to the story, except, in a cunning and insidious manner, Noah Cotter, who left the village in the middle of the night after breaking into the pub and thieving money from Caulfield's cash box.

"It was not for seven weeks until we learned what had happened to him. I had decided to travel again to Bridlington for a few days of solitary diversion viewing the untamed sea that always thrills my imagination. Whilst I was gone, the same two men returned to Carperby and spoke to my uncle, and Caulfield and Grant and whomever else about Cotter. They related that Cotter had been arrested for attempting to sell factual accounts of his childhood acquaintance with Sherlock Holmes to a writer from the Westminster *Clarion*. He was charged with high treason based on the pact's outlines and placed in gaol for twenty years. The men warned us that if anyone else should be similarly found at fault, dire consequences would befall the town, and the horrible fire of 1810 was alluded to. The men then left, but their ghostly presence still permeates the town in the fear that surrounds their dreadful caveat. One last thing, I have always found it a bit suspicious that the two men should return to speak to my uncle and Caulfield and Grant, and whomever else, when I was out of town and unavailable to question or comment directly to them. Though I will say this for the strange, anonymous men—Cotter's wife still receives the twice-yearly payment."

Harry tapped his pipe out on the window sill and sat back in his chair, crossing his arms. "Now I think you know all that I know. What do you think of it all?"

I finished writing, rolled my wrist, and then began to review my scribbling. "I don't know what to think," I said shaking my head. "It's…it's incredible."

"It's that and a host of other words as well," Harry said.

"Have you ever heard from Cotter, or found out where he's imprisoned?"

"We've had no word from him and, to be honest, I haven't endeavoured to uncover within which gaol he languishes. As Sherlock Holmes has grown in popularity, I had, over the years, begun thinking of transcribing my uncle's memory for posterity, and maybe for publication. I made the inexcusably grievous error of letting that slip from my slightly inebriated mouth one night several months ago as I sat drinking with Caulfield and Grant after hours. They took instant umbrage to the idea and last night's argument was just one in a number we have held since then. Things have escalated between us now that Holmes is dead—they worry, and perhaps righteously so, that my resolve grows firmer in the publication line. The fact that I have signed no pact does not move them, and truly, their concern for the town's welfare is one I fully embrace. I should not like to be the instigator of self-serving actions that end with a bonfire of Carperby's homes."

I ran my hand through my hair several times and pulled down on my hidden waistcoat. "This is certainly complicated. We must proceed cautiously."

I looked outside at the dark evening. "It's late, and I should be returning to the pub. However, tomorrow I should like to return to speak to you some more. Please spend some time in continuing to persuade your uncle of the importance that he not go to the grave with his history unspoken. Perhaps utilising the angle that Holmes is dead and his brother a government clerk of unimportance will enable your uncle to see the invalidity of the pact now."

"I'll speak to him," Harry said, nodding several times.

"It dawns on me that we may wish to leave Carperby if your uncle shall take some time in his recollecting. I cannot visit your domicile every day without attracting unwanted notice. I have a good friend in York at whose home we could stay during Uncle Percy's recitation. It is a large city, but perhaps your uncle's reticence of entering a metropolitan area would be modified by his enthusiasm to tell his story in the safest and most convenient atmosphere possible."

I stood up and stretched deeply. Harry and I shook hands. "You'll have to extend my sincerest apologies for not having a conversation with him tonight. Assure him I eagerly look forward to returning tomorrow."

"I will," Harry said, as he led me back down the stairs. It was not difficult to avoid Uncle Percy, as he dozed peacefully in the same chair I had seen him in earlier. Harry opened the front door, and I stepped outside to his whispered "Thank you."

"Good night," I responded. The wind had blown in and I hunched over as I made my way back to the pub. My mind was whirling as much as the snowflakes that danced in the air, and I did not endeavour to pull my thoughts together. I knew endless hours of fascinating rumination lay ahead that night, but for the moment I simply indulged in the fresh, clean air that enlivened an aura of hopeful destiny engulfing me.

The pub was busy as I entered, and I was glad to find an empty table in the back. Once the landlord espied me, food and drink were quickly and satisfactorily procured. As I ate I looked around at the boisterous camaraderie of a warm pub on a cold winter night and was heartened by the sincere air of noisy *bon homie* that filled the establishment. When I finished, I climbed the stairs and repaired to the quiet and solitude of my bedroom. I lit the fire, and as I threw my coat and gloves onto a chair, thought about what I had heard from Harry Brewster, and what I was craving to hear from his uncle, Percy. My God, this biography idea was shaping up to be an exposé of the most revealing and enlightening content! What had at first begun as a difficult posthumous biography of a much beloved, respected, yet extraordinarily reserved private consulting detective was indeed gradually developing into that, but now suffusing the entire investigations was an underlying current of curious and controversial government participation in a singular pact.

It dawned clearly on me that second that I was in this to the finish—every cell in my old reporter's body felt more alive with unbridled anticipation of what the future would unfold than they had in many years. Too many years. I knew that no matter the obstacles facing me, I would proceed along the lines of research I had instigated. However, hearing about the punishment ladled on Mr. Cotter ensured that I would be a cautious man—twenty-six years of life spent among policemen and criminals had taught me about subterfuge and deviousness. Fancying myself a worthy opponent, I sat back against the wall wrapped in a blanket and spent some little time working out a plan of action regarding Harry and his uncle. Hours later I finished, an extremely confident and satisfied man. Letting the fire die out, I lay down upon the bed and dozed fitfully for another several hours until it was after midnight and I was sure the pub was empty.

I arose and dressed fully, except that I wore my slippers and carried my shoes. I then crept quietly downstairs, candle in hand. I went through the kitchen, not even daring to breathe as I passed the small room in which one of Caulfield's sons made his quarters. The old beagle lying on a rug by the immense iron stove of the kitchen did not stir except to open one eye and observe my furtive movements. I reached the door down the slight hallway from the kitchen proper, and, first wiping my sweaty hands on my pants, I unlatched it with deliberate attention to any perceptible creaking. Caulfield was mindful of his possessions, though, and the latch hitch was oiled and smooth and noiseless. I buttoned my coat, put my shoes on, and stuffed the slippers in my trouser pockets, and, hand on the door handle, I blew out the candle. Praying the door hinges were as well cared for as the latch, in one swift and even motion I opened the door, dashed outside, and closed the door.

Though the moon was only a crescent, the sky was clear and there was just enough light for me to see without needing to relight the candle. I did not dally, but strode rapidly back to Harry's house, my exhalations puffing out like the smoke from a train engine's stack. Once at the house I calculated which upstairs window indicated Harry's bedroom and found several small rocks from the ground beside the leafless bushes that in summer no doubt nicely decorated the front of the house. I moved to the side of the house and practised tossing the stones—my arm had never been an accurate one, but the window was of sufficient size that I was optimistic of success.

The first two stones mortified me by cleanly missing the window and striking the stone of the house above and then to the side. Certain unpleasant childhood memories of the cruel nature of young lads' teasing birthed the same shame of incompetence as if I were eight years old again. However, the third stone re-established my self-esteem by surely tapping the pane, and I was hard put not to utter a squeal of glee. It was but a scant moment later that I saw a light flare and Harry standing by the window looking down at me. I waved and motioned to the front door. He waved back and left the room. I darted to the front and within a minute was safely ushered into the house.

Though in a sleeping gown, Harry was far from the groggy state of interrupted deep slumber and his hair was not disarrayed. He had undoubtedly been insomniacal. He led me into the sitting room his uncle had occupied that afternoon and lit a fire to dispel the coldness. Placing a couple of padded armchairs close to the fire, he guided me to one and sat in the other, lighting a second candle and setting it on a table next to his seat. It seemed he could not do these actions quickly enough, and when he was done, he leaned over to me, hand on my knee, his visage that of a child's first view of his Christmas presents, and whispered, "What is it? What brings you here tonight?"

I opened my coat and pulled down on my waistcoat. I related to him my concerns about getting him or his uncle in trouble by the same men who had arrested Noah Cotter. Harry and I spent a good hour formulating a strategy of procedure, and afterwards, we both stood satisfied with our plans and resolute in our commitment to ride forth into whatever battles we might encounter.

"I had some rousing political clashes back in Alberta and earned a respectful reputation for tenacity and honour. It seems this dull life of mine in England is about to end, and as one not afraid of conflict, I welcome this nameless opposition," Harry said. "Especially when I have such a lucky and ingenious chap as a friend and colleague." He patted my back solidly, and I was pleased by his sincerity.

"I'd better head back," I said. "I don't want to be caught tonight by any other sleepless wanderer or meddlesome neighbour. I shall see you again as planned in a couple of weeks."

We clasped hands and then I surreptitiously returned to the inn. To my great relief the door was still unlatched, and I entered, latched the door, put on my slippers, lit the candle, and delicately retraced my steps upstairs back to my room. There I undressed and slipped under the bedcovers, quickly allowing a brief smirk to cross my lips before allowing a deep and dreamless sleep to claim me.

Chapter Four

Percy Brewster

I arose the next day most slothfully, and after a late breakfast and effusive thanks to the Caulfields for their hospitality and generosity of spirit, I secured Williams' horse and carriage and made my way back to Askrigg. I had told the inquiring Caulfields that my one-day ramble around the pleasant environs of Carperby had indeed not sated my appetite to fully explore the area, and that when spring broke warm and fertile, I should return for a more in-depth perusal of the surrounding natural beauty.

A profound apology to Mr. Williams for the unplanned and extended sequestering of his horse in Carperby combined with several extra pounds in payment for its services quickly assuaged all hard feelings he exhibited upon first sight of me once again in his establishment. I collected my luggage and arranged for the long return trip to Yorkshire beginning with the afternoon train out of Askrigg. All went smoothly, and although all the travelling made the day wearisome, by late that night I was happily back in the Grand Hotel in York, enjoying another night of easy, undisturbed slumber.

I telegrammed the Timms the next morning and was rewarded with a prompt reply stating that I should indeed be most welcome at supper. I was glad to read in the tone of the reply that they had not thought my request too forward in its immediacy. I then telegrammed my editors in London relating that I was on the trail of the story and proclaimed that things were progressing satisfactorily. I did not care to be too detailed in the message due to my reporter's instincts for secrecy and a growing paranoia that mysterious men might be watching me. It was difficult for me to appear indifferent to people I encountered or saw when actually I was extremely keen to notice precisely everyone around me. I found it was hard to behave casually and naturally when wondering if that man or this woman was watching or following me in some ugly design to prevent my gaining advantage in this investigation. Ironically, since I knew that lodging a complaint with the police against unknown and unproven potential malefactors would avail me naught, I understood clearly during those hours why men and women would seek the help of a private consulting detective for their bizarre and unusual tales of intrigue. Unfortunately, as Mr. Holmes was the subject for my biography, I was left without a brilliant comrade-in-arms. Therefore I was pleased Harry had shown nerve and a certain strategical acumen during our midnight assignation, and I was hopeful that Edgar Timms would also willingly play the role we had constructed for him.

The day had begun blustery, and then in the afternoon and evening the snow started falling in large flakes, blanketing the city in the pureness of white silence. I had no desire to walk the streets in such weather, and so spent the day reading newspapers and playing cards and chatting socially with other similarly minded residents of the hotel.

I asked the doorman to have a cab ready at 6:15, giving myself an extra twenty minutes to arrive at the Timms' abode. The ride was slow, though we were able to keep moving, and I arrived at Edgar's home right on time. They were waiting for me anxiously, concerned that the weather should not impair my passage to their home or, worse, cause an accident in which I might have been injured. Their concern touched me deeply, and it was a moment or two before I could compose my sensibilities.

Unlike my previous visits, the Timms engaged me in direct conversation about my visit to Askrigg and Carperby following the serving of before-dinner drinks in the drawing room. It delighted me to see their interest and raised higher my expectations that Edgar would be of aid.

"Josiah," Camille said, "I dare say I have the most intractable curiosity. I wonder if you would forgive me for inquiring into your village expedition so immediately and candidly?"

"I should be most glad to share my minor adventures with both of you now, as that was the reason I desired your company tonight," I replied. "For through the telling of my experiences these last days you shall discover the cunning method by which I hope to employ your aid in this matter. The events have been very singular and bid the questioning mind to consider issues far beyond a simple biography."

Camille and Edgar silently turned to face each other with eyes wide and forgotten drinks in hand. As one they then quickly moved to sit, Edgar avidly waving for me to join them in the nearest chair.

"Well, for goodness sakes, man, tell us what happened. I dare say you have our full attention," he said.

I then repeated the narrative I had related to Harry, expanding it to include the plans Harry and I had concocted in response. This took a little time, but so concentrated were the Timms on my words that the butler had to announce three times that dinner was served. Edgar hastily dismissed him telling him we would be late for supper, and motioned for me to continue. As I neared the conclusion, I adjusted my cravat and began speaking of the boon I needed. When I had finished, I sat back and drank fully of the wine they had poured for me almost an hour before.

"So, let me recapitulate for my own clarity," Edgar said, his countenance an eager one. "You have found the butler of the Holmes estate, who, you believe, is ready to be a witness of the Holmes family life throughout the long years of his service to them. However, because of a certain and, I readily agree, fantastical pact made years ago, it seems that an unknown person or persons are involved in preventing the gathering and dispersal of the exact type of information about Holmes you are trying to accumulate."

"Exactly," I said.

"How very singular," Camille interjected. "This grows in interest to me with every passing second. What an enlivening adventure to escape from the dreariness of winter."

"Camille is a child of summer," Edgar smiled. Camille smiled back and took his hand.

"Now, Josiah, tell us how we may aid you," he said.

I pulled tightly on my waistcoat. "It is really quite simple," I said. "I should just like for you to ask one of your friends or relatives in Bridlington to write to Harry, requesting that he and his uncle visit him again. As I said, Harry and his uncle went on holiday to the coast when invited to do so. The other villagers knew they went to Bridlington, though Harry said he and his uncle never shared the names of the friends. Therefore, the other night, it occurred to Harry and me that if they received another invitation to travel east—a letter postmarked Bridlington, for proof—and it was spread around town, no one would be suspicious of their subsequent journeying. But here is our cunning—Harry, Uncle Percy, and I would actually converge privately in Richmond; if anyone did go to Bridlington in search of them, he would come up empty-handed. Of course, Harry will engage his full faculties to ensure that he and his uncle are not themselves followed. Harry knows the Richmond Arms Hotel in Richmond and it is there we shall stay until Uncle Percy has disclosed his full history to us. Harry will spend all his waking breaths on convincing his uncle to talk now that Holmes is dead. If he fails at that, then all this intricacy will have been in vain." I took a deep breath, hesitating in my apprehension. "Do you know of anyone in Bridlington who would help us?"

I had expected the query to render the room silent for a time, in contemplation of both the unethical nature of my desire and of someone who they could possibly induce into such a simple yet false action. To my surprise, Camille spoke at once.

"Edgar, the Forsythes have a home in Bridlington; remember we were there six years ago. Although we haven't maintained connexions with them of late, Horace seemed the sort of sporting man who wouldn't bristle at such a strange entreaty, especially if the cause were shown to be good. And he was ever known to be trustworthy. Do you think you could approach him on the subject?"

My ears seemed to enlarge as I awaited Edgar's rejoinder.

"Well, my dear," he said, stroking his clean-shaven chin, "you may have hit the target with Horace. I had been considering Wilson Taggert, Flora Gardner's cousin, who has a fish distributorship in Bridlington. But, truly, I have only met the man twice, and that for short times only. How absent-minded of me not to visualise Horace in such a role! You are correct, I feel, Camille, that Horace's love of hunting combined with his endearing good-humored personality could very well produce an attitude of compliance."

Edgar turned then to me. "Josiah, tell me, how much had you supposed we would take our acquaintance, whomever it may be, into our confidence?"

I swelled inside with delight at his use of the plural pronoun. "To be honest, Edgar, I should like to tell him as little as possible to acquire our goal. As much secrecy as feasible will best protect both myself and the Brewers and, though I shudder to think it, perhaps even the acquaintance himself."

Camille reacted to my dread utterance with shock. "Dear me, how horrible to hear you speak thus! Do you really feel that Horace could be placed in danger by aiding us?"

"I really do not think so, Camille," I said strongly, honestly endeavouring not to have their obviously avid interest suddenly dissipate out of understandable concern for their friend. "I do not mean to unnecessarily inflate the dangers inherent in writing a misleading letter; even if I am being followed, it does stretch the imagination to broaden the jeopardy to such an innocent as Mr. Forsythe." I was desperate not to lose their good graces, and felt that my injudicious caveat, while based in a sincerity I had felt compelled to express, could in an instant be the death knell of Harry's and my plan. I was fortunate that Edgar had never been a nervous man.

"Although I should never knowingly direct danger to anyone," he said, "I do think any hints of peril in this regard should be obviated. We are simply asking a man to write a letter, so let's not have our fancies run giddy and wild. I, for one, am game to try Horace. Camille?"

I simply beamed as she replied, "I agree, my dear." She turned to me. "This adventure is fully worth pursuing; and as long as you both feel there will be no harm to Horace, I should like to ask him to pen that letter."

"Excellent," Edgar said. He stood and Camille and I followed. "Now, let us attend to our supper before the food is too cold to eat. After dinner we shall put the finishing touches on contacting Horace Forsythe, and…" He held up his wineglass and laughed. "The game shall be afoot!"

It went very smoothly. Edgar posted an explanatory letter to Mr. Forsythe the next day, and a telegram arrived two days later: "Glad to hear all is well. Can say the same from this end. Singular request granted and acted upon; in return demand visit in near future. Horace." Horace Forsythe certainly was a good-natured sportsman! The Timms say I clapped with joy as they read the telegram to me, but I was so lost in the emotion of our success, so unaware of my physical body, that I thankfully cannot recollect such an embarrassing outburst. As we had directed Horace to tender the invitation for two weeks hence, I stayed with the Timms in their home for the interval. Then on the first of March, I hugged Camille tightly, clasped both hands into Edgar's, and departed for another long journey to Richmond. Upon arriving in that town, I checked into the Richmond Arms Hotel under the alias of Adrian Wurther, arranging for an adjoining room for some friends, the Calloways, who would reach the hotel on the following day.

I spent the entire night up in my room, essentially checking my cravat and pulling down my waistcoat so often I would have appeared to be an automaton designed to solely perform inane repetitive movements if anyone had seen me. My dinner did not digest well—a more intelligent man would have skipped the meal—and three generous doses of the stomachic barely contained my intestines from burning irritation. The night seemed interminable besides, each minute appearing endless, each hour an eternity. I thought of Holmes, and the patience he maintained on the numerous watches he engaged in with Wiggins, and tried to draw patience and some composure from his examples. It did not work and I resigned myself to a worrisome night. I tortured myself considering all the ways Harry and his uncle could come to harm during the trip—accidental, or God forbid, deliberately induced by men holding pacts. When that had roused my emotions into a frenzy, I then poured salt into my mental wounds by convincing myself that at the last minute Uncle Percy would recant his offer to act as a witness. As the night progressed and my bodily fatigue increased, my mind, caught in the chaos of unbreakable agitation, began creating the most ridiculous concerns to horrify me—perhaps a bomb should explode in the bedroom we would use to gather in, perhaps food would be poisoned, perhaps we would all wind up rotting in some horrid gaol.

It was truly a miserable night.

The morning dawned overcast and I had a headache. With the increase in light, my mind relented at last and ended its terrible ramblings, and I fell into a chair and entered a brief though deep slumber for a few hours. When I awoke I looked an utter fright and took some time cleaning, shaving, and dressing. My stomach felt better, and handled even the strong coffee I drank at breakfast to aid in rousing my energy and mental clarity. It seemed the nighttime exertions I had suffered had purged me of a great deal of anxiety, and while waiting for the Brewsters'/Calloways' late afternoon arrival, I was able to read the paper calmly and talk with a few people whom I came across in the lobby and restaurant of the hotel. Anticipating the following day, I sent the errand boy for a sheaf of foolscap, a pen, and a bottle of ink.

I saw the Brewsters enter the hotel at 3:45, covered with a light layer of snow from the windborne flakes that swirled up and down the streets. The porter followed with their luggage, two bags, and I approached them as they neared the desk. Uncle Percy moved slowly, leaning heavily on his cane, and it was obvious that the trip had depleted his small reserve of energy. Harry strode slowly along Percy's side, and when he saw me, gave a curt nod of acknowledgement. At the desk they checked in with no difficulty and were in their room with all the speed a tired Percy could attain. Harry's uncle immediately lay down on a bed and Harry and I repaired to my hotel room in consideration for Percy's need for rejuvenating sleep.

Once in my room, we shook hands with strong feeling. "You have no idea how happy I am that you have arrived safely. Was the travelling uneventful?" I asked.

"Well, I saw no one following us, if that's what you mean. Uncle Percy is a steady but slow traveller, affording me a good amount of time to constantly search for mysterious men. I saw none."

"Excellent, most excellent, indeed! And, I assume, you have convinced your uncle to share his valuable recollections with us? He had no compunction about breaking the mysterious pact?"

"We spent some little time discussing it the day after your midnight visit. I did not know, but Uncle Percy had some little affection for Noah Cotter. What happened to Cotter upset him greatly. Ever since then, even though it would be against the government's wishes, he had begun to consider breaking the pact, if only to help restore the name of Cotter as a decent, honest youth. And he does feel that recording the histories of famous men is vitally important to enable people to understand their motivations and personalities. Now that Sherlock Holmes is dead, and Uncle Percy no longer worries about upsetting him, for my uncle held the detective in utmost esteem, he is willing to elaborate fully on the subject of the Holmes household. He said, 'Let them stick me in gaol for good. I can die in a bed at home or in a cell, it's all the same to me,' when I reminded him of the possibility of being punished for treason." Harry rubbed his hands together, smiling widely. "He's game."

"Excellent, excellent, excellent," I repeated. "Harry, we have risen to the heights today! Tonight let's enjoy a hearty supper and an early bedtime; tomorrow we shall begin Percy's dictation."

And so it was that at 9:00 A.M., after breakfasting, we gathered in the Brewster's bedroom, I at the desk, they in chairs. As I endeavoured to write clearly—although my hand shook like a needle indicating the occurrence of an earthquake—Uncle Percy pulled a large number of notebooks from a Gladstone bag, opened up the top one, sipped a little water from a glass, and, occasionally glancing at his reference material to aid his memory, began his recitation.

What follows is his story of the Holmes family.

Chapter Six
The Holmes Family

My name is Percy Brewster, and I was the butler for the Holmes of Hillcroft House from 1840 until its unfortunate but inevitable end in 1872. Before I begin further on the Holmeses, allow an old man to tell a little of himself. I was born in 1810, in Bridlington, the first of two sons of a sailor. My father was a very kindly man and he loved our mother and us lads deeply. It was a terrible blow to all our hearts when, June 12, 1818, we learned that the ship he had joined to travel to Greenland and back had been lost in a storm, and all crew members had drowned. I was eight at the time, and in her grief and despair, my mother made the three of us lads swear to God Himself that we would never make the sea our lives and deaths. Life was very difficult after that; my mother continued her work as a piecemeal seamstress, bringing in pitiful earnings. An apt and interested student, I continued at school until I was twelve, when—through a connexion from my mother's employer—I was hired into service as an under servant by a wealthy importer in Hull. The butler of his household was impressed by my ability to read and write, to do addition and subtraction quickly in my head, and my honest and pleasant demeanor. Of all my siblings, I had inherited the most similar disposition to my father and had that nature nurtured and fortified by the sweetness of my mother. It served me well in service, for I did my work dutifully, abstained from gossip, was sincerely respectful of the upper servants, and caused no trouble. The work was hard, long, and tedious, and my bed was just a cot in the basement, but I worked well and without complaint. At fifteen I was made underbutler and given extra instruction in serving tables and taught how to properly interact with the master of the house and his family. The butler also began teaching me French, for the businessman had a brother who visited from France and who enjoyed ordering about the servants in that language.

Through some great act of fate's whim, I had stumbled upon a career that suited me to a tee. I realised that dignified service to a man and his household, assuming important responsibilities, juggling multiple tasks at once, being organised, calm, these were qualities I thrived upon, and my manner naturally contained the attributes necessary to excel in such a position. Thus I decided to devote my life to service, a decision I have never regretted a day in my life. I stayed with the businessman's family for another fourteen years, until I was thirty, having acted as butler from age twenty-two on, after the death of my predecessor. When I was thirty, my employer died, and his widow decided to move to France. She wrote me an excellent letter of character, and soon found me another situation as a butler in a squire's home in Carperby, Wensleydale. I applied for the position with Mr. David Holmes and was hired on the spot after he read the letter of character and tested my French. I remained there thirty-three years. But enough of me, Mr. Cobbett, let me now move to other topics which no doubt are the true ones preying on your mind.

The pact of which I understand you are fully cognizant, Mr. Cobbett, was not hard for me to make with those two gentlemen at the time. I would have kept my silence about those years due to loyalty anyway; for all Mr. Holmes' faults regarding his sons, he was always good to me, as were his sons. It was only after the poor lad Noah was put in gaol—on the ridiculous charge of treason!—only after that I began to think that the truth should out, that the men I had thought noble government emissaries were nothing less than official bullies possibly acting illegally, though with power and money behind them. But still, my word was my bond, and as I had given the former, I truly was loath to break the latter. As further years passed, however, and worldwide fame and affection attended the activities of Sherlock Holmes, I began to feel that knowing his past as a child would be of great value to those who admired him now and especially to those in the future who would wish to study his method and his genius. However, my respect for him was still the basis for my continued silence, for I felt how improper it would be for me to break a confidentiality he had established so completely in an obvious desire for utter privacy regarding his childhood. As for Mycroft Holmes, he desires the same total secrecy, but truly there is less to tell of him anyway, and fewer persons interested, for he has not the public's ardour as does his younger brother Sherlock.

However, when I was recently stunned to read of Sherlock Holmes' untimely and tragic death at the Reichenbach Falls—he always loved waterfalls—I developed a firm conviction to break with the pact, let my honor suffer the affront it may. Surely your entrance into our lives, Mr. Cobbett, as Harry took me into your confidence, led me to feel that perhaps young Sherlock is not averse to my decision to relate my recollections; perhaps he truly supports it, for one can only believe your appearance was heaven sent. I do not know if all the machinations Harry arranged were necessary, but it is difficult for an eighty-four-year-old man to argue, and so I am in Richmond and here I tell my tale.

I shall start at the pertinent beginning—I shan't tell the whole history of the Holmes in England or the Vernets in France; I certainly won't even pretend to know it all, and the importance of what I have to say does not require a thorough understanding of the family's entire genealogical record. However, I will relate the necessary family background.

Apparently the Holmes line had once been prolific, but for unknown reasons had begun to struggle with maintaining itself since Sherlock's great-grandfather's time, and, I think, maybe even before that. Where some families gave issue to innumerable children per marriage coupling, the Holmes line struggled to produce two or three children per marriage, usually later in life, and some of those were born sickly. Perhaps Mrs. Winters, cook to the household, had views on that as well; a fairy curse no doubt. However much the struggle, though, continuance did occur.

Mycroft William Holmes was Sherlock's paternal great-grandfather, born in 1742. His elder brother died as an adolescent after a fall from a horse and his sister married a man from Canterbury and moved there. Of his younger brother I know nothing but that there were some grave difficulties with his moods, even to the extent that help was sought medically, and that he and his family eventually had a total rending of all connexions. William married Grace Winsby in 1766, and they had their first child eight years later in 1774, Brian Mycroft; their only other child was born in 1778 and was named John Scott. I do not know more of Grace Winsby's family, for I gathered there had been ill feelings among her and other family members, and she never spoke of them, and her children did not know of them. William Holmes farmed Hillcroft House, the large house of the Holmes family in Carperby, Wensleydale of the North Riding of Yorkshire, named apparently in respect of the Pennine Peaks with which the original freeholder had been enamoured. Hillcroft House had been in the family for generations and the family had once been yeoman farmers. Over the years, as a result of a succession of profitable investments, at first in sailing and then mostly in the textile trade of Huddersfield, they had accumulated about twelve hundred acres of land, upon which they had tenant farmers raise horned Swaledale sheep and a good number of dairy cows, and others working the oats and making the hay. They treated the farmers fairly and with kindness and were therefore held in much regard by them. Certainly by William's time, the Holmes were considered the squires of the Carperby, and lived a quiet life of gentry privilege.

The land in the dale is beautiful but rough and isolated; bleak moors are just miles from awe-inspiring waterfalls, and ever the Pennines stand starkly watching over the land and people. Oh my, how we had trouble keeping up with young Sherlock's wanderings! There was not so much industry in Carperby as above in the heavily mined Swaledale; though there were a few small collieries, a slate quarry, and both the Carperby and Askrigg Common Mines in close proximity to Hillcroft House. The family had used admirable foresight in investing early on in the textile mills of Huddersfield, thus ensuring the Holmes' solvency through the collapse of the mining industry in Wensleydate around 1830. The family maintained themselves with respect and the bearing of the area's squire, and not a poor word could have been found against them.

Brian and John were as close as brothers can be. They farmed together in complete harmony, and finished the improvements and expansions to Hillcroft House that their father had initiated, but, due to the debilitating effects of an apoplectic attack in 1799, had no ability to continue to manage. By the time John married Anne Routh in 1801, daughter of a squire in Hawes, the house had reached its full proportions, and two large and comfortable cottages had been added on the outskirts of the small park. In 1802, Brian Holmes married the daughter of one of the owners of a textile firm in Huddersfield and moved there to be manager of the firm. Unfortunately, the pairing proved loveless and childless, and Brian found himself overwrought by city noise and filth. He returned to the farm alone in 1808, ostensibly just briefly to bury his mother, who had died of a blood disorder, but he never did return to Huddersfield or his wife. When William Holmes died two years later in 1810, of another apoplectic attack, his two sons were happy to continue farming and living together in Carperby, Brian returning to Huddersfield two or three times a year to check on the mill. John and Anne had three children: Stewart Mycroft in 1803, Margaret Elizabeth in 1804, and David William in 1812. In 1818, Brian decided to travel to Egypt and there he died four months later, having spent too much unprotected time in the heat. John Holmes deeply grieved his brother's death, finding a weak comfort in the vice of drink, and it was some years before his spirits lifted from a most distressing depression.

Though Stewart was at public school mostly during those years, Margaret and David were affected by their father's melancholy, even though their mother Anne did all she could to constantly uplift her family's spirits. John had no tolerance for socializing with the few friends they had in the surrounding area, though he did not disallow his wife and children visits from their acquaintances. After some difficult years, during which, much to her credit, Anne's love and devotion to him never wavered, John cast off his sad spirits and the family was whole once again.

Stewart, as the eldest son, was raised to take over the farm estate, and after his Grand Tour in 1824, returned to Carperby and Hillcroft House. In 1826 Margaret was married to Vincent Fairburn, a gentleman she had met on a trip to Whitby, and she moved to the coast to live in his home.

Master David, as the second son—and future father of Mycroft and Sherlock—was educated to take over the business responsibilities in the textile company his father had maintained after his uncle's death. This, apparently, was not an unhappy idea to Master David, who had a head for business matters, and who did not especially want to join the military or the clergy. He did well at public school, he was especially proficient in mathematics and French. At college, though, he developed a most unwelcome tendency to drink and gamble beyond the allowance his father had granted him. His weakness for these vices was magnified during the freedom of his European Grand Tour in 1833, and finally his father ordered him and his guardian home, two months early, as his spending had become quite outrageous. It was well known that his father enjoyed his daily imbibing—which had become quite firmly established during his years of grieving his dead brother and never ceased thereafter—but had never let his regular habit embarrass and bankrupt him the way Master David had. In fact, when Mr. Holmes drank, his reaction was, unusually enough, to require quiet and solitude, while Master David became very gregarious. Upon his return to Carperby, after a lengthy chastisement from Mr. Holmes, Master David was forthwith sent to the business at Huddersfield, where his father hoped he would settle down in his duty of accepting the responsibility of managing other people. A portion of his pay from his managerial position was sent home monthly to help recompense his father for paying off the youth's foreign debts. It may be clearly stated at this time that Master David took to his position with noticeable competence and afforded his father no cause for regret or further forbearance.

In February of 1837, Master David travelled to Paris to attempt to expand the textile firm into a foreign market. It was there, while walking in the Le Tuileries park to relax after spending all afternoon in several shops on the Champs Elysées, that he noticed Catherine Simone Lecomte-Vernet, who was taking the air with her friend. Master David was immediately smitten with her graceful carriage and her stunning beauty. He introduced himself—he was quite fluent in French—and asked if he might call upon her the next day. Mlle. Lecomte-Vernet was the daughter of Camille Francoise Josephine Lecomte nee Vernet, the sister of the famous military painter Emile-Jean-Horace Vernet. She accepted Master David's card and his invitation. He began seeing the twenty-two-year-old mademoiselle and was soon spending time with her parents, who appeared to approve of his business acuity, his skill at French, and his genuine affection towards their daughter. Extending his visit in France for some months, Master David contacted his father in England in August not only to acclaim his business contracts with several Parisian stores, but also to announce his engagement to Catherine Lecomte-Vernet.

The wedding was held in in October 1837, in St. Oswald's Church in Askrigg, as Anne Holmes could not travel far without grave discomfort from her rheumatism. It was quite an affair, I understand. M. Leon Lecomte and Camille Lecomte-Vernet, as well as their sixteen-year-old son Charles Hippolyte Emile Lecomte-Vernet—who was to become a famous painter in his own right—were, of course, present at the affair. Horace Vernet was not able to attend as he was travelling in Constantine, creating the paintings of the siege there that he would exhibit at his 1839 Salon showing. Vernet's wife, Louise de Pugol; their daughter, Louise;

and her husband, the painter Paul Delarouche, did attend. Also, other second cousins came, grandchildren of Vernet's aunt who died in the Revolution and were supported by Vernet's father afterwards. Through connexions of Mr. David Holmes, one wound up settling in Lancashire in 1845 under the Anglicised name of Verner.

The marriage was a gay affair lasting for days, and not lacking in expense, I may add. A goodly feast was held for the farmers as well, which they very much appreciated, and there was music and dancing 'til morning as well as a few horse races for ribbons. The happy couple settled in Huddersfield, but unfortunately, that winter, David's unmarried brother Stewart died of a sudden intestinal illness and his father called him home to Hillcroft House to learn to become the squire of the estate. Thus Master Holmes returned to Carperby, leaving his business duties in the hands of his associates and bringing his lovely wife with him. There they began the new routine of their lives.

Life at Hillcroft House was pleasant. The house itself was large, but not exceedingly so, and was very comfortable. It was a square, brick house and consisted of four floors. The entrance hall was prettily arranged with wall hangings and rugs, carved oak chairs, oak table, two umbrella stands, and an oak cabinet containing crystal bowls Mrs. John Holmes enjoyed collecting. There was a blazing, open grate in the wintertime, when also a double curtain of felt was hung on a rod over the front door to prevent the passage of draughts. There had been some deer trophy heads upon the walls from over one hundred fifty years ago before the northern Stainmore forest had been cut for Swaledale's mining industry, but Mrs. Catherine Holmes had requested their removal due to her sensitive nature regarding respect to all of God's living creatures. The two Mr. Holmeses had, perhaps reluctantly, complied. It was not the killing of the animals for food she objected to, but the prideful exhibition of their death. The ground floor contained a library, with a beautiful Turkey rug and rosewood furniture; busts of Shakespeare, Shelley, Hermes, and Socrates above the bookshelves; a bronze grandfather clock; and old family ornaments decorating the chimney piece. The library was well stocked, for the long line of Holmes had always been proponents of education and self-improvement and had been avid readers and collectors. Mrs. Catherine Holmes herself loved the attending and reading of plays, and Shakespeare was well represented on the bookshelves.

The morning room was cheerful and cosy, displaying daguerreotypes of family members, the Holmeses having been early appreciators of that somewhat expensive new field. Once they became parents, they had pictures taken of themselves and Mycroft in Huddersfield and had an expert come to the house once for several more daguerreotypes of the entire family after Master Sherlock's birth. Both the carpet and crebonne curtains of the morning room were bright. There were several chairs of no similar pattern—Mrs. Holmes' favorite was a bergère chair with a rounded cane back. She felt it made up in comfort what it lacked in glamour. A stand was always filled with healthy plants, and, when available from the greenhouse, gorgeous flowers. There was also a piano in this room, and Mrs. Holmes spent many hours entertaining family and friends with her considerable grace and skill in both playing and singing.

The dining room, like the drawing room, had a Turkey rug in it that did not quite cover the entire polished oak floor underneath. The table and all the other furniture were of oak; the sideboard carved with intricate designs was particularly enchanting. There were landscape paintings on the walls, and the leather chair cushions matched the burgundy curtains. Mr. Mycroft William Holmes had added the large ballroom adjacent to the dining room, also with oak floor and chairs around the room's periphery.

Mr. David Holmes' study was also the smoking room, and Mr. Holmes was often to be found in there enjoying his pipe and cigars, reclining in a mahogany armchair with a floral tapestry back and seat. A few deer trophies had been rehung on the walls; the others were in storage in the attic. He also had two desks in the room, from which he directed the running of the tenant farms, the raising of the farm cattle and sheep, the investments in the textile firm, and in general managed the household budget.

At the back of the ground floor was a greenhouse. This had been one of the specific additions to the home when it was enlarged by William Holmes, and it was a marvel to behold. From Grace Holmes it had passed to Anne Holmes, and upon Anne Holmes' death in 1839, it became the loving responsibility of Mrs. Catherine Holmes, and she worked diligently with the groundskeeper to achieve success. She went to flower shows in Leyburn and, through one of Mr. Holmes' University acquaintances in London who was a devoted botanist, was able to specially order some plants not easily acquired in the rural counties. She read books on flower arrangement, and the house was therefore always gaily adorned with bright and pleasing flowers in vases. Other plants in the home were palms, yuccas, and cycads; ivy was framed around picture frames, particularly in the morning and drawing rooms, and even sometimes around windows. New house girls were all carefully instructed in the proper amount of nitrate of soda to add to the daily changed water of cut flowers to ensure their longevity.

The first floor contained the drawing room, which had a number of chairs arranged in perfect readiness for conversation, with small tables interspersed, several whatnots, a corner cabinet which held port, whiskey, and brandy bottles, and other assorted pieces. The master bedchamber was furnished with a large four-poster brass bed with metal mesh springs and a hair mattress. The bed had a pleated red alpaca canopy and fringe around the top. Anne Holmes had been an avid seamstress, and all the family bedclothes were quilts of her hand. Also in the master bedroom were Kidderminster carpets, and floral wallpaper in light shades which was intended to soothe the emotions and promote easy slumber. I often wondered if my chambers had been so decorated would I have had less of a struggle with insomnia my whole life. The bedroom contained a large cheval glass for Mrs. Holmes to dress by, her wardrobe, washbasin, and dressing table with cushioned seat. Off the main chamber there was a smaller dressing room for Mr. Holmes, which contained his wardrobe, dressing table, and washstand with chair. There were four other bedrooms on the first floor, each also of good size, one used by Mr. John Holmes until his death. One each was eventually used by Masters Mycroft and Sherlock, leaving two for visiting family and friends. The first floor also consisted of the large nursery/children's study, at first complete with toys and puzzles, but then soon after, with desks, books, and writing tablets. The second floor contained rooms for the servants and several spare bedrooms for visitors. The attic was used for storage.

As I have hopefully described, the house was comfortably furnished, and never overdone. I have never met an ostentatious Holmes; I do not believe there is a drop of gaudy blood among all those drawn from art.

The servants for the hall were thus: the butler, a Mr. Henry Elmsley up until 1840, when he died of chronic heart arrhythmia, and myself as butler and valet afterwards; Mrs. Winters became cook the same year, and always had a young village girl to help her; Miss Marie Borel as lady's maid; the housekeeper Mrs. Emily Birchall, with one house girl. A new house girl was hired the same week I was originally engaged, Clara Bower, eleven years old. Outdoors servants included the groundskeeper, Mr. Fitch, and assorted townspeople to help him with his duties, and the carriage man, Henry Hawkins.

Daily life was peaceful and generally uneventful at Hillcroft. As John Holmes aged, he suffered digestive disturbances and liver pain that made him dislike the energy and business of a great deal of socializing. Also, he greatly missed his wife after her death and took solace in Bible reading and much solitary reflection. He enjoyed walking his horse, a gentle mare named Rose Lady (his wife had favored roses in the greenhouse) around the land of the dales. He preferred riding alone, or with Hawkins, his carriage man, though on horse, not in his carriage. And for good reason, for the roads of the dale do not always take one where one wants to go with expediency, and travelling over the landscape not only affords one the intimate experience of the beauty and variety of the area, but could also save time if an exact destination, particularly going north or south from Carperby, was in mind. John Holmes had one dear friend with whom he enjoyed company, a Mr. John Chapman of Thornton Rust, a gentleman whom he knew from farming, who was also a widower. Often he would ride over to Mr. Chapman's house, or Mr. Chapman would visit Hillcroft House, and the two men would play chess, smoke pipes, or engage in avid conversation.

David and Catherine Holmes were a most devoted couple, and their enjoyment of each other's company was evident and heartwarming. As much as possible they spent all their time together, and their harmonizing was effortless. They spoke softly and gently to each other, and a natural agreement arose from them so spontaneously that dissension was unthinkable. There were times when they were by design separated: David was often gone checking up on the estate activities, or making the bimonthly trip to Huddersfield to look in at the textile firm and his investments, and he required privacy to engage in the letter writing that constantly arises in the course of business. David, like his father before him, was usually the justice of the peace for Carperby and Askrigg—which capacity occasionally called him to town to arbitrate disputes or had him secluded in his study with the aggrieved parties until the matter had been satisfactorily settled. Like his father before him, Mr. Holmes also sat in on the Quarter sessions, which occurred in Northallerton four times a year. Of those times when Mr. Holmes departed Hillcroft House, I had no indication that he was leaving for any reason other than stated—I never imagined him to be involved in government work, in England or during his trips abroad with Mrs. Holmes. How utterly fanciful it clearly appears now! But let me go on.

Mrs. Holmes herself was involved with caring for the tenant families and helping with the sick and poor in the villages with other area gentlewomen. And Mr. Holmes, when the beauty and mildness of a northern day beckoned, was not averse to dirtying his hands with the farmers in the care of the animals, or in fixing a stone wall. However, much time was still spent together between Mr. and Mrs. Holmes— they were both accomplished riders, and they would often spend a day riding out with a picnic lunch tidily packed in a basket. They also enjoyed long walks together to get some exercise. When the weather did not allow such outdoor activities, they spent the time playing chess, reading, working in the greenhouse, and visiting. Aside from Mrs. Holmes' obvious talents in song and piano, she also dabbled with painting in watercolours, though she did not have, as she said, "the Vernet gift for it."

The Holmes socialised regularly, for it was in Catherine's nature to crave company and it allowed David's conviviality to resurface in a more acceptable manner, through suppers, dancing, repartee, and whist, than it had years previously through drink. Home or away, there were garden parties and dinner parties, musical recitals, readings of plays, and the like. Mr. David Holmes enjoyed a hunting party occasionally—hares, foxes, or grouse—much to his wife's disapproval, although he did not frequent such activities, for, unlike his trophied ancestors, he was a most inexpert shot. Occasionally the men would socialize for whist, and at those times Mr. David Holmes was likely to overindulge in his vice of drink; Mrs. Holmes did not chastise him for it. The Holmes travelled occasionally to the coast to visit David's sister Margaret, her husband Vincent Fairburn, and their children. Every year the Holmeses happily left for one or two months to tour Europe, visiting Mrs. Holmes' relations in France, and then on to new destinations for the enjoyment of different sights and cultures. Catherine also travelled, sometimes with her husband, and sometimes with Mrs. Hastwell—her closest friend—to York, and even to London a few times to hear musical concerts, but more often to engage her passion for plays. Mr. Holmes wrote assiduously to a man he had met at University, a Mr. Robert Sherlock, who was a banker in Plymouth, and with Mr. Holmes' frequent reception of missives from the same gentleman there were no attempts to hide their mutual affection. Once a year Mr. Sherlock would visit Hillcroft House or Mr. and Mrs. Holmes would journey to Plymouth.

It was a happy, calm, and easy life marred by only one particular recurrent anguish—Catherine seemed unable to carry a child to confinement. The Holmeses had wanted to begin having children immediately upon marrying, for one of the many things that had attracted them to each other was their similar desire for a large brood of children running hither and yon throughout the house, a home filled with laughter and joyful noise. After the October marriage in 1837, Catherine had the delight of announcing she was with child in 1838; however, not four months later the child was stillborn and Catherine was weak for a month from the hemorrhaging. Another miscarriage followed in 1839, and 1840—even though during the third attempt she had spent most of the time resting in bed. Each one caused a convalescence of months due to loss of blood and sorrowing distress. Finally, after another stillbirth in the fourth month of a pregnancy in 1842, John Irwin, the surgeon from Burton, told the Holmeses she must give up any hope of a child and urged them to protect her own health.

"Further pregnancies will only result in a similar outcome, and the inevitable weakening of her nerve force may result in permanent disability," the surgeon had warned.

Although such a pronouncement was akin to shooting them both through the heart, their love was so strong that together they were able to continue living fully and without any hint of reproach from either. They thought of adopting a child, but Catherine was of the view that if God wanted them to have a child, they would on their own, and if not, they should not contravene His wishes.

Life continued much the same as before, though Catherine did not conceive again and so was not forced to endure another failed pregnancy. In November of 1845 Mr. John Holmes died of liver failure, his skin the colour of a daffodil. In the last years Mr. David Holmes had frequently requested he stop drinking, and for a few uncomfortable weeks once I was ordered by the son not to serve him drinks and by the father to bring him one immediately. Confronting the son with this impossible situation, he was forced to relent. John Holmes continued his imbibing, much to his physical detriment, for in the last two years of his life he was unable to ride due to the discomfort from the horse's gait upon his swollen liver.

After his father's death, David suffered briefly from the same melancholy John had succumbed to after his own brother Brian's demise, though it was not quite of equal intensity. David had loved his father deeply, and with one less person in the home and no children, he felt it to be unbearably lonely at times. His indulgence of his personal vice was quite regular for several months after his father's death until he spoke with Catherine and they decided to attempt another pregnancy. It was not until February 1846, when Catherine announced she was once again with child, that Mr. Holmes was able to once again refrain from drinking, and it seemed that the Holmeses were once again full of anticipatory worry and joy. And this is where Mrs. Winters comes in, for she was used to leaving food out for "the little people to eat" and swears she heard unusual whispers in the night air weeks before Mrs. Holmes became with child, which she had never heard before. I do not know, for I heard nothing myself, and feel myself to have been born and bred in a more rational age, but Mrs. Holmes carried that baby to confinement and gave birth to him 12 October 1846. Suddenly, after ten years of childless marriage, when she was now thirty-two and Mr. Holmes was thirty-five, they had the wonderful pleasure and magnificent blessing finally to be the parents they had always dreamed of being.

"A miracle," surgeon Irwin claimed. "I would have never thought it possible." Mrs. Winter crossed herself for a week after the child's birth. They held a grand gala for their friends and the tenant farmers and villagers when Mrs. Holmes was recovered. Upon learning of the successful confinement, Mr. Robert Sherlock and his family arrived at Hillcroft bearing the gift of a magnificent steed, which almost made both the Holmeses weep from gratitude, and which they named First Boy.

Chapter Seven
Mycroft

The child was born healthy and plump, with a shock of brown hair already present on his large head, and was named Mycroft Sinclair Holmes. Though Mr. and Mrs. Holmes were both tall of stature, Mr. Holmes was stocky as the Holmeses typically were, while Mrs. Holmes was slight, so it was obvious that the lad had inherited from Mr. Holmes' family side. Mr. Holmes proudly pointed out that fact to every visitor and servant as often as possible, I myself being the recipient of his comment no less than seven times. The lad seemed already to have a fully developed phlegmatic nature and spent more time watching everything around him than in crying or cooing. He seemed contained and content at all times and did not seem to mind if he were held or put in the crib as long as there was something interesting for him to observe. For all his extraordinarily inquisitive mind, however, he also was not averse to sleep. He fell instantly into slumber when put down at night, and enjoyed two to three naps during the day. He excelled at verbal skills at an uncanny pace and by six months he could say "mama," "papa," "nanny," and "sleepy."

As soon as he could grasp objects, he studied them—twisting them around in his pudgy hands to view them from all angles—with an intensity that was highly entertaining to observe. From the moment of the child's birth, a smile as wide as the sea never left Mrs. Holmes' face. Mrs. Holmes had hired a nanny, of course, but then spent all of her time with the boy herself, much to the nanny's disapproval.

"You'll spoil the lad, and then he'll be no good at all, madam," Mrs. Kirby would say.

"Let him be spoiled. I shall love him all the while," Mrs. Holmes would reply, holding and hugging him.

However, aside from a rare giggle, Master Sinclair seemed oblivious to all the attention given him, and mainly spent his time examining anything he could hold onto or that came into his view. Any adult who picked him up soon learned to pay attention to jewelry, watches, and the like. He absolutely loved it when he was taken outside and was able to view the workers and the animals—anything new or unusual delighted him. He would watch everyone he was near; he was particularly enthralled with—one can only say—the scrutiny of all persons, their clothes, their tools, and their activities. Incessant crying episodes in the nursery were soon shown to be immediately alleviated by being placed in a roomful of adults. As soon as his pudgy body was dropped onto a blanket in the corner or on a settee, he would listen to them speak and watch their movements with apparent fascination, and he amazed the Holmeses' friends by his well-behaved span of attention in what they would have assumed should have been of the most dreary and dull interest to a toddler. Sometimes, even as a baby, he would engage eye contact with a person so completely the visitor would find it difficult to break that focused connexion.

Master Mycroft continued his study of objects as well. It seemed he analyzed his toys more than played with them—which drove Mrs. Kirby to distraction—and was adept at figuring out the simple puzzles with which he was gifted. When he was seven months old, he was given a board with holes for circular, triangular, and rectangular shaped blocks to fit in; he seemed to enter a trance while looking at it and holding the block pieces, but then correctly placed each block in its proper fitting without a mistake. Mr. Holmes positively beamed with pride, and lavished him with all types of building blocks and games—though the hobby horses and balls held no interest for him, and he would utter no sounds of delight if rocked on the horse. His true attraction was to people, and when a servant came into the room—for example, the house girl to start a fire—he immediately stopped whatever he was doing and stared at the person so strongly that some complaints came of it.

"He gives me the creeps, he does, sir," Clara reported to me, the first of the numerous complaints I would hear for years from her and other servants, and any workers who came to the house.

"Come now, Clara, he's only eight months old," I said, patting her gently on the arm.

"It's his eyes, sir, they seem to bore right into me bones and blood," she continued. "Mrs. Winters says the fairies made him. Can you please get him to stop staring at me?"

"Uh, I'll look into it," I said. "You go along with your work." And she did, relieved at least temporarily by my support.

Clara's appeasement by such an inane statement as the one I had uttered, "looking into" a toddler bothering her, was amusing to me and I thought nothing further of the incident except to chastise Mrs. Winters for spreading such disrespectful calumny against the child of her employers. Still, it was slowly becoming apparent to us all that the child was disturbingly precocious in his mental development.

His speaking at eleven months old was extremely disconcerting; he had a conception of numbers, colours and time that illustrated his progression into advancement way beyond his tender age. He was not consistent in his verbal abilities, for he added words to his speech at his own pace, some days exhibiting a chattiness that was generally incongruent with his basic personality and then often he would be silent for a day or two as he watched others converse, seeming effortlessly to correctly fathom and institute their vocabularies himself. The first time he said "Hello, Mrs. Birchall. How do you do? I am well myself," to the housekeeper when he was barely a year old, the poor woman was so shocked she forget to dust the morning room.

Once when he greeted his mother in the morning, as Mrs. Kirby was taking him outside in a perambulator on a fine early summer day in 1848, he said, "Good morning, mama. What a lovely green dress that is. What lovely lace."

His mother immediately responded, "Why thank you, Sinclair. I bought it in London two years ago on our way to France."

"Did you see Grandma Camille?" he asked.

"Yes, my mother was—" Of a sudden Mrs. Holmes realised it was her one-year-old child she was speaking to in so mature a manner, and she was struck dumb by the fact.

Master Sinclair patiently watched her slightly pale and then recover with a concentration that seemed endless.

"Yes, well, run along and play, now, Sinclair," she said, waving to him and Mrs. Kirby.

"I want to watch the farmers instead," he said.

"No more sitting around for you, young Master," Mrs. Kirby admonished. "It's a walk in the open air we'll do, to breathe in some fresh summer air."

I must admit that out of all the household I found it extremely ironic that the woman who probably spent the most time with Master Sinclair was the person who seemed the most oblivious to his precocious nature. A severe woman in her forties, her hair already grey and arranged in a tight bun, dressed always in black or brown, Mrs. Kirby had nannied so many children in such a similar pattern that it was impossible for her to acknowledge that this lad fell very much outside her rigidly devised and unchangeable child-rearing methods, even though she was in his presence and conversed with him all day. As Master Mycroft briefly frowned at her, it seemed that he, if not she, realised the faults of her obtuse recognition of his advanced development. But Master Sinclair sat back in the perambulator, and with a quick wave and smile to his mother, exited the house with Mrs. Kirby.

Mrs. Holmes went into the morning room and stood in front of the small mirror on the wall, smoothing down the lace at her neck.

Physically he grew and gained weight well, though he did not seem to have an apt command of his body movements—he had difficulty picking up fruit pieces with his fingers, and was not able to walk until a year and a half old, and then still not with confidence, although his slowness in that regard did not seem to upset him at all. It did concern his father however.

Mr. and Mrs. Holmes, as parents for the first time, did not, of course, really know what to expect of their child. And since their love of their son was bountiful and sincere, they regarded the peccadilloes of the lad with tender hearts. Although their friends and acquaintances, many of whom had children, were struck by the oddities of little Master Sinclair, their comments to Mr. and Mrs. Holmes reflected their happiness for the parents, and not the peculiar and exceptional qualities they noticed. Therefore, when Master Sinclair, at age fourteen months, would say, during a moment of natural silence in the conversation the Holmeses were having with some guests, "Mama, please call nanny. It's two o'clock and I feel decidedly tired. I want to nap," the visitors would voice their praise about Master Sinclair, oohing and aahing as one should expect at such articulate language from a toddler, and no one mentioned the strangeness of it.

So time passed, and although the Holmeses would have enjoyed the birth of another child, Mrs. Holmes did not announce she was with child. Therefore, they focused on Sinclair, who enjoyed the attention, but did not seem dependent upon it. The lad was ever satisfied, alone or with others, if there was something of interest to watch. He most enjoyed seeing new people, and regular visits to Carperby or other nearby villages, or the farms, or the quarry and mine to observe the workers and their actions, or to the homes of his parents' friends had him smiling widely. Once placed in an area where he was able to see the most activity, he could be left alone for hours without moving, though, of course, he never was left unattended.

Although being put on the horse First Boy with his father was terrifying to him, he would do fine if they walked down the road to the farms and town instead of just going in circles in front of the house, which would add irritation to his fear and beget a whininess. He seemed to play exceptionally well with whatever child he was placed with, and spent some time with the children of the friends of the Holmeses, getting along at all times with them, although hardly ever speaking in their company except when endeavouring to be peacemaker when arguments arose.

His mother continued to love him and spend a great deal of time with him, and if he didn't actually demand her attention, he never was averse to it. Mr. Holmes seemed slightly more uneasy with his unusual son than was his wife. Of course, one can expect that every father upon the birth of a first child, especially a son, has ideas and dreams for the child to fulfill. Mr. Holmes had possessed, like his wife, the desire to be very involved in the development of Master Sinclair. It seemed to me that Master Sinclair's disturbingly advanced mentation, and noticeable lack of physical coordination, were the exact opposite of what Mr. Holmes, as a typical farm estate owner, would have appreciated in his son. And one can only say with honesty that, unlike Mrs. Holmes, who seemed to accept her son's unusualness out of limitless love for him, Mr. Holmes was more confused and distressed, though I must say that he was never cross with the lad nor seemed to lose affection for him himself. Things did not improve as Master Sinclair grew, for little by little, he appeared to struggle with an ever-increasing tendency to irritable boredom with the commonalities of life.

Once he seemed to grow a disdain for us servants, muttering as if markedly vexed, "Still the same," whenever we entered the room, and then affecting an attitude of painful ennui until we left. This caused considerable distress for everyone, but once Mrs. Holmes had the intuitive idea to dress us in different clothes from the formal uniforms we had been wearing previously, Master Sinclair once again welcomed our presence. We were all, then, given an allowance to purchase articles of clothing so we could, with taste, vary our attire for the sake of maintaining Sinclair's interest. A pin, or pocket watch, was allowed as well, and I remember passing a room not long after that and hearing a brief snatch of conversation between Mrs. Birchall and Master Mycroft, about the history of the purple family pin she had worn that day on her dress. Mr. Holmes continued to supply Sinclair with toys and books, for the lad did have a habit of attaining a level of apathy with his analysed possessions much quicker than one would have supposed.

Not long after the clothes incident, he became listless and cross upon entering the morning room, in which he spent a considerable amount of time in the company of Mrs. Holmes.

"Mama," he said, "must things always stay the same? It is quite uninteresting."

The ever indulgent Mrs. Holmes had the housekeeper alternate the house decorations from room to room, after Master Mycroft had gone to bed, so the rooms' redecorations would surprise him in the morning. She also engaged the groundskeeper to move the furniture around individual rooms, thus altering their form. She even moved the furnishings from room to room, when it would not ruin the comfort of Mr. Holmes or absolutely undermine the propriety or adornments specific to the usage of some chamber. All this pleased Master Mycroft greatly and he would spend some time studying the rooms as he entered them in contemplation of exactly what had been moved where, announcing his findings with assurance and pride. It was, if I may be so bold, eerie how the lad could discern any rearrangement after but moments of narrow-eyed observation. Certainly, this was all very indulgent on the part of the parents, but so sincerely glad were they to have the child, even if he be occasionally troublesome, all considerations for his desires were foremost in their thought. And also, Master Mycroft was a thoughtful lad, and he earnestly expressed gratitude to his parents for their effort on his part. Let me strongly emphasize that most often Master Sinclair was a very well-behaved, respectful, quiet lad. He still sat maturely, and did what he was told to, although he could have the rudeness to quickly make a face about it if he felt it was distasteful. He did not make messes, was clean in general, put away his toys and books unerringly, was gentle to animals and with other children, shared toys well, and almost never, aside from clumsiness, got into trouble. He ate what was placed in front of him without a peep of complaint.

It was this streak of irritability that was his worst aspect, his seeming impatience at times with people and things and his easily attained level of boredom. And once the lad began complaining, he could maintain the tantrum for a half hour; although it seemed to me when seeing him thus that his eyes were more calculating than aggravated, and never relented from their scrutiny of others. I had the chilling feeling that many of his behaviors, complaints included, were experiments to him to test the reactions of others to his words or moods. I will swear before God Himself that once or twice, as he paused for breath in between statements of, "There's nothing to do or see; it's all the same," and the like, the lad pursed his lips together and emitted a decided "hmm" as he watched whatever adults were nearby endeavour to appease him. It occurred to me the lad was discovering the power he held over those around him. However, if such monstrous demonstrations, contrived or otherwise, could easily be prevented by moving the flowerpot from here to there, the Holmeses eagerly engaged such extra demands for the sake of their ordinarily pleasant son. After some time, I noticed that it seemed Master Sinclair grew bored with his tantrums, as if he had learned what he needed to know, and they ceased, although his parents—particularly his mother— had something in the house rearranged at least once a week. It became part of Mrs. Birchall's morning duties to switch decorations and lamps, and so forth, as she could, and still I was ordered to move around some of the heavier furniture.

In between Master Sinclair's extraordinary verbal communications, and once we all expected his stares and his trance-like attentions to toy or book or person or scene, and as we watched him struggle to kick the ball rolled to him by his father or the groundskeeper, it was not difficult to fall back into the attitude that he really was a normal child with just some slight tendencies to genius. Perhaps readers of this biography might find the Holmeses in error for not fully embracing the genius the child expressed, but in their defence all I can say is that all these two devoted and very decent people wanted was a typical family to love and be with. To have struggled so long for a single child and then see that child lost to them due to his innate natural genius was something the Holmeses, I think, did not want to admit. So as much as possible, Master Sinclair's commonness with other children his age was focused upon, and his precocious nature was known but ignored as much as possible, or treated as something completely normal.

I remember, though, the exact day in late 1848, when Master Sinclair was two years old, that the Holmeses had to give up any pretensions that Master Sinclair was actually a typical child. He was in the library with his mother; she sat reading a book in a chair and he sat on the floor with a book, turning the pages slowly.

I had just brought her in a cup of tea when Master Sinclair stood quite deliberately and walked, on still slightly shaky legs, to his mother, holding the book in both hands. She smiled at him as he approached, but her countenance drained of colour as soon as he spoke.

"I want to be taught to read, Mama," he said to his mother, holding up the book for her to see.

I should have taken my leave, but I must admit I was surely as stunned as Madam and did not seem to have command of my own legs at the moment.

"I'm sorry, what did you say?" Mrs. Holmes asked her son, holding the teacup in a frozen pose.

"I want to be taught to read," Master Sinclair repeated. He pointed at the book-shelves. "There are many books to read. I have a good deal to learn."

"Yes, well, let me talk to your father about it first." Mrs. Holmes recovered a bit. Then she laughed uneasily and lifted him up to her lap. "Are you sure you're ready for it? Wouldn't you rather play with your toys or ride on First Boy with your father?"

"Oh, no, I'm ready to read, I think. I am tired of the toys," he said. "I want to learn to read. And speak French, like you and papa and Mr. Brewster." It was true that the Holmeses enjoyed speaking in French as well as English, for they were both fluent in the two languages, as were a number of their acquaintances, and, as I said, one of the reasons for my being hired was my fluency in French as well. In general, however, they spoke in English to Sinclair, for they thought an average child could only develop one language so young.

Well, you can imagine Mr. Holmes' reaction when he returned home and Mrs. Holmes related to him Master Sinclair's desire; his responses were easily heard from the hallway, and mainly consisted of his repeating "He said what?" "Reading, at his age?" and "I don't believe it. Are you sure, my dear? He's only two years old."

"Well, goodness, David, please go speak to him yourself," Mrs. Holmes said.

"I dare say I must. Brewster, bring me Sinclair," Mr. Holmes requested of me.

The lad was upstairs in the nursery with Mrs. Kirby. She was attempting to interest him in a book she had open that showed different animals on each page. Mrs. Kirby had refused, apparently, still to budge from her set pattern of dealing with developing children, even though we all knew that Master Sinclair was beyond her simple ministrations.

"And this is a cow," she said, pointing out the animal for Master Sinclair.

I have never to this day seen a look of such absolute indifference on a toddler's face—in fact, I never knew that a toddler should be able to create such an impertinent visage. Suddenly he turned the page of the book and one by one quickly pointed to the animals drawn on the facing pages.

"Horse, fox, deer, hawk." He turned the page again. "Dog, duck, chicken, fish." Again, "Elephant, tiger, monkey, camel." He looked at the nanny. "You have shown me this book twice before. Enough."

The nanny stared back at the lad, at first with anger and then with fear in her eyes. I cleared my throat to dissipate the charged energy of the room and said, "Mrs. Kirby, Mr. Holmes requests the presence of Master Sinclair in the library."

"Excellent," Master Sinclair said as he rose from his chair. He walked past Mrs. Kirby and reached up to grab my hand. "Let's go."

"Mrs. Kirby?" I asked, not wanting to create antipathy between us by my participation in Master Sinclair's dismissal of her.

"Ach, take the lad to his father," was all she said as she waved me away.

I did not witness the scene in the library, for I was busy organizing the presentation of supper. However, I was able to observe during the meal a combination of confusion and anxiety in both the Holmeses, and a certain smugness in the lad's expression. Master Sinclair had begun eating with them several months earlier, on his request.

Mrs. Kirby was dismissed two weeks later with a letter of high regard and a quarter year's pay, and at the very beginning of 1849 a private tutor, the former schoolmaster of the free grammar school in Bainbridge, a Mr. Anthony Wharton, was hired. Mycroft was elated and took to his studies with a concentration and quickness that amazed his tutor.

"The lad's a genius, sir and madam, I have to say," he shared with Mr. and Mrs. Holmes after the first month of working with Master Sinclair. "I've never seen anything like it in all my years of teaching. At this rate he'll be reading English by two and reading and speaking French not long after."

"Really," Mr. Holmes said, tapping his pipe out over the fireplace grate. "Really." In his pensive state he absentmindedly maintained the now superfluous tapping.

I noticed Mrs. Holmes had to undo a rare knitting error. "Well, keep going, Mr. Wharton," she said.

For a year, Mr. Wharton taught Master Sinclair every day during the week, for two hours in the morning and three in the afternoon. I'm sure Master Sinclair would have enjoyed lessons with him on Saturday as well, but Mrs. Holmes was of the firm persuasion—along with the former Mrs. Kirby—that a day of play among other children, or spent outside in the fresh air, was more important to ensure his nerve energy was not singularly concentrated in studious endeavours. For Sinclair, although a large, healthy lad with a good appetite, was still awkward in his command of his body and was still, one had to admit, on the clumsy side. He would reach for a cup and knock it to the floor, or stumble for no clear reason into table legs. Mr. Holmes tried to disguise his disappointment in Sinclair's continued disinterest in catching or kicking balls. Master Mycroft would ride First Boy with his father with tolerance, though I feel Mr. Holmes was saddened that he never asked for a ride but always had to be simply placed upon the steed's back.

Master Sinclair was perfectly cheerful when observing a machine or contrivance being fixed, but, if handed a tool to hold, he was bound to drop it on someone's foot. Mr. Holmes bought him a tricycle, and after a few turns around the small drive in front of the house, Master Sinclair would want to nap. When he was with other children running and playing, he would always be the first to drop out and sit for a rest. He truly had no stamina for physical activities, though his parents persisted in forcing him to engage in them—his mother to divert his nerve energy from his brain, his father to try to develop his maladroit capabilities in raising him to be the son who would take over the running of the farm. Master Mycroft did enjoy spending time with his father when the latter was going over the accounts of the farm, or acting as justice of the peace and mediating squabbles, and so his father often included him in those activities.

Sundays were spent in the church, for Mrs. Holmes was a religious woman who preferred attending both the morning and afternoon services in Carperby. Mr. Holmes went at least once for himself, and often twice, the second time only to please his wife. Mrs. Holmes spent the rest of the day reading the Bible, usually to Master Sinclair, who loved being read to.

Master Mycroft spent the first year and a half with Mr. Wharton enhancing his speaking and reading abilities, which by the end of that time were formidable. Mr. Wharton proudly showed the Holmeses the schoolbooks Mycroft was now at—almost the level of the first form; and discussed with fervour the lad's immense interest in history, and politics and government. "He seems to have a bottomless desire to learn how things have been, and are presently run. He knows the kings by heart already, and the important events of all their reigns. I've begun Latin and Greek with him. It's amazing, sir."

"I didn't know all the kings until I was thirteen," Mr. Holmes related to his wife when Mr. Wharton returned to his student.

When Master Sinclair turned three, in 1850, Mr. Wharton began teaching him to write, for it seemed he had finally developed the coordination required to accurately control the pen upon the paper, without spilling the ink jar, or having five words take up the entire page. It was then that he learned his name was actually Mycroft Sinclair Holmes, for one of the first things Mr. Wharton had him practice writing, after the individual letters of the alphabet were soon under his command, was his full name. As you no doubt noticed during my genealogical information at the beginning, each generation of Holmes carried the Mycroft appellation. It seemed the Mycroft designation dated back to the first Holmes who had landed here in Carperby, and who had attached Mycroft to his firstborn son out of joy in living on "my little farm." You must understand that although the Holmes line had, since then, an exacting tradition to incorporate the appellation Mycroft as the Christian or middle name of the first male of each generation, no one had ever actually been *called* Mycroft, due to its peculiar nature. Therefore Master Sinclair had been addressed only as Sinclair his whole life, and he was noticeably surprised to discover his Christian name was truly the ancient, esteemed, yet ignored Mycroft.

I was serving the afternoon tea and scones one Thursday in the drawing room to Mr. and Mrs. Holmes as they sat entertaining Father and Mrs. Metcalfe, when Mr. Wharton took his leave of the Holmeses, and left Master Sinclair in the drawing room as per the Holmeses' desire.

Young Master Sinclair stood before his parents and said, "Excuse me, Papa and Mama. May I talk to you later?"

His parents, in excellent spirits due to the agreeable discourse they had been sharing with their guests, smiled at each other. His father picked Master Sinclair up and placed him in his lap. "Come, lad, speak to us now. We have nothing to hide from Father Metcalfe and his wife, do we?"

"*I* don't, Papa," the boy said.

His father laughed. "Neither do your mother or I. So tell us what you will."

Master Sinclair seemed to take a moment to study his father and mother, and then turned his gaze to Father Metcalfe and his wife. It seemed to me that somehow in his brilliant child's mind he was contemplating the situation, trying to figure out the proper strategy for arranging his thoughts and words. It lasted but a minute, and yet the silence it begat as those four adults waited for this boy to speak was most discomforting.

Finally the lad stirred. "I should like to be called Mycroft, not Sinclair, Papa," he said.

That was most unexpected. His mother recovered first. "Mycroft? But Sinclair, why should you want to be called that? Sinclair is a much more...appropriate name."

"But Mycroft is my Christian name," the lad said. "Mr. Wharton showed me and explained what it means to me. I like it."

Now his father reacted with some anguish. "Good God, lad! You like it? It's a very peculiar name; just a family tradition, but not to be taken seriously. We have never addressed the family member named Mycroft as Mycroft—it's just a ritual formality. That's the way it's always been, son."

The lad again seemed lost in thought momentarily. Then he said, "I'm proud to be a Holmes, papa. I'm proud of the name Mycroft, too. I enjoy the sound of it. It's unusual."

Mrs. Holmes persisted. "But, I fear you shall be dreadfully teased by your friends if you choose to be called Mycroft."

"Don't worry about that, Mama," the lad said. "I don't think I shall ever have many friends."

At that his father's eyes seemed to swell and his cheeks puffed out. "Nonsense, lad. Any son of mine shall be as popular as a warm day in winter." He jiggled Master Sinclair for effect.

Again that disturbingly pensive countenance. Then he smiled at his father, "Yes, I will be very popular, Papa. Perhaps not overtly so, but very popular to those with whom I work. And I will be very important as well." He paused, then continued. "But I want to be known in those capacities as Mycroft Holmes. May I please be called that?"

"But why, child?" his mother asked exasperated.

The lad glanced at each adult in the room then clasped his hands to his chest. "My-croft," he said, pronouncing each syllable slowly and forcefully. Then he spread his arms out to seemingly encompass the room and beyond. "My world," he declared with an absolute confidence and brashness, as if he were laying ownership to what those words represented.

An eerie quiet hushed the room. Mrs. Metcalfe held her hand over her mouth, in awe or horror I could not tell. Mr. and Mrs. Holmes stared at each other, mouths agape. There was nothing more to be said, except perhaps prayers. The child was beyond reach at that moment. And his name from then on was Mycroft Holmes.

Chapter Eight
Deductions

Time passed. Mr. Hawkins left the employment of the Holmeses and a Mr. Wilcox was engaged. Master Mycroft continued his studies with Mr. Wharton. His verbal skills were his best subject; his vocabulary seemed to swell hourly. He also particularly relished lessons in history and politics—Napoleon, Machiavelli, Julius Caesar, Thomas More, Oliver Cromwell, John Adams, the Borgias; his interest in outstanding men of government was notable. He desired to learn of all forms of government and political thought systems. He was exceptional with his English, Latin, Greek, and French, moderate in mathematics and the sciences, and basically uninterested in the arts. However, he would read plays with his mother, as he knew she very much enjoyed his participation. She continued to lavish her love on him, and after the first few initial weeks of adjustment, had minimal trouble in establishing in her mind that he was now her son Mycroft.

As his learning accelerated, so did his habit of immersing himself fully in the observation of others. By 1851 his observations of others assumed grand proportions. He would gaze earnestly at shoes, clothes, cuffs, hats, trousers, shirts, dresses, coats; he would, politely, ask servants and workers to examine hands, faces, ears, hair; he would study tools and machines. Wherever he was taken he would study the dirt and grass and gravel. All visitors would be subject to his stares. He was fascinated by illness and requested books showing people with various diseases. He also requested books on military uniforms, and books with pictures showing workers at their different professions. He read the books on agriculture in the North Riding. "So I won't have to go to the farms to understand their activities anymore. I prefer being at home." When asked why he was so interested in those lines of inquiry, he responded enigmatically, "To figure out, I have to first know."

"Figure out what, son?" his father asked.

Master Mycroft's eyes shone. "Everything, Papa," he said.

This "figuring out" was mysterious to his parents until once when Master Mycroft sat with his mother in the drawing room, his father entered after being gone from Hillcroft House all day.

Master Mycroft observed his father ingress his chair, eyeing him like a lion watching some prey through tall veldt grasses, attuned to everything about his father, as if, like the lion, Master Mycroft's life depended upon it. His father was aware of this scrutiny of his person, but courteously ignored it—as we all endeavoured to, some more successfully than others—as its frequency had dissipated its blatant ill-mannered affront and only its eeriness remained.

"Papa, I think you rode First Boy to meet with Father Metcalfe, and then First Boy threw a shoe coming home. Luckily the smithy was able to fix it quickly," Master Mycroft declared. "Am I correct?"

Mr. Holmes finished the drink I had poured for him in a large gulp before turning to face his son, his visage a combination of curiosity and wariness. "Quite so, Sincl…Mycroft." He handed the glass to me to fill again. "How do you know?"

Even after a year, Mr. Holmes seemed uncomfortable with Master Mycroft's choice to use his peculiar Christian name as his formal appellation. It had been such a blatant switching of family roles—for a child to demand of his unwilling parents that they allow his name to change was quite unforgivably rebellious; the fact that the Holmeses had relented made the situation even more outrageous. It had upset Mr. Holmes to relate to his acquaintances that Sinclair was now formally Mycroft. I fear the change embarrassed him a good deal, because Master Mycroft had exerted power unsettling in one so young. It meant that Master Mycroft had slipped that little bit further away from him as a child. Furthermore, Mr. Holmes worried that use of the singular name would reflect poorly upon him as a parent for having chosen it originally, family tradition or no.

Master Mycroft put his book aside. "I figured it out, Papa."

As Mr. Holmes took another swallow of whiskey, Mrs. Holmes put aside her knitting and asked, "Really, Mycroft, how fascinating. How did you 'figure it out,' as you say, since you were not up when your father left this morning?"

Master Mycroft smiled and reveled in the complete attention he had garnered. "It's really quite simple, you know."

His gentle mother was willing to play his game. "Do tell," she requested, hands clasped together on her lap. At a questioning glance from his son, Mr. Holmes smiled, put down his drink and sat in a chair next to his wife. "Go on, tell us," he agreed.

"Well, here is what I thought," Mycroft said, sitting straight up with each of his hands resting on the arm of the chair. "When I saw you come into the room I noticed the religious tract in your jacket pocket, very similar to the type of tract Father Metcalfe has delivered here a number of times before. I also noticed your pants were wrinkled on the inside, as happens when you ride for a long while. I, therefore, thought that you had gone to Father Metcalfe on First Boy, not your other favorite—Midas. For this morning whilst I lay awake in bed I heard Mr. Wilcox take the carriage out earlier than your departure—no doubt to pick up the packages for Mama that were due to arrive in Askrigg today—and he favors Midas himself. I knew I was correct as I listened to the gait of the harnessed horse; certainly it was Midas' heavier trot." He looked directly at his mother. "Those packages were the dresses you ordered from the London clothesmaker when you and Mrs. Hastwell went to London for a week to see the opera and the Beethoven symphony three weeks ago; you mentioned upon your return that they would arrive today."

Mycroft returned his gaze to his father. "I noticed that your left trouser leg and both boots are filthy from mud, and that your left trouser leg seems to have been immersed in water. The only reason I could imagine that happening would be if you had been riding the steed after your visit to Father Metcalfe and his wife and First Boy had thrown a shoe. Due to your great affection for the horse, you would naturally have immediately dismounted to save him the discomfort of your weight without four even shoes. As we have had some rain recently, there would have been mud and puddles for you to traverse on the road, and no doubt, even with care, it is likely you accidentally stepped into some water. The mud on your shoe is particular to the red clay on the immediate outskirts of town and has been scraped off and dried. I think that means the shoe came off not far from town. You returned to Carperby for the shoe to be fixed by the smithy, where you removed most of the mud, and the heat of the blacksmith's fire dried both your trouser bottom and the mud. This occurred after the visit to Father Metcalfe and his wife; otherwise, as a result of Mrs. Metcalfe's unwavering cleanliness, which you have commented on so often, their servants should have fully cleaned your boot of the mud during your time with them. Once the horse was reshod, you then remounted and rode home, arriving only a little past your normal time of appearance."

He stopped and the Holmeses looked at each other, their de rigueur first response to Master Mycroft's shows of genius. I believe they found comfort in the shared uneasiness their son could create in them. As usual, Mrs. Holmes found words first.

"Well, dear, is Mycroft right? Did events happen as he...deduced?"

At the word "deduce," Master Mycroft took out a pencil and paper and wrote the word down.

Mr. Holmes shook his head side to side, then put his head back and laughed. To my eyes, it seemed as if he was at constant battle with himself—the one part that feared his own son to be a circus oddity, the other the loving father so glad to have a child that he could forswear and accept any behavior from him. I was joyful to see that almost every single time Mr. Holmes' innate goodness shone through and the accepting side was evident.

"I say, lad, it's as if you were there by my side, invisible, yet recording all the events that occurred. Uncanny, I say, quite uncanny. So that's figuring things out, is it?"

"Yes, Papa."

"Well, if nothing else, you've a career on the stage, or at county fairs," Mr. Holmes said, continuing to laugh.

"David!" Mrs. Holmes playfully reprimanded. "What a thing to say! I'm sure Mycroft can devise a more important use for his 'figuring things out' than those low avenues. Isn't that right, Mycroft?"

"Oh, yes, Mama. I shan't be on the stage or at fairs. Though I do not quite know where I will be."

"Well, try to have it 'figured out' soon, son," Mr. Holmes said, his laughter mounting. "After all, you'll be four before you know it."

When I left the room they were all still chuckling gaily, although the lad himself was laughing the least.

Mycroft continued his "deductions," as he termed them afterwards, sporadically. He was often correct, as when he spotted Mrs. Winters taking a break from cooking one afternoon and told her that he was looking forward to the chicken that night, and that he hoped the rheumatism in her right shoulder relented in its pain. As he walked off, I inquired of Mrs. Winters if the lad had been correct in his deductions, and amidst her incessant crossing of herself, she affirmed he was indeed.

One autumn day as he sat watching his mother arranging flowers in a vase in the morning room, he noticed Clara enter. He scrutinized her and then asked her if she had enjoyed spending her day off yesterday in the company of Farmer Horn's son. Clara gasped in shock, burst into tears, and ran from the morning room, leaving the fire unstarted. Miss Birchall did not seem to be able to console her, so I endeavoured to. It took me half an hour to calm her down, assuring her that Mycroft was not a mischievous fairy himself in human guise. That Mrs. Winters! After speaking to Mrs. Holmes I was able to assure Clara that she would not lose her position as a result of her previously private courting's now becoming family knowledge; so long as, of course, she did not find herself in embarrassing circumstances. Composed, Clara went to polish the silver.

I reported back to Mrs. Holmes and told her that Clara was once again fit for work. "Oh dear, oh dear," Mrs. Holmes said.

I heard Master Mycroft ask his mother, "Mama, why did Clara cry?"

"Because, dear child," his mother said, sitting down and holding both his hands, "you made her very uncomfortable."

"I did?" He looked puzzled. "I didn't mean to make her cry."

"I know, Mycroft. But not everyone enjoys your being able to figure things out about them."

"But why not?"

"Well," his mother hesitated, inhaling deeply. "Some people don't want others to know what you may be able to deduce. Clara didn't want us to know she was spending time with Charlie Horn, and so was upset when you figured it out, and told us."

"I see," Mycroft said. He nodded his head in thought. "So it's acceptable to figure things out if I don't always say what they are?"

"Sometimes it is acceptable to share, Mycroft. And other times it's not. You will have to learn when it is appropriate, and when not; and who it is appropriate with and who not. Or else, dear child, I fear you will continually be upsetting people, and that's not right. I know that may sound hard to you, and perhaps unfair, but it is not Christian to reduce servants to tears."

"I'm sorry, Mama," he said softly. "I don't want to hurt people. It's just that people are as easy to read as books to me."

"I know, Mycroft, I know," she responded, hugging him, but the lad did not hug back and after a moment she pulled back to look at him.

"Why am I so very different?" he asked. His mother just held him tighter.

Clara avoided Master Mycroft fervently after that, doing chores in a random manner that enabled her as much as possible to elude his presence. Mrs. Holmes understood and told Miss Birchall to allow Clara her odd cleaning routine.

Occasionally Master Mycroft was wrong in his deductions, and then his self-degradation was scathing. The next winter I returned to Hillcroft House after spending several days with my friends in Bridlington. Master Mycroft asked me how my trip to London had gone.

When I responded, and I must admit that I felt some untoward glee in doing so, that I had been in Bridlington, not London, the lad fell silent, and his countenance clouded over in consternation.

"But those new boots you're wearing; you've said before that they are made only at one boot maker in London on Oxford Street." If I ever had told the lad that, it was when I had purchased my last pair of boots, two years ago. His memory must have been photographic even then.

"And your new coat has a London label in it as well. I noticed that when you took it off." There was a touch of desperation to his words.

"Yes, Master Mycroft, these boots are made at that London boot maker, and the coat, as well. But, in a grand gesture of generosity, my friend ordered these for me from London and gave them to me as I resided at his home in Bridlington this past week."

"I am a fool," Master Mycroft said, and walked off in utter disgust at himself. He was most reserved and pensive for several days after that.

Even Mr. Wharton, whom Master Mycroft respected and admired greatly, was not immune to being the victim of his pupil's now infamous deductions. Usually, he welcomed Mycroft's amazing ability to figure things out; however, Master

Mycroft received another harsh lesson in verbally uncovering what was not desired to be noted.

In late spring of 1850, after the affair with Clara, I remember walking past the door of the nursery, then Master Mycroft's study, and hearing Mr. Wharton speaking forcefully and with some asperity in his tone.

"Really, Mycroft, whether my wife and I had a fight or not is decidedly a matter I should in no way be questioned about by you. While I appreciate the fact that you have somehow brilliantly deduced that my relations with my wife are presently strained, I'll have you know that one, the entire subject is surely none of your business; two, it is rude in the utmost to mention your thoughts to me along this line even if you did discern the truth; and three, I shall be forced to quit my position as your tutor if you ever bring up such impudent observations again."

Master Mycroft barely spoke at all for a week after that reprimand.

In the summer, Master Mycroft decided to preface his comments with "I have a deduction to make about…" and if the person to whom Master Mycroft was speaking allowed him to continue, he did; otherwise, he maintained his silence, although to do so seemed, at times, slightly irksome to him. For example, once during a garden party, he was sitting on a lawn chair as several guests played croquet on the back lawn.

"I have a deduction about Mr. Blade's health," Mycroft said as Mr. Blade patted his brow with a handkerchief after missing a wicket with his ball. The corpulent Mr. Blade was an extremely private and timid, though friendly, man; he heard Master Mycroft, and flushed so crimson a colour I thought he should faint. He muttered "Um, um, um," and whirled his handkerchief most comically until Mrs. Holmes tapped her son on the leg and said, "Perhaps not, dear."

"Yes, Mama," Master Mycroft obeyed. But he climbed down off his chair—jumping was out of the question for him—and walked slowly back to the house, head hanging low.

Some, as one may expect, were thrilled to be the subject of Master Mycroft's knowing eye and quick mind, and each time they visited the house, they deliberately presented themselves to the boy for his inspection, asking "Do you have a deduction to make about me, Mycroft?" Mr. Routh and Colonel Reston were that way, the colonel even going so far as to attempt deliberate obfuscation by carrying false clues upon his person. Master Mycroft was delighted to see either of them arrive at the estate, and made sure they were included in any invitations his parents sent out for gatherings. However, most people, though amused by the lad's gift, did not crave to be the object of his scrutiny themselves. Although the prefacing was very useful in avoiding disagreeable situations, in his brilliance a deduction was suddenly illuminated to him, and occasionally abrupt mistakes were made by his inappropriate declaration of them. However, any person with an obvious dislike of Master Mycroft's clarity of deduction was also the recipient of sincere apologies from the lad. Whenever that occurred, though, the lad would be silent for some hours once they were gone.

Several individuals and couples decided not to return to Hillcroft House, no doubt mortified that the Holmeses would allow their child to sit in the company of adults and that they would not forbid him from speaking at all. Mr. and Mrs. Holmes' allowance of their son's public eccentricities was shockingly against the norms and manners of the times, I can assure you. I wonder if the groundskeeper Mr. Fitch left for that reason—certainly he had avoided Master Mycroft as much as Clara had. Mr. Denkins was his replacement.

The Holmeses were certainly indulgent in both those regards, as they were with many others, but it was solely due to the unique features of their child, not because they did not understand or honor social mores and constraints. For the most part Master Mycroft did sit silently, although he would offer succinct comments about the conversation if he had a valuable insight. Of course, a toddler offering to clarify a view during a discussion amongst adults in and of itself was scandalous, and produced in the recipients anything from bewildered silence to pleasant consideration of his words. He never spoke for speaking's sake, adamantly refused to pay attention to gossip, and, after some time in trial and error, understood among whom he could speak freely and among whom it would be best to observe in quiet.

Most of the Holmeses' friends were loyal to them, however, and faithfully withstood the deductions and comments of their unusual son when they visited, although none extended to the lad invitations to gatherings where his parents were so welcomed.

Another two years passed in Hillcroft House, and Master Mycroft was five. His vocabulary was exemplary; his reading of English the same; his reading, writing, and speaking of Latin and French remarkable. He knew the names and dates of many historical figures and events, from the Romans to the Americans. He focused on Great Britain, though, and his love for his country was illustrated by his referring to it as "this great nation." He continued his lessons in other subjects as well with Mr. Wharton, whose relationship with his wife I was never privy to again.

Master Mycroft, with his schedule, did not spend much time with other children, nor did he seem to miss such contact. He seemed slowly to withdraw from his love of company, spending more and more time with his multitudinous books. He very much enjoyed his lessons and Mr. Wharton's company, and when his studies in the afternoon were over, he joined his mother or father wherever in or out of the house they were located. If they were both gone from home, Master Mycroft was left on his own, but was ordered not to leave the house until a parent attended him. He was fully compliant with his parents' wishes, and still—when other children would be playful from excess physical energy after hours of study—Master Mycroft was no stranger to an afternoon nap of some duration. As always, when awake, he was easily able to amuse himself, particularly with one of his ever-present books.

His parents still travelled to Europe yearly for one month; until he was three years old they hired a woman, Mrs. Thurmingham, a widow recommended to them by Mrs. Hastwell, to care for Mycroft during their absences. By happy chance, Mrs. Thurmingham was of a nature so calm and serene Master Mycroft was unable to ruffle even one of her feathers; even his deduction that she had been extremely heavy as a child was greeted with tranquility. The Holmeses used her whenever they both travelled abroad and left the lad at home.

Master Mycroft loved to travel at first around the countryside and to other nearby towns—for then all he saw was new—but he seemed to tire easily from the extra exertions journeying wrought upon a body; and by four year old, after several trips with his parents within England, he requested he be left at home with Mrs. Thurmingham all the time from then on.

"I shall best learn of the world from books, not trains and ships," he told his parents, and then left for another nap.

"Perhaps he needs some iron, dear," Mrs. Holmes said to her frowning husband.

Mr. Holmes decided to take the lad to a doctor in Northallerton the next time he sat for the quarter sessions. For all his lack of stamina, Master Mycroft had suffered from nothing more serious in his life than a brief chest cold as far as actual sickness was concerned, and had never been under treatment by a medical man. The chest cold had been promptly overcome by some herbs of Mrs. Winters, who, for all her excessive crossing, had real tenderness in her heart for the boy. My belief in regard to Mr. Holmes was that he hoped the doctor would actually find some easily treatable disease which would explain Mycroft's physical lethargy, negating Master Mycroft's own belief that this was just the way he was.

"Quick mind, slow body," he told his father one summer day after he tripped over a croquet wicket his father had just moments ago warned him that he was approaching.

"If he gets any slower, we'll have molasses for a son," I heard Mr. Holmes mumble in response as I served him some iced tea.

The doctor was not helpful, telling Mr. Holmes that his son was just extremely slothful, and that his nerve force must be more evenly distributed between his brain and body to prevent a grave disease or nervous breakdown from developing in the future. He was adamant about prescribing a harsh regimen of outside exercises and stretches, and mandated they should be enforced even during the cold of the winter. Mycroft then deduced aloud his diagnosis of the doctor as being in the first stages of heart failure, and wondered if a prescribed regimen of harsh outdoor exercises and stretches, even in the cold of winter, were good for toning and strengthening the heart. As Mr. Holmes admitted as he retold the story, this outburst brought both a grin to his lips and some small mortification to his sensibilities. They left the spluttering doctor posthaste, and returned home, the quarter sessions being over. Master Mycroft slept the entire way.

"Of course," Master Mycroft said, as Mr. Holmes ended his storytelling, "I'm quite lazy. The doctor was correct about that. But to tell a chilly, clumsy and tired lad to exercise in the cold—how ridiculous!"

At that the room erupted in mirthful head shaking, from parents and guests alike.

That autumn, Mr. Holmes' friend Mr. Robert Sherlock wrote to Mr. Holmes saying he should very much like to see Mr. Holmes—was it a good time to come visiting? He would be coming alone. Mr. Holmes, quite flustered with joy and expectation at this news, wrote back at once to come as soon as possible, and then initiated a somewhat annoying minute double-checking of my household preparations for his arrival. He spoke constantly of Mr. Sherlock to his son, regaling him with stories of their time spent together as "rather incorrigible" college students.

Mr. Holmes and Mr. Sherlock had been inseparable at University for the four years they attended, having met the very first day of classes by being seated next to each other in a philosophy lecture hall. As Mr. Holmes told the story, the heat of the room plus the fact that they both found philosophy interminable produced an inevitable sleepiness, and when they both awoke after the class they were the only two fellows left in the large chamber. Of course, that instantaneously bonded them together as if they had been joined at the hips, and from that moment on they lived, studied, drank, rowed, went on walks, and travelled together. Mostly they drank together, Mr. Holmes admitted.

"I hope, Mycroft, one day you, too, shall have a friend so close that he will be a brother in all ways but actual kinship," he told his son.

Master Mycroft smiled at his father's exuberant spirits, but said nothing.

Mr. Robert Sherlock was the third son. Very averse to a military career, and as a declared agnostic refusing to enter the clergy, therefore he had decided to enter banking. After graduation, he moved back to his home town of Plymouth and obtained a position at the Royal Bank of Devon and Cornwall. He had married the daughter of the vice president of the bank and had four children.

As I mentioned earlier, the two men had kept in constant contact throughout the years, through letters and visits—usually Mr. and Mrs. Holmes travelling to

Plymouth to see him and his family—although they hadn't seen each other for over a year by the time the letter arrived. The last time Mr. Sherlock had journeyed to Hillcroft House, Mycroft had been two, and ill in bed with the chest cold cured by Mrs. Winters' herbs. Therefore, aside from an introduction, and a few minutes spent with the lad in his sick bed, there had not been much contact between Mr. Sherlock and the boy. I was looking forward to Mr. Sherlock's reaction to the lad, although I was sure that Mr. Holmes wrote of him incessantly in his letters to his dear friend, and had no doubt fully cautioned him as to what he would encounter.

It was a warm, rainy spring day in April 1852 when Mr. Sherlock arrived in the carriage driven from the railway in Askrigg. A shorter man than Mr. Holmes, as most men were, Mr. Sherlock was very handsome, with a dark mane of thick black hair, a well-trimmed line of mustache, and gentle brown eyes. He was a slim man, and dressed in country tweeds and long leather boots.

Mr. Holmes greeted him at the door, and the emotions between the men were sincere and effusive. After a good amount of handshaking and shoulder slapping, Mr. Sherlock removed his outer garments and gave Mrs. Holmes a hug. He then turned to young Mycroft, who had watched this affectionate display dispassionately, as if it were a scene in a play he was critiquing. He stood straight, with his hands clasped behind his back, studying Mr. Sherlock with slitted eyes.

Mr. Sherlock was bemused by this not unexpected scrutiny, and stood arms akimbo for a moment looking down at the lad. A sudden bout of coughing struck him, and he politely covered his mouth with a handkerchief. Somewhat embarrassed, he grinned, and said, "Well, young Mycroft. I hope I am not the one with the chest cold this visit. How do you do?" He proffered his hand to the boy, who shook it firmly.

"I'm fine, sir," Mycroft replied.

Mr. Sherlock mildly hacked once more. Seeing a slight concern on the faces of his hosts, he added, "Must be the lack of sea air; I find the salty winds of the southern coast quite healthy. However, I have felt a cold beginning all week, but I shan't let it ruin one minute of our amusement. I have been extraordinarily busy with the bank—hardly have time to enjoy a regular lunch." He patted his lean abdomen. "Laura demands I take time to eat, to keep my strength up, but work has been overly busy of late. I have had to escape to Yorkshire for my fun. Enough of my rambling, dear me; let us repair to the drawing room for some long-sought companionship."

He wound his arm through Mr. Holmes' and led the way upstairs, chatting all the while. Mrs. Holmes followed, smiling at her husband's good cheer at the sight of his beloved friend, and holding Master Mycroft's hand tightly as they ascended. The lad had taken a number of spills on the stairs, going both up and down, but had never been seriously hurt. As a rule, then, if any adult was with or near him as he traversed the steps, they were to stop everything to guide him along. Clara had sought exemption from such duty, but when Master Mycroft promised he would not look at her at all as she helped him, she relented without tears. It was a fair compromise for the lad.

"I don't much fancy tumbling down the stairs and will take what help I can, at whatever cost," he had told her.

I followed in the rear.

As soon as we entered the room, I was directed by Mr. Holmes to pour some libations. The four of them each sat in a chair forming a rough circle in the center of the room. Whilst I stood at the decanter obeying Mr. Holmes' instructions, I glanced at Master Mycroft and saw him refocus onto Mr. Sherlock, as the latter began sharing with the Holmeses about his wife and children. There were warning signs we had all learned to observe with Master Mycroft: the pensive visage, the calculated pause, and the gently nodding head were all signals that an ejaculation of shocking proportions was no doubt being formulated. However, instead of speaking, Master Mycroft, with astounding impertinence, carefully hopped off his chair and walked over to Mr. Sherlock, whereupon he proceeded to circle the unfortunate man in his chair as he slowly surveyed everything about him top to bottom. Suddenly his head snapped up, his brows wrinkled, his eyes went vacant in deep thought, and his mouth opened wide.

Seemingly unconsciously, he whispered "Oh, my..." and then raised his hand to his mouth in a reflex of maintaining silence, it appeared. Although Mr. Sherlock's raised eyebrows, pursed lip, and smirk indicated his comical views of the lad's behavior, it proved too much for his usually very forgiving father.

"Good God, Mycroft! What rudeness!" his father exclaimed, shooting to his feet and standing arms akimbo. "I have never seen the like! Get back to your chair, young man, or I shall have to ask you to excuse yourself from our presence."

Master Mycroft was terribly unfamiliar with anger and admonishment from his parents, and his father's tone seemed to cut him to the quick.

"I'm terribly sorry, Papa," he said as he strode back to his chair and climbed up into it.

"Apologize to Mr. Sherlock, lad. He's the one you've treated like a pig for sale on market day." Mr. Holmes crossed his arms and stood stiffly in his ire.

The lad stood up off the chair. "I offer my sincerest apologies, Mr. Sherlock," he said. Then to his father, "I should not have circled the chair, Papa. You are quite right. It was a shameful and monstrous insult to Mr. Sherlock. I truly regret doing so, and hope all of you will grant me undeserved forbearance."

The look of anguish on the lad's face, mingled with a rare softness of tone, overcame Mr. Holmes' ire. For all we knew him to be extraordinary in his intellect and somewhat separate from his parents due to his independent nature, it was at rare times like this that Master Mycroft showed such intense desire for regard from his parents that he melted their hearts and their full love for him was made evident.

"It's all right, lad," his father soothed. "I forgive you." Mr. Sherlock nodded in agreement. "And so does Mr. Sherlock. However, I should prefer you to treat my friends, and your elders, with more respect."

I found this an apt moment to serve the drinks and then I positioned myself by the doorway as was my usual placement by Mr. Holmes so that I might be available for any needs that should arise in the company. Master Mycroft climbed upon his chair again.

"So, tell me, Mycroft," Mr. Sherlock said to Mycroft, placing his drink on the table beside him and covering a tiny cough with the back of his hand, "exactly what do you see about me that is, apparently, so enthralling to you? Have you a deduction to make?"

Mr. Sherlock did himself much credit in my opinion for handling the situation with such aplomb. He was clearly a good-natured, convivial man—much like Mr. Holmes himself—and I realised how compatible and mutually fulfilling their friendship obviously was.

Master Mycroft cast a quick look at Mr. Sherlock before renewing the analysis of the carpeting he had commenced once his apology had been offered and accepted.

"Yes, I do, but I shall not communicate it, if you please, sir," the lad said. Suddenly he climbed down from the seat again and stood at erect attention facing his father. "I should like to be excused from your presence, Papa. I have some studying to do, and you and Mama have some conversing to do with Mr. Sherlock."

This was a surprise; Master Mycroft typically enjoyed being with adults who welcomed his deductions more than anything else. He still was effusive in his greetings to the colonel and Mr. Brown, even though he generally refrained from being in company. What was this deduction that he didn't want to communicate? He father's lids narrowed suspiciously at the lad.

"Are you well, Mycroft?" his mother asked.

"I feel very well, Mama," he answered.

"Well, then, begone, if that's what you want. Honestly, lad, sometimes you are inscrutable." Mr. Holmes said. "Now you be awake and ready for supper at seven."

"Yes, Papa," Master Mycroft said, as he bowed to them all and exited from the room. Mr. Holmes sent me for a bottle of his best Burgundy from the cellar.

"Most extraordinary, David; most extraordinary, indeed," I heard Mr. Sherlock say as I left the room.

Their jovial and unrestrained camaraderie continued through the evening and all the week that Mr. Sherlock was at Hillcroft. The two gentlemen spent all their time together, riding, touring the estate and the farms and animals, drinking at the village pubs, playing chess, smoking pipes, discussing politics, and reminiscing about their time spent at University and the troubles they had brought down upon themselves. Mr. Sherlock seemed to have changed the most of the two, for Mr. Holmes was always offering drink or tobacco to the man, and although Mr. Sherlock did not abstain, he did not partake as avidly as did his host. The Holmeses had two dinner parties that week, which caused no lack of work for me and the rest of the house staff. But it was a very gay time, with no dissension or unfortunate incident to mar it. By the time the week was over, and Mr. and Mrs. Holmes, and Mr. Sherlock once again leisurely reposed in the drawing room on the eve of Mr. Sherlock's departure, only the pleasant air of well-earned fatigue differentiated the end of his visit from the beginning one week ago.

Master Mycroft had been remarkable by his general absence during the week. Where we would have thought he would revel in the presence of the interesting Mr. Sherlock, and the other guests who begged for his appearance, he seemed morose and preoccupied, and tended to wander off to read in his bedroom or study. The few times the more extroverted and uninhibited visitors invited him to deduce upon their person, he begged off, saying he could observe nothing of importance. Mr. and Mrs. Holmes, though concerned with this sudden change in their child, were too busy during the week to ask him what had prompted it.

He had particularly avoided Mr. Sherlock, refused to even look at him; although the kindly gentlemen was disposed to attempt several times to draw the lad into feeling a part of the crowd, it was to no avail. Mr. Holmes had to assure Mr. Sherlock two or three times that certainly nothing he had said or done was the reason for Mycroft's grim mood. Mr. Holmes' conferring with Master Mycroft in private did not seem to resolve the situation; it was decided the adults would allow the lad his mood while not letting it impinge on their own enjoyment of the week.

So it was that on that last night the Holmeses and Mr. Sherlock were up late, quietly talking in the drawing room, the men sipping on brandies, Mrs. Holmes doing beadwork. The men were both somewhat intoxicated, having been drinking in acknowledgment of Mr. Sherlock's sad leave-taking. It was about 10:00 P.M. when Master Mycroft appeared in the doorway to wish them all good night. He was long accustomed to preparing himself for bed.

"Well, well, young Mycroft, and good night to you," Mr. Sherlock responded. "I am sorry we were unable to spend more time together."

His parents wished him good night, his mother arising to hug and kiss him.

"Shall I tuck you in?" she asked.

"Thank you, no, Mama. Not tonight. You should stay with Mr. Sherlock, as he leaves tomorrow." Mycroft studiously ignored Mr. Sherlock as he hugged his mother.

As the lad made for the door, Mr. Sherlock spoke up. "I say, Mycroft, one favor before you retire, if you please."

The lad stood straight in the doorway before very slowly turning around to face his parents and guest.

"Yes, sir?"

"I'm sure you remember last week, the first night I was here. You told us you had a deduction about me, though you were loath to communicate it. I did not press the point at the time, but now, upon my departure, I do wish you would share your amazing observations with me. I have heard a good deal about them, and would be honored if I should be gifted by your brilliant deduction of myself."

"Thank you for the compliments, sir," Master Mycroft said, shifting from foot to foot in agitation. "However, my attitude regarding revealing my deduction of yourself has not changed. I would be grateful—"

"Nonsense, lad," Mr. Sherlock interrupted, smiling. "Really, I'm most interested. And insistent. What have you detected? That I have two dogs, a collie and a spaniel? That my youngest daughter has beautiful chestnut hair? That I find my co-worker, Mr. Attleson, rather addlepated?"

Mr. Holmes guffawed at that.

Mr. Sherlock continued in his teasing vein, "That I don't like bread pudding? That I broke my right arm as a child? Do tell."

Mr. Holmes chimed in. "Go on, lad, it's all right. Tell us what you figured out."

Master Mycroft looked down at his feet. "I really would rather not," he implored.

"Oh, my, he's uncovered that I stole tuppence from my father once to purchase an incredibly large sack of candy," Mr. Sherlock baited.

Mrs. Holmes endeavoured to rescue the boy. "It is late, dear, and we know Mycroft needs his sleep. Perhaps he should just go to bed, and the next time he sees Mr. Sherlock he may feel more comfortable in bestowing his deductions."

I do not believe I have ever seen a look of appreciation and love more perfectly pronounced than on Master Mycroft's face. Not even the angels in the paintings of Raphael captured such pure intensity of feeling.

However, Mrs. Holmes' simple defence was useless. The two men, gently inebriated and in playful spirits, would broach no dissent.

Mr. Holmes slapped his hands on his knees. "Come, lad, we've begged and pleaded enough. Now, as your father, I order you to reveal your thoughts. And no dissembling of the truth."

"I never lie, Papa," Mycroft said, softly.

"Quite so, quite so," his father agreed. "So, tell us what is to be told."

The two men sat back in their chairs, legs crossed, grinning devilishly at each other; only Mr. Holmes holding a glass of brandy clearly marked them as adults, and not just overgrown boys themselves.

Master Mycroft saw the impossibility of his situation; he did not want to speak and yet he could not disobey a direct command by his father. There was nothing he could do; so, after a quick glance at the three adults, he closed his eyes and softly spoke.

"What I have deduced about Mr. Sherlock is that he has tuberculosis, of a severe and worsening nature."

The smiles on the faces of the men disappeared; Mr. Sherlock flushed. Mr. Holmes, who had been sipping his liquor, swallowed it incorrectly and began hacking harshly. Mrs. Holmes held her arms across her chest as if she had taken a terrible chill. The poor lad looked like he wanted to shrink away to nothing, standing stock still in the doorway. Mr. Sherlock paled to whiteness.

"My God, I never..." he said softly, then seeing Mr. Holmes' condition, leaned over and grabbed the arm of the still coughing Mr. Holmes. "David, are you all right?"

"Fine, fine," Mr. Holmes managed to gasp as the fit subsided. A few more coughs were elicited before he regained his composure. "But what is going on? What do you mean to say, Mycroft, that Robert has tuberculosis? Robert, is it true? It can't be!"

"Easy, David, easy does it," Mr. Sherlock said. "You're upsetting the boy."

Master Mycroft stood watching them, his brows raised in anxiety. As Mrs. Holmes opened her arms to him and said, "Come here, dear;" he strode morosely to his mother. Once by her side, he turned to face the men—his jaw clenched tightly—while Mrs. Holmes rested her hands on his shoulders.

Mr. Sherlock rose from his chair and strode to the mantlepiece, where he stood in nervous agitation tapping his finger along the top of the mantlepiece. Mr. Holmes, still pale and distraught, repeated his previous question with urgency: "My God, Robert, is it true?"

Mr. Sherlock turned back to his friend. "It's true, David. That's why I wanted to come and see you. The doctors think it is only a matter of time before I worsen rapidly..."

Mr. Holmes struggled for comprehension. "Your grandmother. She had tuberculosis, when she lived with you when you were a child. I remember your saying how you would read to her and bring her fresh flowers. She died quickly you said. Oh my God, oh my God."

Mr. Sherlock continued speaking with a resignation and fatigue in his voice
that had not surfaced previously all week. "I have always struggled with my lungs,
ever since a lad. You saw me through a number of severe episodes of bronchitis
at University, David. It has now, apparently, come to a head."

He directed his attention to Master Mycroft, who had continued to stand without moving a muscle. "What I should like to know at this moment, though, is how
you figured out my disease, Mycroft. I had wanted to keep it a secret, so that my
time here with your father and mother would not be spoiled by any thoughts of
my illness. It is only to your credit that you withheld out of sympathy with your
father the unhappy information you determined a week ago. I feel how unfairly I
have treated your most magnificent talent and your compassion tonight—I hope
you will accept my apology. I see now how blind and foolish I was, for even though
I had heard enough from your father about your amazing mind, I never thought
you should deduce my disease. But, now that we have forced your hand, tell us
how you did it, if you would be so kind."

Mr. Sherlock's speech had a tranquilizing affect on Master Mycroft. He pulled
himself out of his solemn immobility and turned his head to Mr. Sherlock, who
remained standing but gestured him to come over to the fire. Mr. Holmes sat forward on his chair, elbows on knees, resting his head on his hands in absolute
dejection.

"Mama?" Master Mycroft asked.

"Go on, dear. You may as well tell us how you figured it all out."

As the lad went to Mr. Sherlock, Mrs Holmes moved over to sit next to her
husband, lending what comfort her presence, and her hands on his shoulder and
thigh, could afford.

Mr. Sherlock sat down on a chair by the fire and Mycroft positioned himself
by the man's side. Mr. Sherlock smoothed the hair on the lad's head, and raised
his chin with his finger.

"What a special lad," he said.

Mycroft said nothing.

"Tell me how you deduced my tuberculosis."

"It was simple, really."

Mr. Sherlock smiled briefly. "I'm sure it wasn't."

"It was. I have made a study of diseases, and tuberculosis, being common,
naturally fell under my perusal. First I noticed your pale face, which is unusual,
as the sun has been generous to England all spring, and I knew of your habit of
taking long walks from my father. In and of itself it is meaningless, but then I
added in the other clues. Your clothes are slightly large for you, not overly so, but
enough that with my observation that you have recently begun using a different
notch on your belt, I deduced you have had some weight loss recently. Your ram-

bling discourse on your absent eating habits only roused my interest that you were attempting to prevaricate. Your slight coughs assiduously covered by your hand-kerchief, and which you tried to pass off as being caused solely by a lack of sea air, were curious, since you placed no importance on the coughs, yet I noticed when I circled the chair last week that the handkerchief—which was visible at your shirt sleeve then—was spotted with small drops of blood. Also it was then I espied the slight swellings of your lymph nodes on the right side of your neck—when you glanced toward my father during my encirclement of you. All these signs indicated to me you are suffering from tuberculosis, and that the disease is, unfor-tunately, in a serious stage of advancement. When I considered your subterfuge with the reason for your coughing, plus the fact that you knew my father was greatly overjoyed by your presence and had a full week of activities set up for your pleasure, I realised that you were not intending to share with him the poor state of your health. Therefore, I decided also to be silent on the issue." He glanced at his mother. "I did not want to hurt anyone."

His mother nodded in return.

"Quite, quite remarkable," Mr. Sherlock murmured.

Mr. Holmes stood and sat next to Mr. Sherlock, whilst Master Mycroft bowed slightly and strode to the doorway, not far from where I remained motionless.

"My God, how simple. I would have seen it myself, if I had not been so delighted to simply have you here with me. When were you planning on telling me, my dear friend?" he asked.

"I don't know, David. I had thought of informing you all along, but then when I arrived and everything was so lovely, I just couldn't bring myself to ruin it all by such an unhappy declaration."

"Will you travel then, to Switzerland, perhaps? What do the doctors say? You're young; surely you can overcome it."

"I never told you this, but not just my grandmother developed this terrible disease—one older brother also contracted it when he was twenty-two, and I but twelve, three years after my grandmother died. He lasted but one year, succumb-ing so speedily even the physicians were surprised."

He paused, slouching back and putting his hands in his trouser pockets. "The Sherlocks have never had strong lungs—I can't tell you how many ancestors died of pneumonia and tuberculosis. And I fear my family's unfortunate susceptibility to the latter affliction is only worsened by our lack of resistance to it once it lands a foothold. I have known of my diagnosis for a year, but have told only my wife. Even in that short time, already the blood I expectorate grows rapidly in amount, my stamina decreases with each passing week, my breath becomes scarcer—David, I am dying. I do not wish to do so in Switzerland, away from my family and friends; I have chosen to remain in England. But that is why I so suddenly insisted to see you. You are closer to me than my own brothers. I feel this may very well be the last visit we spend together, my dear, dear David."

Mr. Holmes said nothing, his face awash with anguish and despair. Master Mycroft cast a glance around the entire room once more and then slipped out the room towards his bedchamber. Mrs. Holmes also rose quietly and, at the door, motioned for me to leave with her, leaving the two men alone with their friendship and their sorrow.

The year passed—in December Mr. Holmes received a letter from Mrs. Sherlock, relating the sad news of the death of her husband from tuberculosis.

Mr. and Mrs. Holmes and Master Mycroft immediately left to attend the funeral in Plymouth—even though the travelling was long and difficult due to the harsh, chilly weather. Mr. Holmes had them all pack bags and worked out the arrangements ahead of time in anticipation of the lugubrious news, for he kept in weekly contact with the Sherlocks by post.

When they returned home a most horrific and frightening change overcame Mr. Holmes. He locked himself in his study and entered into a time of drinking that was so excessive his wife grew gravely concerned. His mood was most irritable when disturbed; he seemed to crave solitude and silence in his grief, much like his father had towards the end of his life. He rarely ate, and hardly bathed or shaved, and seemed to sleep seldom. He smoked so incessantly that his study was filled with a thick fog of fumes. Never had I witnessed such a gross display of relentless woe. After three long weeks of this, during which he forbade visitors, abandoning his responsibilities to family and the estate, Mrs. Holmes ordered me to retrieve no more liquor from the cellar stores for him and then confronted her husband with Father Metcalfe and Mr. Brown alone in his study. They were all there quite some time—Mr. Holmes ceasing his angry outbursts after the first hour—the happy outcome late that afternoon being his led upstairs to a bath and a bed. He awoke the next morning famished and spent another several days recuperating in bed, constantly surrounded by his attentive and ever-loving wife. They spent much time in private conversation during those days. It seemed that their regard for each other seemed to grow as a result of their weathering that hideous month, and they lavished soft words and gentle touches on each other as if they were newlyweds. His indecorous behavior ceased, although strong moments of sadness would arise at times that seemed suddenly to enervate him, and he would sit for a while gazing blankly into a fire, sighing deeply. He maintained his daily drinking at a higher than normal level for awhile, although never again descending into the shocking display of a frankly uncontrollable vice. Then after a few months, even his drinking returned to his previous acceptable habits, and life returned to normal at Hillcroft House.

During his father's grieving, Master Mycroft stayed in the background, saying little, but observing everything. He watched his mother's frantic pacing, the agitation of the servants, myself bringing yet another bottle of wine to his father. He put his ear to the closed door and listened to his father cry and rail against the Creator. Mrs. Holmes had sent a message to Mr. Wharton, politely stating that due to her husband's illness, Mr. Holmes wished no visitors to the estate. He requested Mr. Wharton kindly refrain from tutoring Mycroft until notified to return to Hillcroft House. Thereafter, Master Mycroft entertained himself in his study and read, in those three weeks, seven books. He first approached his father as his father convalesced in bed, and though I did not hear the conversation, it seemed to benefit them both.

Although Master Mycroft continued his habit of pointed observation of people and things, of particular relief to the servants—and I feel to his parents as well—was that he completely stopped communicating his deductions. His father still spent much time with him, as before, taking him to the village and the quarter sessions, allowing him to work on the accounting books, encouraging him to go for walks and ride throughout the countryside.

Mycroft still saw the children of the Metcalfes and the Browns and continued his good relations with them. I believe he never let them know how advanced he was, but instead met them at their level with an adaptability equal to that of a chameleon. He also spent much time in pensive contemplation.

So another year passed, and it was April 1853. Master Mycroft, now age six, addressed his parents as Mother and Father. Two incidents occurred that spring that shook the Holmeses greatly. The first was Master Mycroft's requesting that he be sent to boarding school in the autumn term when he would turn seven.

His parents looked at each other.

"But, Mycroft, we thought you would prefer to remain privately tutored, as you are so far ahead of the students of your age, you would be terribly bored by being in classes with them," Mrs. Holmes said.

"That is true. However, I do not want to attend public schools for the academic education they will provide, for that will be woefully lacking to my needs. Nor, obviously, for the sports. I need to attend for the personal connexions they create and encourage." He stood straight with his hands behind his back. "I shall need those connexions in the future."

"Oh, and what future is that?" his father asked.

"I plan on entering government service," the lad said.

"A politician, eh?"

Master Mycroft raised his eyebrows high. "Certainly not. I do not yet know how exactly I shall shape my career, but connexions formed in public schools and University will no doubt prove essential to me as I eventually decide how to proceed."

"And what shall happen with the estate, then, lad, if I have no son to pass it to?" This was spoken with some bitterness by the father.

"Surely, Father, you have known for some time that I had no intention of inheriting the responsibilities of Hillcroft House as my life's work. For your peace of mind, however, and to ensure there are no hard feelings between us, let me avow that no matter the capacity in which I find myself in the future, when such a time sadly arrives that you—for whatever reason—can no longer act as full patriarch, I shall hire a trustworthy steward to live at the house, and through him I promise to take on and maintain Hillcroft and your investments in Huddersfield. I swear I will not ever renege on my responsibilities to you or Mother."

The speech appeased the Holmeses and they acquiesced—the child had been beyond their comprehension and control from the moment of his birth, though they fully trusted his sincerity towards them. It was clear that he would be terribly unhappy as squire—he was totally unfit for such a career—and they knew that he had potential that could take him very far. His offer to run Hillcroft House by proxy showed his consideration to his father, and ensured his parents they would have a home and steady income when they were aged. It was, therefore, arranged for him to attend boarding school come the autumn.

"In whatever you do, lad, work for justice and good. We have tried to teach you respect and honor; we hope we have set examples in being kind-hearted, patient, and acting in regard for others," his father said when he and Mrs. Holmes told Master Mycroft he was enrolled as desired. If I as butler vividly recalled his infamous "Mycroft, my world," pronouncement, I can only imagine how that may have haunted the dreams of Mr. and Mrs. Holmes. His parents stood with arms intertwined, awaiting their son's reply.

Master Mycroft had risen to his feet when his parents first entered his study; his manners were often impeccable. He straightened his chubby little body fully erect.

"I shall never do the name of Holmes any dishonor, Papa, and neither of you shall ever have cause to be ashamed of me. I swear it," the lad said.

His parents smiled broadly, and Master Mycroft stood observing them, nodding his head in what I may only describe as approval.

One month later, in early May, Mrs. Holmes announced herself as being with child. She was certainly as astounded as everyone else. Mr. Holmes, as she related to Mrs. Hastwell, actually had the pipe fall right from his mouth onto the floor when she told him. As she was now thirty-seven, the situation was greeted with guarded joy. Her history of miscarriage, with subsequent debility, floated heavily in the air of the home, although it was balanced by the fervent hope the pregnancy would lead to the birth of another child. Truly it seemed to me to be a blessing from God Himself, for on the eve of losing their first child to public school—a child whom one could say they never truly had in the first place—here it seemed they were being given a miraculous second child at the instant they so very much would welcome it. Master Mycroft's reaction was unfathomable to me. He seemed happy for his parents, but his own thoughts were guarded beyond any endeavour at intuiting them.

As is usual in a house, as goes the mood of the employers, so goes the mood of the servants. We were all delighted at the news until one evening Mrs. Winters spoke to us as we reposed in the servants' quarters.

"They've been eating more food, they have, lately," she said in eerie tones. "The bones are licked clean. The little people have been busy as bees, I tell you. Go outside at midnight and the whispers will surround you. Oh, it doesn't bode well, I tell you, it doesn't bode well. The little ones have been much too busy." She crossed herself.

"If you weren't the best cook in Yorkshire, Mrs. Winters, I don't believe any employer would put up with your balderdash," I laughed. The others chimed in briefly, but then the laughter died down, and only nervous coughs remained. I'm sure I know what everyone thought: *She has been right before.*

Mrs. Holmes continued with child in a healthy, though tired, state. As the months progressed, her spirits brightened with hope, and only the leaving of Master Mycroft with his father to journey to school initiated recurrent bouts of weeping.

Master Mycroft's parting words of "Good luck, dear Mother. When I return, may I be greeted by the long-sought sight of a healthy sibling," itself engendered a flood of tears from Mrs. Holmes. Her weeping gradually lessened when Mr. Holmes arrived back at Hillcroft, and once again they were bound together by the developing child their love had formed.

Mrs. Holmes entered her confinement the evening of January 5, 1854, but the labour was long, and she did not deliver until the morning of January 6. She was attended by the surgeon from Aysgarth, Mr. Irwin, who delivered unto a nerve-wracked Mr. Holmes at 10:08 A.M. a healthy baby boy, whom Mr. Holmes immediately named Sherlock Scott Holmes.

Chapter Nine
Sherlock the Terror

*B*e was as active and gay a baby as his elder brother had been slow and restful. Born a long though thin baby, six pounds and a half only, and with a light sheaf of wheat-coloured hair, it was clear that he was Vernet in form, which it amused me to hear Mrs. Holmes constantly yet playfully mention to her husband. Oh, I tell you it was a grand time of joy at Hillcroft House! The Holmeses threw a large party to celebrate; all the tenant farmers attended, as well as the Holmeses' friends and acquaintances, and Master Sherlock was shown to everyone as the blessing he truly was.

The boy certainly was active even in the crib, arms and legs flailing around all day. He was easy to get to giggle, and loved to be held and tickled and given attention. He did not sleep nearly so well as Master Mycroft had, though, awakening several times during the night and difficult to put down to nap during the day. Another difference between the two babies was Master Sherlock's finicky eating habits, which caused some concern in the household. The wet nurse did her best, but it seemed to Mrs. Holmes that he did not drink enough, and she even called Mr. Irwin to examine the lad. When Mr. Irwin assured her that Master Sherlock was thriving and growing, she was calmer.

"You cannot base all your children on your firstborn," Mr. Irwin told her. "Sherlock here is of an entirely different nature and may require less food than young Mycroft did—goodness, I must say, and you'll pardon this transgression, madam, but for the same husband and wife to have such different babies…well live and learn, they say."

Live and learn we all did. Master Sherlock was so happy a baby, so alert, and his eyes shone brightly at all times. His innate overactivity was, unfortunately I must report, modified with laudanum to help his nursemaid get some rest at night, and even occasionally during the day when Master Sherlock seemed unlikely ever to nap for more than fifteen minutes. They had never administered that drug to Master Mycroft, and whether that predisposed Master Sherlock to drug addictions later in life I cannot say.

Master Sherlock also observed things, staring at them, but his mien was pleasant, not peculiar, and it was much easier to distract him by holding him or speaking to him. His observations were not judged to be of the advanced type of his elder brother; more those of a typical baby normally examining his environs. The servants reported all this to Mrs. Winters, who enigmatically crossed herself and stood by her position.

"The fairies were too busy. Just you wait and see," she warned.

Of course you can imagine how utterly in heaven the Holmes were with their second child. Mrs. Holmes caused the nursemaid, Mrs. Smythe, no end of consternation by her constant presence with the boy, and really, after his work requirements were over, Mr. Holmes was also almost always visiting his son in the new nursery, the old one being maintained as Master Mycroft's study. They would have Master Sherlock brought to the drawing room after supper, where during frequent breaks from knitting and reading, Mrs. and Mr. Holmes would observe or hold the tittering child.

Again showing his opposite nature from Master Mycroft, Master Sherlock sat himself up at three months, crawled at six, walked holding his father's hands at nine, and was walking skillfully and fearlessly by himself by one year. I cannot adequately relate the intensity of Mr. Holmes' smile, which covered his whole countenance, when he would enter the nursery and see Master Sherlock screaming with glee as he rode the hobby horse. Master Sherlock had as complete a mastery of his thin body as I ever imagined a child could have. He rarely fell, and could climb upon furniture and objects almost as soon as he could walk. Mrs. Holmes developed anxiety over her son's movements, for he was so thin, and with no fat to pad him like Master Mycroft she feared his falling and breaking a bone. But it was rare that he fell. It seemed he would not only be active enough for himself, but would make up for Master Mycroft's years of inactivity as well.

The one way he was similar to his elder sibling was in verbal skills; although not so adept at talking, Master Sherlock still seemed remarkably quick in his grasping of words. Personally I feel that the lad no doubt had the mental ability to learn as rapidly as Master Mycroft, but his initial focus on the physical—that is, playing all the time—hid his innate precocious mentation. Master Mycroft had been content sitting in the drawing room listening to the adults' discourse, and thereby rapidly increased his own exposure and skill in the art of conversation. Master Sherlock, the first time they sat him down similarly once he could walk, was flitting all over the room like a butterfly, lifting up room decorations and putting them back down on their sides, climbing on the sofa, then over the sofa, then dropping to the floor and running across the room past Mrs. Hastwell, who gallantly endeavoured to continue her story about her irresponsible cousin Edward, then back across the room again, up, over the chair, then dashing to Mrs. Holmes and hugging her tightly about the legs, saying, "Mama, Mama, I love you."

You can imagine how impossible it was for the Holmeses, particularly Mrs. Holmes, to discipline the child. He was happy, healthy, alert, and very affectionate to both his parents, and they swelled with love every time they saw him. He ran into his parents' arms as soon as they entered the nursery or as soon as he was taken by the nursemaid to them. His father devoted himself to the lad, for Master Sherlock loved to ride First Boy, and loved to be taken anywhere on the steed, securely held by his father's strong arms. Like Master Mycroft, he craved visiting the villages, the quarry, the mine, the farmers, but he also liked just travelling over the land exploring the beauty and starkness of the dales.

"Today, Papa, let's go climb the Pennines," he begged his father one day when he was a year and a half old as they started out on a carriage ride. Oftentimes they went alone, but sometimes Mrs. Holmes would join them, which Master Sherlock greatly enjoyed. I feel that Mrs. Holmes would have ridden with them much more regularly if she had not recognized her husband's need to have time alone with his son.

"Not, today, Sherlock, my boy. We're off to see Farmer Nobbes about some dairy cows. We'll climb the Pennines some other day."

"All right, Papa. Let's see Farmer Nobbes. He's the one with the two moles on his left cheek, isn't he, Papa?"

Mr. Holmes thought for a second. "Hmm, indeed he is, lad."

"Oh, I like him! Too bad about his eye! Let's go!"

And they would take off, Mr. Holmes' briefly wrinkled brow, and glance to his own leg, and pensive visage immediately giving way to the exuberance of his son as the horse began his gentle walk.

Master Mycroft returned home from school in early July 1855 for the two-month summer holiday after a year of outstanding performance at the school. The other holidays of the year he had spent at the homes of assorted school mates, which both pleased his parents—for his making of friends—and saddened them with his absence. He was happy at public school, and doing well, and so it was decided he would continue his education there. "Connexions have begun" was all he would enigmatically state about his time away. If coming home to a household devoted to his new younger brother was difficult, I cannot say, for the lad had become even more reserved than before. However, it was clear that Master Mycroft was at first a little wary of his young brother—for example, he was uncomfortable holding the lad, and was not interested in holding gewgaws over him or rocking him on the hobby horse.

"Isn't he adorable, Mycroft?" Mrs. Holmes asked Master Mycroft as they stood by the drugged, sleeping lad a few days after his return. Mr. Holmes stood nearby.

"He is underweight," the lad answered. "Clearly Vernet in appearance. Beware the overuse of Godfrey's Cordial; one wonders of the long-term health effects of laudanum with regular administration." At that the lad walked off.

Mrs. Holmes watched him and then returned her glance to her newborn. "Do you think that means he cares?" she asked Mr. Holmes.

"Who on earth could know?" he replied, his narrowed eyes on his elder son's retreating figure.

Master Mycroft seemed more interested in his books, in fact, than in anything else, brother included; even though the summer was pleasant and warm, the lad mostly read. He would occasionally go for a ride on First Boy—with his father on Midas—and only fell from the gentle steed once, luckily not injuring himself. He took frequent walks with his mother, and even if he was not talkative it was apparent he enjoyed her company. If his parents had hopes that the lads would bond closely, there was no indication on Master Mycroft's part that any such intimacy had developed. However, each time Master Sherlock saw his older brother and yelled out, and I do mean yelled, "Hello, Mycroft! How do you do?" the elder lad stared at his sibling with some intensity. Whether he just disapproved of the volume of voice or was trying to uncover deeper layers to the lad, I do not know.

"I'm quite fine, Sherlock," Master Mycroft would invariably answer.

"Read me a book?" the younger lad would ask.

"I don't think—"

"Oh, go on, Mycroft," Mrs. Holmes would plead. "It would so please Sherlock if you did."

So Master Mycroft would sit down and read whatever book Master Sherlock gave him. He would never have won any awards for vivacious renderings of the literature, I can assure you. If the younger lad realised the coolness with which his brother held him, it did not lessen the lad's affectionate regard for his elder brother, who hugged him as strongly when he left to return to school at the end of August.

Of course, it is easy to criticize from hindsight. It is easy to judge, and to ridicule, and to point a finger and say. "How obvious; how did you miss it?" But at the time Master Sherlock was two, and the fact that his speech was advanced, though not so like Master Mycroft, and that he was observing things, though again not as blatantly or intensely as his brother, well, all that was submerged by his activity and personality. It was easy to ignore the obvious mental precocity in young Sherlock, for he did not focus on it as had young Mycroft.

Whereas Master Mycroft had stared at people until their neck hairs stood on end, and then pronounced some exacting deduction, playful Sherlock would be kicking a ball all over the house, chased by the chastising nursemaid, encounter me suddenly in the hallway, and state, "Mr. Brewster, you had insomnia last night, again." As he noticed the nursemaid spy him from the morning room and leap out to grab him, ordering "Stay still, I tell you," he would run for the stairs laughing and yelling back at me, "You may try my cordial, if you like!"

It was easy, as I stated, to lose the incredible genius in the overtly innocent lad. It was what Mr. and Mrs. Holmes had dreamed of when they had married seventeen years ago—a household of happy children running hither and yon—except they hadn't expected that one rail-thin toddler would encapsulate the activities of all the five children they had imagined. In between times when Master Mycroft was home, Master Sherlock and his delightful, uncontrollable manner dominated the household.

Oh my, what a little terror he was! By the time he was two the whole household was geared to look out for him, although by no means was he a mean, devious, or destructive child. He had mastered walking, and the stairs, with a grace Master Mycroft had not attained even at age five. Let me explain a typical day regarding the young lad. He slept alone in a bed in his bedroom, for, by one year old, he could climb up and over the crib walls, and so, of course, he did. It was, therefore thought that climbing out of a bed would entail a lesser possibility of injury than up and over the crib poles. He was still often given a teaspoonful of laudanum to put him to sleep; otherwise, he would be up and wandering the house at night. I have two memories of times when an experiment was attempted to curtail the administration of laudanum. The morning of the first attempt, Clara found the two-year-old Master Sherlock alone in the library, sitting on the floor chattering to himself about the pictures he saw in the book he held, a lit candle by his side—my God!—and a considerable number of other books strewn all over the floor. The other time I remember he was discovered in his father's study, emulating him by sitting in a chair with an unlit cigar in one hand and an empty whiskey glass in the other. So laudanum it was, and a locked bedroom door.

He was often awake when the nursemaid came to him in the morning and he was energetic from that moment on. He was washed and dressed. He was then taken to breakfast, which was often with both his parents, if his father had not had to leave early for business matters, as they lavished their attention on an all-too-accepting Master Sherlock. He sat without a bib at a child's table by his parents' side; he was too finicky and slight an eater to require a bib. It was all they could do to force him to eat; he would pick at his food with utensils he had already learned to use, placing miniscule pieces of food in his mouth.

"For goodness sake, Sherlock, eat some more porridge," his mother would implore.

"All right, Mama," he would say, then place less than a spoonful in his mouth, his shining eyes seeking approval.

If the nursemaid, Mrs. Smythe, endeavoured to remove the spoon from his hand and feed him herself, Master Sherlock would drop the spoon into the porridge and cover his mouth tightly with both hands.

"I can eat by myself as my parents do!" he would declare to the portly, ruddy-faced woman with her blonde hair up in a bun. Her cheeks would frequently glow even more redly as the lad removed his hands from their obstinate placement to make his forceful comment, only to immediately replace them before she could put some food into his mouth.

"Dear me," was Mrs. Holmes' usual comment.

"Let the lad be, Mrs. Smythe," Mr. Holmes said. Then leaning over to his son, whose hands were still plastered over closed lips, he would add, "You must finish the porridge before we ride First Boy wherever you like."

Once I timed it—an entire bowl of hot porridge neatly eaten in twenty seconds.

After breakfast, the day varied somewhat as could be expected with the changing demands of business for Mr. Holmes, the societal obligations still maintained by Mrs. Holmes, such as caring for the poor and sick, and the general socializing that took the Holmes away from Hillcroft House and brought others to it.

Ostensibly, Master Sherlock was in the care of the nursemaid, but he was a handful to be sure. It was true that he could easily play by himself or with Mrs. Smythe in the nursery, but his constant activity tired her out. At those moments when she understandably took a brief rest from full attention to her charge, Master Sherlock would be gone from the nursery, rambling through the house; or, if a chair could be put by a door without anyone seeing, the knob was turned and he was outside in a flash. No doubt you can imagine the unendurable agitation this caused his parents, Mrs. Smythe, and all the servants who were then to stop everything and help find the lad. He almost always walked to the stables to see the horses. When orders from his parents did not end the conduct, removing the chair from the hallway brought that most frightful behavior to an end. He was not yet strong enough to quietly lift a chair, or drag one, from a room and carry it to the entrance to the house.

Oftentimes he would merely find his mother and stay by her side. He was very attached to her, called her "my dear mama" to her utmost delight, and desired to observe and learn all that interested her, from her perfumes, to her flower arranging, to her piano playing—he especially loved to hear music being played—and her play reading. When he was alone with his mother, those were some of his quietest and most relaxed times, and when the nursemaid found him, Mrs. Smythe was dismissed from his care until later. Mrs. Holmes and the lad would spend hours chatting about her interests. If she was visiting with a friend or several, Master Sherlock, and the rest of the house staff, would be most disappointed. Although he could be well behaved and attentive when he had his mother solely for his own, when others commanded her attention, Master Sherlock had not the calmness constantly just to sit in a group of adults as had his brother Mycroft. After more directions from his parents to the effect that he could not enter the room in which visiting adults were situated and cause distractions, he would come upon his mother sitting with guests, morosely greet them, and then leave the room to cause distractions elsewhere in the house.

I do not mean to imply that Master Sherlock was a blatantly disobedient child. When corrected in some errant activity by his parents, he was usually most responsive to their disciplining. He usually put his toys away, washed, and got ready for meals and bed with admirable promptness. In all the little ways a child is ordered to obey, Master Sherlock was impeccable in his adherence. He was open and friendly, and, one may only say, a character. It was his innocent playfulness that got him into the most trouble, and it was solely in that arena where his parents and he struggled for clear lines of behavior and usually ended up compromising. His parents never were harsh or violent in their exhortations, for I feel that they were actually quite happy to have to give them. Master Mycroft had never really required corrective talks—he had been too phlegmatic to instigate reprimands along the lines of overactivity, and too precocious, well-behaved, and independent for his parents to feel comfortable advising him, except where his inappropriate deductions were concerned. That their younger son was much more along the lines of necessitating actual parental input from them made them feel needed and important; and a compromise was better than not needing to institute rules to begin with. Their gentle natures never departing from them, most of the times they initiated a disciplinarian encounter with Master Sherlock by sitting him down and discussing with him how and why he had to modify his behavior. It was mostly during those times that his advanced language skills were made evident; however, his parents treated his uncanny capabilities as things common and uneventful.

"Sherlock, we must speak to you of your ball playing and of your appearance," his parents began once when the lad was two and a half. They were sitting in the drawing room, having just heard the thirtieth complaint from the exhausted Mrs. Smythe.

"As you wish, Papa," the two-year-old child said, standing at attention, hands straight down his stick-like legs. His hair, beginning to thicken and darken in colour, was completely disarrayed, his shirt hung partly out from his pants, his waistcoat was half unbuttoned, and one shoe was untied.

"Well, dear," his mother began, "we must very much insist that you contain the kicking of your ball to the outdoors." She paused, then quickly added, "Of course, you must only go outdoors when you are allowed to and are supervised by someone."

"But it is quite good fun to play with the ball inside the house, dear Mama," Sherlock countered.

"Yes, but things may continue to break, as did the Chinese vase in the morning room two months ago, and the two matching statues here in the drawing room, only yesterday. You must appreciate and respect that we cannot have our household belongings destroyed by your unwarranted ball kicking in rooms not designed for such merry fun."

"I'm sorry I broke those things, Mama. If you like, I shall work off the cost of the shattered items by helping Mrs. Winters with the dish washing, or by polishing the furniture with Clara."

Where children come up with their comments! Mr. and Mrs. Holmes stifled their mirth with a control much to their credit; Mr. Holmes clearing his throat to hide his snicker, and Mrs. Holmes inhaling deeply for some breaths.

"That shall not be necessary, Sherlock," Mr. Holmes continued. "However, to prevent further inexcusable breakage, you must follow your mother's and my command to restrict your ball playing to the outside."

"Perhaps you would allow me to play with it also within the confines of the nursery?" the boy asked.

His parents looked at each other. "Well, I suppose that would be acceptable," his father said.

"I do so enjoy bouncing the ball off of the steps of the stairway as well, and have never caused anything to break in that way, as aside from the cabinet in the hallway with its enclosed fragile items, there are no other breakables in the area. Perhaps, Papa and Mama, you would be so gracious as to allow me to maintain that pleasurable sport? At least on rainy days, when proceeding outside would be frowned upon?"

His father clenched his teeth and rubbed his forehead. His mother reinstated her deep inhalations. Mr. Holmes spoke, "Very well, you may also bounce the ball on the stairs on rainy days. But those are the only areas of the house where the ball may be used. Is that understood?"

"Certainly, Papa."

The Holmeses nodded at each other with a look of delighted satisfaction and confidence. Suddenly their visages were cracked open when, in a genuinely curious and angelic voice, Master Sherlock asked, "If, however, on the off chance that the ball is found in a forbidden room of the house, perhaps along with myself as the bringer of it there, what do you suppose might be the punishment I would expect to receive?" As his parents turned back to him, he continued in a rush, "As justice of the peace, Papa, and a member of the quarter sessions, how would you fairly gauge the severity of the crime, and what punitive measures would you recommend be taken?"

"I'd...I'd...I'd smack you on the bottom, I would, for your insolence if nothing else," his father spluttered, bending over the wide-eyed Master Sherlock with open hand, less coherent and rational than his not-quite-three-year-old son.

"Goodness, David, calm yourself," Mrs. Holmes said.

Mr. Holmes sat straight, adjusted his tie, closed his eyes, and shook his head back and forth. After a minute he began smiling, and soon after a laugh erupted. He opened his eyes and saw his son clinging to his mother's legs.

"Lad, come here," he said with open arms. Master Sherlock rushed to them, and his father picked him up, setting him on his lap. "You can be as exasperating as your brother, you know."

The lad said nothing. Then, "You wouldn't really hit me, would you, Papa?"

"No, no, Sherlock, I'll not ever hit you. But don't play with the ball except in the nursery and on the stairs, all right?"

"Yes, Papa. I promise...mostly...to do that. Did you want to speak to me about my appearance, too?"

His father put him down. "Not now. Run along to the nursery, won't you? I should wish to speak to your mother alone."

Sherlock hugged his father's and mother's legs. "I love you, I love you," he said. They returned the sentiments entirely. The lad ran full force from the room, his usual travelling speed.

"I will...mostly..." his father muttered through a grin. "Good God, he's wily."

"Well, David, at least he seems commendably honest, if disobedient," Mrs. Holmes said.

"Remember, he comes from your side of the family," her husband teased.

"We must address his appearance next," she remarked.

"It could be worse," Mr. Holmes said. "He could have been twins."

Chapter Ten
Sherlock's Genius

Years of speaking to Master Mycroft as an equal made the Holmeses comfortable with speaking to their younger son in so adult a manner, and the fact that he fully understood them and could relate back to them in such a discourse was just taken as a matter of fact. I began to think that when the Holmeses saw other children, they ascribed to them a certain dullness and backwardness of intellect rather than acknowledge the unusual and unbelievable circumstance (fairies or not) that they had two genius children with communication skills much beyond their tender years. In fact, Mr. and Mrs. Holmes had clear difficulty speaking to other young boys and girls, for they had had no real experience with the simpler words and sentences required by all other children.

Although not interested in sitting still in company, Master Sherlock increased his verbal abilities and vocabulary through the times he spent with his parents, who so easily spoke to him as an adult. He also spoke to myself, the other house servants, Mrs. Smythe, the groundskeeper and carriageman, the farmers, and all visitors he could pull aside. Mr. Cornelius Brown and Father Metcalfe would always give the lad their time in discourse, and he loved to hear Mrs. Hastwell describe the museums she had been to all over the world. He was not at all a shy lad, but seemed to benefit most from conversing with people one on one, instead of just sitting and listening to a group as had his older brother.

If Master Mycroft had been content to learn from passive hearing and books, Master Sherlock preferred to experience himself what was to be learned. He would rather see how Clara cleaned the fireplace grate and started the fire than just read a book on how it was done. Oftentimes he would ask to do the work himself, and pestered his parents into allowing the servants to show him the proper way to mop and clean, polish, do the laundry, and so forth. Mr. Wilcox taught him to brush down the horses, although he had to stand on a chair to do so. Mr. Denkins had him plant the lettuce, and showed him how to shear the sycamore and briar hedges, and plant traps for weasels, stoats, and carrion crows. Mrs. Winters—after crossing herself—showed him how to pluck a chicken, light the cast-iron stove, and cook it; he also helped her with the making of the oatcakes.

His mother taught him how to arrange flowers, and the basic knitting strokes, though that brought a rare frown to Mr. Holmes' face. Mr. Holmes showed him how to shave, how to sit properly on a horse, how he did the accounts, and let him watch him in his role as justice of the peace. Yes, yes, it is true that the lad had an interest in hearing about crimes from the start.

Master Sherlock showed no compunction in walking up to anyone and asking them to show him what they did. That he confronted people with a winning smile and bright, shining eyes asking them to explain what they were doing, instead of staring at them silently and analyzing their every move, promoted a friendliness and openness in others that enabled young Sherlock to learn as much as his brother had, but without the negative feelings and unease Master Mycroft had created. In fact the opposite often occurred. For example, after meeting Mrs. Winters two or three times in the kitchen for some cooking lessons, he began to cross himself whenever he ran into her, or whenever her name was mentioned, which caused no end of hilarity for all the house staff. His precocious nature was aligned to a personality that ingratiated, not alienated, and that difference in temperament from his brother endeared him to the servants as well as his parents.

Master Mycroft returned home for the Christmas holiday in 1856; his brother was ecstatic to see him. Since Master Sherlock had been born when the Holmeses were quite past the usual age of childbearing, their friends' children were mostly all considerably older than Master Sherlock and spent their time at home with tutors, or, more usually, also away at school like Master Mycroft. The young Sherlock still was not yet engaging in his wanderings of the dales, to his parents' future exasperation; therefore, he had not yet made friends with the poor farm and village youths. The lad spent a good deal of time by himself or with the other adults he watched and emulated. Seeing his brother brought him into solid contact with someone relatively close in age. Besides, this good-natured lad liked everyone, and his brother received his affection wholeheartedly. In fact, Master Sherlock seemed to elevate his brother to hero status due to his abilities to observe and deduce.

It was one afternoon during the Christmas holiday of that year when Master Mycroft was again home, that he became, finally, very interested in his younger brother. It was a mild winter, and so Mr. and Mrs. Holmes had taken their sons on a long ride to Leyburn on market day to look at the Winsby furniture that was exhibited by the esteemed family craftsmen in front of their shops. Mr. Holmes was of a mind to order a new mahogany wardrobe, a couch for the library, and some cabinets for the kitchen. Being very satisfied with the birch chairs with hair cushions he had purchased from Thomas Winsby years ago for the morning room, he decided to visit Winsby's again, and thought an all-day outing with his wife and sons would suit him. As I heard the tale from Mr. Holmes after they had returned home late that night, and the lads had gone to bed, when they entered the town Masters Mycroft and Sherlock became immediately enthralled with all the artisans and people thronging through the streets.

"Mycroft, how can you tell the difference between a wheelwright and a blacksmith?" the near two-year-old Master Sherlock asked his brother. "They both have similar arm muscles and broad backs."

Master Mycroft shot his two-year-old brother a look and blinked several times. "What did you say?"

"Dear Mama says you're good at observing things. I like to notice whatever I can and try to tell things apart, too. I like to meet everybody and see what makes them different, but I'm not so good at it yet. How would you tell a wheelwright from a blacksmith?"

"Sherlock, I didn't know you were interested in such things," Mrs. Holmes remarked.

"Oh yes, Mama. It's fun."

Mr. Holmes reported that Master Mycroft showed a look of sheer glee on his face, though I personally feel that saying Master Mycroft rubbed his hands together slyly is no doubt an exaggeration.

"Of course the musculature will be similar, Sherlock," he began. "They are both involved with heavy, onerous work. You must seek differences elsewhere, then- –use your brain to discern what your eyes see. For example, with your simple question, there are several obvious answers: such as check for the blacksmith's apron; if he doesn't wear it but still you suspect that is the man's trade, check for the clothes to be dirty only in the lower legs and on the sleeves, the areas where the apron does not protect the blacksmith's clothing. Also, it is possible to see a cleaner area around the back of the neck where the apron loop sits. A wheelwright will have sawdust on his clothes; the blacksmith will not. It is also not uncommon to observe a plethoric countenance on blacksmiths due to years of being so near a hot fire. Look for tools contained on their person; they will often be conclusive in and of themselves. Learn all you may of tools."

Mr. Holmes reported that Master Mycroft lapsed into a loquacious display never seen before, and spent the rest of the day instructing his younger brother— whose eyes were wide as saucers for the entire day—on the intricacies of all the people they saw, even during the trip home.

"It was a long ride," Mr. Holmes said. "I tell you, Brewster, Mrs. Holmes and I felt superfluous to Mycroft's deductions at times. I...worry about Sherlock."

"Sir?"

"One genius is enough for me," he said. That night he stayed up quite late and slept in until the afternoon the next day. Upon noticing it first thing in the morning, I dutifully refilled the whiskey bottle in the drawing room, and spent the day being perfectly attentive to the slightly solemn Mrs. Holmes.

As for Master Mycroft, another year at school had not really changed him; his observances continued, as did his incessant book reading, his stockiness, and his lack of desire for physical activities. He was more silent though, and neither wanted nor unwanted deductions escaped from his lips in company. Master Sherlock adored him; he was like a small greyhound puppy darting up and over his brother's large, bulldog composure. However, after Leyburn, Master Mycroft did not seem to mind his younger brother's constant attentions; in fact, the two of them were often secluded in private discussions. Master Sherlock craved to hear all about his older brother's adventures at school, and showed him all that he knew in Hillcroft House. The younger lad even was able to persuade his brother to go on walks around the park, and to ride with him in the carriage to the village. After a couple of those trips, I was surprised to hear Master Mycroft ask Sherlock if he wanted to go again, which the latter readily and joyfully agreed to do in an instant.

It disturbed their parents a little to have the two sequestered in either of their studies; what could they possibly be talking about for hours at a time? I think that the Holmeses feared somehow that Master Mycroft would change young Sherlock, make him more inscrutable, separate, like their elder son was—more unarguably different. For to everyone now, even Mrs. Winters, Master Sherlock was still more amiable lad than unapproachable genius, and no one wished for him to change into Master Mycroft.

Master Sherlock's relationship with his brother was made glaringly clear in a terrifying episode. One day Mrs. Holmes had felt slightly indisposed with a cold—she was the most susceptible to colds in the household—and I had brought her breakfast to her on a silver serving tray. Upon hearing that his mother felt poorly, after breakfast, which not even his brother could entice him to eat, Master Sherlock was excused by his father to attend to her upstairs. Master Sherlock spoke with her for half an hour, and then, sensitive to his mother's need for rest, bade her good-bye and took the tray to return to the kitchen, saving Miss Borel the effort. At the top of the stairs his innate impulsivity reigned supreme, and, placing the dishes and cutlery safely on the floor, he endeavoured to sleigh down the stairs on the tray. He made it about one-third down, before the tray hit a step top and the lad and the tray both rolled down the entire rest of the way. Goodness! It made a God-fearing clamber and racket the entire house heard, even Mrs. Holmes, who arose from her sickbed to investigate the disturbance.

The family and the staff converged in the hallway, where Master Sherlock sat, arms firmly planted on the floor to keep himself upright, his head whirling around in small circles on his thin neck. A large bruise already swelled and discoloured the middle of his smooth forehead. The dented tray lay over his splayed legs. His father scooped up his dazed son and ran into the morning room, laying him upon the sofa, while his mother dashed down the stairs, almost tripping herself on her untied dressing gown, joining her husband in a state of frantic anguish. Meanwhile, Master Mycroft lifted up the tray and examined it closely.

A glass of water was fetched and a bowl filled with a cloth and cool water. The wrung-out cloth was laid on Master Sherlock's injured forehead.

"Sherlock, are you all right?" his father cried. He examined him in a fearful manner for broken bones or lacerations.

"Oh, my God," his mother wept. "What happened? David, is he all right? Brewster, send Wilcox for Mr. Irwin." I moved to the hallway.

"Wait, Brewster, wait. He seems to be coming around. I don't think the boy broke anything, Catherine. Sherlock, can you hear me, lad?"

Master Sherlock's eyes thankfully regained their focus. He put a hand to his head. "Ow," he moaned. Then he noticed everyone standing over him in concern. "Uh-oh, did I crash?"

Before anyone could speak, Master Mycroft's voice rang out derisively. "Of course you crashed, Sherlock. How could you not? From my analysis of your handprints and scuff marks on the tray, it is obvious you were kneeling forward on it, a position from which it would be impossible for you to descend the stairs effectively. If you wish to ride a tray down the stairs, you must sit with your weight on its back end, not the front, thus elevating the front end of the tray above the edges of the stairs. Only sitting so would you avoid an otherwise inevitable hitting of a step on your descent, and the following dangerous forward flight of your body onto and down the stairs. You're an impulsive fool, Sherlock; use the brain in your head the next time you attempt a stunt like that."

The dressing down silenced not just Master Sherlock, but everyone in the room. I did see Mr. Holmes' face scrunch up during the speech, but with irritation or impatience or some other emotion I do not know.

Mrs. Holmes spoke. "That's enough, Mycroft. I'm sure Sherlock has seen the error of his action. We are just thankful he appears only slightly worse for it."

"I have, Mama, and I'm sorry. But Mycroft is right, I was kneeling on the front of the tray." He looked at his brother with adoration. "I'll think first next time, Mycroft."

"Good! I should not like to see a brother of mine doing something so stupid, and almost dying as a result."

Mr. Holmes stood up brusquely. "Well, well, the excitement's over. Everyone back to work. Catherine, back to your sickbed. Mycroft back to your books. And you," he said, pointing his finger at his youngest son, "it's two days in bed for you, my lad."

He lifted up the boy and had Clara follow with the bowl of water. Mycroft volunteered to sit with his brother during those days, freeing the nursemaid from her duties, which both pleased and unsettled their father. He was certainly glad that even though their age difference was somewhat large, the boys were attaining a true closeness; however, I imagine he did not want to consider what other lessons Mycroft was imparting to his willing and eager younger brother. The rest of us no doubt silently worried about that as well. When Master Mycroft left to return to school, yielding to a long embrace by Master Sherlock, I believe the air in the house palpably lightened.

Not many days after Mycroft's departure, Master Sherlock asked me to bring his parents to him when they returned from their lunch at the Metcalfes. I did as he asked and brought them to the nursery after they arrived home. His parents approached their young son and asked him what he wanted.

Master Sherlock—all two feet and thirty-five pounds of him—stood on a chair, placing a tenth wooden brick on the pile he had built up from the floor. He stopped for a moment in thought before reaching for number eleven from the bricks he had placed on the chair seat around his feet. He then pronounced, "Mycroft said it's time for me to learn to read. Will you please engage Mr. Wharton as my tutor? Mycroft recommends him highly."

His parents' faces paled. I am as sure of what they thought as if they had screamed it into the high heavens: "Now we will lose another child to his own genius."

"You want to learn to read?" his mother asked, glancing at Mr. Holmes.

"Yes, Mama," Master Sherlock said, placing the eleventh block successfully on the column. He pointed at the column to his parents, chest swelled with pride, then reached down for the twelfth block. "However, if it's acceptable to you, I should only like to study reading and writing, Latin, Greek, and French. Otherwise, I still just want to play, even though Mycroft disagrees. He won't say exactly, but I think he worries of my impetuosity. He would rather I study all the time, as he does. But such is not my nature."

His parents stood watching him silently as he focused on the blocks. They were utterly speechless for the moment, a whirlwind of emotions fluttering over their features.

The twelfth block perched precariously on top of the others, and the column began swaying back and forth. With an eagle eye, Master Sherlock stood surveying his tower. "Eight seconds," he stated. As one, we all stood still watching the tower and the clock standing on a table. After eight seconds, the tower tilted too far to the right, and the blocks crashed to the floor.

"Ha!" Master Sherlock exclaimed. "It is possible; Mycroft was right."

"Mycroft," Mr. Holmes finally muttered. And the next day there was an empty wine bottle to remove from his study.

They engaged Mr. Wharton again, who was only too glad and amazed to begin tutoring a second mentally precocious child.

"I've never heard the like," he stated to the Holmeses when he visited them to begin teaching Master Sherlock. "Geniuses do come and go, you know, but for you to have two such children; why it beggars the imagination. I should write them up and submit it to someone for publication."

The force of Mrs. Holmes' ejaculation stunned Mr. Wharton, Mr. Holmes, and no doubt herself. "You'll do absolutely no such thing, Mr. Wharton. I absolutely forbid you from ever mentioning such an absurd idea again. We should be quite content if you simply tutor our sons and remove all thoughts of any publication of their abilities from your mind!"

They had a hard enough time keeping their children to themselves; the last thing the Holmeses desired was the prying interference of unwelcome scholars.

Mr. Wharton was quite contrite; he agreed forthwith and I led him to the nursery, where Master Sherlock awaited him for his first day of instruction. As per Master Sherlock's request, Mr. Wharton was only to teach him for three hours in the morning, nine o'clock to noon; the afternoon was allotted for him to play and explore inside and out the house.

More time passed; it was late spring of 1857. Master Sherlock could read and write, was excelling at memorizing conjugations, declensions, and so forth in Latin grammar, spoke French impressively with his parents, and worked on his Greek. At almost three feet tall, Master Sherlock was of a height to open doors without the aid of chairs, and by the age of three had lost any childlike apprehension of the outside of the house. In fact, the lad was truly fearless. This proved to be the beginning of a long horrific nightmare for his parents; for in the midday, if he was not with one or both parents, the nursemaid was supposed to be watching him, even if he was in the presence of another person, such as a servant. Mrs. Smythe, only thirty-six, but corpulent and easily tired, did not have the stamina to keep up with the lad. It was a game to Master Sherlock to run away from her, hide, lose her completely, and then duck outside and begin exploring the land by himself. He mainly stayed around the house and the park, occasionally wandering to a farmer's field. The entire staff would be mobilized to find the lad on the days he surreptitiously left the house, and sometimes it would take an hour or two to locate him. The fact that he hid from his searchers as well did not amuse the Holmeses at all. Nor did it amuse them the time he jumped down from a tree right in front of his mother, scaring her terribly. For a three-and-a-half-year old, Master Sherlock's stamina was legendary—naps were out of the question—and it was at the end of August that he was brought back to Hillcroft House by the blacksmith. He had walked the two miles to town by himself—his worried parents smothered him in so many hugs that he resurfaced positively disheveled.

He slept well that night, the nursemaid actually having to wake him up in the morning. They had long ago stopped the laudanum, even though his sleep was still restless, for Mrs. Holmes had worried about the effects of the medication on his health. They had not, though, stopped locking his door.

"You'd best keep locking it," Master Sherlock had said. "Or I'll no doubt find it irresistible to leave the room, and I fear admonitions not to do so may well prove to no avail."

They kept the door locked.

"Well, at least he's honest," Mrs. Holmes told her husband, as he pocketed the key in his trousers.

"Your side of the family," was the familiar rejoinder.

In this latest episode, however, no one thought that exchanging a toddler's restless night of sleep for his fatiguing himself in wandering the roads by himself a good idea. Least of all his parents.

"Don't you ever, ever, do that again!" his father scolded him the next day as the three stood in the morning room.

Master Sherlock regarded his parents. He thought for a minute before speaking. "I cannot promise I shall not repeat yesterday's escapade. I found it enjoyable beyond measure."

"Yes, dear, and in return you had us distraught beyond measure," his mother answered.

"I truly apologize for that, Mama. But, really, you must understand that I am not afraid and can take care of myself."

This cut his parents to the quick. No doubt they had hoped that Master Sherlock would have developed his independence after some more years of childlike play. Now they were in danger of losing this most precious second son as well; this son who had at least allowed them to treat him as a child, and who had given and received love with abundance.

His mother sat down heavily in a chair and burst into tears. Mr. Holmes quickly sat down next to her, gently whispering "There, there," to her. Master Sherlock was remarkably affected by her weeping, his eyes widening and his pose frozen.

"No, Mama, don't cry," he said very softly. When she continued her crying, he threw himself at her legs.

"I'm sorry for making you cry, Mama. I won't go out walking by myself anymore. I promise I won't. Oh, please, don't cry, Mama," he implored with all his heart.

His mother took him up into her lap, smiling through her still-falling tears. "Oh, thank you, Sherlock. Thank you so very much," she said, hugging him tightly. "I love you so fully, I shall die of worry if you go out alone."

"I promise I won't go out alone, Mama," the boy repeated.

"That's a good, lad, Sherlock," his father added, and there was a catch in his voice as well.

Arrangements were made to the satisfaction of all. Mrs. Smythe was let go, like Mrs. Kirby before her, with a quarter-year's pay and a letter of recommendation. She was no longer needed to help the lad wash and dress, as he could do that himself now, and she was obviously unable to keep up with Master Sherlock's love of activity. A lad—Hank Cotter—was hired to help Mr. Denkins and Mr. Wilcox, though his primary duty was to attend Master Sherlock on any walk he wanted to take, if neither of his parents were available or willing to go.

At this time Clara also left the household to marry Bart Pruitt, the son of a sheep farmer. A new girl, Eliza Williams, age twelve, was engaged. Upon meeting her Master Sherlock deduced that she had broken her arm recently, and requested of Mr. Holmes that her chores still be on the light side for another month or two. This embarrassed the girl greatly, for it was true, yet she had sworn to be perfectly healthy when applying for the position. She expected to be let go at once, and began to cry in shame. When, instead, Mr. Holmes acknowledged his son's cogent observations calmly, and then told Mrs. Birchall to allow Eliza no heavy duties until such time as her arm would allow, Eliza was so flabbergasted she could not even collect herself to express her gratitude. Mrs. Birchall lead her away still blubbering.

His deduction that Hank, age fifteen, drank consistently at night when off duty, was greeted less charitably. It was only Master Sherlock's growing friendship with Hank's youngest brother Noah, that enabled Hank to maintain his position once he swore off drinking to Mr. Holmes. When asked several months later, Master Sherlock assured his father that Hank drank only occasionally.

It was no doubt Master Mycroft's advice that Master Sherlock followed in remaining silent generally about his observations and deductions. By the time Master Sherlock was sneaking outside it was no longer possible to avoid acknowledging that he had the similar double gifts of incredible intelligence and the flair for "figuring things out."

"Told you all," Mrs. Winters said. "Fairies."

However, coached as he was by his reclusive elder brother, Master Sherlock had never developed the tendency overtly to demonstrate his fantastic sharpness of mind by indiscriminately analyzing people. Even when visitors to the house deliberately asked Master Sherlock for a deduction—for his parents had shared with their friends their son's gift—it was rare that he obliged. This added to the staffs' favor of him; they felt their secrets were safe with him.

How closely Master Mycroft was involved in grooming his brother was made evident only to me, I think. At the large Christmas party the Holmeses threw when Sherlock was almost four, I was kept, of course, extraordinarily busy in my duties.

However, during one brief break in the festivities, I removed myself from the drawing room to stand in the hallway and take a rest. As I leaned against the banister in repose I heard the boys discussing the guests as they sat on the step at the bottom of the staircase.

"Mr. Metcalfe, the man with the balding head and the grey suit with high collar, suffers from a headache he tries to hide, no doubt to maintain the holiday cheer of his wife, and he has two cats," Master Mycroft told his younger brother.

"I saw the signs of the cats, the two different types of cat hairs on his trouser legs were obvious; but the headache—is it because of the way he slightly stiffly holds his head and subtly rubs his brow when no one pays him attention?" Master Sherlock asked.

"Yes, that, and also how he sits at the edge of the circle of chairs, away from the smoke of Father and Mr. Brown, and with the largest group of candles to his back. Very often light aggravates the pain in migraine victims."

"I see," Master Sherlock said, nodding his head.

"Now," Master Mycroft commanded of his attentive younger brother, "tell me how we can deduce that Mr. Blades was in the navy as a youth. You have been perusing the books I recommended, haven't you, the ones with pictures of military uniforms and decorations?"

"Whenever Papa takes my ball away for a while, I look at them."

"Good. Then tell me what you can."

I stood in rapt attention, listening to them analyze Mr. Blades and then many of the other guests; they could discern something about most of them. Master Mycroft then began deductions about the servants. I would have listened to them all night, if I had not been called back to serve some more drinks. I could only wonder at what they knew of me.

Chapter Eleven
Sherlock's Wanderings

aster Sherlock and Hank Cotter went on regular walks almost every day when the weather permitted, and occasionally when it did not. For all his thinness, Master Sherlock was warm-blooded and hardy in the cold. Outdoors he was generally more inhibited by the layers of clothes his mother forced upon him than by the bitter northern winds.

Although he still spent a good deal of time with his parents, either with one or the other or both, due to the nature of Mr. and Mrs. Holmes' standing in the community and their public and private obligations and socializing, the times they were available for a walk were infrequent. Besides, childlike wanderings did not really interest either of his parents. Chasing after rabbits, or having a snowball fight, or leaping about in a creek was best relegated to Hank Cotter's presence than theirs; and anyway, it afforded Master Sherlock opportunities to meet with other children, albeit poor village folk.

As he grew older and was able to travel about the land, Farmer Baynes and his sons showed Master Sherlock how to milk a cow and carry the milk from the pasture to the farmhouse in a can on his back; and Mrs. Baynes and her daughters showed him how to make butter in the winter, and mild Wensleydale cheeses from spring through autumn. He cut peat with Farmer Harland, watched sheep washings and shearings, darkened his finger with sheep salving, helped Mrs. Postlethwaite salt a pig, helped Farmer Terry with haying and with mucking—that is, spreading manure—although his mother made him swear upon the Bible never to do the latter again. When in town he would visit every tradesman he could: blacksmiths, saddlers, shoemakers, tinsmiths, tailors, wheelwrights, farriers, joiners, roofers, stonemasons. Anyone, really. He'd engage them in—to their surprise—articulate conversation about their trade, and ask to see their hands and arms, their feet and shoes, their tools, and so on, then respectfully request that he be allowed to aid the tradesman in any capacity his tall, thin body and brilliant mind might permit.

It was on a walk to town with Hank Cotter one day that Master Sherlock met Noah Cotter, Hank's youngest brother, as I mentioned. As both the children were four, and slight of build, and good-naturedly mischievous, they immediately became boon companions. Certainly you may be thinking it highly unusual for the squire's child to play with the village children, and of course you would be right, but the Holmeses had long ago ceased to worry about all the proprieties when it came to their children. They were delighted their son had a good friend—didn't that make him quite typical?—and hoped that his contact with others would stanch the desire to become ever more like his elder brother. Mostly Mrs. Holmes worried he would contract a disease from the poor folk, and so Master Sherlock was forced to bathe upon his every return home from playing with Noah. This did not upset the lad so much, for he reasoned that since he was to bathe anyway, he should make the most of it and become as filthy as he could. This greatly pleased him and his friends, but not so the servants or his parents. The only illness he caught was the measles, and his recovery was quick. Yet it took all Mrs. Holmes' strength of spirit to overcome her fears and allow him to return to play with the village children.

Noah's father was a farm hand who did odd jobs as dictated by a farmer's needs and the season; the Cotters had a tiny plot of land they used to grow vegetables themselves. There were six children—Hank, another son, two daughters, Noah, and another daughter—ages fifteen to two. A couple had gone to school for a year or two but had then stopped.

After a while, Noah by himself, or with a group of lads from the village, would occasionally appear in the afternoon at Hillcroft House timidly knocking on the door. When I answered it and was greeted by a gang of scruffy boys pushing each other to the front to talk to me, it was all I could do to step aside quickly enough to avoid the exceedingly rapid egress of Master Sherlock to join them. They would play on the lawn, hitting each other with croquet mallets (although that was quickly stopped once Mrs. Holmes espied them out the greenhouse windows), visit the horses in the stables, play football with one of Master Sherlock's ubiquitous balls, pretend to be knights and kings and villains, or criminals like Dick Turpin, or the Norse Vikings by whom, Master Sherlock informed his mates, the town of Carperby was originally named, or engage in any other of numerous games young lads enjoy. Master Sherlock consistently outpaced the other boys in races, a fact that Mr. Holmes thought was frankly wonderful.

I must say that for a boy such as Master Sherlock, who was interested in everything on God's green earth, Carperby was idyllic for him. In his home he had his tutor to promote his intellectual gifts, his parents to encourage proper respect and formality in social situations, and his mother to foster a spiritual connexion with the Bible and the goodness of God. The world outdoors came complete with all the activities of the different tenant farms—to which he had full access as son of the squire. There were the multiple fairs country villages are always having, market days in various villages—Thursday was Carperby's—gypsy caravans, drovers from Scotland, and so on.

In fact, the only thing that could tear the lad away from his friends was the two trips he made with his parents that year to London, during which he saw his first plays—*Twelfth Night* at Sadler's Well in early January for his birthday, and then later in the year at the Princess Theatre, Charles Kean as Bolingbroke in *Richard II.* How they got the lad into the plays I do not know, children generally not being allowed at such productions. "Money screams where rules whisper," was all Mr. Holmes would say. The lad's desire "to be an actor just like Mr. Kean" was not so keen to his parents; neither were his repetitive outbursts of "O villains, vipers, damn'd without redemption! Dogs, easily won to fawn on any man! Snakes, in my heartblood warm'd, that sting my heart!"—I forget the rest of the quote. After some time back home, though, the call of his friends outweighed the call of the stage, and he forswore Shakespeare for puddle jumping.

Master Sherlock always exhibited a tender heart, and injured birds or animals that he carried home were placed under Mr. Wilcox's care, though the boy would hover over them for days, feeding and watering them by hand. We soon learned that his natural compassion extended to human beings as well. Mrs. Winters was responsible for uncovering this, for she reported to me that food was disappearing from the pantry mysteriously—a little at first, then growing in amount—and she was none too happy about it. Mrs. Winters' domain was inviolate; how dare an intruder penetrate her realm! After questioning the other servants, all of whom pleaded innocent, I was forced to notify Mr. Holmes of the disappearances and state my belief that the servants were not to blame. The Holmeses exchanged knowing glances just as Master Sherlock entered the drawing room to bid his parents good night. His sleep was deeper now that he regularly expended considerable physical energy, and he might even, every now and then, decide for himself that he was sleepy and should retire. His parents still kept his door locked, however.

"Sherlock, I think we should like to speak with you," his mother began.

"Yes, Mama?" the lad asked.

"Dear, Mrs. Winters feels that there is…well, that food is somehow disappearing from the pantry. No servant admits responsibility, and certainly your father and I are not the culprits. Dear, are you secretly taking food?"

"Yes, I'm taking the food, Mama."

"But, why, lad?" His father asked. "You may eat as much as you like at meals. You've no need to hoard comestibles. If you feel hungry in between meals you've but to ask Brewster to serve you a sustaining bite." Actually, Master Sherlock's hunger had greatly increased over this last year, and his eating had doubled. His parents were relieved to see him finally develop a hearty appetite, and though he grew, his still stayed rail thin.

"I don't take the food to eat it myself, Papa. I take it to give to Noah and the lads."

His parents raised their eyebrows simultaneously.

"Noah and the lads, dear?" his mother reiterated.

"Yes, mama, they hardly get enough to eat. There are six children to feed in Noah's family, and Noah's father is only a farming assistant for a couple of farms; that's hardly likely to earn a wage equivalent to the needs of such a large family. So, seeing that Noah is my friend, I thought I should help him out a little. Then I realised Jimmy and Peter Burton would benefit from extra food as well. So I've taken more."

"You've stolen more, you mean, Sherlock," his father stated sternly.

Master Sherlock looked down at his feet. "Yes, I stole the food, Papa. But for a good cause."

His mother spoke. "For an excellent cause, Sherlock, and how proud it makes me to see you have such a giving heart. But we cannot feed the entire village."

"You must separate yourself from the lads you play with, son." His father stood and continued, "Though your friends, they are not of our class. We take care of the sick and the destitute, and help pay for the education of some of the villagers, but you cannot expect us to allow our own larders to be depleted in the warmth of your compassion for those of the lower classes."

"But everyone should have food to eat, Papa," the boy said.

"Yes, everyone should; and one day God will provide such a Heaven on earth. For now, we must realise that pitiful discrepancies exist in the world. While we should not ever harden our hearts against the poor folk, and should always be open to helping them as we can, you must learn there are practical and financial limits to our giving."

Master Sherlock said nothing for a minute. Then he asked, "Would it be practical and financially sound to give just one sackful of food a week to my friends—perhaps a few loaves of haverbread, and some cheese?" He did not ask it sarcastically or viciously, but softly and with his hands deep in his trouser pockets and his sight centered on his shoes. Then he looked up and coquettishly grinned. "If you like, I shall work off the cost of the dairy products by milking the cows myself and churning the cream into butter. Mrs. Baynes has showed me how."

Mr. Holmes' head turned to the right, so he was viewing his son from out the left sides of his slitted eyes. He held up a finger to him, and then dropped it back down to his side, noisily slapping his leg in the process.

"Your side of the family," he grumbled to his wife as he sat down.

Ignoring her husband, Mrs. Holmes was left to deal with their son. They were used to compromising by now, as it allowed them to exert some power and authority while not chasing their precocious yet endearing son away from them.

"You may take one sack," she paused, thinking quickly, "of which we will decide the size, to your friends each Sunday as we go to church. You may repay us by cleaning up your study each day before you go out to play." (He *was* a messy boy.)

"I should rather milk the cows," the lad said. A throat clearing from Mr. Holmes, and several deep inhalations from Mrs. Holmes, ensued.

"Charity begins at home, Sherlock; the sack shall be filled dependent upon the cleaned room," his mother declared.

Master Sherlock pursed his thin lips. Of a sudden he stuck out his open right hand. "You drive a hard bargain, madam. I am helpless but to obey."

He shook his mother's and then his father's hand, and then bowed to them both. "Good night fair parents; I bid you adieu." He ran from the room like a cannon shot.

"My side of the family," Mrs. Holmes positively glowed, before they both burst out in laughter.

Another year passed, and it was 1859. The reading of plays with his mother became a favored pastime for both. Attending to the roles of Shakespeare, Master Sherlock's energy was well spent, though at first he could easily become meretriciously silly in his interpretations. After making a tormented Macbeth cringe in terror at the sight of Banquo's ghost, he then ran from the room waving his arms and fanatically shrieking at the top of his lungs "Avaunt! and quit my sight! Let the earth hide thee!" Mrs. Holmes patiently explained, once her nerves had settled, that the scene was ruined due to an excess of misapplied fervour.

"You must realise the beauty of the parts for themselves as written, Sherlock," she explained patiently. "While each performer does lend his personal stamp of interpretation to the story, one must ever be mindful of the limits of believability and good taste."

"You don't think, dear Mama, that a person might run screaming from a room if he saw the ghost of the man he had respected, yet killed, returning from the dead to curse him?"

"Many persons might indeed run," his mother agreed. "I just do not think Macbeth would have, as William Shakespeare meant it."

Master Sherlock nodded his head. "I see."

He developed a love for plays that equaled his mother's. Again that year the Holmeses went to London for a trip, and Mrs. Hastwell went along as well. Mrs. Holmes, Mrs. Hastwell, and Master Sherlock went to the Princess Theatre and saw Charles Kean and his wife in a lavish production of *The Merchant of Venice*. He spent the weeks after they returned asking anyone who came into the house, "If you prick us, do we not bleed," soon changing it to, "If you cut off our arm with a butcher's knife, do we not bleed?" until Mrs. Holmes very sweetly but firmly requested he stop.

Most evenings after supper if the Holmeses were at home alone, Master Sherlock divided his time between playing chess or cards with his father, reading plays or playing music with his mother, bouncing his ball on the stairs, or reading books. One spring evening, as they all sat quietly reading in the drawing room, Master Sherlock requested that his parents get him a dog.

"A dog?" his mother asked.

"Yes, any kind that can walk for distances will do."

His father put down his paper. "I see no reason why you shouldn't have a dog. I'll purchase one on the morrow, as I know that Mr. Brown's collie has had puppies."

"A female should be best, for Noah's spaniel is female, as well."

"A female it shall be. Fancy a game of chess?"

Master Sherlock shook his head and held up the book, *Linley's Strategies of Chess*. "Not until I have discovered how to immobilize your precious rooks." He returned to his reading, adding, "I think I shall be ready by Saturday."

He did beat Mr. Holmes quite soundly on Saturday.

The new puppy was of a gentle yet excitable nature, and therefore fit well with Master Sherlock. It grew quickly in height and weight, and by the end of summer had attained its full size. The spaniel, named Daisy by the lad, accompanied Master Sherlock and the village lads who joined in on his tours of the countryside. A system was worked out in the house between Master Sherlock and his parents— if he were leaving to play with his friends, he could travel solely with the dog; if he were leaving to traverse the land randomly, he was to take Hank Cotter with him as well. If the journey were over four miles, he and Hank were to saddle up First Boy and ride him. These plans required some forethought from the lad, which he understood was good to help him control his impulsive nature, and which he knew would be approved by his older brother.

The land around Carperby was and still is rich in scenic wonders, with its gentle hills and dales, pastures with wild flowers, beautiful valleys, Bolton Castle, the river Ure, and the Pennines in the far distance. However, the multiple waterfalls of the area most enchanted the lad. For most of its length the river Ure is a tame body of water, yet at Aysgarth it is released from its bonds of civility and plunges over a rocky gorge, falling two hundred feet in a series of three gorgeous and awesome falls. When the weather was dry, the Ure could be low enough for Master Sherlock to play on the flat rocks in the middle of the river, surrounded by the lush beauty of the trees lining every inch of the water's edge. When there had been many rains, or during the spring melting, the river there rushed in a dangerous torrent.

There were also three waterfalls by Askrigg: Millgill Force, with a vertical drop of about thirty yards before it flooded down the rocky bed of a ravine; one mile farther was Whitfield's Force. Five miles up the Dale from Askrigg, journeyed to only by horseback, was Hardrow Force, a singular falls where the water rolled off a perpendicular rise of rock one hundred feet in height, tumbling to the placid river below in one wide sheet. As spectacular as the waterfall was the chasm after it, three hundred feet long and bounded on both sides by massive boulders. There was a deep recess behind Hardrow Falls, where Master Sherlock was allowed to stand with Hank to observe the wonder safely. The Holmeses had been to all the waterfalls with the lad for picnics, and Master Sherlock had been enamoured of them immediately.

These were some of his favorite spots where he would play and think. For while Master Sherlock was not solely of a contemplative nature, as was his sibling, there were times since he had begun his studies with Mr. Wharton when he, too, stopped his almost incessant activity and sat and pondered such things as I only wish I'd been privy to. He related to his parents—when they inquired why he returned so often to the falls—that he found the background noise of the waterfalls conducive for deep meditation; also, there were plenty of rocks to throw to strengthen his arm and sharpen his accuracy.

"I find the water enthralling; the air stimulates and clarifies my thoughts. The Yore bridge by the Aysgarth Falls is a terrific spot to have a sword fight with Noah. The decorations on its side are lovely to behold as well, and I fancy the ancient craftsmen of the bridge were justified in their pride upon the bridge's completion."

Another keen interest of Master Sherlock's were the cases his father heard as justice of the peace, and during the quarter sessions Master Sherlock was taken to Northallerton for the sessions, as Mycroft had gone, after much pleading, and with promises to be "mostly well-behaved." He surprised his father greatly by sitting quietly in a seat in the corner, captivated by the stories of crime and the entire justice process. His father brought Master Sherlock articles and books about famous crimes and criminals—such as *A Penal Reform in England, Scotland, and Wales,* and the lad attacked them with relish. He desperately wished to see a criminal hanged at Newgate; his parents adamantly refused. Once a simple wayfarer was brought before Mr. Holmes, charged by the mercantile owner in Carperby with shoplifting two cans of beans. The gaunt man admitted his theft and asked for leniency. Mr. Holmes let him go, whispering to me to give him some bread and cheese before he left. The store owner was enraged. Master Sherlock, who had witnessed the scene, related it later that evening to his mother.

"Mr. Bigelow said, 'You can't do that! I caught him plainly with my goods in my pack. He's guilty as sin.'" The lad added, "I daresay his face was red and swollen as a tomato."

He continued, "Papa was grave. 'The crime I have just heard, Mr. Bigelow, is that you couldn't find it in your heart to ask a poor, lonely fellow to supper with the missus. His sin, if we should term it such, is abject poverty; your sin is callous pettiness and cold-hearted avarice—tell me, if you were justice of the peace, whom would you think the greater criminal?'

"Mr. Bigelow stormed out of papa's study—it was all Brewster here could do to hand him his hat before he stomped from the house."

A mirthful moment passed, and then Mr. Holmes pointed his pipe at his son and said, "Justice is subjective at times, lad. True, the man shoplifted and therefore broke the written law, and should have been fined or put in gaol. But always remember, Sherlock, that to a good, upstanding man, his conscience should weigh more heavily in his decisions than the words in a dusty book on a barrister's shelf. I have the lawful edict to judge criminal situations. That may lead to bending the law occasionally, but sleep is a dear commodity to me; I'll not lose it satisfying the odious and spiteful Mr. Bigelow's need for vengeance over such a sad affair. In some cases, 'There but for the grace of God go I' should suffice in pronouncing judgments."

Master Sherlock drank this in, then spent the next several weeks often in silent contemplation at the waterfalls.

That year Mrs. Holmes' mother passed away and she and Mr. Holmes packed bags to travel to Paris to pay their last respects. Master Sherlock wished to go, but his parents did not feel he was of a manageable temperament for them to take with him. Master Sherlock pursed his lips together tightly, and then nodded his head several times. "You are absolutely correct," he admitted. "I would indeed be a great deal of trouble. Please give my regards to the family, and enjoy a safe and pleasant trip."

His parents' smiles illuminated their entire faces. It was one of the first times the lad's innate honesty had actually worked in their complete favor.

The days were busy and full for Master Sherlock—studies in the morning and playing in the afternoon. There were his village friends, his dog—who never left his side; she even slept with him—his books, his ball, his walks and rides around the towns and countryside, his chess playing with his father, his play reading and acting with his mother, and his thinking sessions by the waterfalls.

By then, Noah was allowed in the house if he was immaculately clean before his entrance. He did not come in too frequently, although one time he looked positively scrubbed, and he and Master Sherlock had a grand time around the house. I remember the ball was taken away from him that day by his father. The lads finally made it to the kitchen, where they both crossed themselves upon seeing Mrs. Winters. She crossed herself back, and then served them bowls of soup and bread. She left them to go outside for a breath of fresh air for about twenty minutes, her last respite before the push to prepare the evening meal.

The kitchen was in the back of the house on the north side, down a small staircase from the ground floor. Mrs. Winters had a witchstone pegged up on the wall, that being a piece of limestone with a water-worn hole in it to ward off evil. The kitchen had three rooms attached to it—the well-stocked wine cellar, the pantry, and a warm though simply furnished servants' room. The kitchen was a comfortable place smelling of good food, havercakes with crosses on them as a charm against witches, and candles hanging by wicks from the ceiling. One door led from the kitchen up to the outside of the house for deliveries, and another, forbidden one to several passages, one of which wound its long, dark and dank way to a stall in the stables; an ancient escape route it appeared. Where the other passages went no one knew. Which path was the correct one to the stables, no one knew. I had also heard rumors that the paths had hidden in them deep pits lined with spikes, leg traps as laid for animals hidden by a thin layer of dirt, and legions of starving rats. It was thought that the first settled Holmes may have had an enemy or two, though, as far as I can recall, no Holmes ever had to make use of that miserable passage, which was said to have many confusing branches containing dangerous traps for those unfamiliar with the one correct path. The escape route theory is the best one the family had for why the kitchen was not on the ground floor, to be able to grab some food in a hurried departure. The door to the subterranean maze was padlocked closed.

When Mrs. Winters returned, she saw a frightened Noah standing by the opened door off the kitchen, peering into the escape-route passageway.

"Sherlock, come back!" he yelled down the path.

"Lord God, have mercy!" Mrs. Winters gasped. Noah swung around to face her. "Lad, tell me now and tell me true, has Master Sherlock gone into that tunnel?"

Noah began crying. "He told me about it and I dared him to go. So he ran and got the key to the lock that his father hides in his desk drawer. I said I'd follow, but I'm too scared. He took a candle, but I can't see it now. I'm sorry, I'm sorry." Tears flowed onto his shirt.

There was no time to placate the lad. Mrs. Winters flew up the stairs and found me in the dining room, roughly grabbing me in her strong, flabby arms. In her utter concern, she was incoherent, hysterical, and I had to sit her down forcefully in a chair and serve her a brandy from the fine liquors and wines on the sideboard—a major transgression, though necessitated by the intensity of her emotions. After several rapid swallows, she relayed to me Master Sherlock's situation, bemoaning that she had let Marianne—the local girl who helped her—have the day off to look after her sickly mother, therefore leaving the lads alone in the kitchen.

"Oh, my dear God," I said, my stomach transforming itself into a large, heavy weight.

It was fortuitous that both the Holmeses were home, sitting on the back lawn with the Metcalfes, enjoying the sunny spring day. Though an undignified action, I ran as hard as I could to them and told them the dreadful news; Mrs. Holmes paled so drastically I thought she would faint dead away. Then she shot ahead like an Ascot racehorse, and it was left to the rest of us to follow in her stead. In very short time we had plunged down into the kitchen and dashed to the door where the weeping Noah still stood. Somehow Mr. Denkins was with us; he probably had seen us running and had joined the mad scramble to investigate.

"Denkins, find Wilcox and make sure nothing obstructs the end of the tunnel door in the stable floor," Mr. Holmes said to the gardener.

"Where does that door lay again, sir?" he asked.

"In the last stall from the doorway, I believe. Hurry man, hurry!" Denkins darted up the stairs. He then sent me for as many skeins of yarn from his wife's knitting basket as there were. I returned within three minutes with six large skeins. Mr. Holmes had emptied out a grain sack and placed five skeins in them. With the sixth, he tied one end to the door handle and held it in his hand, to unroll it as he progressed down the tunnel.

Mr. Holmes lit two candles and put them in a holder. He shoved more into his pockets. He kissed his wife, who held the lad Noah to her dress, fear distorting her countenance.

"I'll use the yarn to prevent getting lost. I'll find him," he said.

"Have you ever been in the tunnel yourself?" she asked.

His face was grim. "No. But I'll find him."

"Be careful," she whispered.

Mr. Holmes brushed aside some cobwebs and entered the passageway. We could feel the damp coolness of the air and that, combined with unrestrained worry about Master Sherlock, chilled me, and I'm sure all of us, to the core of our bones. Suddenly a squeak was heard from nearby in the darkness, followed by the sound of Mr. Holmes' scuffling and "God!" as a rat ran from the route into the kitchen. Mrs. Metcalfe fled upstairs as I grabbed a skillet and chased the rodent into the servants' quarters, closing the door behind it. I dealt with the foul beast later.

Master Sherlock had now been in the terrible passageway for half an hour. From the kitchen to the door in the horse stall, I would estimate, was about three hundred feet, for the kitchen was placed at the back right of the house, if viewed from someone outside facing the house, and the stalls were about fifty feet from the house on the left. The exit to the tunnel was in the last stall of the stables, apparently. If the lad found the right path, and survived whatever traps may have been set there hundreds of years ago, it still might be hours before Master Sherlock found the door and unlocked it with the key he held. By that time his candlelight could run out, and he could succumb to the cold, or the horrors of the utter darkness, or both.

Father Metcalfe had begun praying in a hushed voice.

Mrs. Holmes kneeled down by Noah. "Noah, it's very important you remember—did Sherlock take any extra candles or matches?"

The lad, still holding tightly to Mrs. Holmes' dress even as she knelt, continued crying. "I don't know. I don't know."

Mrs. Holmes never lost her gentleness even in the midst of her anguish; I was never as proud to be her butler as I was then.

"Please, Noah, we're not mad at you. You shan't get into any trouble for Sherlock's decision to enter the passageway. But, try to remember—did he take any extra candles?"

Noah took several jerky breaths to compose oneself. "I...I think he did, ma'am. I think I saw some candles sticking out from his trouser pockets."

That news removed one slight edge of fear from Mrs. Holmes' countenance. Now the five of us, Mrs. Holmes, Father Metcalfe, Mrs. Winters (in a crossing frenzy), myself, and Noah had nothing to do but wait. Father Metcalfe continued his hushed praying. Mrs. Holmes stood again, and Mrs. Winters took her hands.

"The little folks will look out for him; don't worry, Mrs. Holmes. He's born of their work, and they won't let him fall to evil."

Mrs. Holmes smiled at Mrs. Winters, a tear trickling from her eye. She knew of Mrs. Winters' view of her children's connexions to mythical beings and also knew that the cook was very fond of young Master Sherlock.

"I wish they had given him more sense," she said.

"Fairies are not known for their sense, ma'am," Mrs. Winters rejoined, smiling back.

Fifteen more minutes passed, an eternity. Noah still clung to Mrs. Holmes, who had not moved from the door; neither had Father Metcalfe . Nervous energy had driven me to pace the kitchen floor; meanwhile Mrs. Winters had begun preparing the evening meal, in hopeful anticipation of a happy outcome to this dreadful affair, and, like me, feeling the need to do something.

Suddenly a strident voice cut through the oppressed atmosphere of the room. "Mama!"

Five people turned as one and were greeted by the sight of Master Sherlock poised on the stairs to the outside door, thin as a stick, wet and filthy as a pig in a mud puddle, breathing so hard his chest seemed to expand to twice its size with each inhalation, eyes so opened they seemed to cover half his face.

"Mama!" he yelled again, as he leapt down the three last stairs and ran to his mother, who enveloped him into her body until he all but disappeared from view, dirtying her clothes as much as his.

"Sherlock, Sherlock! Oh, thank God, thank God, you're all right, oh, my God, you're all right…" she went on and on, kissing and hugging her son, the tears she had managed to suppress bursting forth like one of Sherlock's waterfalls. In a moment she stopped and drew back, holding him at arm's length. "What an awfully bad thing you did! How could you do this to us! How could you be so thoughtless! We were worried sick about you!" Then she grabbed him for more hugging and kissing.

"I'm sorry, I'm sorry, Mama. I was always curious about the tunnel, and then when Noah dared me, why, I had to go. I took extra candles, and watched for the traps…I'm sorry I made you worry." He noticed the yarn on the door handle, and then, with effort, extracted himself from the clutches of his mother to look down the tunnel.

"Papa's coming back," he yelled, pointing down the route. Looking past the door I could see a dot of light growing in size. Within two minutes Mr. Holmes was back in the kitchen. He barged into the room obviously upset.

"There's a locked door in the tunnel that I couldn't get past; Sherlock has the only key…"

His son threw himself at his father. "Papa!" For a moment Mr. Holmes was too shocked to move.

"Praise God!" Mr. Holmes said as he lifted his son and clasped him firmly to his breast; his clothes would need a good washing as well. He then held him in one arm as he hugged his wife in the other. Mr. Holmes placed Master Sherlock on the ground.

"You are in more trouble than you know," he said gravely, pointing his finger at his son. "Where is the key to this forbidden door?"

Master Sherlock took a large key from his pocket and gave it to his father.

Mr. Holmes removed the yarn from the handle and then closed and put the padlock back in place, locking it firmly. "Let us leave the kitchen and allow Mrs. Winters to work in peace."

"Papa," Master Sherlock said softly, "you should probably let Mr. Denkins and Mr. Wilcox know I'm out of the tunnel. I did not come out through the horse stall."

How the lad knew both those men were there, I do not know. But Mr. Holmes sent me to inform them the lad was safely accounted for; I then returned to the house to see the Metcalfes out. They had judiciously decided that the Holmeses required privacy to deal with their errant son and had therefore decided to return home. I am not so sure, but the fact that there was a large rat in the house was no doubt also a strong impetus for Mrs. Metcalfe fairly galloping from the premises. Noah was also sent home.

Master Sherlock was taken to his bedroom, shorn of his wet clothes, placed in a hot bath, and then dressed again in fresh clothes and returned to his parents. Mr. and Mrs. Holmes did not immediately address their own dirtiness, which signified to me their marked aggravation over their son's action. The Holmeses went into Mr. Holmes' study, where Eliza had lit a fire; I poured Mr. Holmes a drink and then was ordered to leave the room. I did so; however, I then stood by the slightly ajar door to enable myself to eavesdrop on the ensuing conversation. As much as I am loath to admit, this is not an uncommon practice in many household servants, and while I always prided myself on a compelling dignity and grace as butler, I did engage in this unpardonable behavior throughout my service to the Holmeses. I cannot deny that the peculiarity of the lads intrigued me, and I desired to be privy to conversations involving them. Before you judge me harshly, let me say that without such shameful behavior, I would not have this tale to tell you. Although oftentimes I was allowed to stay in a room where the Holmeses were conversing—if I had no other pressing matters to attend to—and even though Mr. Holmes was not averse to speaking with me intimately about his thoughts and concerns, as you can imagine, several of the anecdotes I have related could only have been heard through this unattractive manner of adhering my ear to a door.

There was silence in the room for some minutes, and I could detect impassioned pacing, clearly by Mr. Holmes.

"I promised I would never hit you, lad, but if ever a son deserved a smack, it surely must be you," he finally said.

Master Sherlock, showing more wisdom than precociousness for once, remained silent. More pacing.

"God knows you have the brains of your brother, and your studies and deductions are almost his equal; but your very annoying habit of allowing your impulsive whims to overpower your intellect at times will drive your mother and me into an early grave. You must not turn your brains off so easily."

"But, Papa, I didn't turn my brains off in the tunnel. I used them to get out so quickly."

"If you had used them to begin with, I should like to think you wouldn't have gone into the tunnel in the first place. If you had stopped to consider the terror you would inflict on us by your escapade in that hideous passageway, I can only pray that your loving regard for us would have overcome your selfish need to prove a dare by a peasant boy too fearful himself to follow you."

The lad spoke after a long pause. "You are right, Papa. I'm sorry I was…selfish…yes, that's the correct term; you're right. I have had some little curiosity about the tunnel for years. Noah's dare was a mere catalyst for an action I fully knew one day I would take, even though that action was clearly forbidden, for obvious reasons of safety. Although I did think things through enough to take extra candles, which came in most handy. I really am extremely sorry for your anguish over me, Papa, and dear Mama; I really am extremely sorry."

"Your apology is accepted, Sherlock, though your explanation is contemptible in its utter disregard for following the rules of this house. Therefore, in punishment for this outrageous deed, you shall not be allowed to leave the house for a month."

This was most unusual—a punishment. To my recollection, the Holmeses, in their kindness and acknowledgment of their odd sons, had never initiated a punishment for their behavior once the episode had been discussed and a sincere apology offered by the offending lad. Those episodes had been rare with Master Mycroft; they were more common with Master Sherlock, though taking his ball away for a day was not nearly as severe as this proposed chastisement. A month of seclusion in the house during the height of early summer, when Master Sherlock would have been out every day playing or wandering about, was harsh indeed.

"I must protest your decision, Papa," Master Sherlock said. "A month's seclusion for my reproachable behavior of this afternoon is needlessly extreme. I can assure you that reentering that dark passageway is definitely not in my immediate future. If you insist on my not leaving the house for a month, I, and both you and dear Mama, will become so miserable, this home shall lose the joyful essence which permeates it normally and shall itself become as terrible as the dark tunnel which sits locked below it."

Was that Master Sherlock or Mycroft speaking? Only at times like this, when Master Sherlock was verbally at his most intellectual, did his parents have to abruptly realise his great mental powers. As Mr. Wharton was in charge of his advanced mental development, the Holmeses could often deny this aspect of their second child; due to his openness and playfulness, they much preferred their attitude that he was an active, mischievous lad. Master Sherlock had developed, thanks to his brother's coaching, an incredible control of his great mind. His was a nature to endear himself to others, and so he often hid his intellect—when it came out so purely it simply took one's breath away.

I heard Mr. Holmes slump heavily into a chair. "I suppose you'd just escape anyway, disobeying that command, too."

"If the weather holds as beautiful as it has been, I would certainly escape as often as I could. Probably through my bedroom window. I have hidden a length of rope in my closet for that very purpose, though have not as yet attempted a descent down the outside wall. However, bedsheets might work, if you took the rope away. Of course, walking through the front door, or the greenhouse door, or the outside kitchen door, when no one was observing are other available avenues, though not nearly as challenging. Really, there are innumerable ways to leave the house."

The lad's honesty was astounding, as was his inability to adhere to rules he did not want to follow. That was his worst fault, and the one that brought trouble upon his head consistently—he was a lad who always did first and foremost what he wanted to do, rules and laws aside. If, after he was in trouble, a compromise could be reached between his parents and himself in regard to subsequent similar affairs, fine; if not, such as the restriction with the ball in the house, he continued to disobey parental objections. The fact that the lad was loving and gentle, as were his parents, assured all that his behaviors would be injurious to no one, but possibly himself, or the house decorations and furniture. For all his amiability, though, he was certainly harder to control than Mycroft, who possessed neither the energy nor the desire to create disturbances, especially as he had grown older and more reserved.

For the first time, his mother spoke. I'm sure she thought a change of subject to be most welcome at the moment. "Sherlock, if you did not exit the tunnel by the door in the horse stall, how did you get out?"

I could sense Master Sherlock's eyes glow, and his voice betrayed an excitement he had suppressed much to his credit, for it would have surely further inflamed his father.

"I came out through the old well by Denkins' cottage," he said, adding, "which is where I had expected to."

His father remained quiet.

"Really? Tell us of your adventure," his mother said, evenly.

"Papa?" the lad asked.

Mr. Holmes' voice sounded weighted with fatigue. "Do as your mother requests, lad," he intoned.

The boy began speaking rapidly. "Well, of course I knew of the tunnel; Mrs. Winters had told me what was behind the door the first time I entered the kitchen three years ago. I did not give it a second thought until earlier this year when my interest in the tunnel increased. In visits to the kitchen, I noticed the door was pad-locked, and the lock rusted, although upon close examination it appeared that the lock was not inoperable. I thought the key would be among Papa's effects, and once, as he opened the drawer of that table by the lamp, I espied a large key of clearly the same age as the lock. Surreptitiously, the next day, I was able to remove the key from the drawer and satisfy myself that it would open the lock on the door, which it did with a little effort. I relocked the door, replaced the key in the drawer, and waited for warmer weather to undertake my excursion.

"I was aware that the wooden door in the far horse stall floor was the assumed exit from the tunnel, the door being apparently locked from the tunnel side, for no handle or lock is found on the stall side. It appeared to me that would be a poor choice to end an escape route. Since the horses are in the stables, any attackers would go there immediately upon entering the domain of an enemy, to steal the means of escape. Oftentimes the stables would then be set on fire, for the wood of the stalls and straw for food and bedding make excellent tinder. If a person were fully aware of advancing attackers, and therefore could make it to the horses unbidden before they arrived, no secret escape would be necessary, for surely it is faster and more efficient to just run out of the house to the adjacent stables. No, no, if an escape route was created, it was because our ancient ancestor feared a stealthy, overpowering attack of a number of men, when a tunnel from the bowels of the house would afford the only available avenue for retreat. It seemed to me, then, the utmost folly to end the route in the middle of either a number of your enemies, particularly if they were absconding with your horses, or setting the stables into a roaring conflagration, and I believe that is a purposeful deception.

"The true exit, I deduced, would logically have been placed at some distance from the house and outbuildings. I spent some time walking the periphery of the land, and came upon the old, broken well by Mr. Denkins' cottage, both of which had laid in utter disrepair until your grandfather, Papa, began the restoration of the cottage. The well was left alone, unused. It is not overly deep, as you may know, and contains only whatever rainwater and melted snow accumulates there. I have never heard of it being used, even during great-grandfather's time. I examined tree stumps, the several boulders by the edge of the garden, and other landscape items, though my mind kept returning, for some reason, to the well. I begin to feel I have some instinct in these matters, as does Mycroft. There are metal handles in the brickwork on one side of the interior of the well; I climbed down these one day in March, about ten feet, until I got to the level of the water. I did not observe anything of import."

"Of import?" his father asked.

"The main bricklayer of the well was left-handed and irregular in his working patterns."

"Oh. Quite." His father did not ask how his son knew that, and Master Sherlock did not offer to tell.

"When the opportunity came today for me to enter the tunnel, mostly sparked on by Noah's offhanded dare, I took it. I knew both of you were sunning with the Metcalfes. Mrs. Winters had taken her repose outside, and her helper, Marianne, was home tending to her sickly mother. I dashed upstairs, took the key, dashed back downstairs, and unlocked the door. I lit a candle and put several others in my pockets with some matches; the key went into another pocket. I knew for all his bluster that Noah wouldn't follow me, but I entered the tunnel anyway. Luckily Daisy was on the lawn resting by both of you, for I didn't want her along. If I was correct, and the well was the exit column, Daisy would not be able to climb up the metal handles.

"I was aware of the rumors of branches of the trail leading to dangerous and fatal traps; I engaged all my powers of observation in my forward progress, analysing on each stretch of dirt the floors, walls, and ceiling. What I am about to relate to you I shall do now in a calm manner; for my fear evaporated when once more I stood on the earth and felt the bright sun warm my body. But I do not wish to portray a false picture, however I may have presented myself in the past as brave and capable. Although I seem to be drawn to thrilling adventures, I am not wholly fearless. Even though it may rekindle your anguish or ire, I will not dissemble; my anxieties were fever-pitched throughout my experience.

"I did not like the tunnel; the dampness, chill, and the dark surrounding the light from the candle all conspired claustrophobically to agitate my nerves highly. The floor and walls were dirt, and only wooden beams spaced evenly kept the earth from falling in. Not infrequently I saw worms in the dirt walls. I must admit that several times I came quite close to turning around in defeat, but I persevered. However, I have gained new admiration for those miners who toiled in such foul conditions their whole lives.

"I wished to run, but did not as I feared encountering a trap at a speed at which it would be unavoidable that I should fall victim to it. After thirteen minutes, by my pocket watch, I arrived at the door which Papa mentioned when he came out of the tunnel. It's a thick wooden door, with a lock in it that my key also fit; when the lock was turned, I was able to push the door open. I did so, taking the key out of the lock, as I imagined I might need the key for other doors to come. When the door swung close, I heard the lock engage. It was a foolish mistake on my part not to place an impediment in the closure of the door. There was no way to open the door on my side; I was fully alone.

"I kept walking, my heart beating loudly enough that I felt myself the inspiring drum roll of an advancing army. In just a few more minutes I encountered a splitting of the path. This was not at all to my liking—I had hoped that the rumors of branches and traps had been mere chimeras to avoid unwanted trespassing by house servants or visitors. I was beginning to regret my impulsive action seriously."

"Once again?" his father asked, dripping with sarcasm.

"Yes, Papa, once again. Although I found that to remain oriented under the ground was difficult, there had not been any drastic turns or curves in the route so far. Since the path to the left would, if straight and accurate, take me to the area of the well, and the path to the right apparently to the carriage house, not the stables, I decided on the left. There was no draft to aid my decision. I started off to the left and forthright tripped on a rock. I stumbled and fell, extinguishing the candle on the damp ground. I do not believe I have ever done anything as quickly as light another candle, which I thanked God that I had brought. The wick of the first was covered by dirt, and I do not believe I would have maintained the calmness of mind in the utter blackness to have cleansed and relit it before losing my senses completely to fear. With the candle lit, I stood, kicked the rock as hard as I could down the way I had come, and proceeded further, at a quicker and less rational pace, traps or no.

"As I had expected, I did not encounter any traps. What family fleeing in terror for their lives would want to endanger themselves by the placement of traps in the tunnel, slowing down their movement, and possibly leading to fatalities of the very kin they were trying to protect? If the traps were not there previously, but had been set during their flight, I wondered what family in a dire forced escape situation would wish to stop to dig a pit and place spikes at the bottom, or burden themselves carrying animal traps to place behind them instead of clothes, money, and valuables? No, that would be nonsensical. Perhaps at least the animal traps were there already and only needed to be set; if that was the case then I should only encounter closed traps, if I came to one, for as far as we have ever known, the escape route had remained unused. Continuance has occurred on this spot for the Holmeses for two hundred years with no record of warding off attackers. I therefore had some confidence that the traps were deliberate falsifications; the multitude of hungry, carnivorous rats I thought a farcical fabrication as well."

"I found a rat in the tunnel," his father said.

"You…you did?" Sherlock asked, his young voice rising even higher in tone than normal.

"Yes, it ran into the kitchen, where Brewster sequestered it in the servants' quarters. Denkins has been called to kill it."

"Praise God I encountered none. I should have surely lost my composure if I had."

"Pray continue, dear," his mother quickly stated.

"Well, it was approximately fifteen minutes before I came to a third door; my key fit that lock as well. I opened the door, but placed a rock to prevent its closure, though there was no real point to do it then. I walked forward a few feet and was able to discern a rounded brick wall where water soaked through and trickled down; an old metal sledgehammer hung from the dirt wall to the left of the brick one. It was definitely chillier here, and the ground was full of puddles. If I was right, this was the brick wall of the well, and the rusted but still usable sledgehammer would be used to knock out some stones; thus, freedom would be attained. There was a small problem to this aged plan, however; I had not the strength nor height to heft the hammer and swing it forcefully into the wall. I studied the wall, and found a central area where the bricks had been apparently broken out and then restored with only a very light dollop of mortar—I realised that should be the striking point. I placed the candle in a holder I found in the wall. More fearful of not getting out of the awful tunnel than of incurring an injury, I lifted the hammer, holding the head of it out in front as a battering ram. Stepping back several feet, I ran at the wall. I connected with a jolt that rattled my teeth, but also did actually move the bricks a little. I repeated the process three or four times until two bricks fell out of the wall and water came pouring in, entirely dousing me. I retreated but slipped on the muddy ground and fell, thus adding to my soiled state. The water stopped flowing and I ran back to the well using my hands and the hammer to knock out enough bricks so that I could climb out. The glow of sunlight through the opening brought immense relief to me, and warmth to my chilly body. Bending around the opening, I grasped the metal rungs as I swung my legs out onto them. Soon I was climbing out of the well. I rejoiced momentarily in the lovely day, and then ran as fast as I could to the kitchen. As I ran I then had the presence of mind to think about how events had unfolded at Hillcroft. I imagined that Mrs. Winters had returned to a distraught Noah and had discovered my trespass; she had then informed Mr. Brewster, who then informed both of you, and inadvertently the Metcalfes. I imagine all of you ran to the kitchen, which Mr. Denkins, who was working in the garden, would have witnessed with alarm. He naturally would have followed the five of you to the kitchen, where I reasoned Papa would send him to fetch Mr. Wilcox and go to the horse-stall door while the rest of you waited in the kitchen. When I saw the yarn tied to the handle and only your absence in the kitchen, Papa, I obviously knew you had gone after me, and would return when you reached the impasse of the first locked door. Therefore I discerned that the candlelight in the tunnel was yours. And here we are."

He paused. "I do wonder where that other branch leads to…"

His father shot to his feet. "If you ever—" he began threateningly.

"Pace, pater," Master Sherlock immediately interrupted. "As I have tried to make clear, my enjoyment of the confines of the tunnel was minimal at best. My attraction to danger and my innate curiosity are satisfied enough on the matter, and in no way do I intend to enter that dismal corridor again."

"Good. That's settled then," his father declared. There followed the notorious Sherlockian Pause, as I had titled it to myself.

"At least not for a number of years," the lad added.

Mr. Holmes' spluttering sounded exactly like a heavy full-window curtain being blown in and out by a fierce wind.

"At least he's honest, dear," Mrs. Holmes said, trying to placate her aggravated husband.

The very next day Hank Cotter and another man were engaged to help Mr. Denkins fill the well completely with large rocks. Mr. Holmes had Master Sherlock watch the affair all day. "Full of rocks," Denkins reported to me that Mr. Holmes had told his son when it was done. Several days later a load of bricks arrived from Richmond—the three men then bricked up the entrance to the tunnel, making a wall two feet deep into the corridor. Master Sherlock was ordered to watch the men work for the two days it took to finish the barrier. "Thick brick wall. Extra mortar," Mr. Holmes told his son when the wall was done. The door was then closed and mortared shut at its edges. "Mortared door," Mr. Holmes said to the lad. Lastly, a brick floor was laid over the wooden floor of the last horse stall and then large rocks were placed upon the bricks. "Rocks on the brick floor," his father pointed out to Master Sherlock. "Just in case."

"That is that, then," Mr. Holmes said, walking off and rubbing his hands together.

His son called after him, "But now we shall never know."

"Exactly," was the reply.

I can report that Mr. Holmes was immensely pleased with himself for a number of weeks after, his cigar smoking much increased, and he even read a play with his wife. It was the first time he had ever truly got the better of one of his sons, and that probably irked Master Sherlock more than a month of seclusion would have done.

Chapter Twelve
Happy Home Life

Another year passed and it was 1860; Master Mycroft turned thirteen and returned home during holidays only occasionally, still preferring to stay at the homes of acquaintances he met at school at Eton, which he now attended, if he were invited to do so, which seemed to occur with unusual frequency. Master Sherlock, age six, missed his brother at those times, but had so rich a life otherwise his mood never dropped into sadness as a result.

Master Sherlock indeed had a busy and full life. He continued his studies as before—Mr. Wharton in the mornings Monday through Friday. He had progressed into other subjects with Mr. Wharton, including mathematics, which he apparently excelled at; history and politics, in which he held much less interest than his brother; and the arts, which he loved. He still had an undying fascination with criminal anecdotes; he was always in his father's presence when the latter was called to adjudicate in his public role of justice of the peace, and travelled with Mr. Holmes to Northallerton for the quarter sessions. His father bought him books—lurid tales of past crimes and criminals—which he cherished and memorized astonishingly quickly, though it displeased his mother greatly. Criminals from all over the world interested the lad, and he soon became expert on foreign characters such as Cartouche and Schinderhannes, as well as fictional criminals such as Fagin and Sikes in Dickens' novels. It upset Master Sherlock to see his mother so perturbed by his hobby, and so, to appease her, he spent Sundays with her in both church services and then spent the rest of the day absorbed in Bible studies. Each Sunday as she joined him in the library for religious reading, he made a proud showing of lifting up the H. Hopwood's *Progressive Exercises on the Church Catechism* that Mr. Wharton had given him. It pleased him no end to see her smile after he recited verses he had memorized as easily as the lives of criminals.

When Mr. Holmes told Master Mycroft the tale of Sherlock's trek into the tunnels beneath the house, the lad said nothing, but his eyebrows knitted together darkly. He spent a good deal of time alone with Master Sherlock that night after dinner and the next morning Master Sherlock requested to speak to his parents after breakfast. They repaired to the morning room.

"I should like to begin taking lessons in the violin," the lad stated, hands clasped behind his straight back.

"The...the violin?" his mother asked.

"Yes," the lad continued. "Mycroft thinks that learning an instrument, since I enjoy classical music so avidly, will help me expend some of my energy in a more acceptable fashion, unlike sneaking down into a forbidden and dangerous tunnel. We chose the violin as we feel it somehow best suits my temperament, being as it is, perhaps, the most emotional of instruments. I think it is a smashing idea, for then, Mama, we can play lovely music together."

The Holmeses looked at each other, the idea obviously not an uncomfortable one for them.

"The violin it will be, lad," Mr. Holmes smiled.

Mr. Holmes had a violin specially made for the small lad on his next trip to Huddersfield several weeks later. It was half the size of a normal instrument. Mrs. Holmes knew of a retired music teacher in West Burton, a Mrs. Willoughby, whom they hired to visit the house weekly to give lessons to Master Sherlock. From then on the rough strains of the bow resonated clearly throughout the house, not uncommonly putting teeth on edge. The lad took to the instrument keenly, and to the irritation and surprise of the household, had the concentration to practice for thirty to ninety minutes a day.

Master Sherlock travelled to Huddersfield with his father a few times that year, Mrs. Holmes preferring to stay at home, to observe the textile firm which garnered the Holmeses a good portion of their yearly income. As his brother had, Master Sherlock enjoyed those trips very much for the opportunity to study the workers in the mill—their hands, arms, backs, feet, and the like. He was much less interested in the running of the business, and when he learned all he could watching the mill workers and managers, he would slip into the streets of the town and walk from shop to shop, staring at people through the windows. His father, knowing it would be impossible to prevent his leaving Vickerman's, had initiated a compromise with the lad that he should stroll the street no further than half a mile each way, and would return to the factory by five o'clock. A few times Mr. Holmes had finished his work at the business early and had gone out looking for his wandering son. To his slight mortification, sometimes he would discover his son in a shop that had particularly interested him, happily involved in the repairing of a boot, or preparing leather with alum and salt, with the charmed and accommodating proprietor by his side.

Mr. Holmes related such stories to his amused wife.

"I suppose one day I'll find you selling apples out of a cart," his father chided as the three of them sat in the drawing room after returning from a journey to Huddersfield.

The boy affected a bemused look. "Perhaps you shall, Papa. It is the best way for me to observe; books do not satisfy me as they do Mycroft."

"Well, Sherlock, just don't seek any criminals to observe their trades," his mother said.

Master Sherlock raised his eyebrows high as he glanced at his mother. "I have no immediate plans to do so, Mama."

His parents looked at each other, mouths agape. No immediate plans? They mutually and silently agreed to discuss other matters.

He continued his association with his impoverished playmates and very often was off in the fields or the village with them and Daisy. As I mentioned, most of the lads didn't go to school much, though they did often have to help in the fields with harvesting and many other chores; some they enjoyed, some they hated. When very unlucky, one was assigned to guard the seeded fields from birds, which was dreary work. Master Sherlock still brought food to them on Sundays, although the cleaning of his nursery as an inducement had not lasted long. From birth, that boy was messy and untidy with his belongings, another total difference from his most fastidious elder brother. Although, due to his mother's continued insistence that he be scrubbed clean head to toe upon returning from playing with his lower-class mates, he had grown used to, and seemed to favor, as Dr. Watson described it, a "cat-like" cleanliness in regards to his own person. Aside from the food parcels, I believe that Noah Cotter's father received a slight payment from Mr. Holmes to enable his son to be available for frolicking with Master Sherlock instead of working. Hank Cotter was still employed occasionally when Master Sherlock wanted to wander further, especially when a horse ride to the Hardrow Force for his meditations was required. From spring to autumn, the lad was at one of the waterfalls at least once a week. His parents once endeavoured to uncover from their son the exact nature of his ruminations.

"I just work through my head all that I have learned and observed. I think about my studies, the criminals, the lessons of the Bible. I ponder the unending possibilities of the future. I have begun contemplating life, how it unfolds in its infinite varieties. I have not yet begun contemplating the meaning of life, but that will not be long in coming." He shrugged. "Nothing too *recherché*," he added. His parents would have agreed if he weren't only six years old.

Although he was the quickest lad in town, and one of the tallest, he was still extremely slight in build. His health, like his brother's and father's, was generally excellent, and colds were quickly overcome. I remember he a very bad sore throat not two weeks following his sixth birthday. After two days when no progress had been seen in his health, Mrs. Winters called on him in the morning and gave him some herbal tea to drink and a tincture that was "an old family recipe, and no Winters lives to see less than seventy of the same named seasons."

"I shall rather live to sixty-nine than take that odious mixture again," he whispered hoarsely, as she leaned over his bed to serve another teaspoonful at lunchtime. Mrs. Winters had refused to allow anyone else to give Master Sherlock the medicine—"the little people wouldn't like it"—and much to the silent good humor of everyone, the sick lad and his healer engaged in identical crossing of themselves each time she entered his sickroom.

"Take it, Sherlock. When Mycroft was sick once, Mrs. Winters' herbs had him on his feet in no time," his mother said, knitting by his bed.

Seeing the concern on his mother's countenance, Master Sherlock swallowed the proffered liquid. Many unnatural and frankly fantastic contortions of his face followed, succeeded by a general shaking of his whole thin body.

"Eeyuck!" he protested.

"I'll return after supper, Master Sherlock," Mrs. Winters threatened as she left the room.

"Is her Christian name Torquemada?" Sherlock asked his mother after gulping down his third glass of water.

"Son, that is very disrespectful," his mother rejoined, but her grin betrayed her.

"Well, I thought Genghis too masculine for a woman," he muttered as he sunk down into his bed, eyeing the clock by his bed warily.

He was well by the next day. At least he said he was.

The lad maintained his independent nature, except for the way he doted on his mother. Still he loved to be by her side, to play music with her, to read with her, to act out plays with her, to learn about plants and flowers with her. They went on walks together, to church twice together on Sundays—Mr. Holmes only went once. Although the affair with the tunnel had ended with the permanent blockage of all avenues into the forbidden route, Mrs. Holmes had experienced horrifying nightmares of her son's demise for many months after Master Sherlock's trip through the passageway. The terrors filled her mind even after she awoke, and her appetite and nerves suffered; she lost weight and became somewhat pale and wan. Master Sherlock was wracked with guilt at her state, and swore his behavior would never again cause so severe a shock to his "dear mama." At that she began to recover, and the relationship between him and his parents grew even closer. A trust was established between them and their son that had never existed before, and his relentless code for honesty demanded his behavior actually be noticeably modified. His parents were able to leave his bedroom door unlocked, and when he left his room, he was found serenely reading in the drawing room, or smelling roses in the greenhouse. He broke no ornaments with his ball. He did not climb trees blindfolded, charge bulls like a matador, try to cross the river Ure when it was swollen after weeks of rain, nor attempt to drive the carriage by himself.

Mrs. Holmes in return conveyed an affectionate regard for her son that seemed limitless, and spent more time in his company than in that of her other friends and acquaintances. While she had never refrained from her warmth and tenderness toward either of her sons, Master Mycroft rarely seemed to require it. Master Sherlock imbibed it as a fish does water, but his mischievous actions had always limited their total closeness. Now that it was certain the lad would not dash off on his own for possibly days, Master Sherlock was able to accompany his mother on shopping trips and holidays in large towns. He abstained from wandering off down the street to investigate all manners of tradesmen in order to avoid upsetting Mrs. Holmes. The lad and his mother had grand times together—poor Mrs. Hastwell felt positively deserted—and many hours were spent recounting their adventures to Mr. Holmes on those times he could not join them in their fun. The family travelled again to London. The grandest times for Master Sherlock were when he was taken see plays with his mother, and I recall that from the summer of 1860 until that horrible, horrible autumn of 1861, the lad went again to the Princess Theatre, saw one symphony, and a couple of violin recitals. They never did travel overseas with him, though.

One time, during a break in their reading of *Romeo and Juliet,* I heard Master Sherlock tell his mother, "Mama, I hope I shall some day find a woman just like yourself to marry."

"What a rare and fine compliment, Sherlock. Thank you," his mother blushed.

The lad's Romeo was masterful that day, his "Here's to my love—O true apothecary! Thy drugs are quick.—Thus with a kiss I die," and his graceful fall to the floor almost brought tears to his mother's eyes.

Master Sherlock divulged deductions when asked, and rarely otherwise, unless it was an observation of import, or he was overly excited, or he was well away from the person he was commenting on. Mr. Holmes told me of a magnificent example of his mental powers after the lad's first visit to the textile mill and the environs of Huddersfield, a trip lasting only three days. As Mr. Holmes and his son travelled back on the train, Master Sherlock gave a detailed accounting of the floor manager, five of the women who worked on looms, two of the dyers, the banker who came to the business meeting, the policeman who patrolled the street the firm was on, and a number of other individuals he had observed and docketed, including four shopkeepers and three young female waifs!

When Master Mycroft did come home for the long Christmas holiday in 1860, I think he must have felt at first like a foreigner in his own home, even though his younger brother expressed no end of delight at his presence, and his parents displayed sincere interest in his schooling, his friends, and his thoughts. Since his phlegmatic and reserved nature did not fit into such a merry and active family with ease, it took some little effort on the Holmeses' part, and Master Sherlock's, to convince the senior son to participate in their amusements. I imagine if not for their persistence, Master Mycroft would have simply stayed in his study reading untold numbers of books. But his family insisted he join their walks, their church-going, the play readings, and their other activities. His father even held two gatherings in the ballroom, inviting adults and their children, to see if Master Mycroft would enjoy other male, or female, company of his own age. In return, the lad received invitations to other parties at other households in the area, which, surprising to us all, he attended.

Master Mycroft partook of all this enforced company good-naturedly, even at times laughing and chatting gaily with his family and visitors. No doubt he had learned some social skills from his years of mingling with the other lads at school. He had grown some and was already a tall lad, though he still had not lost his chunky build. He danced with his mother only upon her approaching him, and, more out of fear of ungainliness than shyness, I think, did not himself ask anyone to dance. He certainly kept his deductions under the control he had imposed upon his younger brother, and no slips occurred. He even had developed an ability to soften his penetrating eyes, to relax them, I should say, so his gaze did not bring discomfort to all he looked at. Still, to my feeling, even in his most extroverted moments, there was in his presence a slight taint of falsity, of awkward insincerity, of endeavouring to act the part of companionship instead of entering into it wholeheartedly.

He and Master Sherlock still spent much time together, the latter regaling his elder brother with his observations during his travels and his activities with his friends. Somehow, in his exuberance, Master Sherlock even got his brother to meet Noah and the others in Noah's small house on the edge of Carperby. The two lads took long walks to the other nearby towns, no doubt sharing their rapid observations of people they saw, as I had come upon them doing covertly during a break at the Christmas party years ago. Master Sherlock showed his brother his skill on the violin, and for two days they spoke only in French, as they sat together again in their unsettling seclusion in one of their study rooms. It was still evident that for all their differences in personality, there was a strong connexion and affection between them; more so, I dare say, than Master Mycroft had with his parents. Master Sherlock, having the same touch of genius, and being able to discuss it as a selfsame participant and not as an onlooker gazing at an aberration, was therefore the only person in the world Master Mycroft truly felt comfortable with, even though their natures were as night and day. Mr. and Mrs. Holmes, however, were more relaxed around their eldest son this visit for several reasons: his attempts at conviviality, his softened eyes, and their confidence that Master Sherlock had his own unique disposition and was not going to suddenly change into the twin of his brother by spending time with him.

I heard only one disagreement, though mild, between the brothers. It surfaced during dinner one night when the Holmes were home alone.

"So, Sherlock, you shall be seven tomorrow. Have you decided to follow me to school next autumn?" Master Mycroft asked.

"Certainly not, Mycroft," the lad answered. "I should never be able to stand the rules and regulations; I do not like to be ordered about. Surely you know that. It would not be in my best interest, I fear."

"I strongly feel it is in your best interest to learn some discipline, and to learn how to mix with others of our class, and above. Those connexions that you establish there may prove invaluable in your future. The food is edible, and there are sports galore to deplete your excessive energy."

"I like mixing with the friends I have; I don't care about their class. I don't care about my future at the moment, either, although I will admit to a certain curiosity about where I shall find my place. I am not a sluggard at my studies, dear Mycroft, but still enjoy my friends and my sporting with them, my wanderings, my waterfalls, my devoted Daisy, and my dear parents. So long as Papa agrees, I shall choose to continue my education at home."

"You may stay at home until you're ready for University, Sherlock," his father declared. I'm sure it must have slightly galled Mr. Holmes to be heretofore left out of this discussion of their youngest son's future.

"There, then, it's settled," the lad said, slapping the edge of the table for emphasis. Then he frowned. "My only concern with remaining at Hillcroft House is becoming ill enough to require more of Mrs. Winters' medicines."

"Sherlock!" his mother tsk'd lightly.

"That, my dear brother," Mycroft concurred, "played an integral part in my decision to leave home. Having that loathsome mixture in my mouth once was enough for me in this life. You may very well find yourself reconsidering your resolution tonight the next time you are struck by a savage cold."

Master Sherlock's mouth grimaced in disgust and his head shook violently as he thought upon that statement. "My dear Mycroft, you may very well be right."

It made me happy to hear the family so joined in spirit.

This is the last episode I have to relate in this first section of Master Sherlock's life. It occurred in April of the year, when the Holmeses and Master Sherlock had gone on a walk one sunny yet blustery afternoon. Several weeks earlier the flu had come to Wensleydale and Eliza's mother and one of Noah's brother's had died of the disease—Master Sherlock had been spending time with both since, observing and helping out as he could. Master Sherlock had watched Eliza silently, and had taken to giving her bouquets he arranged himself from the greenhouse flowers. To Noah he gave his nicest ball and the new shoes his parents had just bought him. He spent the weeks otherwise walking alone with his dog in the country, and on the few warmer, sunny days, at the Askrigg Falls sitting pensively with Hank Cotter sleeping nearby.

Although Master Sherlock began his walk racing ahead of his middle-aged parents, the three returned home with Master Sherlock holding a hand of each of them as he walked in the middle. His face beamed with such joy I thought he should burst from pleasure. As they stood in the entrance, removing their outer garments, Master Sherlock laughed in his high voice.

"That was great fun! I should like to walk with you forever, Papa, and dear Mama. You will promise, will you not, to walk with me forever?"

"Forever is a very long time, lad," his dad said offhandedly, leaning backwards, hands on hips, to stretch out his back muscles. "Your mother and I are getting on in years, as this aching back frequently reminds me."

Suddenly the boy, at his father's words, seemed to grow fearful, and his grand smile fled his countenance. Perhaps for the very first time, he realised their approaching old age, and it seemed to terrify him.

"Promise," he now pleaded, laughter vanished. "Promise you'll be with me forever."

Did his parents notice the switch from "walk" to "be"? How could they not? They exchanged confused and anxious looks; their son was too smart not to realise that death would strike them as it had recently struck others. It was true they were approaching fifty years, and Master Sherlock was only seven, though the difference in those ages had never arisen as a sign of concern before. His parents generally enjoyed the excellent health that Master Sherlock did, aside from Mrs. Holmes' penchant for catching several bad colds a year. Was his father's bringing attention to stiffening muscles, though, the first time it had ever clearly dawned on him that his parents were aging, and would one day die as he now understood it truly happened?

The lad was close to tears. His mother panicked at this alteration of her son's mood, and like all mothers everywhere first faced with the same question by their sons, her answer flew from her mouth unbidden.

"Of course we'll be with you forever, Sherlock," she assured him, kneeling down and holding his bony shoulders.

"Promise it," he begged.

Mrs. Holmes paused for a moment—she knew how intensely he honored promises. Could she, therefore, so willingly lie? Her personal code of honesty was as strictly adhered to as her son's. But here was her little boy begging for relief from appalling images of his parents dead and buried. How could she deny him such solace? When they would finally die years from now, he would understand her dissembling to him now, and would probably view it gratefully and tenderly, not critically.

"Of course I promise," she said, hugging him tightly. He held her for a long time before letting go. "Now, let's not talk of such dreary things and let's see if Brewster here might be able to uncover a biscuit or two for you."

Relief flooded the lad's face, and his eyes shone again. "Yes, a biscuit sounds quite lovely." And he led them off to the morning room.

Chapter Thirteen
Mrs. Holmes' Death

I have been endeavouring with my recollections to establish the personalities of the members of the Holmes family, particularly of the two lads. This has been important, I feel, because only by knowing all the Holmeses so fully beforehand will the changes that occurred, especially to Master Sherlock, ring true in all their devastating power. The gentleness and kindness of Mr. and Mrs. Holmes, combined with a natural unease around their precocious children; the reserved stiffness of Master Mycroft; and the most wonderful of them all in my mind, Master Sherlock. Dear me, how things did change.

It breaks my heart to be forced to relate to you the following events that scorched and finally burned to the ground all the hope and promise and love that family had created among its members. It truly pains me as much as if I were actually reliving it all those years ago. Yet this information is really the important history you have patiently waited these last days to hear from a wordy old man, and so I will not delay you any longer. I will start with the tragedy that irreparably cracked the foundation of the house of Holmes—the death of a beloved wife and mother, Catherine Holmes.

It was late September of 1861, and the winter winds had hit early that year. Though there was no snow yet, the feel of the air was of harsh and bitter cold months to come. Although I have not the photographic memory of the lads, I remember the date as clearly as my own natal day. September 21. That day Master Sherlock, after practicing his violin, convinced his mother to join him for a brisk walk in the dreary, overcast day.

"It will stir our blood and vitalize our wits," the lad stated.

"I'm not sure, dear. I'm comfortable here by the fire with my knitting."

"I shall wither away from loneliness on the road to Carperby, dear Mama, if you don't accompany me."

His mother smiled at his extremely thin body. "You're withered enough for my taste as it is. Very well, I'll join you."

They dressed and proceeded out. About forty minutes after they left, however, the winds changed, it grew dark, and a downpour of freezing, biting rain began. Some long minutes later, Mrs. Holmes and her son returned at a run to the house thoroughly drenched and chilled. They were both ushered upstairs posthaste, removed of their wet clothes, placed one by one into a hot bath—Mrs. Holmes insisting her son be first—then placed in beds with blazing fires and hot water bottles.

All the time the lad protested.

"I'm fine, I'm fine," he said, brushing aside attempts to have Mrs. Birchall relieve him of his soaked shirt. "I've been rained on before, you know. This is England. Look after my mother."

He hated being treated delicately by anyone but his parents, hated admitting any complaint that would relieve him of his independence, and only complied with the ministrations of the servants after his mother strongly asked him to. He lay in bed for exactly one hour and then arose, dressed, and went to see his mother.

Mrs. Holmes did not fair as well as her young son; remember, she was forty-five by now, and was more prone to the ill effects of wet and cold, having as I have stated before a tendency to take cold several times a year. The chill she caught entered her system and laid claim to it; even hours later she lay in bed shivering, and only desired a little soup for supper.

How graphic do you need me to be, Mr. Cobbett? Do you insist I spend hours going over each minute of those last days of Mrs. Holmes' life? Do you want every word spoken, every cough expressed by her as she began dying? Do you want to hear every plea from the young lad and his father for her to recover and thrive? Do you need me to weep over how often Master Sherlock cried out his guilt over taking her on that walk? I will attempt to do so to clearly paint the picture of that terrible time, yet it tears my protesting heart apart even now to think about it.

Mrs. Holmes awoke the next day feverish, aching all over, and with a cough. She had no appetite, though she did accept the soups and teas that were brought to her. She was chilled to the bone with the ague, and her bedroom fire was kept blazing so her healthy family had to sit far from the fireplace after a short time in the room. Mrs. Winters was summoned to administer her mixture—Mrs. Holmes took it without complaint. As yet the household was not overly concerned; not out of a lack of sympathy with the discomfort madam was in, but due to the belief that this was only a cold from which she would quickly recover. Still, Master Sherlock spent the afternoon reading in his mother's bedroom as she restlessly slept.

By the next morning, the household was more alarmed. Mrs. Holmes' fever seemed higher, though her chill was still deep, as was her cough, which Mrs. Holmes suffered in paroxysms that left her weakened and created a thick expectoration. Mrs. Holmes was thirsty and continual bowls of hot vegetable soups and chicken broths were brought to her. Mrs. Winters maintained her medicinal applications—tincture and tea—and fashioned a mustard poultice that she applied to Mrs. Holmes' chest for fifteen minutes, then repeated on her back. That seemed to relieve Mrs. Holmes; by the afternoon, the household was anticipating her rallying through the disease. You can imagine the crushing disappointment when her fever soared again at nightfall and her coughing resumed with an oppression in her lungs that necessitated her sitting up in bed on pillows to ease her efforts at respiration. Mrs. Winters was awakened, but a second mustard poultice did not appease her this time, and a greatly distressed Mr. Holmes sent Wilcox to bring Mr. Irwin to Hillcroft, even though the hour was late.

Master Sherlock had not eaten all day for worry over his dear mama. He had apologized to his mother and father probably ten times for his taking her out for a walk. Of course, no one blamed the lad, then, for his mother's condition, but his father, his nervous energy focusing on his beloved wife, after a few "It's all right, lad"s to his son, had no more ability to console him at that time. Master Sherlock moved his chair from five feet from his mother's bed to right next to it, and never left that chair, withdrawing entirely into silence.

When Mr. Irwin arrived, I directed him upstairs to Mrs. Holmes' bedchamber. He dashed his thin, slightly bent body up to her room, clutching his large, black doctor's bag. He was a welcome sight to everyone, and immediately sat down on the bed next to Mrs. Holmes and began an examination of her. He took her pulse, felt her head, thumped on her chest, and then, as I—the only male servant in the room—left the room briefly out of decorum, listened to her chest with his stethoscope. During his actions the room was absolutely quiet, though the distress in the atmosphere hung like heavy smoke, and our breaths seemed to come in gasps like that of Mrs. Holmes. She bore the examination well, although her breathing was laboured and several times she had an attack of coughing; after each paroxysm she smiled at her husband and son, who held her hand the whole time.

After Mr. Irwin finished his examination, he took out from his bag some powders and an empty bottle; he placed several different powders into the bottle and shook it gently to mix them.

"Mix one teaspoonful in a little water and administer every two hours," he said to the room in general, not knowing to whom to direct his order: the pale Mr. Holmes, or one of the numerous servants who stood in the room or by the entrance awaiting the doctor's prognosis.

"I am not so ill as concerns my family, am I, Mr. Irwin? Assure them I shall recover in good time; it pains me to see them so gravely affected by such a trivial affliction," Mrs. Holmes said. She held Master Sherlock's chin in her hand, her thumb stroking it. Her obvious fatigue after such a short comment left us feeling anything but relieved by her words. Mr. Irwin stood and motioned for Mr. Holmes to follow him out the door.

"I shall do just as you request, madam," he assured her, patting her arm. "Now rest."

In the hallway, Mr. Irwin's countenance changed into one of dire worry. "She has pneumonia; it appears to have settled in both sides of her lungs."

Those words struck Mr. Holmes as a bullet. He struggled to maintain his composure. "Pneumonia? But it was just a little rain! How could this happen?"

Mr. Irwin did not speak, for it was clear that Mr. Holmes' cry had not been directed at him, but at faith in the goodness of the heavens. Mr. Holmes covered his eyes with his hand for a moment and then looked again at the doctor.

"Will she live? Tell us what we have to do. We will follow your orders to their exact specifications. She must live! Tell us what to do!"

"I cannot make promises. I do not know if she will live. I will stay with her, watching her from now on. We must continue the broths and soups and teas. She must have fluids. The mustard poultices your cook has administered should be continued, alternating as she did on her chest and back. The herbal mixture, too, let us continue with it as well, whatever it is; we will use all our forces to strengthen Mrs. Holmes' vitality."

"Then there is some hope?" Mr. Holmes asked.

"There is always hope…" Mr. Irwin said. I heard in my head the rest of his unfinished sentence: "Even if it appears futile." It was then I noticed Master Sherlock out of the corner of my eye; he had snuck out of the bedroom unnoticed and had been listening to the conversation. His father saw him then, too, kneeled and opened his arms—Master Sherlock ran into them, tears streaming down his face.

"Everything will be fine, lad. Don't worry," his father said, hugging his son.

"She promised me she'd be with me forever. She has to live, Papa. It's my fault we were in the rain. But she promised me. She never breaks a promise." The lad was distraught, and his sentences jumbled one into another.

"Hush now, Sherlock. You must wear a brave face for your mother. It upsets her to see you so disturbed; that shall not aid her recovery. She needs to focus her energy on her health, not on worrying about your spirits. Affect a loving attitude; hide your fears; then let us return to her as gay company to enliven her mood and ease her mind. She will rally the better for it." He wiped the tears from his son's face with his handkerchief.

"You speak wisely, Father. I will contain myself as best I can…"

"A valiant statement, for we all know how difficult containment is for you," his father interrupted with a smile.

His son grinned back—it was the last smile I saw on the lad's face for a long time.

She died five days later, the phlegm rattling so in her chest it was impossible for her to inhale any air. Her lips and fingertips turned blue. She became too weak to continue her restless agitation, or even to cough, so she could not expectorate the bloody, thick mucous. Master Sherlock had valiantly controlled himself as his father had requested for four days, visiting his mother in a chatty, nonchalant manner during those brief times she felt strong enough for visitors. But, since earlier that morning when it was evident that Mrs. Holmes' health had definitely worsened, his true emotions came to the fore and he begged and pleaded for her to live.

"Fight this illness, Mama," he implored. "Please, dear God, it was just a little walk. Don't die, Mama! Mama, don't die! Don't die!"

I doubt she was aware of his pitiful entreaties, due to her fever and her delirium. Master Sherlock's words grew in frantic pitch as his desperation and despair now flew unbidden from him. "I'm sorry, I'm sorry, don't die, oh God, don't die. I'm sorry for the walk. Forgive me for the walk. Mama, Mama, please forgive me! Forgive me! Forgive me!" He shook the bedclothes over his mother's arm, craving absolution, but with a hideous gurgle that has haunted me for thirty years, she expired. At that moment, all of Mr. Holmes' respected composure died too, and he fell sobbing on his wife's body.

At the instant Mr. Irwin pronounced her dead, and closed her eyes, the young lad sat stiffly in his chair, trembling as if an earthquake were occurring beneath his seat. His eyes stared into nothing for some minutes. There was something about him that frightened me, and it was fortunate I continued observing him after chasing all the other servants except Miss Borel back downstairs. Mr. Irwin left the room, too, and I accompanied him to the front door as he went to notify Father Metcalfe to prepare for the funeral. I entered the Holmes' bedroom once more to be sure that Mr. Holmes desired privacy and no other services; Miss Borel was leaning forward, hands covering her face, as she wept gently in a chair. Master Sherlock was not in his seat; I looked to the side and my stomach turned to clay. He had opened the window and was preparing to leap from it.

I have no wings, but I tell you, I flew across that room, screaming "No!" and grabbing the lad about the waist the moment he launched himself into the air. I dragged him twisting madly into the room, set him down by his wide-eyed father, who through his grief was just barely able to comprehend what Master Sherlock's intention had been.

I ran back to close and latch the window. Mr. Holmes suddenly realised what had just taken place and grasped his son by the arm; the lad struggled to remove his father's firm grip with his free hand.

"Let me go! Let me go! I killed her! I should've died, not her—I never promised to live forever; she did. I want to die too! I want to be with her! Let me go!" In his hysteria the lad had begun hitting his father, who warded off his blows by enclosing him in a tight immobile hug.

"No, you can't kill yourself, lad," he said. "Your life is not your own, as your mother's was not hers. We may not understand it now, but there must be meaning in all that happens. Her death and your continued life is what the heavens decree—you cannot force the issue, for that is the worst sin of all."

"But I should have died instead of her. I killed her. I took her for a walk in the freezing rain."

"You both went on a walk and then it rained. It was not your fault, Sherlock. The worst consequence of your mother's death, the worst way you could dishonor her and what she was to you and taught you, would be for you to kill yourself."

There were no sounds but the sobs of the boy for a while. Then he moaned, "But she promised me to be here forever. She never breaks a promise."

"You knew that promise was impossible to keep, lad. Everybody dies. Even those we love most in the world."

The lad's next words caused my heart to bleed for him. "Then I shall never love again."

"Don't say that, lad. Of course you will. Time will heal us. Somehow it will. Promise me you shall leave your life alone. Promise me you will never take your own life. Promise me." Mr. Holmes held his son by his upper arms, and shook him not from anger, but from trembling at a ghastly vision of losing a dear son as well as a wife in the same horrid day.

The lad would not meet his father's eye, even through the shaking, would not notice his emotional distress. Finally his father grabbed his chin and forced the lad to see him.

"Look at me, Sherlock. Promise me, now. Promise me." The boy tried to focus on the lamp on the table, on the picture of horses in a field on the wall, on the post of the bed. Soon, though, his eyes did indeed fall on his father and observed the fear in his countenance and tension in every fiber of his body.

"I promise, Papa," he said, and his father took him in his arms.

Master Mycroft arrived that afternoon; his father had hired a special horse courier to rush a letter to the lad after Mr. Irwin's visit when it became clear that Mrs. Holmes was desperately ill, and the lad left at once upon receiving the dreadful missive, but the trip from Eton to Carperby took two days by train. Mrs. Holmes' relatives in France were also notified, as were the Holmes' friends and acquaintances.

Master Mycroft found the household in total disarray, the servants barely able to uphold their responsibilities and his father and brother inconsolable in their despair. They both continued their vigil in the bedchamber, which is where Master Mycroft found them. I do not know what passed between the three of them, but the elder son stayed in the room as well until far into the evening. Finally he came out and requested I bring some sustenance to his father and brother. He made me assure him I would see that Master Sherlock ate at least half of the proffered food, "For I observe he has not eaten anything for approximately thirty-six hours. You have my permission to force it down his throat if necessary." Master Mycroft then went downstairs to continue to arrange the necessary affairs.

It was not that the older son wasn't deeply saddened by his mother's death; it was obvious from his firmly pressed lips, lugubrious tone, and slumping posture that he was greatly depressed by her untimely death. However, Master Mycroft had been apt at concealing himself from others almost since his infancy, and his reserved nature served him well to hide his melancholy spirits in organizing the details of the preparations for his mother's funeral with efficiency and expediency. The lad was only fourteen, true, but was well able to assume the mantle of patriarch as his father lay insensible from grief upon the bed on which his beloved wife reposed lifelessly. Bearing the food tray, the very one Master Sherlock had used as a sleigh so few happy years ago, I found the lad sitting on the floor, leaning against a wall, his elbows on his knees, his eyes cupped by his hands. I put his soup, cheese, roll, and glass of milk on the chair seat next to him; and put his father's food on a seat next to him.

I returned to the lad. "Master Sherlock, your brother strongly insists you eat at least half of your food. I have been ordered to stay here until that occurs." Of course, those were not the exact orders, but I had no intention of forcing food down the lad's throat if he were to disdain his brother's command. The lad did not respond to my words at all for a good number of minutes, did not even move a muscle, and I began to feel uncomfortable standing by him. Also, unlike Mr. Holmes and Master Sherlock, I was not wishing to spend much time in the room with the deceased Mrs. Holmes; though my personal grief for her death was considerable as well, I am of a nature that prefers to avoid the face of death. I wanted to leave that room as quickly as possible.

Mr. Holmes, who had been nibbling at his meal, came to my rescue, arising from his chair, and coming to his son to sit next to him on the floor. "Eat some food, Sherlock. I and your brother request it. Would you faint away from lack of nourishment during the funeral, thus transferring all thoughts of those attending to yourself, removing your mother's predominance from their minds on her burial day? You are a finer son than that. Eat some of the food."

The lad said nothing, but slowly reached for the soup bowl and placed it by him on the floor. Enjoying not a swallow of it, he ate it, and the roll, and a few bites of the cheese. Then he drank the milk. I removed all the bowls, plates, utensils and the like from him and his father, and left the room. It was all I could do not to run.

Chapter Fourteen
Sherlock's Depression

The funeral was well attended, as they usually are by the tenant farmers, villagers, acquaintances, and friends when a member of the well-liked and honored gentry dies. Mrs. Holmes was buried three days after her death, and though few of her French relatives were present, Mr. Holmes received letters of condolence from all of them over the next weeks. The aged M. Leon Lecomte was deeply grieved by the passage of his only daughter, so soon after his wife's death, and regretted that his ailing health prevented his journeying to Yorkshire to visit her grave. Mrs. Holmes' brother, Charles, sent a lovely letter of purest emotion to Mr. Holmes, but, due to the demands of his work, was unable to come as well. Only Mrs. Holmes' cousins, the Anglicized Verners living in Lancashire, and two of their four children, came to Carperby in time for the funeral, after Master Mycroft alerted them to the sad event by a letter sent by special horse courier. Mr. Holmes' sister and her husband were also absent, as they were travelling in Europe for several months, and Mr. Holmes did not know exactly where they were at that time. The lads' cousins, the Fairburn children, situated far away in Cornwall and London, did not appear at the funeral either, but also sent their heartfelt condolences.

The lads were doubled up in Mycroft's room, to enable the Verners and their children room in the house. This was to Master Sherlock's benefit, for his brother was then able to attend to him, making sure he was washed and ready for bed, and on the morning of the funeral, making sure he was properly dressed and ready to go on time. I'm sure it also gave Master Sherlock someone to talk to if he chose to speak, which he had not done in my presence since his mother's death. Master Mycroft was the one person who no doubt understood him better than anyone, and who, in his own noneffusive way, exhibited a constant regard and caring for his younger brother that Master Sherlock could not help but notice. The lad now ate dutifully when ordered to; otherwise, he ate not at all. He had not slept more than a couple of hours each night since the day before his mother's death, and by the second day after her demise, he had large dark circles under his eyes, and a lethargy I had never thought to see in this endlessly energetic lad. Master Mycroft ordered the laudanum then, and administered it to his brother in a dose sufficient to have him sleep solidly through the night. He recommended to his father that he ask Mr. Irwin for a sleeping draught as well, but Mr. Holmes did not. Mr. Holmes slept himself in his study, which was very unusual.

The funeral was a terrible affair. It was held in the church in Askrigg, which was packed to standing room only. Although it was chilly and drizzling outside, the number of people inside the church left the air stifling and suffocating. There was much crying. The eulogy was really the most beautiful I have ever heard, and rightly so, for Mrs. Holmes shone like a unique and treasured star amongst all who knew her, rich and poor.

The rain still fell at the graveside service, but I do not think the family and friends noticed it, so numb they all were from disbelief in the finality of this ritual. She is dead and is now being buried; that is her coffin; here is her grave. That was all, I'm sure, their minds registered, and if a horde of savage barbarians had come on a rampage at that very minute, this group of woeful mourners would not have turned a head to see them.

Back at Hillcroft, although there was food and drink laid out, few partook of the refreshments. The afternoon seemed interminable, and after hours of pretense, the painful remembrances of Mrs. Holmes and the now bittersweet anecdotes were too much for him and Mr. Holmes excused himself and retreated to his study, where he then sat alone behind a locked door. Master Sherlock had long before gone up to his brother's room, and it was left to Master Mycroft to provide the proprieties for the guests and visiting relatives, which I must report he did admirably and much to his credit. One by one the guests left, and the relatives ascended to their rooms to prepare for their early departure the next day. It was not a home, at the moment, whose ambience encouraged undue lingering. Miss Borel was returning to France as well, with a very generous payment from Master Mycroft for all her years of devoted service to his mother.

By ten o'clock the following day, the house was once again occupied by the Holmeses only: Mr. Holmes still in his study, where he had spent the entire night; Master Sherlock now back in his own room, refusing to leave his bed; and Master Mycroft endeavouring to act as counselor and aide to the two of them through the solemnity of his own pain. He was unsuccessful with his father, who refused him admission to his study all day; the lad spent most of his time in Master Sherlock's room. Master Mycroft then held a meeting with Denkins, Wilcox, Mrs. Winters, Mrs. Birchall, and myself to reassure us that we would all be retained as servants. He discussed how to organize the household so it should continue to function when he left to return to Eton and his father and brother were still incapable of assuming responsibility for the daily running of Hillcroft. We assured him that we could provide all services to the house on our own, in a trustworthy and efficient fashion, as we had already done for years. I was instructed which types of letters to forward to Master Mycroft if it seemed as if his father were neglectful of their contents. I was told to contact him if his father was unmindful of the needs of the farmers, neglectful of the estate accounts or his business in Huddersfield, or if any other problem arose at Hillcroft. Master Mycroft had thought to spend the Christmas holiday at the home of the son of the Earl of Kennington; he would now probably return home instead. He then dismissed us and went off to check on his brother again.

"He's a cold one, that lad is. The little people went too far with him, I say," Mrs. Winters murmured, crossing herself as he left the room.

"It's like he lost a book, or the key to his trunk, not his mum," Denkins agreed bitterly.

"If it was a book he lost, he'd no doubt be wailing to beat the sinners in hell," Mrs. Winters said. We arose, nodding our heads in disgust, and returned to our duties. I did not like to think so cruelly of Master Mycroft, but the lad's attitude these last days had been inscrutably unflustered. I had at first seen grief in his demeanor, I had thought, but maybe I had been mistaken. Perhaps he had just been exhausted from his rushed travels. Perhaps his duty to his brother and father was nothing more than that—cold, impersonal, callous attention to duty. Perhaps his genius had taken over his entire personality, I thought, stamping out any human-ity his parents had tried to impart to him. It left a bitter taste in my mouth.

It wasn't until late that night that I, in my insomnia, arose and decided to go to the kitchen to warm some milk as a sleep aid. I heard the repeated crack of light-ning and thunder as I held the glass and wandered through the darkness of the house as was my sleepless habit. As I entered the entrance hallway, I heard gen-tle weeping coming from the library. At first I thought Mr. Holmes had left the solitary confinement of his study, but then I recognized that the voice of the lamenter was too high pitched to be his. I crept closer to the entrance to the library and could discern a speck of light inside it. Between the weeping some muffled words of awful grief reached my ears. I felt a flood of remorse course through my body; it was clearly the voice of Mycroft Holmes. I repaired to the drawing room with the lad's sobs pounding in my ears. I sat in the dark until I heard Master Mycroft enter his bedroom, and then I lit a candle. I stayed up reading for hours, though each page was reread many times.

It had rained all night and was still drizzling in the morning. Master Mycroft woke early, and after some earnest yet fruitless attempts to persuade Mr. Holmes to open his study door, he went into the morning room to read for an hour until breakfast was served. At that time, he ascended to the first floor to wake his younger brother.

After a few minutes he approached me in the dining room, actually running. Daisy trotted by his side. "Sherlock's not in his room, though Daisy was locked in it. He's not in the study, or my room, or father's, or any other room of the house that I searched. I perceived from his room that he arose and dressed hurriedly..." Suddenly Master Mycroft darted to the hallway; only my hand on her collar kept the dog by my side. I heard his yell from there. "He's taken his coat! He's left the house!"

He ran back to the dining room at a gait he was unaccustomed to, which left him almost out of breath even from that short distance. "Brewster, did Eliza see my brother leave this morning? She's up earliest, isn't she?"

"Usually, sir. I can check with her. However, I was up most of the night from about 3:00 A.M. due to my insomnia. I spent some time in the kitchen, but then wandered about the house. I eventually settled into the drawing room to read. I did not see nor hear him leave during all that time." I am sure that Master Mycroft then knew that I had been, therefore, awake during the time he had allowed himself to express his grief; however, neither of us mentioned it further.

"Indeed?" was all the lad said. "Then he left earlier than that and has been in the rain all night." He returned with urgency to his father's study, pounding on the door with an energy that was not common to his nature.

"Father! Father!" he yelled. "Open up the door. Sherlock is gone—I believe he's left the house!" After another moment, his pleas took a very surprising turn. "Father, Sherlock has spent the night in the rain. Open up the damned door now!"

The door opened, and Mr. Holmes appeared—red-eyed, unshaven, tie removed, shirt partly unbuttoned, hair out of place. He was not inebriated, though he held his forehead as if he was surely suffering the effects of an overindulgence the previous night.

"What the hell are you yelling about, lad?" he grumbled roughly. "Go away and leave me alone." He made to re-enter the room.

Anger flared in Master Mycroft's visage. Nearly his father's height already, he grabbed his father by his jacket and pushed him back against the wall of the hallway. "Don't you dare go back into that room. Your youngest son left the house during the night; Sherlock is not here. Were you too intoxicated to notice the tempestuous weather that howled all through the hours? Sherlock has been out in that, alone!"

The lingering effects of the alcohol dissolved as Mr. Holmes comprehended Master Mycroft's words. Slowly his face, which had been scrunched up from irritability and sensitivity to the light, widened and expanded into a visage of fear. Master Mycroft released his hold on his father as he observed the change in attitude.

"What? What are you saying? Where is Sherlock? How do you know he's not in the house?"

"I went to rouse him for breakfast. He was not in bed and I observed that he had dressed in a hurry. I have checked the rest of the house and he is nowhere to be found. Brewster has been up since 3:00 A.M. due to insomnia and did not hear nor see Sherlock depart after that time. I can only deduce that he left the house even earlier than that."

"Oh, my dear God," Mr. Holmes exclaimed. "But he promised."

"I do not think his behavior was based on suicidal intent. He promised you, and I fully believe he will forever follow his word. No, I have no proof, but I strongly feel his departure was impulsive, not premeditative." He paused to allow his father a moment of understanding, then continued. "I thought at first we should organize a searching party. But now I realise there is only one place the lad would have gone to."

"Where? Noah's cottage? One of the waterfalls?"

The lad shook his head. "No, Mother's grave."

There was a hushed interlude among the three of us.

"God preserve him," his father said. He rushed to the entranceway, put on a heavy coat, gloves, and hat, and dashed outside to the stables. Master Mycroft put on his outer clothes and followed Mr. Holmes, the two of them riding off quickly down the road in the light rain. The visits to his aristocratic friends' homes had certainly garnered Master Mycroft, if nothing else, the ability to command a horse.

They returned home almost two hours later, the wetness of the roads having slowed them down considerably in reaching, and returning from, Aysgarth. As Master Mycroft had suspected, they had found the lad awake, soaked to the bone, lying in a puddle curled into a ball next to the gravestone on his mother's grave, shivering uncontrollably. His eyes were blankly open; his right hand had dug into the dirt of the grave and was clenching a fistful of dirt. A spent oil lamp sat in the dirt nearby. The lad had apparently fled to the cemetery, a distance of six miles, by himself, in the middle of a night brought forth by Lucifer himself.

His father scooped him up, ran back to his horse, mounted, and rode off again holding his limp son in one arm and the reins in another. Master Mycroft rode by his side.

When they entered the house, a bath was drawn and a blazing fire kindled in Master Sherlock's bedroom. The apathetic Master Sherlock was stripped of his clothes and placed in the hot water. There he was kept for half an hour, the water continually rewarmed, until his shivering ceased. He was fully washed by his brother, who refused to allow anyone but himself to do it. He was fed a good deal of hot soup by a cup, which his brother held to his lips, and which Master Sherlock seemed to drink without comprehension. He was bundled to bed, given a dose of Mrs. Winters' mixture, and some of the powders left over from Mr. Irwin's bottle of medicine, both of which he swallowed without complaint or physical reaction. This numbness to external stimuli was very unnerving and left us all in quite a state of dread that the little lad had suffered a horrendous nervous breakdown.

We now began our second desperate vigil in as many weeks. Master Mycroft stayed by the side of his brother, his phlegmatic temperament allowing an ease of sitting quietly for long times. Mr. Holmes, nearly out of his mind with concern, paced throughout the house after he had locked the study door, given me the key, and ordered me "on pain of death" not to return it into his possession. I was glad for the command and readily avowed my compliance. He had sent Wilcox once more for Mr. Irwin. It was all I could do to convince him to take his own bath, shave, change into the fresh clothes I had laid out for him, and take some nourishment. When the doctor arrived very early in the evening, in rumpled clothing after spending the day delivering a baby in Askrigg, confusion and concern suffused his countenance. Mr. Holmes fairly pushed the elderly man up the stairs as he explained the dangerous expedition and subsequent unreactive mood of his youngest son.

Mr. Holmes continued his propulsion of the doctor in the hallway and it was all the poor man could do to stop his assisted forward movement before actually hitting the closed door of Master Sherlock's bedchamber.

"I say, Mr. Holmes, breaking my nose on the door frame shall in no way enable me to aid your child more speedily," he protested.

Mr. Holmes removed his arm from the doctor's back. "Oh. Sorry," he mumbled as he reached around and opened the door. "Forgive me. Please go in."

The doctor straightened his freed shoulders and entered the room. The lad still lay in bed, resting on his right side, his face to the far windows and so out of our sight. Daisy lay on the floor at the foot of the bed. Master Mycroft sat facing his brother and put down his book upon our entrance. He stood and reached out a chubby hand to the doctor.

"Doctor Irwin, thank you for coming so soon after your delivery of a newborn." Mycroft narrowed his brilliant eyes. "It was a boy, I perceive."

Mr. Irwin was taken aback at Master Mycroft's deductions; he had not been a sufficiently frequent visitor to the house to have experienced the lad's genius firsthand.

"Why, yes, but how do you know?"

Master Mycroft waved his hand to the side. "That is not important." He held his finger to his lips and led them back outside into the hallway, closing the door behind him. "What is important is the state of my younger brother's physical and mental health. Both, I fear, may have suffered severely from the consequence of his ill-judged compulsion to lie upon the resting place of our mother through the duration of an inclement night. He has slept up until forty-five minutes ago when he awoke in much the same benumbed condition as he exhibited earlier. He has not spoken, although I have attempted several times to draw him out. Aside from a slight fever and a desire for many covers, he shows no sign of physical illness, yet…" He let the last sentence drift away. It was simple for us to end it silently in our own heads; yet, that was how Mrs. Holmes had begun.

A hushed melancholy encircled the group of them, broken only by the doctor's throat clearing. "Let me examine the boy," he said.

They re-entered the room and proceeded to the far side of the bed. The lad lay impossibly still, so small and vulnerable, so unlike anything I had ever expected to see from him, that it broke my heart to pieces. This affectionate and wonderful lad, so devastated by the death of his mother, so guilt-wracked, had withdrawn into a shell I never should have thought the lad had the ability to create anymore than I would have expected the sun one day to rise as an uneven lump of charcoal, unable to cast light and hope upon a needful world. Mr. Holmes stood back from the bed, nervously gnawing on a fingernail, a habit I had never seen him engage in before. I stood by his side while Master Mycroft and Dr. Irwin approached Master Sherlock.

His eyes were still blankly open and did not follow Dr. Irwin's hands as the latter passed them back and forth across the lad's face. Master Sherlock did blink regularly, though, so I was relieved to think he had not developed some frightful catatonia. As he began to examine the boy, Dr. Irwin spoke gently and compassionately, explaining all he was doing, the reason for it, and constantly checking to ensure the lad was not in pain. He took the pulse, noted the respiration, felt for fever, poked and prodded his abdomen, thumped his back, listened with his stethoscope to his lungs, placed a tongue depressor in his mouth, and tried unsuccessfully to have Master Sherlock say "ah." Throughout all the examination, Mr. Irwin moved the enervated and objectionless lad as if he were no more than a rag doll stuffed with wadding.

When he had done he repositioned Master Sherlock on his side, then covertly took a needle from his bag lying behind the boy and in a one smooth motion jabbed it deeply into the lad's leg. I believe Mr. Holmes almost attacked and throttled the man as he realised the doctor's intent, but I firmly touched his arm and whispered "Sir, do not." It was a considerable breach of my decorum, though it saw him through his momentary ire at the doctor's bold, yet understandable, behavior. There swept through the room as the needle sank into the lad's flesh, for me, a sensation as if time itself had slowed down its passage to witness Master Sherlock's reaction to the painful jab. A flash of comprehension struck my mind in the instant of Dr. Irwin's action—the lad's prognosis was somehow intrinsically bound to that tiny needle. A reaction would mean the lad was not beyond the reach of the hands of those who stood with arms outstretched to help, that he had not withdrawn so fully into himself he was in another world where he could truly not be contacted, where he was drowning in a sea no one but he was afloat in, too far from those on land to notice. Time seemed to crawl and the suspense compressed my stomach into a small rock. I beseeched heaven to bring its blessed grace into the room.

"Ow," the lad said, grabbing his thigh, and, to our great and thankful relief, and in answer to our ardent prayers, he began to weep softly.

The doctor removed the needle, and smiled at Mr. Holmes, nodding his head curtly. Mr. Holmes went to his youngest son and sat on the bed, putting his hand on Master Sherlock's side. A tear slid down his own face. Master Mycroft sat again in the chair next to the bed.

"It hurts," Master Sherlock whispered. "It hurts." I knew he did not refer to his pricked leg.

I led the doctor outside the room. He told me Master Sherlock needed plenty of rest and fluids. He recommended we continue the administration of his powders and Mrs. Winters' herbs, though he assured me that the lad's vitality should easily see him through this slight fever, that his lungs were clear of disease, and that we should expect it to break in a day or two. He stressed the utter importance of calm and relaxation for the boy, and requested he be notified immediately if the lad exhibited any signs of a deepening infection. I assured him that we would do our utmost to ensure the lad was not exposed to any excitement at all. I could only wish that one day soon he would drive the household to distraction once again with his antics.

"I should rather he not even be allowed the company of his friends, and he should fully avoid his studies until he is himself once again."

I asked him how long he anticipated his recovery should take.

"I don't really know. The lad has suffered a terrible shock upon his mother's death, a nightmare of guilt and sorrow. I should think it could take months for his nervous system to re-establish its proper functioning, and his spirits to be buoyed."

I summoned Wilcox and had him take the doctor home. I then relayed the positive prognosis regarding Master Sherlock to Mrs. Birchall and told her to share it with the rest of the staff. Mr. Holmes slept with his son that night, and for weeks afterwards. The lad's fever broke in the two days the doctor had said to expect, though the same could not be said for his melancholy demeanor. It gripped the boy like a choke hold from which he could not escape, destroying all his vibrancy and reducing him to a mere shade of his former self. He spent the entire next month in bed, barely speaking, and eating just enough to keep him from truly withering away. Daisy oftentimes lay with him, and that constant presence was soothing to him, I think, as was that of his father and brother. After that month in bed, the young lad was able to come down to breakfast one morning with his brother, though he did so in his nightgown and slippers, refrained from uttering a word, and barely touching his food. He was pale, his thin lips almost bloodless. His hair was unbrushed and hung from his head in a wild manner that many weeks ago would have brought splendid amusement to all; that morning it only caused one to suppress tears of sympathy. He spent his days moving from chair to chair in the house, doing nothing but absent-mindedly stroking his ever-present Daisy, morning room to library to study; and then when the memories and guilt seemed to overwhelm him, he secluded himself once again in his study or returned to the bed in his chambers.

Master Mycroft had spent a good portion of each day in Master Sherlock's presence, initiating conversations; though it seemed that the elder lad did the majority of the talking, Master Sherlock obviously craved his brother's presence, and would drag himself into a sitting position when he came into the room. Master Mycroft also held daily private discussions with Mr. Holmes. Although I tried to eavesdrop on the discussions Master Mycroft had with his father, I had been unable to hear them, for in the somber atmosphere of Hillcroft House, voices were rarely raised to normal levels of speech. I like to imagine that the lad continually implored his father to control himself for the sake of Master Sherlock, his dear son, who needed him as a strong guiding presence to overcome his recent descent into a debilitating neurasthenia. As the love, compassion, and patience of Mrs. Holmes had been successful in pulling Mr. Holmes out of his previous overindulgence in the evils of drink, and afforded him a tender escape from his sorrowful loss of his friend Mr. Sherlock, I enjoy thinking that Master Mycroft asked for Mr. Holmes' love, compassion, patience, and abstinence in assuring the renewal of the youngest, and most fragile, Holmes. And I believe that it was only Mr. Holmes' pure and complete love for his younger son, who was struggling so in the throes of his own depression, that enabled Mr. Holmes to abstain as well as he did from his usage of alcohol in managing his own sorrow. I may be wrong in my assumptions, but I do know how well behaved Mr. Holmes remained for a good while.

Two weeks after Master Sherlock's nighttime return to his mother's grave, Mr. Holmes requested his study key from me, as he had estate business to attend to and account books to review. I returned the key to him, and was glad to see he did not drink. Mr. Holmes went out for a daily ride as well, and would be gone for hours at a time, carelessly ending up wet and cold at times upon his return, although he did not fall prey to an illness. He also spent hours a day with his youngest son, oftentimes using the lad's chambers as his reading room, and frequently sharing with the usually silent lad tales of his own days as a youth as he stroked Master Sherlock in his lap.

At night, all three of them isolated themselves in a bedroom or in Mr. Holmes' study for an intimate family discourse, or just to sit for comfort in the presence of the others. It seemed that through the direction and mediation of Master Mycroft, and through the love of Mr. Holmes for Master Sherlock, the house was returning to a somewhat normal state of affairs, although all the colour and gaiety with which these rooms had formally overflowed was replaced by a stagnant mood of sorrow and greyness. Those visitors who called were seen only briefly, and mostly by Master Mycroft, Master Sherlock being totally incapable of socializing and Mr. Holmes preferring not to. Even Father and Mrs. Metcalfe lasted only an hour in the drawing room before sensing that their presence caused more discomfort than succor, and they courteously bid farewell. Noah Cotter came once to the door, washed as clean as the queen herself, ratty hat in hands, to give his condolences to his friend. That touched me deeply, and although I explained he could not see Master Sherlock, I thanked him sincerely for his kind concern and gave him a sack filled with food.

At the end of that first month, not long after Master Sherlock began to leave his bed, Master Mycroft announced he would be returning to Eton. For some reason a sense of dread entered my bones at those words, and from the depths of my mind arose such a "God help us now" that I briefly considered begging the lad to stay. I can only declare that I felt Master Mycroft to be the main thread that was now holding the tapestry of the Holmes family together. I feared that after his departure the two remaining Holmeses would begin to fray again. I held my tongue, though I had no doubt that I exhibited unknown clues that enabled the observant Master Mycroft to perceive my worry.

"Do not forget our discussion of a month ago, Brewster. Contact me immediately if trouble arises, if responsibilities are neglected, letters are not attended to, or if illness occurs." He shook my hand. "I am hopeful that things shall be smooth in the household, even if a predominantly dismal mood shall prevail for some time to come."

Again he seemed detached from the recent grief, from the remaining anguish of his father and brother; he related those words so matter-of-factly that if not for the memory of his hidden outburst of despair, I could have hated the lad, and again thought him some sort of unfeeling monster. His eyes bored into me, and I turned my head away in shame. His next words seemed to come from far away.

"Brewster, thank you for…your silence," he said.

Great remorse filled my breast once more. "I…I don't know what you mean, sir," I mumbled.

He observed me again—the hairs raised on the back of my neck. Suddenly he astonished me by holding my arm tenderly; the lad almost never initiated physical contact with anyone. "Take care of them, Brewster. They worry me greatly. Keep me informed." Concern knit his brow into wrinkled lines.

How great a reserve this lad had been born with to hide such a heart so completely! Was it solely his immense genius that prompted his emotional isolation? Did his feeling of being so absolutely different from everyone else, as he had mentioned only that one time when he had upset Clara, led him so stringently to repress emotions I now knew he fully possessed? At least in regard to his family, I understood clearly there was love in his heart. If Master Mycroft desired total privacy in those matters, I would not be the one to publicize his feelings.

"I will watch out for them, sir. I promise it," I said.

"Thank you, again," Master Mycroft responded.

Two days later, Master Mycroft left, shaking Mr. Holmes' hand and having to pry his younger brother off him arm by arm after offering himself up for a rare hug.

Chapter Fifteen
Enter Mrs. Fairburm

After Master Mycroft's departure, we all had hopes that Mr. Holmes and Master Sherlock would maintain their improving state of mind. Indeed, after another three weeks of continued listlessness, Master Sherlock, while still not tutoring with Mr. Wharton, reinstated his by now skilled violin playing. The music he created, however, rang out in notes so sublimely tragic that it seemed to stop my blood from flowing. Once or twice he attempted sonatas he had played with his mother; he never finished them. For hours in the afternoon he would dabble on the violin in his study or bedroom, rarely bothering to dress until his father asked him to. Otherwise his routine of sullen inactivity remained. He ate a little at mealtimes; we should have liked his appetite to be twice what it was, but he ate, and it had to suffice. He read some, slept some, wandered the house like a ghostly waif, watched the servants in their activities though did not join in, read the Bible frequently, and spoke rarely. Occasionally through his bedroom door I could hear him crying. Still, there were many days when he did not leave his bed, or sat all day in the chair by the window, Daisy loyally by his side.

Mr. Holmes gave his son freedom to cope as he would, though took him for a walk several times a week as weather permitted around the land of the estate or to a farm, which was when Master Sherlock was required to dress. He always spent a good deal of time with the boy in the evening and as he was put to sleep at night, which was still induced with laudanum now and then. A few times they went for rides together, the lad now able to control his own mount. I think the boy gained great solace from his father's company. Once more, unlike his elder brother, Master Sherlock was in dire necessity of a parent's attention, help, and love; and Mr. Holmes, though decimated himself by the cause of the need, took responsibility to care for his son. I think in his own grief Mr. Holmes had not the full energy to devote to promoting Master Sherlock's recovery, and so would not overly press the lad to arise from his bed, nor constantly endeavour to stimulate the lad's interest in returning to his previous ways. Mr. Holmes himself welcomed days of lethargy and inactivity, as a result of either the drink or his enervated psyche. Yet, even with the lackluster yet constant attention given him by his father, Master Sherlock began little by little leaving his seclusion to shadow his father as he had done with his loving mother. The lad followed him wherever he went in the house, oftentimes sitting unobtrusively in a chair of Mr. Holmes' study petting his dog as Mr. Holmes spent hours doing his paperwork, smoking a pipe, or reading. If Mr. Holmes' attention was not engaged elsewhere, they spoke a little, but there was not much either one really had to say. I feel they were mostly just needful of each other's company, and if all the energy they could muster was sitting somewhere together, it was enough for them. Visitors were still not encouraged and Mr. Holmes left the house only for business purposes, declining any social invitation that arrived.

By the beginning of December, the lad showed up dressed first thing in the morning at least half the time, though nothing else about him or his solemn routine changed. Still, as you may expect, simple things such as that quickened our hearts with the optimism for full recovery.

Mr. Holmes imbibed alcohol in a controlled fashion at first after Master Mycroft left, though one night just a couple of weeks after his elder son had returned to Eton he did drink to inebriation and spent the night in his study. From that time on, Mr. Holmes regularly indulged to utter drunkenness at least once a week. He would begin after Master Sherlock was put to bed and would continue clear through until early morning hours. Those disagreeable events, however, would mostly last but one night—occasionally they lasted two—so Mr. Holmes was rarely negligent in his responsibilities to his son or as squire. I did not feel the need to contact Master Mycroft. Usually in the morning after a night of debauchery, which always occurred in the seclusion of his study, Mr. Holmes left the room of his own accord, ascended to the first floor to attend to his toilet and change into the clothes I had laid out, and then went about the day normally, if averse to open drapes on sunny days. As this unfortunate routine was established, my initial anxiety at Mr. Holmes' behavior settled into an accepting judgment on the weaknesses of man. I remember the first time, after a night of total intoxication not long after he began these episodes of drinking, Mr. Holmes met Master Sherlock on the stairs as the lad descended to breakfast. The lad silently observed his unshaven and unkempt father, who avoided the eyes of his son.

"Mrs. Winters has herbs for a headache, Papa," the lad said.

"Quiet shall suffice, lad," his father answered shortly. Stung by his tone, the lad continued his descent to the ground floor. His father called after him, and the lad stopped and turned back to Mr. Holmes. His father said, "Sherlock, forgive me. It's…it's…nothing, son. Go have some breakfast; we'll play some chess later." He began again to climb the stairs heavily.

"It's all right, Papa," the lad called after him. "I understand. I'm sorry. I'm sorry. If I hadn't taken Mama for the walk, you wouldn't need to…"

His father stood still for a moment. "Blame no one for the vagaries of cruel fate, lad," and then resumed his slow pace. I saw the tears on the lad's face as he reached the ground floor.

They spoke of it no more that day, nor during any other time it occurred. However, when Mr. Holmes overindulged for two days, Master Sherlock would hardly leave his room.

Mr. Holmes' sister, Margaret Fairburn, returned with her husband from their long trip in Europe several weeks later, very near the time that Master Mycroft was due home for the Christmas holidays. She immediately wrote her sincere condolences, and offered her home up for the convalescence of their spirits. Perhaps, she suggested, a change of scenery would do a world of good, removing them from the home that overwhelmed them with memories? She was sure Mr. Fairburn would allow them to visit at this time. Mr. Holmes wrote back, thanking her for both her condolences and her offer, which, after a brief discussion with Master Sherlock, who had neither desire nor energy to travel, he gratefully declined. "Then, David," she posted, "I shall come to you."

Mrs. Fairburn arrived two days later, with several bags and her lady's maid, a Miss Winston, indicating that she was to stay awhile, "until you're back to running around us in circles," she told Master Sherlock, enfolding him in her arms, although he did not raise his arms to return the embrace. Mrs. Fairburn had almost the height of her brother, being only several inches under six feet. Her inherited stockiness, though, appeared on her as a pleasing plumpness. Combined with her bright eyes, gay aspect, and shining green dress with matching earrings and necklace, the house immediately regained an essence of colour and life. She swept upstairs to a spare room for herself, which filled up the first-floor bedrooms, as Mr. Holmes had moved into a spare bedroom on the first floor—leaving the master bedroom empty—and each lad had his room there. Mrs. Winston was given a room on the second floor.

The dinner was rather gay that night, as Mrs. Fairburn had flowers from the greenhouse brought in for decoration. She chatted incessantly about her family and her children, a girl and a boy, and told of the interesting and remarkable sights she had seen on her trip with her husband throughout Europe and parts of Arabia. She had a fantastic ability to digress from her main subject onto several other often unrelated topics, and then find her way back to the original subject exactly where she had left off as if it had been with her all along. Yet her tales and descriptions were clear and detailed and compelling, and her enthusiasm for sharing her experiences was so contagious it seemed even the flowers leaned over to hear better. She laughed at each instance in her tales where one could have thought she'd endured some awful hardship, dismissing it with little gibes such as, "Well, next time we shall jolly well know not to eat those!" or "When the rash came out I wondered which dress would match it." What she evidently lacked in intelligence she made up in a insouciant, and good-natured, acceptance of all that occurred to her. She was the least prepossessing woman I have ever known. I noticed Master Sherlock glance up once or twice at her as she regaled us with her anecdotes, expansively waving her arms as she spoke. Mr. Holmes even began asking her questions about her travels, the first interest he had shown in any socializing since Mrs. Holmes' death. She endeavoured to include Master Sherlock in the conversation, but to no avail.

"Tell me what you know of the Great Pyramids of Egypt, Sherlock," she asked.

The lad built up his remaining mashed potatoes, forming the pile into a soft, white pyramid. Mrs. Fairburn observed him, then pointed at his creation with her fork. "Oh, excellent! Now do two connecting parallelograms. You do know what a parallelogram looks like, don't you?"

The lad glanced at her and then returned to playing with his food. His father allowed him his deplorable table manners; it was enough he was out of his room, dressed, and eating part of the food.

"I just love that word, parallelogram. Mr. Fairburn excelled at math at college and has all kinds of books around. I don't read them, mind you. Reading is so dreary. But every now and then I take one off the shelf and glance through the pages. Mainly when it's raining and there's nothing else to do. That's how I learned what a parallelogram is, by looking through one of Mr. Fairburn's old math books. But don't ask me to spell it! I should struggle through spelling 'cat!'" She tittered and waved her fork back and forth. "Well, enough of that—let me tell you about the pyramids then. They lay in Giza…" She continued speaking for another forty-five minutes, until supper was over. The lad jumped down from his chair when his father dismissed him and went upstairs; the adults would still be served some fruit and cheese. I picked up Master Sherlock's plate and froze at the food left on it. "Aheming" delicately, I interrupted Mr. Holmes' story of a day of amusing mishaps in Rome when he been there with his wife on one of their trips to Europe.

"Yes, what is it, Brewster?" he asked. I showed them the plate, with the mashed potatoes formed into two parallelograms connecting at one end into a right angle.

"Goodness," Mrs. Fairburn said, turning to her brother, "perhaps he should consider a career in art. It could run in the blood, you know. Of course, it's not very respectable—no, it's not respectable at all—but if he has the talent of his forbears, he could make some money at it, David."

"Are you here to keep me from, or drive me to drink, Maggie?" Mr. Holmes grumbled, though I thought I saw the slightest twinkle in his eye.

Although Mr. Holmes and his sister had not visited each other with frequency—due to a falling out the Holmeses had with Mr. Fairburn after a visit with Master Mycroft once—I know they had kept in contact regularly through the post. It was obvious there was an affectionate regard between the two of them, although Mrs. Fairburn's loquacity did occasionally send Mr. Holmes out for a ride or a walk;

however, generally they were fond of each other's company. Master Mycroft returned home for the Christmas holidays pleased with his father and younger brother, both of whom had caused no real trouble in his absence. Upon direct questioning by Master Mycroft in privacy, I reluctantly told him of his father's lack of abstinence, which brought no reaction but firmly pursed lips. Master Mycroft joined his father and brother for their walks occasionally, and strode about alone with Master Sherlock frequently. I imagine they observed and deduced everything throughout the countryside. In regards to his relations with his father, looking back on it, I must say that Mr. Holmes was not so warm around his elder son; I think it may have been out of his own embarrassment at his habit of drinking. Needless to say, while not contentious, the relations between Master Mycroft and his father were somewhat distant. Master Mycroft spent pleasant times with the talkative Mrs. Fairburn, as well; the lad had his own flair for approaching people at the exact level he needed in order to gain their confidence and their favor of him. He deduced nothing about her out loud, though once, two or three days after he had returned home, I heard him with Master Sherlock in their study telling him that from his observations their aunt, like their father, was developing rheumatism in her legs.

"That is unfortunate," Master Mycroft continued, "as she enjoys walking along the beach for several miles every day with her maid, and might have to give up that salutary exercise in the future due to advancing stiffness."

Master Sherlock said nothing.

"The maid, by the way, Sherlock, has recently met a man on her day off, a clerk at a shipping office, I think, and considers leaving her position with Aunt Margaret if he will offer her marriage. She worries that this will greatly upset Aunt Margaret, who has been good to her. Tell me how I deduced those aspects of her. Surely you have perceived the same observations; have you made the correct deductions?"

"I don't know, Mycroft," the lad said languidly.

I heard a sharp intake of breath followed by a forcefulness in Mycroft's voice that astonished me—it was even rougher and sharper than when he had castigated his younger brother for his tumbling down the stairs.

"For God's sake, Sherlock, don't eat, don't sleep, don't speak, don't play— let your body emaciate and your blood dry up into dust. But never ever allow your mind to weaken, your brain to slow, your thoughts to fade away! Whether it was fairies dancing in the night, or no doubt the Vernet line in our blood, we have inherited singular abilities that must be used and honored. Our brains are who and what we are, and if you lose sight of that fact, Sherlock, you have truly lost everything. Observe! Deduce! With those abilities we will always have a beacon of self-awareness around which we can thrive when all else in the world is chaos and grief. With those we can accomplish anything."

Master Sherlock began to weep. "What is the value of accomplishment when it cannot be shared with Mama?"

"Share it with me, Sherlock. Share it with Father. Share it most of all with yourself. Rekindle that immense self-reliance which so very recently was the core of your soul." He paused for a moment. "Share it with Mother, too." Another pause. "I have done that of late, and it brings me…momentary peace."

The lads sat for some minutes in silence.

"Sherlock, I know your promise is your bond. I know of no one whose word is more sacrosanct than yours. Promise me this: that you will never forswear your constant attention to observation and deduction. That whatever happens, you will never lose yourself as a result."

"I cannot promise that, Mycroft. If something should happen to you or Father, I don't think I could prevent a cessation of thought; I would welcome it, I think. With Mama's death it almost happened." He had come so near to embracing that terrible emptiness right after Mrs. Holmes' death, it frightened me to hear him speak so. "You are stronger than I. I cannot shut out my emotions so easily, and…it all gets jumbled up inside, and I can't separate my feelings from my cognition. Stopping them both at least temporarily shuts out the…feelings, the loss, and…the guilt. Mycroft, you cannot comprehend my guilt. Sometimes it seems that is all I am—remorse incarnate. I need to have iron control of my emotions, as you do…"

"Observation and deducing can afford you that."

"Your intellect is greater than mine, and my emotions deeper than yours. Both are strikes against me in the application of my gifts. The depressions consume me and my thoughts as well." Again they sat without speaking.

"Very well, then. I will not force the issue, but think on what I have said here today, brother mine. Now let us return to discussing Aunt Margaret and her maid. I am assuming you have some perceptions about them."

Master Sherlock sighed. "I have noticed one or two trivial things."

Then Master Mycroft spent some time analyzing Mrs. Fairburn and Mrs. Winston's hair texture, colour, and style, facial skin, and robustness as clear signs of walking in the sea air, Master Sherlock adding, to Master Mycroft's vast approval, "and in her haste to pack, the maid was negligent in cleaning all the sand off their walking shoes." They discussed the daguerreotype of her uniformed beau that the maid tried to hide, but constantly took out of the book she carried around and looked at longingly; they made observations about the necklace the clerk had obviously given her, the way she held and caressed it. They exchanged observations of her affectionate attitude towards Aunt Margaret and Aunt Margaret's dependency on her maid in all things. By the time I tiptoed away from the slightly ajar door and returned downstairs, Mr. Holmes was fairly fuming in my tardiness at retrieving his pipe from the drawing room.

Christmas and the New Year were uneventful that year; Mrs. Fairburn's suggestion of a large dinner party was gently and graciously refused, as were the several invitations they received from friends. Mrs. Fairburn stayed with us, for her children were grown and married with families of their own, and her husband did not like Master Mycroft, and therefore, by extension, anyone from Hillcroft House. Mr. Fairburn was one of the people Master Mycroft had very much alienated by his unwarranted deductions of him. As the terse note which came from her husband read, "I'll not come to that house and I'll not invite them here; if you stay, you stay alone."

"Goodness, what a mood he must have been in when he wrote this!" Mrs. Fairburn giggled as she waved the note around after reading it out loud to Mr. Holmes and his sons in the drawing room. The two elder Holmeses sat reading; Master Sherlock lay across a sofa, petting Daisy who sat next to him on the floor, resting her chin on his stomach. I dare say if Mrs. Fairburn had read the message first to herself before grabbing the envelope from my hand, opening it, and blurting out its contents, I still think she would have lacked the self-control to refrain from relating its rude contents.

"He has the gout, you know," she continued, "and that fouls his temper considerably. When it is just his toe, well, then he is only grumpy; when it flies up into his knees, he is a positive beast." She tore the note into pieces, handed them to me, and brushed her hands together. "Well, we shall just have to make do on our own."

"It was your deduction that he had done manual labour when young, Mycroft, that turned him against us," Mr. Holmes said calmly, smoking his pipe. "You do remember, don't you? It was when you were four, and we were in Whitby for the wedding of your cousin Mary."

Master Mycroft continued his reading.

"Of course," Mr. Holmes went on, "I did observe myself that his face swelled and reddened dangerously when you added 'probably with pick or shovel.' I believe it was only the fact that you were four which saved you from getting a punch in the face."

Master Mycroft studied his book as if completely deaf and oblivious to Mr. Holmes' words.

"'It is rare indeed when one falls into the hands of a rich benefactor, and one can rise from street urchin to the head of a firm,' you said next. Good God, lad! Then the final 'You have been a lucky man.' Steam was rising from the top of his head after that coup de grace. If ever a man escaped from imminent apoplexy, it was he." Mr. Holmes puffed twice on his pipe. "I feel he is a very private man who is ashamed of his impoverished past."

"Oh, you don't know the least of it," Mrs. Fairburn exclaimed. "Why he hardly tells me anything about his past, or even of the present, and I'm his wife of twenty-eight years! He broods and sulks as gloomily as one can, but he won't even tell me where he's off to. Sometimes I don't know if he's going to his office or to China!" Mrs. Fairburn stood arms akimbo, shaking her head side to side, "Oh, well, there's nothing one can do but persevere. Now, what shall we have for Christmas dinner?"

"Goose," Master Mycroft said, turning a page of his book. "As for the rest, we should be quite delighted if you chose the menu, as you so skillfully can, and surprised us with a delicious repast."

"Why…why, I'd love to. Mr. Fairburn hates goose, you know. Can you imagine? I think it's luscious," she said. She went over to Master Sherlock and sat down by his feet on the sofa, resting her hand lightly on his shin.

"Is there anything special you would like at our Christmas dinner, young man?" she asked tenderly. Her attentions to the lad were constant and delicate, though never unwarranted or excessive. Her sympathy for the lad, and her caring nature were, bit by bit, opening up Master Sherlock to allow her entrance into his life. "I remember you were ever so fond of plum duff when I visited here several years ago. Is that still a favorite delicacy of yours?"

The lad looked at her genuinely kindly visage. "Yes, it is," he said quietly.

"Then that shall be our grand dessert," she smiled. "We shall prepare enough to eat for weeks to come."

"Thank you," the lad said, and I believe it was in reference to more than just the sweets. Mrs. Fairburn stood and leaned over the lad and kissed Master Sherlock on the forehead.

"Of course, dear child," she said and then left the room to confer with Mrs. Winters on the rest of the holiday dinner. Mr. Holmes watched her leave with a countenance transformed by warmth and tenderness.

The room was quiet for a minute.

"I always meant to ask you, Mycroft," Mr. Holmes murmured, breaking the silence as he resumed perusing his newspaper. "You did it deliberately, didn't you; made those deductions of Mr. Fairburn where so many could hear your observations? You knew he would become enraged. You wanted him to break from us."

"The man is odious, Father. Aunt Margaret would do better to run off with a chimney sweep. Now we are forever spared from suffering his wretched company again."

Mr. Holmes puffed on his pipe. "Quite so, yet quite cunning," he murmured.

Master Sherlock turned eight on January 6, 1865. A large cake was made. His father offered to allow his poor friends to come to the house for a party, washed or not, but the lad still did not have the heart for it. So, there was just Mr. Holmes, Mrs. Fairburn, who seemed in no rush to depart for Whitby and her disagreeable husband, Masters Mycroft and Sherlock, and the house staff, including Denkins and Wilcox. He received as gifts a book on crime in America from all the servants, three sweaters from Mrs. Fairburn, a book of mental exercises and puzzles from Master Mycroft, and tickets to both a London concert featuring the music of Wagner, his favorite composer, and to a London production of *Macbeth* at Drury Lane from his father.

The lad looked at the group of boxes and wrapping paper littering the floor of the morning room, and then at the group of people who stood and sat around him.

"Thank you all very much. It's really quite wonderful, all of it."

It was so lovely to hear his voice, his sweet, high-pitched voice. The lad's personality had so completely changed after his mother's death, from unstoppable energy to enervated weariness, from a love of discussion to an avoidance of all conversation, any of us would have given our right arms to restore him to the wonderful youth he had been.

"You're quite welcome, lad," his father said. "Happy birthday."

Master Sherlock looked at his father, then lowered his head and closed his eyes lightly. A tear fell from one eye, rolling down his face to fall onto the tickets he held. The room grew tense.

"Well, let's cut the cake, shall we," Mrs. Fairburn declared. "My stomach cries out for food. I must have a piece soon or I shall turn positively criminal myself. The temptation is too great not to steal a tiny slice. Sherlock, will you please cut the first piece so your poor aunt won't wind up in gaol, breaking rocks to pebbles with heavy hammers. I haven't the knees for it." I was beginning to think that her convivial airiness was magnificent in its ability to defuse a worried atmosphere. I was also beginning to appreciate that Mrs. Fairburn was more canny and astute than she led others to believe. The lad remained motionless.

Mrs. Fairburn took her handkerchief and gently wiped the lad's face dry. "Please, Sherlock, do have the very great kindness to feed me. If you do, I promise I'll not buy you sweaters for your birthday next year."

At that I do believe I was able to espy a subtle grin shape the lad's lips for one brief second. "Very well, Aunt Margaret," he said.

He stood and proceeded to the wooden table on which sat a large cake with white frosting. He took the knife from Mrs. Winters and deftly sliced a large piece of cake which he placed on the plate Mrs. Birchall held, and which was transferred to the hovering Mrs. Fairburn.

"Do you know," Master Sherlock asked no one specifically, "that in 1784, in Aberdeen, a man killed his wife and two daughters because he didn't like the cake they served him at his fiftieth birthday party. 'Caustic and bitter,' he called it, after tasting the first piece and having the deplorable manners to spit it out into the punch. He was infamous as a vindictive, bitter, loathsome man, who had been known to treat his family horribly." The lad returned to cutting the cake, everyone held spellbound by his sudden and inexplicable verbosity. "One would certainly assume there had been numerous suspicions in the man over the years and a considerable accumulation of distrust to have fostered such an excessive reaction of the husband—that is the slaying of his wife and children—in regards to the distasteful cake, which, did I mention, he assumed was therefore poisoned." Master Sherlock paused for a moment before resuming his deft handling of the knife. "Of course, it was found to actually have been poisoned, but done so by the cook, who had, for reasons that were never made entirely clear at the trial, developed an intense enmity for her employer, and who avowed the wife and daughters were absolutely guiltless of conspiring with her to arrange the man's death. 'I done it on my own!' she repeated endlessly. Her irrational endeavour to murder him using a birthday cake intended for the consumption of thirty people, instead of, for example, putting the strychnine solely in his particular bowl of soup, is a clear illustration, I think, of how important it is to ensure that all cooks must be taught the basics of Cartesian logic. Only then should they be granted a license to prepare food for others. Only her utter incompetence in assuring the murder weapon—that is, the cake—was still delectable, and therefore undetectable, after adding the poison, prevented even more innocents from dying.

"Mrs. Winters," he said, crossing himself for the first time since September, as he sat down with his own large piece of cake, "pray tell, what do you think of my idea of making all cooks study Cartesian logic?"

Mrs. Winters crossed herself several times. "I think it was the fairies."

"It is the art in our blood," Master Mycroft interjected. "And the organization required to ensure that every cook in Great Britain was instructed and knowledgeable in Cartesian logic is staggering, Sherlock. I dare say well nigh impossible. Surely that is not really your point in detailing to us so unusual a criminal exposé."

"Mrs. Birchall and Mr. Denkins claim it was the fairies, too," Mrs. Winters interjected with temerity. The two she mentioned instantly tried to melt into the woodwork.

"Really?" asked Mr. Holmes. "Well, I haven't made up my mind yet. Brewster? What do you think?"

This was a most embarrassing spot I found myself in. As butler and valet to Mr. Holmes, I was naturally expected to agree with him, yet I did not know his opinion on the matter; then again, as head of the servants, it would create a smoother working situation if I sided with the other staff.

"I think the fairies stimulated the Vernet gifts and brought out talents heretofore unmanifested in the family line." That seemed to go over better than I had hoped, and there was general head nodding and chin stroking while people fell into temporary deep thought.

"What do you think, Sherlock?" his father asked after rousing himself. A roomful of eyes fell onto the skinny lad who sat feeding his piece of cake to Daisy; his lighter mood of a minute ago had fallen back to a moroseness only the dog did not seem to notice. The lad allowed his pet to lick the plate, and then spoke, his face towards the floor.

"I think it is meaningless at times to ever have hopes of comprehending the reasons for what occurs in life. Take the trial of my aforementioned travesty: a cook charged with attempted homicide given life in prison; her victim, a cruel, vicious man, survives, yet is hung for murder. Those sentences are understandable. But what of the three innocent women killed for no reason? How can we explain their deaths? What was the purpose of such a meaningless series of events in which only the innocent suffered unrighteously? Why is this pattern repeated so endlessly in life? Why does bad befall the good?" The room once again grew deathly quiet. I saw Mr. Holmes standing frozen, helpless in his empathy and shared grief.

"Definitely fairies," Mrs. Fairburn said, as she bent down and kissed Master Sherlock's head, her hands resting softly on his shoulders. She then stiffly kneeled in front of the lad and opened her arms to him.

Master Sherlock gripped her in a hug; she immediately embraced him back. Tears once again fell from his eyes. "Art in the blood," he whispered.

Master Mycroft returned to Eton, leaving his father, brother, and aunt at Hillcroft. Mrs. Fairburn apparently had no intention of returning to Whitby soon. "It's not the fashion scene of London," she said of Carperby one day, "but it will do just fine. Besides, I never spent the season in London anyway. Mr. Fairburn hates the noise."

Master Sherlock improved slowly, but, we could see now, surely. He dressed himself daily upon arising and left less food on his plate at mealtimes. The three of them left for two weeks to go first to Huddersfield to visit Mr. Holmes' business, and then to London for the shows Master Sherlock had received as birthday gifts. Though he was not exuberant in anticipation, the lad was packed and ready to depart on time. I had offered to pack for him, of course, but he declined, and I did not press the issue. I felt that if he were beginning to reassert his independence in this manner, I was loath to interfere with its blooming.

They returned on time, the first week of February. I was greatly relieved, as there had been some snow, and I did not know if the trains had been detained. I should have praised God if the lad had dashed into the house straight for his dog, speaking at a pace too quick to understand, telling about the trip and the concert and show with an enthusiasm and delight that had imprinted itself upon my heart. But it did not happen that way; although, as his dog ran to greet him, the lad did call out "Daisy!" and spent some time petting it. But then he turned to his father and aunt, who were busy removing their coats and organizing the packages and luggage they had returned with, and said, "Thank you again, Papa, for the lovely tickets. Both the performances were excellent."

"You're welcome again, lad. Now, go and have a bath." Eliza was sent to heat the water, and Master Sherlock and Daisy went upstairs. Mrs. Fairburn and her maid also ascended to rest from their travels.

I related to Mr. Holmes that all was well here, showing him the letters that had arrived since he left, and telling him who had visited in his absence. He shared with me that the trip had been uneventful. In Huddersfield, Master Sherlock had been content to stay in the hotel room reading while Mr. Holmes was at the factory, although Mrs. Fairburn had dragged him from his solitude for walks in the city on the less blustery days. In London, the three had attended the shows, eaten at several restaurants that business associates had recommended to Mr. Holmes, visited some museums—the British Museum had particularly enthralled the lad, his father beamed—and met with Mrs. Fairburn's son and his family.

"Unfortunately," Mr. Holmes murmured to me, after first checking to see that no one else was around, "my nephew George has turned out to be as completely odious as his father. If we've got fairies in our blood, they must have gargoyles in theirs." I could not refrain from a brief snicker, though was uncomfortable at my loss of control. "However," Mr. Holmes added, "Sherlock has ensured we will not ever have to suffer through another hour with him. Between the lads we shall probably one day have no family connexions left at all."

"He deduced?" I asked.

Mr. Holmes shook his head. "Not exactly, although Mycroft can be a terrible influence on him at times, don't you think?" It was like asking someone if they had ever noticed that the moon comes up at night. He realised the rhetorical nature of his question at once.

"Of course you do. Anyway, no, he didn't deduce anything—he was just honest. Here's what happened, Brewster. Nephew George is a wealthy barrister, and lives on Bruton Place in Mayfair in a house with his timid wife, four shy daughters, and four miserable servants. He was obligated to invite us over once his mother contacted him and told him we were in town, and we were obligated to attend. The afternoon was dreadful. Stifling conversation abounded—the man has no insights that shine with brilliancy or even originality. He is curt to his wife, abrupt to his daughters, tyrannical with his servants. He has noxious breath—forgive me my graphic description, but it is as if there were a tiny abattoir in his mouth. Unbearable! He immediately followed his mention of Catherine's death by demanding a cigar be brought to him. I have never wanted to throttle a man so, Brewster. I did not dare look at Sherlock. Poor Mrs. Fairburn was horrified by her son's behavior, but she held her tongue, too. Supper, though the food was excellent and plentiful, was made unpalatable by the cold, unloving atmosphere the man had created in his house. That was when things came to a head. Sherlock had not even touched the food on his plate; of course, George was incensed at that perceived affront to him as host.

"'Eat your food, boy!' he ordered. I was about to defend the lad, when Sherlock and I exchanged a glance and I realised he had no intention of letting this man command him to do anything.

"'I shan't,' Sherlock said, pushing the plate away. 'It is impossible for me to do so without upsetting my digestion. I find you too unpleasant a host, Mr. Fairburn. For one must agree that to eat with someone is to accept them on some level—and I cannot accept anyone with such an appalling personality, who ruins his home by ruling it with a hand so tight it strangles the life from all who live within.'

"Brewster, George's eyeballs almost burst from his head, they bulged so. He had only met Mycroft before, when the lad insulted his father, and was unprepared for a similar experience with Sherlock. I don't think anyone had spoken to George like that in a long time. My sister did not know whether to laugh out loud or grab a fork to defend Sherlock from a physical attack from her son.

"George shot to his feet and slammed his fist down on the table. 'How dare you, you insolent brat!'

"Sherlock calmly addressed our outraged kin. ' "Insolent," I cannot deny. My words do slam against the pillars of propriety. However, "brat" I strongly contest.'

"George was sputtering so that spittle flew from his odoriferous mouth. He turned to me in fury. 'Get out of my house. Take yourself and your brat and get out of my house this minute.'

"I could not help twist the knife, Brewster. 'He's not a brat,' I said. 'Unless your definition of brat is one who tells the truth to someone who does not wish to hear it.'

"George's yell was heard three streets over, I should think. 'Get the hell out!'

"We left, Sherlock, Margaret, and I. As we were going out the door, before he slammed it shut and bolted it, Sherlock added, 'I just hope your cook is well versed in Cartesian logic.' "

Mr. Holmes lit his pipe and puffed several times, which is hard to do with such a large smile on one's face. "Let the bastard think on that."

For all his interaction with his cousin, and his apparent enjoyment of the trip and the concerts, Master Sherlock still was quite withdrawn and sullen at home. He found comfort in the garrulous Mrs. Fairburn, though, and would follow her into the greenhouse when she went to work among the plants and flowers that had lacked caring attention since Mrs. Holmes' death. She must have spoken to Mr. Holmes about the lad, for she once approached Sherlock to read plays with her. He started at the suggestion, and seemed to favor the idea for a moment, but then politely declined her invitation. He did allow her entrance into his bedroom when he practised the violin; she sat sewing as he played. She did not play an instrument herself. I strongly feel that it pleased both Mr. Holmes and Master Sherlock to have her happy presence in the house. While she was at Hillcroft, Mr. Holmes still drank frequently, though he never overindulged in his consumption.

Mrs. Fairburn returned to Whitby at the end of February, although over the next eleven months she visited Hillcroft regularly for several weeks at a time. Mr. Holmes became inebriated as soon as she left, I am sorry to report. After that immediate reaction to her departure, he resumed his erratic drinking schedule of before, imbibing to drunkenness once or twice a week. We servants, and I am sure Master Sherlock as well, looked forward to Mrs. Fairburn's returns with a desire hard to express. It seemed she was the rock around which Mr. Holmes had anchored himself to prevent his sailing away into utter debauchery. I believe she knew it, and that was one reason she made Hillcroft House her second home; the other ones were her unhappiness in her marriage, and her clearly developed affection for Master Sherlock, to whom she devoted the vast majority of her time.

In March, Master Sherlock asked his father to contact Mr. Wharton to reinitiate his morning study sessions, and at that, the spirit of the house rose like an arrow shot into the sky. Mr. Holmes did so immediately, and the day Mr. Wharton arrived at Hillcroft to instruct Master Sherlock again, Mr. Holmes invited me to share in a glass of wine with him at lunch.

Spring broke in April, sun and sky beckoning Master Sherlock outside with his dog, and then with his friends, who were delighted to play with him again. They were pleasantly dismayed to see that the months of self-imposed seclusion had not decreased Master Sherlock's envied running speed. The lad returned to the waterfalls, and his contemplation of ideas, perhaps adding in the recollection of his mother. He also made a point of visiting his mother's grave when he felt strong enough emotionally. It was not unusual to see his eyes red and swollen after spending an afternoon alone at the cemetery or waterfalls. Even if he had been out with Hank and Noah—the only two lads he would take with him to a waterfall—the evidence of tears was overwhelming. He was not consistent in his recovery; he would have two or three good days, or even a week sometimes, when his spirits were enlivened; then for no reason I could tell, he would fall again into a depression which stole all the energy and gaiety he had seemingly attained. On those wan days he would still see Mr. Wharton, but he would spend his afternoons in heartrending violin playing, or sit quietly in the privacy of his study or bedroom. If his melancholia were great on a weekend when he did not see Mr. Wharton, he could spend the day in bed. He reinstated his churchgoing, his father going to the first service with him, and I believe the lad even held a few private talks with Father Metcalfe, but about what and to what advantage I do not know.

Mr. Holmes resumed most of his normal activities. His continued reticence in regard to socializing after his wife's death seemed to me probably an inherited trait from his father, for I remembered how his father had developed into a quiet, secluded man upon the death of Mr. Holmes' mother. However, Mr. Holmes did uphold his duties to the farmers, and as justice of the peace, and continued his regular trips to Huddersfield. He kept up a steady correspondence with his sister, and his mood would always be agreeable on the days he received a letter from her. Mr. Holmes did reassociate himself occasionally with one friend, Mr. Routh, a fellow estate holder from Wensleydale, and enjoyed the chess games they engaged in, and the smoking and conversation.

As I said, both Mr. Holmes and Master Sherlock looked forward to the return of Mrs. Fairburn every six to eight weeks; both of them would become agitated and restless the day or two before she was to arrive. After the first return visit, as she hugged them each good-bye and promised to return again as soon as possible, they watched Wilcox drive her off to the train for as long as possible, even stepping into the front yard to afford themselves a further view of the carriage trotting down the path. Master Sherlock stayed outside for an hour with Daisy after she left, whilst Mr. Holmes retreated to his study and his wine. After her May visit, on the morning she was to depart, Master Sherlock silently seated himself in the carriage with his dog and rode with her to the Askrigg station, returning with Wilcox after she had boarded the train.

Arriving again in July, she leapt off the carriage as soon as it came to a complete halt by the entrance door. The day was windy and rainy, but the broad smile on her face as she strode stiffly yet quickly through the door overcame any hints of the dreariness of travelling in such weather.

"You shan't believe my words," she began, speaking to her brother and nephew even before I could fully remove her coat and take her gloves. "You can't believe the scandalous event that has occurred, the incredible event. I daresay I myself have not fully recovered from the shock of hearing the news a fortnight ago."

"What is it?" Mr. Holmes asked, leading her into the morning room.

"It is…well, I can't say the man has not brought it on himself. He deserves it," she said glancing around conspiratorily. "And I of all should know. You shan't believe my words, I fear, though it is all true. I thought of telegramming immediately upon learning of the amazing affair, but then decided that since I was returning to you in so short a time, I should very much enjoy relating the entire thing to you both in person."

She pointed a finger at Master Sherlock. "Especially to you, young man, who set the wheels in motion on a very creaky machine that should have been oiled a long time ago." She smiled at him broadly.

Mrs. Fairburn looked at Mr. Holmes and Master Sherlock, who stood observing her calmly. By then, they had achieved a peace of sorts with her method of discourse, realizing that the bonfire of her speech did not need to be fought with verbal buckets of inquisitory water, but would just in time consume itself, leaving the remnants of the main subject revealed. Yet, oddly, Mrs. Fairburn paused for quite a time, until the silence agitated Master Sherlock's curiosity.

"Pray tell, what news of cousin George do you have, Aunt Margaret?" the lad asked.

"Oh, you've guessed who it's about, have you?" Mrs. Fairburn said as she sat down and crossed her arms in feigned irritation, her grin belying her true reaction.

Master Sherlock stroked his dog. "I never guess. Mycroft says it is destructive to the mental faculties."

"Yes, yes, no doubt," Mrs. Fairburn said, brushing away his words with a stroke of her arm. Then she added playfully, "Well, then, can your mental faculties tell us the nature of the information regarding my son that I was about to relate?"

Master Sherlock glanced at his father and then looked up at his aunt. "I believe I can; however, I should be loath to detract from your evident pleasure at conferring such information upon my father and myself."

Mrs. Fairburn put her hands on her hips and affected a pout. "Well, I appreciate your consideration, although it still 'detracts from my evident pleasure' knowing you already know what I am about to say." Of an instant her inherent good nature once more manifested. "Oh well, that's what we get when we have geniuses for relatives. You're still in the dark, aren't you, David?"

Mr. Holmes had lit a pipe—now that his wife had died he did not refrain from smoking anywhere in the house. He took a long puff, and exhaled. "No one has ever called me a genius, Maggie. Go ahead and let me in on the extraordinary secret."

Mrs. Fairburn's eyes twinkled as she sat down in a chair in front of the two. "My son's wife and daughters have left him, and returned to her parents' home in Birmington."

Mr. Holmes' eyes widened. "I do say, that's news indeed."

"And it's all due to him," Mrs. Fairburn finished, leaning forward and slapping Master Sherlock on the knee.

"Sherlock is responsible for their leave taking? But, how do you mean?" Mr. Holmes raised his eyebrows as he glanced at his son.

Mrs. Fairburn clapped her hands together. "I shall tell you how. You're quite the hero to them, young man. Quite the hero. It's all due to his words with George when we visited them. Somehow Sherlock's awful denunciations of George's character, given in so brash and courageous a manner, deeply affected Agnes, my daughter-in-law, and brought forth her decision to leave that brutal and impossible man. When she saw this young boy stand up to her husband so confidently, it solidified in her a faith that she could take steps to quit the situation she had abhorred for so long, but had endured in silent obedience. She described it to me as if something just changed inside her, something imperceptible and unexplainable, when Master Sherlock challenged her husband that night, and from then on she knew with finality she would leave my son."

"Most extraordinary," Mr. Holmes said.

"But that's not the only thing! Oh no, oh no!" Mrs. Fairburn ejaculated. "Last week, only one week since she and her daughters left him, George sent her a note asking her to meet with him at a hotel in Birmingham where he was staying and where they should discuss the concerns she has regarding him and their marriage. He had travelled there to see her, you understand. He wrote, 'I am most willing to learn the nature of your heart and the reasons for the drastic action you have deemed so necessary to embark upon. I am most interested in succeeding in a happy reconciliation of our marriage.'" She paused and looked at them. "You do comprehend his motive, do you not? He is endeavouring to make amends! He wants to initiate proceedings to have them return to London. I may be so bold as to imagine he is quite contrite, and is re-evaluating his entire method of running his family and household. This is all due to your refusal to eat his dinner, Sherlock. How can I ever thank you, my dear, dear boy?"

Master Sherlock's countenance softened at her sincere gratitude, and he said, "I...I was just being honest."

"Yes, but it was your courage to be honest that fueled the courage in Agnes. I do not feel that my son is as horrible as he appears to be. I fear he mimicked his father's harshness but that inside his heart is innately of a gentler disposition. But all patterns assert themselves if repeated too frequently, and my son's disposition became uglier the more he grew, until he left our home a man molded into a form he could no longer reshape. I feel only this crisis with his wife and children has been strong enough to break the mold. Your words have set in motion a series of events and changes I can only describe as long due, groundbreaking, and absolutely wonderful in what I believe will be their final outcome—an eventual reformation of my son's nature, and the saving of a marriage."

She grabbed the lad and hugged him side to side with such strength I feared he would die of suffocation. "Oh, you amazing, lovely boy." She let him go. "You truly amazing, lovely boy," she repeated. "Thank you so very much."

Master Sherlock closed his eyes for some moments. When he opened them they were moist. "You're…very welcome," he said.

Mr. Holmes took the pipe from his mouth. "And," he added, playfully nudging the lad on his shoulder, "you might very well have saved a roomful of innocents from a poisoned cake as well. Not bad for a brat."

Master Sherlock looked at his father, blinking rapidly. And then he did something I had longed to have him do for nine months—he heartily laughed. He spent all the rest of the afternoon at his aunt's side.

Chapter Sixteen
A Happy Home Again

Master Mycroft returned home from Eton at Easter to a house not entirely as of old, but closer than ever in its recovering atmosphere. Master Sherlock, as always, spent a great deal of time with his brother, and the two embarked on visiting the villages, farms, collieries, and the like, deducing all they could from the people they observed. They maintained their private discussions in their study. However, the youngest Holmes—as well as his father—continued his time with his aunt, looking after the flowers of the greenhouse, and riding in the carriage, which Wilcox was teaching him to drive. They went on walks in the countryside with Daisy.

Not infrequently, I would hear Mrs. Fairburn express her amazement to Mr. Holmes, after Master Sherlock had gone to bed, on his deductions about the village folk they saw, and upon his remarkable general knowledge.

"David," she began one night, as the two of them sat in the drawing room, and I poured them a glass of port, "Sherlock's intelligence is really quite beyond measure. You are so inured to it, having been exposed to sheer brilliance already for fifteen years, first with Mycroft and now with Sherlock, that perhaps you have been dulled to the heights to which they so easily soar. Edward, my daughter's boy, is nine, also schooling at home with a tutor, and is struggling over Latin, mathematics, and reading, and he often fights with his younger brother over who shall have possession of what toy. When I have visited my daughter and her family, and I sit to talk with Edward, we speak of how he hates mathematics, how his siblings so irritate him, how he shall be the best forward on the rugby team at Harrow, how good the tarts are from Fleet's Bakery, and how he should like to sail to Bangkok on a pirate ship. And I cannot fault the lad for that, for it is what every nine-year-old boy talks about. But, my goodness, do you know what Sherlock and I spoke of today as we sat at Aysgarth Falls?"

"No, Maggie, what?" said Mr. Holmes. He smirked a little, and I could tell how he delighted in the awe and respect Mrs. Fairburn obviously felt towards his unique children.

"We spoke of Christianity, and of how he didn't know if the concepts and views of the religion were truly satisfying to him. Dear me! We discussed several ideas Christianity propounds—sin, redemption, good and evil, heaven and hell. He honestly wanted my input in the conversation, my opinions and beliefs about Christianity and any other religions I knew about, but I felt a number of times that

I was more in the dark, less insightful, and less of a valuable communicant than my eight-year-old nephew." She shook her head back and forth. "Astounding! And to think I thought connecting two parallelograms a great show of genius!"

"He has always wondered over spiritual matters, Maggie. As soon as he could read—"

"At three months?" she interrupted with a giggle.

"At a little over two years old, he began to read the Bible with Catherine, and he has always been of a questioning nature regarding spiritual and philosophical matters. It seems that since my beloved Catherine's passage, Sherlock has intensified his search for answers to our most basic spiritual questions."

"And Mycroft, does he question, too?"

Here Mr. Holmes darkened a little, pausing to tap out his pipe into an ashtray. "Mycroft questions nothing of the sort." He faced his sister again. "His interest is the world of men and politics, and mastery of the knowledge within it for his own mysterious purposes. My only calming thought about him is that he has promised to use his powers in just and honorable ways."

"So he will not be taking over the world?" Mrs. Fairburn asked, hiding her frivolous countenance in her beadwork.

Mr. Holmes stared at his sister lost to memories—"Mycroft, my world." I wonder if he recalled the declaration as clearly as I did. He took a deep breath. "He has not the energy for it, of that I am sure," he said.

"And Sherlock?" his sister asked.

Mr. Holmes began cleaning out his pipe. "I don't think he has the desire." After silently twirling the pipe cleaner through his briar, Mr. Holmes continued. "Sherlock does well with you, Maggie; you offer sincere solace and affection. His sleep, appetite, indeed his spirits would never have improved as vastly as they have if not for your repeated visits to Hillcroft. I alone should never have been able to help him recover so quickly. My gratitude is limitless."

"David, the pleasure is mine as well. Mr. Fairburn is a man from whom I desire to be absent, however horrible that sounds, and I so enjoy Sherlock, and Mycroft as well. If my little presence may afford those two precocious lads some succor from the indescribable grief caused by their mother's death, then I would be content to be baffled by a genius at a waterfalls all the days of my life."

Mr. Holmes lay down his pipe on the table, stood, and crossed over the room to sit next to his sister. She stopped her stitching, and he took her hand. I left the room then to afford them their privacy, though stayed close enough to the entrance to break into it.

"I am not a strong man, Maggie," Mr. Holmes said, "and without you I fear in my inconsolate despair I would have utterly succumbed to the vice which tempts me daily. Only when you are here do I find it easy to avoid the drink. When you are gone, I must sadly admit, I fall ignominiously to the bottle with a frequency that shames and angers me. Mycroft spends a good deal of time when he is home from Eton pleading with me to stay sober for Sherlock's sake. I am embarrassed to say that without you it would be impossible—even though I know I should be strong for the lad. Your presence here has been a godsend for us all." He squeezed her hand, and then stood and walked to the doorway. I darted down the hallway, rubbing the second floor railing with my cloth.

"Good night and God bless you," Mr. Holmes said without turning around.

"Good-night, dear David," I heard her faintly answer.

A few days later, as I walked past the morning room, I heard Mrs. Fairburn and Master Sherlock reading *A Midsummer Night's Dream.* Although Master Sherlock was not leaping over the furniture in his usual portrayal of Puck, the fact that he was involved in an activity so associated with candid memories of his beloved mother invested in my being a wild hope for full recovery that I had not dared allow flourish until that moment. Master Mycroft, home from school for the summer, spent time politely with Mrs. Fairburn but did not seek her out as avidly as did his younger brother. Master Mycroft was as reserved and inscrutable as ever. Aside from time spent with his various family members, his attention was attuned to the small trunkful of books without which he never travelled. His interest in reading was only equalled, I believe, by his desire to demand stringently that his brother focus on mastering the use of his own fantastic intellect.

"What are you reading now, Mycroft?" Master Sherlock asked early one evening, as he came across his elder brother reposing in the drawing room.

"About minerals and jewels, their historical foundation, their individual values, and where each has been and is presently successfully mined," his brother answered without lifting his head from the page.

"Oh," his brother nodded. "But why?"

Master Mycroft laid his book down on his lap. "Why? Tell me, Sherlock, why do you think I chose such a topic to peruse?"

The lad shrugged. "I don't know." Knowing his brother's hatred of that phrase, he added quickly, "I mean, I suppose you have developed some interest in it."

"Really?" Master Mycroft's voice dripped with sarcasm. "How brilliant you can be at times, Sherlock." He returned to his book.

Master Sherlock's face flushed crimson, and through his thin face I could see the muscles of his teeth clench tightly together. He stared at his brother, and then sat down in a chair opposite, bending his legs so that his arms enfolded them and his chin rested on his knees. He sat in thought for a good long time; long enough for me to leave and return almost an hour later to find him completely unchanged. At suppertime he spoke not a word, and hardly ate any food, even though a good amount of his favorite Wensleydale cheese graced the table. The lad spent most of the meal absent-mindedly tapping his fork on the table, until his father dismissed him and he went upstairs. His father then queried his elder son as to the reason for Master Sherlock's behavior.

"He's pondering the reason for my interest in a certain literary subject," Master Mycroft said, removing himself from the table.

"What subject is that, dear?" Mrs. Fairburn.

"Minerals and jewels."

"Oh. Those interest you?"

"In some regards greatly, in others not at all. It is for Sherlock to cogently unearth the former, while disallowing the latter. If you will excuse me, I should like to return to my reading."

"Of course," Mrs. Fairburn said, adding after Mycroft left the room, "Quite an unusual form of sibling interaction, David."

Mr. Holmes reached for a piece of cheese. "He's been administering lessons to Sherlock ever since the lad was one year old when he perceived in Sherlock a kindred mind. Sherlock has always been enamoured of his elder brother's expertise in observing and deducing, and his softer heart thrilled to the attention of his generally distant sibling. Catherine and I used to fear Mycroft's power over Sherlock, but I now see Mycroft exerts no malevolent influence on the lad; he merely compels him to use his brains. Sherlock seems to thrive on his instruction. He has a remarkable capacity for deductive genius as well as Mycroft, I feel, though it does not come quite as easily to him. And he has not Mycroft's…impenetrable wall around him."

"Quite, quite extraordinary," was all Mrs. Fairburn could think to say.

When the adults ascended to the drawing room after supper, they found the two brothers again seated exactly as they had been beforehand. Mr. Holmes sat down to read, Mrs. Fairburn took up her sewing, and they chatted a little as the evening progressed.

Finally, at eleven o'clock, one hour after Master Mycroft had gone to bed, Master Sherlock's legs unfolded abruptly and he sat straight up in his chair. "Ha!" he cried.

"Figured it out, eh?" his father smiled as he lowered his book in an adjacent chair, throwing a clandestine wink at Mrs. Fairburn.

The lad didn't answer, but rushed down the hallway towards his brother's bedroom. The three of us followed him, very interested in what the young lad had to say.

"Mycroft, wake up! Mycroft, I've figured it out. Mycroft!" Master Sherlock called out, pounding on the door.

His elder brother opened his bedroom door and stood in his sleeping gown, more than a foot taller and about five stone heavier than his younger brother. Master Mycroft rubbed his eyes and then stared down at the lively lad.

"Well?" he grumbled, sleepily.

"You want to go into government service, and serve in some as of yet ill-defined capacity, which you might possibly create using your deductive abilities. To create such a position of importance for yourself, it would be to your benefit to do several things: attend public schools and University to attain the appropriate educational credentials, and cultivate the friendships of well-placed peers, both of which you have been doing for years. You would also need to have as much information as possible on all topics which have in the past, and no doubt very well might in the future, impact on our government and the constantly changing decisions that our nation's leaders have to determine correctly. Certainly throughout the ages various minerals and jewels have consistently led to international conflicts, and to national and international economic fluctuations of grave import; the failure of the coal- and lead-mining industries here in the North Riding, and the resultant migration of workers to Lancashire and the South Riding, is a small example solely confined to England of how those products can seriously affect market economies. A comprehensive understanding of minerals and jewels would impress upon the leaders of the country that you are an invaluable asset to them, and create a deep body of knowledge from which to draw your wide-ranging deductions and state your advice for their policy decisions."

Master Sherlock had spoken quickly in his excitement. When he stopped, he stood waiting for his brother's reaction. Master Mycroft continued to look down at him, long enough to cause the lad some discomfort, and he put his hands in his trouser pockets and watched his right shoe kick his left shoe repetitively. His head lifted suddenly at his brother's words.

"Quite right, Sherlock. In all regards correct and complete. But next time try to think it through more quickly so you can speak to me before I am in the midst of welcomed slumber."

"I'll do my best, Mycroft. Sorry. Good night." The young lad waved to his brother as the elder boy closed the door with a "Hmmff!"

"Don't let the bedbugs bite!" Master Sherlock finished loudly, cupping his hands around his mouth.

"Well done, lad," his father said, draping a hand onto his shoulder as he walked back to him. "Well done, indeed."

"Very impressive indeed, young man," Mrs. Fairburn added.

As so often happened after a happy event with Master Sherlock, I would see his triumph change in a moment to grief; grief, I believe, at not being able to share his joy with his mother. It was horrible how the lad's mood could and so often did transform itself instantly from joviality into solemnity; he teetered precariously in his emotions. The lad closed his eyes and his head sank.

"Thank you, Papa and Aunt Margaret," he said, his voice a bare whisper alongside his loud ejaculation of but a moment ago. "Good night."

"Good night, lad," his father said sadly as he watched his son slowly walk down the corridor, and enter his bedchamber, shutting the door softly behind him.

"Good night, good morning, good afternoon, good night—another day passes," Mr. Holmes continued. "The lad's spirit goes up and down to make one dizzy. But at least he has some true times of exhilaration. For me, one lonely day melds into the next, and still she lies in her grave." He went back into the drawing room and sat down on the sofa, slouching against the cushions. "Why don't you go to bed, Maggie? I fear all hints of conviviality wisp away from me like a piece of paper blown by the wind across the loneliest moor."

"Are you sure, David? I do not mind your moods. Even in your silent brooding, a sister's love can deliver a touch of benevolence."

"No, please, I should prefer solitude now."

"As you wish." She arose and kissed his forehead, and then retired, having the sweetness to smile and nod her good night to me as she passed by.

"A sister's solace spreads wide, Brewster, but thinly, though ever she grows more dear to me. And Sherlock has claimed her for his own as well." He rubbed his forehead until I thought he might scrape some skin away. "Brewster," he said, "I am not feeling well. Please give me a glass of port. But give me no more than one."

In August, Master Mycroft returned to Eton, hugging his brother, or rather being tightly hugged, I should say, and bowing his good-byes to his father and aunt. September was noteworthy both for the absence of Mrs. Fairburn, who returned to her husband for some weeks, and for the sadness that the anniversary of Mrs. Holmes' death stirred anew to a dreadful, yet thankfully, temporary pitch in Master Sherlock and his father. Mr. Holmes drank to excess six times in two weeks, and Master Sherlock hardly left his room. But once Mrs. Fairburn returned in early October, they were able to overcome their depression through her cheerful aspect and bearing. She picked up her activities with Mr. Holmes and Master Sherlock, the walks, the flowers, the play reading. She enjoyed carriage rides to the Tuesday market at Hawes, which Master Sherlock always attended to make use of the free subscription library there. Master Sherlock continued to take Mrs. Fairburn to a waterfall with him—a passionate homage to the respect and comfortable regard in which he held her. And still there were studies, his friends, his dog, his violin, and his activities with his father. Mr. Holmes, Mrs. Fairburn, and Master Sherlock shared meals together, and in the evening usually sat together playing cards, a board game, or followed their own interest in the company of the others. Even visitors were allowed somewhat, particularly Mr. Routh, Mr. and Mrs. Cornelius Brown, and Father and Mrs. Metcalfe. Mrs. Fairburn and Mr. Holmes rarely went out to socialize; however, Mr. Holmes did venture to the farms and Huddersfield. If it was a somewhat boring life, it seemed to suit them.

Mrs. Fairburn visited as I said in early October, mid-November, and early January each time for a week or two; after her departures, Mr. Holmes spent the first night or two imbibing in his study, and continued sporadically thereafter. He gained a fair amount of weight as a result of his lack of regular exercise and his drinking habits. Master Sherlock learned to avoid him during those times, never knocking on the study door, for Mr. Holmes wished only for privacy when he drank and was irritable with any who crossed his path. After he regained his sobriety, Mr. Holmes would endeavour to expiate his guilt by lending his full attention to his son, which the lad received graciously and gratefully, and which went far to assuage Master Sherlock's anguish at his father's avoidance of him.

I am sure that Mrs. Fairburn desired to stay at Hillcroft permanently, though her obligations as wife to the odious Mr. Fairburn and as a woman of charity in her home community demanded she return to the coast regularly.

I remember she flew through the door like a bullet when she appeared in November, as excited as I have ever imagined a human being could become. Her hands fluttered like butterflies, and she fairly danced around the entranceway exclaiming, "Dear me! Dear me!"

Mr. Holmes and Master Sherlock stood off to one side casually watching her with an air of humorous puzzlement. When she caught sight of them, Mrs. Fairburn pounced upon the two.

"Guess what fantastic thing has occurred! Oh, joy is my heart; God has answered my prayers!" she giggled, still wearing her coat, gloves, and hat.

"I never guess," Master Sherlock said.

"I do, but I haven't a clue," his father added.

"Clues, clues, who needs clues? It is gloriously clear for all to see once I tell them. Shall I tell you? I must or I will positively burst," Mrs. Fairburn said, rambling in her gaiety. She grabbed hold of each one by an arm. "Come with me; you must sit down. Let us repair to the morning room, where I shall tell you the astounding news."

They allowed themselves to be led to the sofa once again where they were pushed into sitting shoulder to shoulder. Mrs. Fairburn remained upright. She suddenly noticed her outer garments and removed them quickly, placing them on a chair. I swept them up and took care of them and then rushed back to the edge of the morning room to listen to her words.

"So, it's about cousin George, is it?" Master Sherlock murmured, stroking his dog's neck.

"Yes, it is. He's—That's not nice," Mrs. Fairburn pointed an incriminating finger at her nephew. "I should very much appreciate it if you kept your deductions to yourself, Sherlock, my dear lad. It is not often I have such good news to share; I should drop to the floor in utter dismay if you ruin it for me." She pouted, though it was clearly in good sport.

"I shan't say another word, Aunt Margaret, I promise," the lad insisted.

"Hmmf. Good. Well, here it is. Finally, after all these long months, my daughter-in-law and granddaughters have chosen to move back to London with my son."

"Well, well, how did he ever manage that?" Mr. Holmes queried.

"By swearing to turn over a new leaf. It has taken him these long months to convince them that he has learned temperance and humility, and that his horrible behavior to them was to be no more. He has met and spoken with Agnes numerous times; in fact, he even took a room at a hotel in Birmingham for permanent residence whilst they lived at the home of her parents. Finally, he has persuaded them, and they all leave for London tomorrow."

"What happy news indeed," Mr. Holmes said. If he was a little lackluster in his exuberance, I can only imagine that it was due to his own thoughts that things had not worked out so happily for him.

"I was in Birmingham last week and saw my son and daughter-in-law, and they have asked that I give young Sherlock this gift in gratitude." She opened up her handbag and took from it a small box covered in red wrapping paper, tied with a gold ribbon. "After all, their future happiness together might never have come about if not for your courage and honesty, my dear boy." She held the box out to him, but the lad sat still.

"Take it, son," his father said. "It's a blessing to have helped others, even if done innocently and through a discourteous confrontation. Your mother smiles in heaven, I dare say, at this astounding turn of events, and your pivotal role in the circumstances cannot be denied. Sometimes immediate actions have the most long-lasting effects. Open up the box; let's see what lies within."

The lad took the box and removed the ribbon and paper. Opening it, he took out a pocket watch of excellent quality hanging on a gold Albert chain. "Hallo," he said softly.

"They noticed you did not wear a watch when you visited last February," Mrs. Fairburn said. Indeed the lad's watch had been broken in a wrestling match with Noah the summer before his mother died. The Holmeses had decided to wait in purchasing another until he was sure he would not break that one too, which he could not at the time promise. Master Sherlock put the watch in his waistcoat pocket and threaded the chain through the buttonhole, putting the end in his other pocket. He took the watch out and popped it open.

Mr. Holmes whistled. "That's quite a watch, son."

Master Sherlock set the time from the clock on the mantle, and then reinserted it into his waistcoat pocket. He eyes were lost in thought for a moment and then he spoke to his aunt, "I should very much appreciate the address of Mr. and Mrs. Fairburn. I must express my gratitude to them at once. If I have helped them, I did so only by chance; it was not my intention to assist them when I spoke as I did to cousin George. However, I must admit that I feel a certain pleasure upon believing that I was of aid to them. I feel especially moved receiving this gesture of gratefulness, and I hope I may, in some capacity, be of aid to others in the future."

I tell you, I almost wept myself at the sincerity of his words and the goodness of his heart.

By next February, the year being 1863, Mr. Holmes was fifty-one, Master Mycroft was sixteen, and Master Sherlock nine. Mrs. Fairburn spent a delightful two weeks with us in February, and would have spent more if an urgent note had not arrived one evening reporting that Mr. Fairburn had taken a fall on some ice and had broken his ankle. She was requested to return to Whitby at once. Her maid packed their bags and there she was leaving Hillcroft House the following morning. Master Sherlock and she had made plans to read and act out Shakespearean plays all that afternoon, and he was noticeably sad to see her going.

"Don't worry, my dear Sherlock. I shall be back in no time at all, you'll see. We'll conquer *Richard III* and put Edmund Kean to shame in the process. For now, I must care for my husband; however, I shall be tending the greenhouse flowers and sitting by your beautiful waterfalls before you even begin to miss me."

"I miss you already, Aunt Margaret," the lad said quietly. "Do come back."

Mrs. Fairburn lifted the boy in a hug. "I will be back as soon as possible, I promise. Let us hope it is only a minor fracture so it heals quickly. Then I will fly back to Carperby with the speed of Mercury." She placed him back on the floor and ran a finger down his nose. "You *are* dear to me, Sherlock Holmes. I shall miss you terribly." They hugged each other for a long time, and when the lad stood back he wiped a few tears off his face.

Mrs. Fairburn said her farewells to Mr. Holmes as well and then she and Mrs. Winston climbed into the carriage and Wilcox flicked the reins to start the horse walking. Master Sherlock would have run after them if Mr. Wharton had not arrived just then on his large, black mare.

The next week passed uneventfully. It was not until eight days after her departure on another snowy day that a note arrived, written by Mrs. Winston, Mrs. Fairburn's maid. The contents of that letter were the roaring boom which began the avalanche of destruction that crushed the house of Holmes.

Chapter Seventeen
Another Tragic Death

Nine-year-old Master Sherlock was out playing with Noah in the village when the baker's lad delivered a letter from the postal drop in his father's shop in Carperby. I brought it to Mr. Holmes in his study, where he sat reviewing the costs he was incurring by fixing the cottage roof of a tenant farmer before going out to talk with him.

"Sir, the post," I said.

He took the envelope from the tray and began opening it as I departed. I had walked a good many steps into the hallway when I heard an exclamation of dire anguish.

"Oh, my God! No!"

I rushed back into the study and found him sitting forward in his chair, his face hidden by his hands, one of which still gripped the letter. I approached him anxiously and could see his whole body was trembling.

"Sir, forgive me. What is the matter?" A cold stone sat heavy in my stomach. When he did not answer I wondered whether to stay or go. "Sir?" I repeated.

His voice was muffled and choked. "She's dead, Brewster. My sister is dead."

My knees weakened and my head whirled, and even though I had not been given permission to do so, I sat down out of sheer necessity. My stomach, my heart, all my organs seemed to be of such a weight that I felt myself sinking lower than the claustrophobic tunnel below the house. Some time passed before I managed to speak.

"Dead, sir? But, how?"

"A horse kicked her in the chest." He held the letter out for me to read. I took it and he arose, pushing himself up from his chair and then lurching to the fireplace, tightly clutching the mantlepiece with both hands as if he were dangling from a cliff edge and holding onto the marble for dear life.

I was not able to save Mrs. Winston's letter, but I will always remember the contents of it. Mrs. Fairburn had arrived back in Whitby and had been walking through the train station to meet her coachman, who was to drive her home to the invalid Mr. Fairburn. Mrs. Fairburn had met a lady on the train from York, a stepsister to an acquaintance of hers in town, with whom she engaged in conversation the entire train ride. They separated upon leaving the train to meet with their individual parties; however, at the front of the station Mrs. Fairburn spotted this woman once more and gaily waved to her. At that moment everything went horribly

wrong—a dog got loose from its handler and ran at the front legs of a skittish horse
that stood harnessed to a carriage right behind Mrs. Fairburn. The driver struggled
to control the scared horse but it grew frenzied as the dog bit at its front legs. As
she heard the barking and the fearful cries of the horse, Mrs. Fairburn turned around
and was struck in the chest by the suddenly terrified and rearing horse before anyone could pull her out of harm's way. She fell backwards from the force of the
blow and her head savagely struck the edge of the kerb, fracturing her skull. Death
was instantaneous. Mrs. Winston had been hysterical for several days and was
only now able to contact the Holmeses. Mr. Fairburn, in his spite, the dear maid
had written, would have never contacted the Holmes family, and forbade his children from contacting them as well. Since she was leaving the service of the Fair-
burns, Mrs. Winston was under no such compunction herself. She informed Mr.
Holmes that the funeral had already occurred. Mr. Fairburn had buried his wife
within two days of the dreadful accident, barely enough time for her children and
their families to arrive; the maid herself had not been able to attend due to her disturbed mental state.

"How horrible!" I cried, looking at Mr. Holmes.

"Bloody hell!" Mr. Holmes yelled, throwing a bust of Apollo across the room.
He then went on a rampage, and as I watched in shock, broke several more items
and kicked over chairs and tables. It was only when he hefted the oil lamp from
his desk and made to throw it against the mantle that I felt it was of the essence to
intervene. I grabbed his arm, crooked to release the lamp, with both of mine, for
he was a strong man.

"No, sir, don't! You'll set the house on fire!" I implored.

We struggled for a moment, until reason once more descended upon his mind
and Mr. Holmes allowed me to wrestle the lamp from his grasp and replace it on
the desktop. He stood still, his chest heaving, and then stumbled over the debris
on the floor to the small sideboard upon which lay his bottles of alcohol. He poured
a large whiskey and gulped it down in one swallow. As he poured himself a second one, the memory of Master Sherlock racing after his aunt's departing carriage
filled me with abject sorrow as I heard Mrs. Fairburn bend down to the lad and
say, "I will be back as soon as possible, I promise."

I found myself at Mr. Holmes' side as he poured yet a third glass of whiskey.

"Sir, please! I beg you to control your drinking. You have to inform Master
Sherlock when he arrives home."

He took the bottle and his glass and sat in a chair in front of the fire. I moved
to his side. "Sir, the lad," I begged, but was then lost for words that might persuade him to follow another course of action. I felt absolutely helpless.

"Go away," Mr. Holmes mumbled, rubbing his eyes with his hand. "Write
Mycroft and inform him of his aunt's death. Let him tell Sherlock."

"But, sir, that will take days. Master Sherlock is sure to know immediately that something is drastically wrong. He shall need your support."

Mr. Holmes took another large swallow of the alcohol. I thought of ripping the glass from his hand and adding it to the breakage already present in the room, but, of course, I did not.

"At the moment, Brewster, I have no support to give. I am drained and weary and can offer Sherlock no consolation. The lad requires too much. Mycroft is the strength of the family; write to him at once. Have him come home for his brother's sake."

I left the study, and heard him lock the door behind me.

I wrote at once to Master Mycroft; here is a copy of that letter I sent:

Dear Master Mycroft,

It is my sorrowful duty to relate to you the tragic news that your dear aunt, Mrs. Fairburn, met her death in a sudden accident eight days previously. Your father was just informed of this by a letter sent by Mrs. Fairburn's devoted maid, Mrs. Winston. As a result, I dread to report that Mr. Holmes has sequestered himself in his study and is drinking heavily. He desires you to inform Master Sherlock of his aunt's untimely passage, as he feels incapable of doing so. As I write, the lad is away in the village with Noah Cotter.

Please accept my heartfelt sympathy upon your aunt's death. I speak for all the servants in offering our sincerest condolences. We await your arrival and further orders. Forgive me this breach of formality, Master Mycroft, but do hurry home. I fear for your brother and father.

Your humble servant,

Percy Brewster

I gave the letter to Mr. Wilcox to post, then alerted all the house staff of the appalling loss of Mrs. Fairburn, Mr. Holmes' seclusion in his study, the impending return of the unaware Master Sherlock, and the quick note I had jotted off to Master Mycroft. A sense of morbid apprehension seemed to substitute itself for the air in the house, and each breath I took filled my mind and body with deeper draughts of anxiety and distress. I found myself unable to concentrate on my tasks, and I wandered about the front of the house, constantly glancing out the windows for the sight of a bundled-up Master Sherlock with Daisy coming back to a presumed warm and safe home, one where promises once again were held sacrosanct. I wished for time to stop its progression, for each minute to become a year, so that the relief of death claimed me before I had to face the grey eyes of that extremely intelligent and equally sensitive boy.

At twilight, I saw Master Sherlock approach, cavorting in the light snow, throwing a stick for Daisy to chase. He had lost his hat and his scarf was loose, but he did not seem bothered by either in the cold. I checked my appearance in the looking glass in the hallway, searching for clues that the lad might very well discern from my features or my bearing which would at once alert him to the sorrow he was destined to experience anew. I motioned for Mrs. Birchall and Eliza to vanish, for I trusted their talents for deception even less than my own.

As I heard the lad trampling his feet on the doorstep, knocking snow off his boots as he was requested to do, I opened the door. A slice of cold air entered with him and combined with the chilliness already present within me, I was hard put not to shiver. I closed the door and began to help Master Sherlock with his outer clothes.

"Is my father home, Brewster? I have not checked the stables to see if he has returned yet from his visit to farmer Nobbes," he said, once divested of his winter garments.

"Yes, he's home, Master Sherlock. He decided to wait until tomorrow to visit Mr. Nobbes. Would you like some milk and biscuits? You must be hungry after playing all day with Noah and the lads."

"No, thank you, Brewster. I shall be fine till supper; I ate the havercake and cheese Mrs. Winters gave you to place in my coat pockets."Very often Cook and I conspired to hide food in the lad's coats and his rucksack in the hope he would eat more and possibly gain some weight.

"Very well, Master Sherlock," I said.

Was it the slight tremor in my voice, or his notice of Mrs. Birchall's haphazard dusting of the furniture in the morning room that inflamed his suspicions? Was it some telltale way I stood, the tense air of the house, or some vague otherworldly sense that alerted his perceptive genius?

He stood still, his active eyes noticing Mrs. Birchall—whom I made a mental note to speak to about not vanishing as I had ordered—then glancing around here and there before exploring me so intensely the hairs stood on my neck as they had not done since ten years ago when Master Mycroft had peered so acutely. He turned his head slightly, as if to attune his ears to discern sounds he alone could hear, and I wondered what he detected within the hushed walls; perhaps the hard pounding of my heart. He took a few steps towards the morning room, and then stopped and faced me again.

"What's wrong, Brewster? Something's wrong. I can feel it." The high-pitched modulations of his tone quivered enough to betray his concern, but otherwise he held his body tightly.

I had no choice. "Nothing's wrong, Master Sherlock," I lied.

He bore his eyes into me without a pinch of antipathy, although I knew he was aware of my dissembling. Instead, worry covered his countenance, and I broke eye contact as casually as I could, walking to the cabinet in the entranceway and removing my handkerchief to clean from the panel glass a nonexistent smudge.

"Brewster," he said, his breath coming faster, "where's my father?"

I did not know what to say. For the first time in my years of employment with Mr. Holmes, I felt anger and frustration towards the man for the untenable position in which he had placed me. Although I believe it was only mere seconds I stood mute before perfectly clear glass uselessly rubbing a cloth upon it—my mind too chaotic to arrange a cogent sentence—it was enough time for the lad to observe and deduce.

"He's in the study drinking, isn't he? That's clear enough from your awkward silence. But what is the reason for it? If this lapse is just another in his recurrent failures to ward off the latent vice that has hounded him since Mama's death, you would not be affecting such a wary and perturbed attitude. No, you would have just delicately mentioned he was in his study desiring complete privacy, as you have before when this has happened. No, no, something new and awful must have compelled him to seek such release. Your every mannerism, and those of Mrs. Birchall in the morning room and Eliza's on the first-floor landing, indeed the very atmosphere of the house, describes an event of grave and dreadful character which you are endeavouring to keep from me. Pray, Brewster, I order you to tell me the truth."

I had kept my back to the lad as he spoke, and my eyes had been closed, my handkerchief still moving aimlessly. Opening my eyes narrowly, I turned slightly and glanced up the stairs and saw Eliza polishing the brass on the decorated wooden poles of the handrail, her focus on Master Sherlock; I had not noticed her there before. I let my eyes dart down the hall to the closed study door, and then they settled on the lad, standing straight in his capacity of authority, his right hand holding Daisy's collar. Damn Mr. Holmes and his alcohol, I silently cursed, damn Mrs. Fairburn for dying, damn the women for their obvious and inept eavesdropping, damn me for not having the brains to have said Mr. Holmes had just fallen prey to his whiskey as normal, damn the lad for noticing everything, and damn God Himself for all the misery in the world!

What difference did a few more days make? Master Mycroft would receive the letter in two days and arrange to return home as soon as possible. Then he would tell his younger brother what horrible fate had befallen his aunt, and what would occur, would occur. If I told Master Sherlock now, would he act differently than if his brother were here relating the information instead? Would his reaction be tempered by the presence of his elder brother giving stoic comfort and guidance? Or would it be more kind of me to tell Master Sherlock now, before his brother arrived, than to let him wonder for days what had driven his father into such a state. Besides, when he learned his brother was arriving, wouldn't Master Sherlock immediately deduce that the bad news was in regard to his dear aunt, the only other person his father now cared enough about to be driven to such *angst* if she were to die? At least I could offer the news with a tenderness and sympathy that might alleviate a little of the tremendous grief he was to feel whether I or his deductive genius, or perhaps even his brother, informed him of the facts.

All that ran through my head as the lad and I stood together in the cool hallway, looking at each other as though only we, and no other person or object or world, existed around us.

He broke the spell with a single word, "Brewster?" spoken as a sensitive command, as if he were ordering me to shoot an animal dying in pain.

At once my courage failed me. I am not ashamed to admit it; it was solely due to the love I felt towards the lad. His joyous life had been ripped into bleakest depression on the death of his mother; slowly and painstakingly it had been patched together like a blanket once rent into pieces and then darned completely, and although it would never be mistaken for the beautiful covering it once was, at least it now kept him warm again. His aunt had been the seamstress for much of that mending, and the lad had developed a dependency on her love for security and happiness; now she too had been torn from his life for no reason, no reason at all. It was all so meaningless and destructive—my head began to spin.

"Oh, lad, oh, lad," I cried, reaching out for the wall to lean on, "I don't know how to tell you. Let your brother inform you; he should be here in a few days."

A moment's relief illuminated the lad's visage. "Thank God," he whispered as he understood his brother was not the subject of the matter. Then he went blank for a moment, and I knew his mind was actively involved in answering the mystery which surrounded him. It took but another moment, and then his bearing expanded into pure fear and despondency—the blood drained from his face, and he stood absolutely stationary with his hand over his mouth, pupils dilated, tears forming. There was no sound but a whimpering from his dog, who sensed the changed mood in her master. Seeing the boy's need, I felt my strength return and I knelt down by his side.

"Master Sherlock, come into the morning room. Come, sit down." Idiotic things to say, but what would have been better? All words were superfluous as he stood there, now a line of wetness falling from the outside of his eyes.

"She's dead?" he asked me.

There it was, so simple and so final. I truly had no choice then.

"Yes," I told him. I reached out to hold him, but he jumped away shaking his head back and forth, one of his tears landing on my forehead. There was not an adequate sentence in the all the English language I could think of to share, so I simply said, "I'm so very awfully sorry."

So simple and so final. Out of the corner of my eye, I saw Mrs. Birchall and Mrs. Winters standing together watching us. Mrs. Winters came nearer. "Young lad, give us a hug," she said, arms outstretched.

"No! No! Stay back!" Master Sherlock yelled, and then turned and ran for the stairs. His speed was truly remarkable and, taking the stairs two at a time, he was on the first floor before I could blink. "Leave me alone!" He ran to his door, opened it, then slammed it closed, Daisy left outside the room barking loudly in dismay.

The sound of the door forcefully shutting echoed through my veins. After many minutes the dog stopped her barking, and the house sank into the silence of a tomb.

Chapter Eighteen

A House of Sadness

I butlered to no Holmes that night. Both wracked with grief, they stayed secluded in their personal gaols, admitting no one, eating nothing. Through the ground-floor door, crashes occasionally could be heard; through the other, sobs that turned my blood to acid. We servants were stricken with melancholy as well for two reasons: because Mrs. Fairburn had been kind to us and earned our respect and tender regard, and because all good-hearted people sincerely weep as calamitous misfortune befalls those who deserve it not. For all their unusual family and social interactions, we servants had developed a love of the Holmeses. They had been good to us. They had been forgiving, undemanding, considerate, and gentle employers, and had paid wages well above the standard prices to ensure we were recompensed for any inconvenience or irritation their sons caused us. I received the very generous wage of twenty pounds per quarter, as did Mrs. Birchall, and Cook received fifteen. These were not wages to be found elsewhere for our positions, I daresay, and our loyalty to the Holmeses, and the axiom that hope springs eternal, were the reasons we stayed in the house to the very end.

The lad had locked his door, as his father had, and neither left their rooms that night or all the next day. Daisy maintained her vigil, leaning against the door, whining every now and then for her master. As best we were able, given the dreary mood affecting us, the servants cared for the dog, and managed the house as usual. We had the horrible burden of waiting five days for Master Mycroft's arrival. My relationship to time was thus the exact opposite of the previous day; as soon as each morning broke, I could not wait for the minutes to pass quickly enough for Master Mycroft to appear. Although he would not be riding on a donkey, I felt his impending presence was to be as great a savior to us all. Each day Mr. Holmes and Master Sherlock refused all three meals I brought to them; Mr. Holmes at least would yell, "Go away, dammit, and quit the bloody knocking." Master Sherlock said nothing to my entreaties, and finally I took away the lunch I had placed on the floor by the door and put his dinner there instead. I was concerned greatly with the lad not eating anything, for he was thin to start with and had few reserves upon which to call if he maintained this self-imposed starvation. A vision of his lying catatonically on his bed, open eyes unseeing, ribs outlined clearly on his chest, filled me with horror, and it flashed through my mind to have Denkins and Wilcox break the door down. Perhaps I should send for Mr. Irwin? Or just force food down his throat as his elder brother had ordered me to do a long year and a half ago?

No, as much as it pained me to, I left the lad alone with his devastated psyche and waited desperately for Master Mycroft's heavy tread in the entranceway. I took some comfort in the knowledge that there was plenty of fresh water in the lad's water jug, a large bowl of fruit and some havercakes and cheese on top of a table. We were always trying to aid the lad's weight gain; if the food had not been in Master Sherlock's room, I certainly would have felt compelled to have Denkins knock the door down after the first day or two of the lad's seclusion.

Master Mycroft finally arrived after an infinity of five days, in the early evening. He leapt off the dogcart Mr. Wilcox had used to drive him to the house before it was even at a full stop—an athletic feat that expressed to me his total concern. I had the door open for him and he rushed in, Mr. Wilcox following at a leisurely pace with his two bags.

"Thank God you've arrived, Master Mycroft. It's very bad, very bad indeed," I said, even as I helped him off with his coat and hat.

"Very bad?" he repeated, his eyebrows raised in a rare demonstration of anxiety. "So, Sherlock deduced the news himself?"

"Yes, Master Mycroft. And then I felt I had no choice but to substantiate it." I stood facing the lad, who stood over me in height, and who, already at only seventeen years old, commanded a confident and authoritarian manner.

"Of course," the lad said, nodding his head, once more retreating into his typical air of detachment. "I believe it went thusly—no doubt you and the other servants were unable to portray to Sherlock a picture that nothing was awry when he returned home from…playing with Noah, I believe you wrote. When you reassured him that I was not the subject of the morbid taint in the house, Sherlock then correctly reasoned that only his aunt's death would elicit such sordid behavior on Father's part and such edgy trepidation in the servants. He then fled into his bedchamber. They are both secluded in their grief, are they not, Father in his study, Sherlock in his bedroom?"

One thing about Master Mycroft—explanations and descriptions of situations never took very long. Even if his cold and calculating way of stating his accurate deductions left me once again wondering if he had a living heart in his stocky chest, at least the circumstances had been quickly detailed for everyone's comprehension.

"It is all as you have stated, Master Mycroft," I said. "Neither has come from his room since the letter arrived, and Master Sherlock especially is causing us grave concern."

Master Mycroft stood staring up at the first floor, as if he could see clear through the bedroom door of his younger brother and visualize his skinny body motionless and helpless. I saw his lips tighten, and a momentary moistening of his eyes before they drew hard in their greyness again and all intimations of tears were arrested as if they had never begun to form. The lad directed me into the morning room and then had me sit adjacent to him in the cushioned chairs that faced the large front windows.

"Tell me how she died," he said.

I related to him the information the maid's letter contained. As I spoke, his countenance betrayed no emotion, his limbs no agitation. It took me but a few minutes, and when I was done, he rubbed his chin and lost himself in anxious thought.

"This is very serious, Brewster," he said. "Another meaningless death."

I said nothing. He ran his hand through his thick brown hair, and then stood to pace back and forth, his hands clasped behind his back. In the first gesture of questioning uncertainty I had ever witnessed in the lad, Master Mycroft stood with his brow furled in thought for some long minutes. Mrs. Birchall and Mrs. Winters appeared in the doorway of the morning room; I indicated they should come in and sit on the sofa, and they unobtrusively did so, although Mrs. Winters first crossed herself once. We all sat anxiously awaiting Master Mycroft's orders.

"I don't know what to do. I don't know what to do," he admitted. Then added strongly, "This is the worst thing that could have possibly happened to the both of them. I might be able to figure out the situation in my head on the train home, but I cannot change it. I can do nothing about it."

I dared to speak. "But surely, Master Mycroft, you shall have similar success in mitigating the mourning of your father and brother at this time, as you did after your mother's death."

"I fear it will not be so," he answered, still standing. I was too uncomfortable seated with his standing, and stood as well. I motioned for the women to remain on the sofa.

"What anchor has my father now to help him weather this foul storm of death?" the lad asked. "He capsizes as we speak and I know of no port in sight for him to seek shelter. I was previously less successful than you think, Brewster. If not for Aunt Margaret joining the household, the slight gains he attained after Sherlock's dash to the cemetery I am sure would have been eventually lost to his compulsion to drink."

"Surely, his concern for Master Sherlock will once more reinstate his sobriety, even without Mrs. Fairburn," I implored.

Master Mycroft took a daguerreotype of his mother down from the mantlepiece and gazed at it with his back to us. His father had placed a beautiful Italian cameo brooch of Mrs. Holmes next to the daguerreotype, and Master Mycroft gently held that as well for a few moments. He then placed them back down next to a daguerreotype of the entire family, taken when Master Sherlock was two years old. He turned back to us.

"No, I don't think it will," he said, sighing deeply. "I fear the worst."

I felt as if my throat had closed off and air could not reach my lungs. Somehow I formed words, "But it did last time, through your impressive efforts. We cannot be sure he would have forsaken his sobriety if Mrs. Fairburn had not arrived. You can convince Mr. Holmes again. You must. Master Sherlock will need his affectionate regard; the lad…" I could not finish, and did not need to. Master Mycroft looked at me and I could see that he understood everything, more so than I, and it was creating a frantic fear in him that he was using all his powers to control.

"Sherlock," he repeated softly. "I must see to him." He faced Mrs. Winters. "Mrs. Winters, would you be so kind as to prepare some hot soup and bread for him?"

"I should be delighted to, sir," Cook answered. "I'd cook all night if the lad would only eat some warm, nourishing food." She stood and smiled at him. "I'll cook an egg or two as well. He surely loves his eggs."

"Thank you."

She left the room for the kitchen.

Master Mycroft took a deep breath, and with force of will regained all his usual composure. "Well, I'd best see to my father first. If nothing else, he has a master key that we can use to unlock Sherlock's door if my brother declines to do so for our benefit. Mrs. Birchall, do you wish to return to your chores?"

"No, sir, if it's all the same to you I should like to stay on hand in case I may be of service to your brother. I'm so worried for the young lad. I couldn't concentrate on the dusting, now, sir, with things so up in the air."

"Very well, you may remain vigilant here in the morning room. Brewster, please stay with Mrs. Birchall whilst I confer with my father." I read the meaning clearly: don't eavesdrop.

"Yes, sir." As he left, I sat down next to Mrs. Birchall and endeavoured to alleviate her worry by taking her hands in mine. That somewhat calmed me as well. I could not hear the words, but the sounds told the entire episode: the knocking and then pounding on the door, the murmured attempts at persuasion followed by angry pleadings from Master Mycroft, the slurred, scathing bellicosity from Mr. Holmes, followed by a respite, then a short outburst of heated ranting again by Mr. Holmes, another murmuring from the lad, and finally a door slammed loudly.

Master Mycroft returned to the morning room, his normally slow and measured gait almost plodding in nature. He sat his tall body down in his cushioned seat as though he was a boulder falling into a mound of dirt from a great height. He closed his eyes and rubbed his forehead, his elbow resting on the arm of the chair.

"Master Mycroft?" I asked.

"A complete failure in all ways but one, Brewster." He pulled a key out of the breast pocket of his jacket. "The master key."

After a time he stood and drew in a deep breath. "Let us go."

He led the way into the hall, up the stairs to the first floor, to the door of Master Sherlock's bedroom. Without hesitation, he tried the doorknob, and when he found it still locked, he knocked forcefully on the door. Daisy sat up in eager anticipation of seeing her master again.

"Sherlock, it is I, Mycroft. Open the door." I believe he did not use the master key at once as he desired to know if his younger brother would indeed admit him on his own. When nothing happened and no sound could be heard from within the chambers, he knocked again briefly and repeated his entreaty, "Open the door, Sherlock."

Again his words were futile, and he took the master key from his pocket and unlocked the door, opening it slowly, and stepped inside. Mrs. Birchall and I followed a few paces behind him; however, when I saw the room in complete darkness, I hurried in and lit the candles on his dresser and on the table beside his bed. Light flared harshly into the room, and the sight it revealed was both a comfort and heart-wrenching.

The lad had not killed himself, which I admit now had been a grave fear of mine, even though he had promised to his father never to partake of such a final and awful action. I should have had more faith in the lad, for, although he was not amenable to trusting the promises of others from this event onwards, for ever and ever his word would be true. What internal or religious tenets adhered him so strictly to the concept of honesty I never was able to discern—perhaps, like his brain and his heart, it was something he was simply born with—but I never saw the lad renege on any promise in all my service to the Holmeses. At that moment in his room, I was most grateful for it.

Master Sherlock lay on his bed, uncovered, curled onto his side; Daisy leapt up to lie beside him, licking his face first, to which the lad did not respond. Again the lad's eyes were open and unseeing, large dark circles surrounding the lids, redness marring the whiteness of his eyeballs, his pillow wet from tears. His face was horribly gaunt.

"Sherlock?" his brother whispered as he approached his younger brother. "Sherlock, it's me." He moved his stocky frame with a smooth tenderness he rarely exhibited. Master Sherlock did not respond.

Master Mycroft pulled a chair to the side of the bed where the lad lay. Reaching over, he easily turned his brother onto his back and sat clasping the boy's hand in his. He leaned over and brushed some hair out of the lad's face.

"It's all right, Sherlock. I'm here," he softly reassured his brother.

For some minutes the boy lay limply on the bed. Then he raised his other arm and draped it around his brother's thick neck, burying his head in Master Mycroft's chest.

"She's dead. She's dead just like Mama. Why do they always have to die?" Master Sherlock moaned, as he then covered his eyes with his hands.

A look of pure relief was exchanged between Mrs. Birchall and myself at hearing Master Sherlock speak. Mrs. Winters arrived with some warmed soup from supper, bread, and soft-boiled eggs. I put the tray on the bed.

"Leave us alone," Master Mycroft said hoarsely, and we servants left the room, closing the door behind us.

Mrs. Winters and Mrs. Birchall went to bed. I stayed up another hour to ensure Master Mycroft would have no need for my services. I went and blew out the candles downstairs, checked to see that all the doors and windows were locked, then spent the rest of the time standing in the hallway by the stairs, staring down into the darkened house, remembering the gay times that had so enlivened this home for, unfortunately, too few years. I realised that those happy recollections were not to be enhanced by any new memories for a very long time, if ever again, and on that sour and disheartening note, I retired to a night of relentless insomnia.

Chapter Nineteen
Mycroft Takes Over

Master Mycroft resumed control of the household. He spent most of his days in his brother's room sitting by his silent side, feeding him, talking to him, and giving him the medicine that Mr. Irwin had prescribed. After being called for and informed of recent events, then visiting and examining Master Sherlock, that kindly and sagacious man led Master Mycroft and me outside the room to discuss his findings and opinions.

"The lad is physically well, though he must be urged to partake of food regularly, and nothing too fancy, mind you, no spicy food, and few sweets. We must keep his weight up, for he is underweight as a normal status, and a further loss shall only enervate him and promote a deeper ennui. Feed him his favorite foods to encourage his appetite." As we nodded our understanding and agreement, he continued.

"As for his mental state, it is not good at the moment, although he is responsive to his environment. I fear the lad suffers from some inherited tendency to severe depression that his mother's death initiated, and his aunt's death has rekindled. He very well might struggle with these terrible melancholic moods his whole life, made worse by his innate sensitivities and the fact that already, at his young age, the latent melancholia has surfaced. I believe it is instigated and propelled by his genius. If the lad wasn't so advanced in mentation, I do not think his suffering would be so deep; it rarely is in children. But he seeks meaning where other young ones do not, and where there is none to be found. You are lucky to have escaped from such a deep pit of grieving yourself, Mr. Holmes."

At that Master Mycroft stood as if he were cast in bronze. The doctor finished his report.

"Certainly his aunt's death has negated the gains the lad had made in this last year and a half, and while I do not doubt a full recovery shall occur, it will be a long and slow process, and he will need vast quantities of patience and compassion to ensure it occurs. I have left a tonic on the side table; give it to him daily to aid in the reviving of his spirits. Allow him his whims and moods; do not force activities nor company upon him. Time shall do the rest, and a long time I fear it shall take. If you plan on returning to Eton, Mr. Holmes, you should seriously consider engaging a nurse or private assistant to care for him daily. Especially if your father…well, if he is not able to assume those responsibilities."

Master Mycroft thanked the man and paid him. Before he left, Mr. Irwin, at Master Mycroft's request, had briefly endeavoured to have Mr. Holmes unbar his study door for a discourse on his own and his youngest son's health. At the sound of an object thrown against the door, the aging physician had shaken his head, mumbled some forlorn words to Master Mycroft, and departed. It was decided by the lad that obviously no one was able to travel to Whitby to pay their respects to the grave of Mrs. Fairburn; thus, Master Mycroft posted a letter of condolence to his uncle, not revealing from what source he had discovered his aunt's fatal accident. I was impressed by the lad's restraint in this action, for he displayed, publicly, no anger or contempt for the man's outrageous and inexcusable behavior in not conveying to them the information himself.

Each day Master Mycroft approached his father three times: when I brought meals and clothes and alcohol to Mr. Holmes, and Mrs. Birchall simultaneously went in to replace the chamber pot, remove any old clothes, and fill the washing bowl with fresh water. We would knock several times and then enter, using the master key if Mr. Holmes did not allow us in himself. At these times, Mr. Holmes remained sitting in his chair, speechless, sometimes too inebriated to notice us; if more sober, he would studiously avoid any eye or verbal contact. He ate little. He had not shaved or kept up with his toilet. Sometimes he changed into the fresh clothes I brought him; other times he wore the same clothes for days. Master Mycroft would enter with us, standing quietly to the side until we servants left the room, and then would attempt to converse with his father or would just sit with him as he also sat with his younger brother. Usually within an hour, some communication would begin, soft at first—it would grow inevitably loud and antipathetic and Master Mycroft would leave. He took some of the estate books with him and his father's private stationary, and overtook to see the duties of his father were discharged as needed. Otherwise he was in his brother's room.

Master Sherlock did not leave his bed. He lay there in his nightgown, pale as fresh snow, his thick brown hair matted, saying almost nothing, sleeping much, eating just enough. He would lie in the dark if someone did not light candles, and would let the candles burn in broad daylight if someone did not put them out. He seemed consoled solely by his brother's presence, and only in his presence did he not weep.

Once as I entered the room with Master Mycroft, to bring out the lunch tray, Master Sherlock lay in his customary position, on his right side facing the far wall, and I heard him whisper "Papa?" at the sound of both our treads. I stood still and exchanged a glance with Master Mycroft. The elder lad went around the bed and sat in the chair.

"No, Sherlock, it's Brewster and myself," he said. "Father has a heavier step than Brewster, as you have observed before, due to his weighing three stone more than our butler, and a quicker gait than I." He nodded at me to take the food tray and leave.

As I bent to pick up the tray from the table, the young lad whispered again, speaking as if a full voice required more strength than he would ever have again. "Papa?" he repeated.

"Still he drinks," his older brother reported softly. I left the room before I almost began weeping myself.

During the second week of his father's constant intemperance, Master Mycroft had me post a considerable number of letters for him, not mentioning their contents to me. A few letters arrived for him a weeks later, and again he promptly posted other missives, receiving replies anew. At that time, with his father still drinking in seclusion, Master Mycroft asked for assistance from Mr. Routh and Father Metcalfe. They arrived one afternoon, pleased to be able to lend assistance, for both men held Mr. Holmes in high esteem, and they understood that buried under the vice that obsessed him was a decent man worthy of much effort on their parts to reclaim. The three spent some time alone in the library while Master Mycroft fully appraised them of his aunt's death and the troubled reaction of Mr. Holmes. Then they went to Mr. Holmes' study. After a short knock, Master Mycroft used the master key and announced his and the guests' entrance. I left the door slightly ajar so I could listen in on their discussion, though I could not see any of them.

Master Mycroft began. "Father, I have brought Mr. Routh and Father Metcalfe to speak with you this afternoon. Please do not be angry with me for this action. I did it solely out of concern for you. If you wish, I shall leave the study and allow you private discourse with them."

I did not hear a reply.

"Very well, then," the lad went on. "I shall stay. Gentlemen, please be seated." Some rustling of leather occurred and then another silence ensued.

Father Metcalfe cleared his throat and began first. "David, let me offer my sincerest condolences on the death of your sister. I understand your relationship with her was most intimate, and that she was extremely dear to you. While none of us can ever comprehend why she was destined to die so early and in such an inexplicable manner, you must not let the seeming meaninglessness of her passage weaken you to the extent it has. For those who still live, life must go on. You have responsibilities to yourself, your estate and farmers, your business in Huddersfield, and, most importantly, to your youngest son, who languishes in a grief so deep he lies motionless in bed. David, you must put aside the sin of overindulgence, and reclaim your soul from the bottle. For the sake of your beloved wife, you must attend to Sherlock, and channel your sorrow into nursing him back to health."

When there was no response, Father Metcalfe asked, "David? What do you say?"

"Easy words for a man with a wife." I barely made out Mr. Holmes' gruff, slurred, despondent tone.

"David," Mr. Routh interjected, "you know my first wife died in childbirth two years after our marriage, the infant girl dying with her. Six years after I remarried, my second wife died of influenza after a trip to London, leaving me with two children. Although I felt as if my world had ended with her death, and wished for myself the oblivion of death, I knew I had to be strong for the sake of my children, who are now grown and have children of their own. Let Sherlock be the inspiration for you to put aside your drinking, thus reaffirming your strength of character to him and to yourself. I have every confidence that with our support and your love of both of your sons, you will at once resume your affectionate and sober nature. I dare say no one would state I am a better man than you, and I was able to do such a thing."

It went thusly for a while, back and forth between the two men, whilst Mr. Holmes sat mutely. Master Mycroft allowed his guests to make many ideal points before he, too, spoke.

"Father, I have not much else to say to you than what I have been trying to unsuccessfully relate these past three weeks. Sherlock needs you, and, I must admit, so do I. Certainly no one here is endeavouring to begrudge you your feelings of gloom and dejection upon Aunt Margaret's death. Certainly not. However, you have been drinking alone in your study whilst your youngest son lies abed one floor above in grief, utterly disconsolate, and whose one word of speech is, repeatedly, "Papa." I implore you now, as I have for three weeks, to walk out into the hallway, resolving to save yourself for the sake of yourself and your family."

The three men sat still, awaiting Mr. Holmes' comments. "I…can't stop drinking," he finally said. "Don't ask me to."

"Of course you can, David," Mr. Routh countered. "We'll help you. You're a strong man."

"No, no, I'm not. Ever since college I have desired to drink. It is like a poison in my system, a demon craving I no longer have the vigor to fight. When I lived in Huddersfield, I had my youthful aspirations and my job. Then I had my wife, then my sister—I drew temperance from them and so could usually control my ever-present longing for alcohol. With them gone, so is my strength. Besides, I find comfort with drink. I want to drink. I have fought it, and now welcome it. It is all I want to do. Leave me be."

"You can find comfort in caring for your sons."

"I have not the energy to do so. I have no energy but for lifting a glass, and no motivation but for doing so. It is all over, but the drink is never-ending. People die, but the grape lives on. If others are better than me, then let them care for my sons now. Leave me be," Mr. Holmes repeated in growing annoyance. I could feel the room grow tense.

"David, listen to yourself. What can you mean by your words?"

Mr. Holmes' voice grew in pitch and passion. "What do I mean? I mean leave me to my wine, and let the lads and their brains fend for themselves. Go away. Take over the world, Mycroft; you never needed me. I fail to believe that you truly need me now. Sherlock, on the other hand, needs too much. He needs your strength, not mine, your guidance. I have nothing to give. No wife, no sister, no strength, no genius. Only the alcohol is mine."

"This self-pitying attitude saves not yourself, nor your sons, David," Father Metcalfe said. "If you feel weak and despairing, draw your strength from God. Pity for oneself can lead nowhere but to personal destruction. God will grant you abstinence, if you but ask for his help."

"No! Get out and leave me be! None of you know, none of you! What have I now? Genius sons, one with a steel backbone, and one with none at all. One with no needs and one with unending ones. No wife, no sister. My anger at everything grows and drives me mad. Why these sons? Why all this death? Well, to hell with God and all of it!" He was standing now, lurching forward and back in his ravings. "To hell with all of it. I won't see him now. I can't. Go away." When they made no move, he actually screamed, "Go on, get the hell out!"

I closed the door at that point, and was standing down the hallway when I saw it open and the three file out morosely. They withdrew once more to the library and sat down, fatigued from their unexpected defeat.

"It's a shame, an utter shame," Mr. Routh said.

"Let us not give up hope. He has fallen into drink before and then found sobriety again. I have faith that in several weeks...or months, he will be able to see young Sherlock," Father Metcalfe offered. "I will visit him several times a week, if he will allow me to do so, and continue our efforts along those lines. Mr. Routh, your occasional presence will certainly be welcome as well. He cannot live in a study forever. In the meantime, Mycroft, what will you do?"

Master Mycroft sat in a chair facing the fireplace, his back to the men. "I shall do what I have to, and what I can."

Master Mycroft extended profuse appreciation to each of the men as he shook their hands in parting. Both were granted unrestricted visitation rights, if they would be so kind as to come and endeavour to persuade Mr. Holmes to change his attitude about drinking and about his sons. After they departed Master Mycroft had a light supper, and then had a tray prepared for his brother, which I carried upstairs to the lad's bedchamber, where he still lay in his bed. Mrs. Birchall had entered earlier and lit candles in his room.

"Sherlock," his brother said, "we've brought you some supper." I walked around the bed and laid the tray on the table near the bed and the chair that Master Mycroft always sat in. "Sherlock, you must sit up and eat some food," his brother softly ordered.

With effort, the lad sat up. He looked small and pathetic, almost gaunt in his mourning. "I'm not hungry," he said, with a hollowness that echoed the small voice around the room.

"You must eat anyway. Here." Master Mycroft handed him a spoon and put the bowl of soup in his lap. With interminable slowness and lackluster movement, the boy ate most of the soup. It flashed through my dejected mind that once he had eaten a bowl of oatmeal in twenty seconds. After the soup, Master Mycroft was able to force him to partake of some of the meat and potatoes, and several bites of the cheese. It was not much, but it was enough to keep him from the harsh consequences of starvation. When he was done, he sank back under the sheets.

I collected the items and the tray, and was almost at the door when I heard Master Sherlock ask his brother, "Papa?"

Master Mycroft's hesitation floated in the air like noxious smoke from a fire, and had the same deleterious effect on his younger brother, who began to weep. "Not yet, Sherlock," was all his brother could say.

Another week passed with no change in either of the bereaved Holmeses. Master Mycroft had spent his time in the bedroom of his younger brother and occasionally in the study of his father, who allowed him to visit for advice if some business needed attending for which Mycroft needed direction to fulfill properly. One day, after he had received several letters that he greeted with satisfaction, Master Mycroft went for a long ride on a horse, then called Denkins, Wilcox, Mrs. Birchall, Mrs. Winters, and myself into the drawing room. When we entered he had us sit by him, but before he began to speak he stood and began pacing around the room. Again I felt uncomfortable by the awkwardness of our positioning, though I remained seated.

He turned, and his grey eyes bored into us as of old. As one, we shifted in our seats, squirming as delicately as we could under the intensity of his gaze. Upon Mrs. Winters crossing herself, he seemed to realise he was discomfiting us, and looked away. When he once more faced us, his eyes had softened only minimally, but enough to set us at ease.

"I am sorry to have to speak to you about household matters as I had to a year and a half ago. But, as before, I need to return to Eton, and seem to be doing no real good here at Hillcroft anyway. The mental states of my father and brother are not relieved by my presence this time. Therefore, I am anxious about leaving, as you may well imagine, without either my father or my brother able to care properly for themselves, for the estate, or for the business in Huddersfield. Perhaps you think me selfish, but I have no desire to serve in the capacity of permanent squire, nor does my temperament flourish in the midst of the countryside. However, I once pledged to my parents always to care for them and the estate if, due to death, injury, or illness, they were unable to manage the duties themselves. Therefore, I have decided to hire a steward for the estate and a caretaker for Sherlock; the one will administer to the needs of the farms and the Huddersfield firm, the other to the needs of my younger brother. Until such time as either my father or brother improves from his melancholic incapacitation, those men will remain in the roles which I have described. As before, I greatly hope all of you shall stay at Hillcroft in your respected and established roles—I will offer a wage increase of five pounds per annum if you agree to do so. Although I do not think the house will be a source of joy as of old, I am hoping that you consider remaining engaged here for the sake of my family, who are both familiar and comfortable with you and your personalities. Will you stay?"

We affirmed that we would—none of us could think of leaving the Holmeses in such distress.

"Thank you very much." He took the letters he had received that day out of his jacket pocket. "These letters are from the two men whom I have already engaged in the capacities of which I have just spoken. I have made many connexions and met many people, at and around Eton and among my classmates, and it is through some of those people that I hired these well-referenced, competent, and highly regarded individuals. The manager and caretaker should arrive in two days. I will stay until it is clear that they are both knowledgeable of their duties; then I shall return to Eton. Of course, I still request, Brewster, that you contact me at once if any crisis arises, or if you feel the men are not acting in the best interest of the estate or my brother. I will let them know that I authorize you to be intimately informed of all they do—you shall be in charge of them. Is that agreeable to you?"

I was touched at the implicit trust he was placing in me. "It is, sir. Thank you, sir."

"Good." He paced back and forth for a few moments, then stopped and spoke without looking at us. "I should be eternally grateful to all of you if you were to treat my father and brother gently and with compassion, even if they prove to be very difficult for some time to come."

I spoke for the group. "Of course, sir. That goes without saying."

He waved us away, still with his back to us. "That is all. Thank you."

We arose and left the lad to himself. This time, not one of the servants said he had a heart of stone.

Chapter Twenty
Mr. Hathoway Arrives

The caretaker arrived two days later. He was a middle-aged man, a green-grocer by trade, Mr. John Hathoway by name. Fifteen years ago, Mr. Hathoway had sold his mercantile when he began to act as caretaker to his younger brother after a carriage accident in which his sibling had lost the use of his legs. He tended his sibling for ten years, until his brother passed away, and then he was hired on in the same capacity as full-time caregiver for the grandfather of one of Master Mycroft's classmates. He was with the grandfather for four years; the elderly man had passed away from heart failure several months ago, and so Mr. Hathoway was contacted for this position, which he accepted. He was of slightly less than average height and, though of medium build, he was developing a midriff paunch. His hair was already fully grey on his head and his full, bushy, black mustache and sideburns were following suit. His hirsuit appearance in no way detracted from the gay shine in his eyes, and his open and amiable manner, his lips ever willing to swing upwards in a pleasant smile. Oddly enough, he was missing the first joints of four fingers on his left hand. Mr. Hathoway arrived with a large number of boxes, some quite heavy. He requested I store them in a private area exactly per his instructions as to how they should be segregated, and followed me upstairs to a spare room on the second floor to ensure they were arranged correctly and "safely." His anxieties in regard to the boxes made me curious as to their contents.

After the introductions to the staff, he was taken to the drawing room for refreshments. Master Mycroft spent some time apprising him of the full situation in Hillcroft House for the past year and a half, and where things stood presently. Then Mr. Hathoway was shown to the study to be introduced to Mr. Holmes, whom I understood had full knowledge and approval of Master Mycroft's plans. I held my breath during the time he was with Mr. Holmes, but apparently all went well. After that, Mr. Hathoway was taken to see the young lad. I took his bags up to a spare bedroom, and then found myself at the entrance of Master Sherlock's bedroom, watching his brother introduce Mr. Hathoway.

The lad sat in a chair looking out the window. Master Mycroft had placed him there after breakfast the last several mornings. He was in his nightgown, slippers, and dressing gown, and a blanket covered his lap and legs. A book rested on top of the blanket, but I doubted whether the lad had even looked at it. Wonderful, loyal Daisy, sat by his side.

"Sherlock," his brother began, Mr. Hathoway by his side, "this is Mr. John Hathoway, the man whom I told you about. He has come to care for you during my absence."

The lad ignored his brother's words, though by his slight hunching over, it was evident he had heard and comprehended them. Master Mycroft took a deep breath, and walked over to his brother, nodding for Mr. Hathoway to follow. He sat down in a chair next to Master Sherlock.

"Sherlock, I have to return to Eton, you know that. Mr. Hathoway will take good care of you, I pro—" He caught himself, though not quick enough to avoid causing his younger brother to stiffen. "He will take good care of you. Come, at least have the good graces to bid the gentleman good morning. Notice him; there are some pertinent features of interest, and later we will discuss your observations and deductions." Mr. Hathoway's quizzical countenance at those last words was expected, yet still I found it a little amusing.

The lad looked at his brother, who raised his eyebrows and flicked his head in Mr. Hathoway's direction. Master Sherlock followed the head motion and wound up timidly viewing his new caretaker.

"Good day to you, young son," the man said genially, bowing forward a bit, a smile lighting up his face.

"Hello," the lad said softly, looking again at his brother, who mouthed "Observe." The lad reinstated his gaze on Mr. Hathoway and this time spent a few moments letting his eyes take in the gentleman from head to toe. During that time a subtle energy seemed to suffuse the lad. Mr. Hathoway, unused to such a minute examination of his person, withstood the silent scrutiny with a stoicism and bemusement that engendered a remarkable admiration for the man on my part. When the lad was through, he once again assumed a flat and tired affect. His eyes fell to his dog, and he mumbled to Mr. Hathoway, "Thank you," though did not elucidate for what exactly he was thankful.

"It…it was and is my pleasure, Master Sherlock," the man said, impressing me with his genial nature.

"Let me show you the rest of the estate," Mycroft said to the caretaker, as his brother resumed his blank staring out the window. "Then, we shall luncheon here with Sherlock. We'll be back in about an hour, Sherlock. Think upon your observations."

I led Mr. Hathoway to the door and Master Mycroft followed us. I glanced back at the young lad and saw only half his face, the other half hidden by his profile. His eye was closed and tears fell down his face, noiselessly. I instinctively stopped abruptly and Master Mycroft walked into me; his immediately irritated mien was dissipated by his notice of the subject of my vision. He looked back at his younger brother and I saw his jaw clench tightly.

"Walk, Brewster," he commanded softly yet stiffly in my ear. We left the room, and Master Mycroft closed the door behind us, his hand resting momentarily on a panel of it. "Let us start in the kitchen," he then said, and we proceeded down the stairs.

Since I was to be directly over Mr. Hathoway, I joined them in the tour of the house; and as the day that end of March was fine, sunny and not too chilly, we walked the land of the estate as well, stopping at the stables, where to his evident pleasure, Mr. Hathoway was requested to ride the horses, if he were able, to help keep them exercised. We strode to the cottages of Wilcox and Denkins; at the well full of rocks, Mr. Hathoway was told by Master Mycroft the story of Sherlock's adventure in the escape tunnel, which sent the man into a stream of "Oh, my, my, my."

When we returned to the house, Mrs. Winters had luncheon ready. We carried our separate portions on individual trays, Mrs. Birchall with Master Sherlock's food. As we stood in front of the door, Master Mycroft asked Mr. Hathoway if he would mind if he and his brother discussed various aspects of his life and his past, endeavouring to deduce important facets about him from clues they had discerned on his person and by his bearing. The man naturally was surprised by such a question, but admitted his curiosity at Mycroft's words and granted permission. Master Mycroft thanked him and then strongly requested that neither of us speak until we were pointedly addressed. We both acquiesced and then we all entered the room. We found Master Sherlock in exactly the same spot and pose as we had left him, though his weeping had ceased. After putting the lad's food down on the table by his chair, Mrs. Birchall took the dog out to feed and walk it. Master Sherlock maintained his wan affectation and listless perusal of the world outside the window which I knew held no interest for him. Master Mycroft sat down by the window next to his brother as before; Mr. Hathoway sat in a chair at a right angle to the two, and I sat on the foot of the bed by the new caretaker.

"Sherlock, eat some lunch," Master Mycroft ordered, beginning his own attack on the steak and kidney pies Mrs. Winters had prepared. The lad did as told but at a torturously laggard pace. We three had already finished our entire meal by the time the lad laid down his fork, only half of the pie consumed. Master Mycroft was content with his brother's intake and began to converse with him.

"Now, Sherlock, let us turn our attention to the accommodating Mr. Hathoway, shall we? You have had some time to ponder the observations you made a little bit ago; what have you to deduce of your new caretaker? Don't worry; the agreeable gentleman has sanctioned our discussion of him." Master Mycroft leaned forward, his eyes alight with anticipation. "Well, tell us your deductions."

The lad kept his eyes on the mildly wintry scene beyond the window. "I don't..."

"You do know, Sherlock. Don't say you don't. I know you better than that. Tell us."

Master Sherlock faced his brother, despair punctuating his words. "Why? To appease you by showing you I think? To smother my feelings in the consummate cognition which you hold highest above all things? To use my intellect as a 'beacon of self-awareness around which I may thrive when all else in the world is chaos, and grief?'"

Master Mycroft sat resolute under this attack by his brother. Perhaps he had even deliberately planned to ignite his brother's pain and frustration, for this was surely the longest speech Master Sherlock had spoken in a month. Perhaps he wanted to ignite some flame, any flame, in his younger brother on the nearness of his leave-taking, hoping it would lead to a fuller fire of life in the boy. I cannot believe that there was not some motive behind his machinations, as I watched him calmly respond to his brother's ire.

"Yes," Master Mycroft said simply.

Master Sherlock burst into tears. "I can't."

"You can," his brother urged. "Focus on observing and deducing, on learning and studying; the emotions will fall to the rapt attention to your intellect. They will not disappear, but will lose, even if for but a moment, their destructive claim on your being. Your nature is one of a loose manifold of burgeoning sensibilities; they will continually plunge you down into this melancholic abyss if you allow them full ownership of your soul. Think, Sherlock. It is the only way you shall escape from your depression. I have said it before, and aver it again now. You cannot bring the dead back to life, but you can lift your veil of grief through your unique power of ratiocination. Escape your sorrow in this next moment, brother mine—tell me about Mr. Hathoway."

The lads let their eyes drift away from each other, Master Sherlock renewing his glance out the window. He suddenly turned toward his caretaker.

"I perceive that Mr. Hathoway was born in Canada," he began, "where he suffered frostbite at an early age, losing the tips of four of his fingers as a result. I imagine he might also be missing parts of some toes as well, although that is mere speculation. He is a bachelor, enjoys carpentry and birdwatching as hobbies, and up until lately had been in the habit of taking frequent brisk walks among the hills of northern Wales. He is a man who does not clamor to uphold societal status, even though he has the monetary means to do so, preferring service and comfort to the rigid standards of intransigent decorum. Beyond that, Mycroft, I cannot say."

Master Mycroft's grin was huge. "Excellent, Sherlock. You have only missed his problems with his teeth, which are particularly troublesome on his right side today; his dabbling with chemicals as another hobby; and his frequent use of snuff."

"Oh."

"Oh? Hmmf, I should have thought you'd have a more articulate response than that. However, by my observation of the surprised Mr. Hathoway, I feel it would only be fair if we explained to the man the reasons for our comments about him. They are correct, are they not, Mr. Hathoway?"

"Surprise" did not exactly cover Mr. Hathoway's reaction—I would have used "flabbergasted." His eyebrows flew up his forehead and his mouth dropped entirely open. Apparently his personal knowledge of the Holmes children was nil before he had received his invitation for employment at Hillcroft.

"I say, that's quite, quite extraordinary! Quite extraordinary indeed. I feel bared to the bone. You do this often, do you, the both of you? I was informed of your intelligence, but this, really, it is quite beyond the pale!"

"The lads' singular gifts are quite renowned in our small circle, Mr. Hathoway," I said. "Most of us in the villages in this area have been the vic—have been on the receiving end of their observant peering and remarkable deductions. It...does take a while to become accustomed to."

"Indeed. Well, then I suppose I shall become familiar with it as well. I feel utterly transparent! So, please, clarify for me how you deduced what you did about me."

Master Mycroft brought his brother back into the conversation. "Sherlock?"

The lad brought his legs up to his chest and clasped his hands around them. Speaking in a monotonous tone, he amazed the caretaker and myself with his explanation. It was a thing that never ceased to amaze me.

"You dangle a Canadian coin from your watch chain, Mr. Hathoway, and frostbite would be the most obvious deduction when several fingertips are missing, and there is a barely perceptible smallness to your left hand, the hand that lost three of your four tips, compared to the right. Canada, especially the northern climes in that already northern country, would be an obvious place for a child to suffer such severe exposure to the cold. The fact that it also slightly affected the growth of your left hand indicates that the exposure was in childhood; otherwise, if it happened when you were an adult, the difference in hand size would not have occurred."

I had spent more time with Mr. Hathoway, and only now, as he held he hands up for his own inspection, did I perceive the difference in the size of hand and fingers between the two appendages.

"When I see such marked effects of frostbite upon someone's hands, I would naturally speculate that some toes may have been removed as well."

"I lost three toes as well, it is true," Mr. Hathoway said. "It was in Toronto, Canada, where we lived until I was twelve. I was frostbit the winter before we left for England."

The lad continued, "The bird watching was simple to deduce by observing you from my window as you walked around the estate. Your frequent lifting of your head to glimpse whatever bird appeared was simplicity itself to deduce. Your hands are well calloused, and I noticed as you grew uncomfortable under my scrutiny, your eyes flitted avidly around my bedroom, landing on the beautiful grain of the wainscotting, the two antique tables on either side of the bed, and the decorative bedpost. When I further perceived your distaste of the scratches in the wood of my dresser—an early habit of my dog Daisy which we have trained her not to do—I knew I had a carpenter in my room. Your legs are muscular and strong, and your lean build suggests a tendency for exercise. As I knew you were for some years caring for a man in Bangor, which in general is a sedentary occupation, it seemed to me that you took regular walks among the hills in the area to maintain your conditioning. Of late, however, since the man's death, you have allowed your exercise to lapse and by the tightness of your clothes it is clear you have gained"— the lad's eyes narrowed to slits "—ten pounds. As for the last deduction, that of your disavowal of societal dictates in favor of service and comfort, your suit is of excellent quality though somewhat out of fashion lately with the tethered studs of your shirt and your embroidered Comprino braces. Your continued wearing of it illustrates that comfort is more important than following the fashion season each year. Your very high quality and expensive boots, however, do signify you have the money to follow the latest clothing designs, if you so desired; and that you have the money to do so, on the wages you are paid, shows you probably have no wife or child to care for. Of course, the lack of a wedding ring and the fact that you came here alone are obvious indicators as well. The fact that you choose to work aiding others—a rather lowly occupation for a man with your education— illustrates that yours is a heart dedicated to the service of his fellow man, and you are indifferent to how others judge you." The lad rested his head on his knees, exhausted by his long explanation, and closed his eyes.

Master Mycroft reached over and placed his hand on his younger brother's shoulder for a second, and then detailed his added deductions.

"You have lost several teeth, and I imagine you desire the bushiness of your mustache, in one regard, to cover up the problem. I noticed during lunch that you chewed only on the left side of your jaw, so your right side is paining you today. The discoloration of your fingers appears to be from chemicals. I also noted a slight odor to your coat, from a sulphur compound. Since sulphur is not a medicine one has general use for in daily life, I believe you enjoy dabbling with chemicals in experiments of your own. As for the snuff, I can see the container outline in your waistcoat pocket and the slight discoloring of the skin by your right thumb where the snuff is laid. Your barely perceptible fidgeting after lunch is typical of a tobacco user who is not able to indulge his habit at the usual time after a meal.

In your case, no doubt you felt it might appear impudent to do so, as I, your employer, do not smoke."

Mr. Hathoway had sat, riveted to the words of the lads, and now, as Master Mycroft finished, the man was awed by what he had heard.

"I can't believe it! You both were correct in every instance! Absolutely fascinating. It will be an honor to care for such an outstanding lad as Master Sherlock." That was an unexpected though warming sentiment from the man.

Master Mycroft stood and turned the bed down, and then lifted up his brother and put him to bed. "Let us let him sleep," he said and we took our trays and left, I carrying mine and the young lad's. As we exited, Daisy entered, hopping up onto the bed and lying next to her master. Mrs. Birchall took the trays from Master Mycroft and Mr. Hathoway, and we left, the caretaker and the elder lad going into the drawing room.

"Tell me more about your brother, Master Mycroft," I heard him say, as I and Mrs. Birchall removed the trays to the kitchen. I liked Mr. Hathoway and was reassured by his desire to learn more about his fragile charge. The two spent hours discussing Master Sherlock.

Later that day, Mr. Goff, the manager, arrived, tall, balding, wearing spectacles, with a long, narrow face pinched at the mouth. "Horrible cold," were the first words I heard him say as he entered the house, although the weather was actually mild. I had Wilcox take his bags up to his bedroom on the second floor, and I ushered Mr. Goff to the drawing room and introduced him to Master Mycroft. Mr. Hathoway was unpacking his bags in his chambers.

Master Mycroft rose to greet the man, using his powers to study him, I could tell. Neither extended their hand to shake, which was normal for the lad, who was averse to almost any form of physical contact.

"Good afternoon, Mr. Goff," the lad said. "Won't you be seated?"

"Thank you," the man said, "but I prefer to stand. It is quite a journey to reach these netherlands."

"Indeed," the lad agreed, sitting down himself, and crossing his legs. "Brewster, you may sit, if you like." Although I usually would prefer to stand in such a situation, I felt that my sitting would clearly align myself with the lad, and not the gentleman of whom my first impressions were disagreeable. I sat, stiff and straight in the chair, for I did not want Mr. Goff to feel I was lax in my attitude or carriage as butler.

"Thank you for coming, Mr. Goff. My classmate Egbert Eddleton's father recommended you highly for the management of their country home and farms in the Cotswolds."

"So I understood, sir," the man answered.

"I have written in detail the situation and your duties here at Hillcroft, your wages, our full expectation of your confidentiality, and the fact that Brewster shall have the authority, at all times, to check that your work, especially at first, follows the normal method of administration of my father. I do not know the length of time for which you shall remain employed; my father may discharge you upon a moment's notice. However, I do guarantee wages for at least six months with a month's severance pay, even if you do not stay engaged until that time. Do you have any questions?"

"Is Mr. Holmes then, still…incommoded, sir?" That calculated pause in his sentence seemed to me an opprobrious judgment of Mr. Holmes and solidified my initial impression that I did not like the man.

"Yes," the lad said, his face betraying not one emotion. "I shall spend the rest of today and most of tomorrow showing you your responsibilities and going over the account books; I should also like to introduce you to a few of the farmers who have been with the family for generations."

"I hope the weather tomorrow is more conducive to being outside than it is today, sir."

Master Mycroft ignored that comment. "Let us now introduce you to the rest of the household staff and give you a tour of the house. Your workroom shall be in the library. First, do you require any refreshment or washing up after your trip?"

"No, sir."

The lad stood and we repeated the process we had followed that morning with the infinitely more amiable Mr. Hathoway. However, I had to keep reminding myself that the Holmeses were hiring this snarly man for his qualifications in managing the farms and business, and not to entertain us with convivial repartee.

Master Mycroft took him to see his father without me, and again I was buoyed to hear nothing but murmuring in the study. The lad took Mr. Goff to see Master Sherlock, but after brief introductions they left his room. It did not take a genius to know that Mr. Goff would not welcome being examined by the lads. His introduction to Mr. Hathoway at supper was formal and uninviting, and their conversation was stilted. After supper, Mr. Goff was left to his own devices. He read a book in German in the library, whilst Master Mycroft and Mr. Hathoway took Master Sherlock his food. They did not stay long, for the lad was still debilitated from that afternoon. By eleven o'clock, everyone was retired for the evening. I was the last to enter my chambers, and as I walked the house checking that it was secure, I remembered when the heavy silence of the house was a welcome switch from the joyous noise of the day, and I prayed that soon such happy sounds would return.

All the next day the house was very busy. Master Mycroft spent many hours with Mr. Goff, carefully and painstakingly going over all the books and reviewing the philosophy of management he wanted to see Mr. Goff uphold, especially after Mr. Goff saw the amount of money Mr. Holmes used to help the farmers with repairs, with illnesses, and in feeding Noah's family, and commented, "Too generous with the peasant class." Master Mycroft expressed in a very forthright yet even style that such benevolence was to be maintained. He then forced the caustic Mr. Goff to brave another mild Yorkshire day in touring the estate lands and visiting some farmers. On top of this Master Mycroft took meals in his brother's room with Mr. Hathoway, who already was beginning his gentle caretaking of the lad, bringing him his food, changing his nightgown, washing him, and just being there with him for silent fellowship. The lad stayed in bed and did not speak that day at all, and I know his brother's departure was preying heavily on his mind. As I walked past the room once, though, I heard Mr. Hathoway reading a riddle to the lad from another book of puzzles his brother had given for his birthday earlier this year, as he had the previous year. Force him to think, I thought, it may be his only salvation. It encouraged me that Mr. Hathoway was so attuned already to following Master Mycroft's ideas in healing the depressed lad, and I hoped he matched in persistency what he obviously had in intuition, for I felt it would be a long and tedious process working for the lad's full recovery. Especially if the lad was not to be consoled by his father's presence. I think it was quite brilliant of Master Mycroft to hire a man to watch over the young boy, for I doubt Master Sherlock would have wanted a woman as his temporary guardian; that sex had caused him nothing but devastating depression. I had no doubt that Master Sherlock would benefit greatly from his male companionship when Master Mycroft left. My stomach twisted into a knot when I hypothesized on what the house would be like without his crucial control. His leaving would create a vacuum, and who knew what would fill it? We servants dreaded his return to Eton.

Master Mycroft spent several hours after dinner alone with his brother. And then he pulled me into the drawing room and we reviewed my duties, and what events would necessitate an immediate message to him.

"What do you think of Mr. Hathoway?" he asked, when our business was completed.

"He seems perfect for Master Sherlock."

"I agree. Until father can resume his patriarchal role, I think Mr. Hathoway shall be of utmost value and importance to Sherlock."

That was my opening and I took it. "Does the lad miss his father much?"

"Yes, greatly so, as you would expect and have noticed. It is as if he has lost his father concurrently as a result of our aunt's death. But I have explained to him that Father secludes himself out of grief, as he himself is doing, and that until Father has his drinking once again under control, he is not much good to anyone. I have tried to allay Sherlock's fears that he is the cause for Father's avoidance of him, that somehow he is truly the one at fault. Although, to be honest, Father does seem to have an aversion to Sherlock, as a further drain on his own minimal nervous resources, perhaps. I have not yet been able to fully understand Father's point of view. The damned alcohol has magnified all his weaknesses. We shall just have to wait and see. Sherlock knows I have hired Mr. Goff to manage things until Father is able to reassume his role as squire and businessman. And as long as Mr. Hathoway doesn't die on us, he may be of great benefit to my brother. I expect no miracles in life, but if one wishes to occur in regards to my suffering family, my cynical mind would truly welcome it."

That last was spoken with a truthful bluntness that illustrated to me Master Mycroft's worst fears for the lad. I had noticed over these tumultuous weeks that Master Mycroft had never referred to his own mourning.

I decided to pursue that thought. "And what of yourself, Master Mycroft?"

"I am of a different ilk than my father and brother, Brewster. My aunt was dear to me as well, but…incapacitating grief is not a problem I think I shall ever experience." We let the uncomfortable subject die, the unspoken implication of his words being, "Because I will never allow emotions to overshadow my intellect." By choice, I wondered, or by victim of his genius? Master Mycroft changed the subject. "What are your perceptions of Mr. Goff?"

"I am sure he is competent in his work."

"Though invidious in personality?"

"If I may say so, sir, markedly."

Master Mycroft yawned. "I need more sleep than I have been getting. Yes, I agree Mr. Goff has some serious flaws. Try to keep him away from Sherlock, although I do not think they should have much natural contact. He does come with extremely good references, you know; he only left his position of years to help his sister's son set up a business in Portsmouth, so let's give him a chance."

Then he caught me off guard by offering his hand. I shook it, touched by the gesture.

"I'm depending on you very much, Brewster."

"You shan't regret it, sir," I answered, and he went to bed. I spent a restless night with my insomnia.

Chapter Twenty-One
Master Sherlock and Mr. Hathoway

Mycroft's leave-taking was uneventful, though traumatic for the staff, and even more so, I imagine, for his younger brother. He bade good-bye to his father in the study, then the servants, Mr. Goff and Mr. Hathoway, and again to me. He spent half an hour with his brother, and when he left the room, his jaw was clenched. He asked Mr. Hathoway to go sit with Master Sherlock, descended the stairs solemnly, entered the carriage, and was taken away by Wilcox.

The next two days proceeded smoothly.

Early in the morning of the third day, before breakfast, I could not believe my eyes when I saw Mr. Holmes walking unsteadily down the hall towards me, holding an empty bottle in his hands. He fell against the wall, and then in the common way of drinking men, pulled himself straight with an air of dignity and nobility that his very inebriation belied.

He leaned forward to me and whispered in a conspiratory manner, "So, Mycroft's gone, has he?"

"He has returned to Eton, yes, sir," I replied, a bit taken aback.

"He's smart, that one, and cunning." He tapped his head, and gently belched. My heart cried in sympathy for him. "Those gentlemen still here?"

It had only been three days. "Yes, sir, they are."

"Mycroft hired them, eh?"

"Yes."

"He's cunning, that one. It's better to stay away from him. It may well be that the fairies have him under their control; Vernet in the blood alone cannot explain it."

I said nothing. It was only a year ago at Master Sherlock's birthday party that Mr. Holmes had declined to share his opinion on the cause of his sons' peculiar genius. It disturbed me to hear him state such an odd view on that topic, and to hear him cast aspersions on Master Mycroft. Looking back, I see now that the alcohol was already playing havoc with Mr. Holmes' mind, and that those beginning suspicions were the heralds of a whole collection of future calumnies and conflicts with the innocent lad. Mr. Holmes looked up and down the hallway as if he had never been in it before, swaying off balance and using his hand upon the wall to finally stand steady. I would have given my right arm to hear him mention Master Sherlock with concern.

"I suppose I'll take a bath, Brewster. Warm some water for me, will you?"

I was more than glad to have one drawn for him. He had, I shudder to relate, not fully bathed since his sister's death, weeks ago. "Of course, sir." Aside from his desperate need to cleanse himself, he had to pass Master Sherlock's room on the way to the bathroom.

"Here," he said, handing me the bottle. "Get some more of this wine. It's good and doesn't give me heartburn. I'll be waiting in the morning room." He stumbled there and sat heavily on the sofa.

Eliza had already lit the fire in that room and was cleaning the grate and light-ing the fireplace in the drawing room. I redirected her to draw a bath for Mr. Holmes; her eyes widened and she left to do so. I got some hot coffee from Mrs. Winters and brought it to Mr. Holmes, who reclined snoring on the sofa. I woke him gently and gave him the cup, which he drank. I affected my best nonchalant attitude and asked, "Shall I tell Master Sherlock to prepare for a visit from his father?" I had absolutely no right to query him so, but I needed to for my peace of mind.

Mr. Holmes put the empty cup down on the saucer. "No," he said.

Here I almost made the biggest mistake of my life. "But, sir," I blurted out, "he needs you!"

It was only due to our long and comfortable association that he did not dis-charge me outright, but instead flared into anger.

"How dare you speak to me so!" he yelled.

Then he completely deflated and spoke as if he hadn't slept for months, his words delivered in even tones void of inflection. "He needs me? He frightens me, Brewster! I have nothing to give to him." He paused, his head rocking back and forth. "He reminds me of my wife and sister. And he's too much like Mycroft, whom I never have trusted. They stand beyond the mark of reality, one a brick, one a tear. Their oddity chills me now, and seems to carry with it a curse. I'll have no more to do with them. No, no, I just can't see him." He fell back against the seat and closed his eyes. "I dreamt Sherlock pulled me down into a hole and there we lay among the screams of Hell, and I escaped by climbing out on a ladder of bottles. I think I dreamed that. The drink is my shepherd; I shall not want. I hate the world and all the false hopes in it, Brewster. That Hathoway chap is all Sher-lock needs. Besides, if the lad had not taken her out for a walk..." He was not aware of the tear falling from one bloodshot eye until he felt the moisture hit his lip, and then he reached up and roughly wiped his face dry. "Just like him, dammit, just like him." He leaned forward, elbows perched on his knees, resting his head in his hands. "I need a drink."

I stood there frozen in place. His muffled voice appeared from under his hands. "Do you like Mr. Hathoway, Brewster?" he asked.

"Yes, sir."

"He seems...to care for Sherlock?"

"Yes." But, I added to myself, he is not his father.

"Leave me until the bath is ready. And never speak to me of this again."

I did as I was told.

In the next months, things went well, and things went poorly. Now that Master Mycroft was back at school, Mr. Holmes left the study a good deal, although that was still his principal room of habitation. It was evident that he viewed his oldest son with suspicion, for Mr. Holmes spent numerous afternoons in disparaging contemplation of Master Mycroft's motives for his actions.

"What does he want, Brewster?" he asked me once in regard to Master Mycroft, as he sat drinking whiskey in the library.

I responded, "For you and Master Sherlock to be happy and healthy again."

"Mycroft's happiness depends on his mind, not his heart. He does not love, but schemes," Mr. Holmes scoffed. "Always he has been distant, involved solely in his mentality. I fear he plots subversion, perhaps with Mr. Goff."

I said nothing. I realised how little he actually knew of Master Mycroft, and how what little he did know was being twisted by the insidious effects of his intemperate consumption. I wanted to tell him of Master Mycroft's weeping after his mother's death, but could not. I considered that a confidence between the lad and myself and did not want to break that bond without his permission. Perhaps that was also a mistake at the time; it was very hard to know what would be the best thing to do sometimes, so I would just say nothing.

Outside the study, Mr. Holmes wandered the house aimlessly, oftentimes enmeshed in an alcoholic stupor. He might sit for hours in the library or drawing room, with his ever-present bottle or glass. He was rarely fully sober, and then not for long. Wilcox endeavoured to dissuade him from riding his horse the first time he returned to the stables, but he angrily brushed aside Wilcox's pleas and rode anyway; to our relief he did not fall.

Father Metcalfe and Mr. Routh did call on him as they had promised, two or so times a week, usually individually, but also together on occasion. During those visits they found him unwilling to participate in conversation, unwilling to discuss his addiction to drink, unwilling to visit his son, unwilling to play cards, and unable to play chess. He might go for a walk, though his rheumatism had considerably worsened over the last year and he had no desire for long strolls. I was eternally grateful for the indefatigable perseverance of the two men, for their visits were often unappreciated by Mr. Holmes, yet still they returned regularly. I feel

Mr. Holmes seemed to want their company at first, for he did not turn them away when they visited, yet something held him back from joining in their proffered healing friendship. It was a wariness of fellowship, I feel, a desire to avoid the pain of loss—if they stopped coming by, or if they, too, died.

Mr. Holmes began to demonstrate anger in small ways, pushing away Wilcox; a curt and harsh tone of voice when requesting anything; a countenance full of glowering frowns and darkness. Only Mr. Goff was not a victim of his unpleasantness, for, as a direct agent of Master Mycroft, whose imagined machinations still oozed like poison in Mr. Holmes' thoughts, the estate manager was avoided by Mr. Holmes, and viewed with narrowed, suspicious eyes. Oftentimes Mr. Holmes avoided meeting Mr. Goff, and would only go to the library when Mr. Goff was out on a visit to the farmers, or in another part of the house. Mr. Holmes still ate his meals in the seclusion of his study, and he did not visit his son.

Master Sherlock struggled to overcome his depression, but it was not at all easy for the lad. In a span of less than two years, he had lost to death his dear mother—a guilt he still had not expiated from his conscience—and his dear aunt, and his father had fallen victim to the scourge of drink. The lad could hear his father walking the house through his bedroom door, I am sure, and to never hear his knock must have been unbearable for him. For two long months the lad stayed in his room, and Mr. Hathoway was there with him. We all thought that walks in the spring sun would benefit him, but Master Sherlock had absolutely no desire to leave his chambers, and was not forced to do so. His was occupied by Mr. Hathoway quizzing him on puzzles, playing chess with him, or reading to him. Mr. Hathoway ordered papers from York and London to read to the lad of various crimes and criminals; he had certainly done his homework with Master Mycroft. Sometimes Mr. Hathoway would just speak quietly to him, or sit with him patiently as the lad spent hours looking out the window. Master Sherlock's violin lay unplayed upon the dresser. At first, nothing seemed to interest him, albeit he did pay close attention to the criminal news. The words of his brother to use his mind to overcome his emotional distress seemed destined to fail again before the lad's tremendous ennui. He had heard similar words from his brother upon their mother's death, but it had been more natural for him to use his growing love of his aunt to lift him out of his deep melancholia. Now, with this gone, and his father unavailable, the lad was enmeshed in sadness, and had to learn slowly to focus on his genius, and not his spirits, to return to life.

One day, Mr. Hathoway had me bring down to the lads' study a number of the boxes he had arrived with and which we had stored so cautiously on the second floor. This I did with much anticipation. He then cleared off the large table that sat in the center of the room in between the desks of Masters Sherlock and Mycroft, removing the errant papers and books and placing them on Master Sherlock's desk where a little more clutter would go perfectly unnoticed. He then unpacked the boxes, placing on the table all manners and shapes of small and large glass containers, tubes, rubber corks, clamps, tiny spoons, a scale, round oil lamps, and bottles of chemicals. He fit this tubing here, and this glass column there, until a small laboratory sprang to life. He lay charts on the chairs and notebooks on Master Mycroft's empty desk. Several other boxes were full of books, as the ache in my back attested to.

"Well, what do you think?" Mr. Hathoway asked, standing proudly by his creation as if it were his child dressed to visit the queen.

"It's...quite impressive. Do you propose to introduce Master Sherlock to the workings of this intricate apparatus?"

"Yes, to have him use his brain in studying, safely, mind you, various chemical reactions."

"Indeed," I said, nodding, fascinated by the coloured substances and the connected glassware. "When do you think to start?"

The man rubbed his hands together and his eyes shone as he grinned. "Right now," he said, leaving the study. At the door he stopped and turned back to me, brows knitted together. "Um...is Mr. Holmes around?"

"He is in his study presently."

Mr. Hathoway's face lit up again. "Good," he said, and left.

I had some household responsibilities to attend to, but I was anxious to see if this unusual laboratory would interest the lad. I looked down the hall at Master Sherlock's bedroom; the door was ajar. I waited some minutes, my lack of attention to my duties preying upon my mind, when, quite miraculously, I saw Mr. Hathoway carrying the lad from the room towards the study, one hand covering the lad's eyes. I was indignant at first, my initial thought being that he brought the lad against his will, but then I saw that the lad was allowing himself to be conducted so. We must force the lad to eat more, and to take walks, I reprimanded myself on his weakened condition. I stood back against the wall of the study, not wanting to interfere, although I knew my presence would be noticed immediately. If they requested I leave, I would.

They entered and Mr. Hathoway sat him down in a chair by the table. He then lifted his hand off Master Sherlock's face and swept his arm to the table in a grand gesture. "Ta-da!" he exclaimed grandly.

Master Sherlock stared at the small chemical laboratory now gracing his study, his wide eyes flitting back and forth over the entire structure.

"So, what do you think, Master Sherlock?" Mr. Hathoway asked, winking at me behind the lad's back. "Shall we concoct some mysterious powder that causes cows to sprout tiny wings? Or shall we make some odious fumes rise up from boiling red liquid? Or just blow up most of Carperby by mistake? Do you know that

Justus Liebig, the renowned German chemist, as a young man once took off a good part of his roof attempting to prepare silver fulminate? We can do that here."

It was very difficult to contain my mirth and I was compelled to compress my lips together. I found myself appreciating Mr. Hathoway immensely.

Master Sherlock remained enthralled by the bottles and tubing. He reached out a thin arm and delicately touched a glass column, and then let his hand fall to a bottle of white powder.

"Calcium chloride," Mr. Hathoway explained. "When mixed with sodium borate, it creates a precipitate of calcium borate."

"I should like to see that occur," the lad said.

"Of course," Mr. Hathoway said, pulling up another chair. "I will show you how. But first, let me introduce you to all the components of chemical experimentation, and to the many readings on it, for much knowledge is essential to conducting safe experiments. Even the esteemed scientist Bunsen lost an eye through an explosion of cacodyl cyanide, although the vast majority of experiments are not so volatile." He took a book out of the box. "I have always had a tremendous interest in chemistry—ever since I worked at an apothecary as an assistant while I was going to school to earn a science degree. I even considered making it a career, and travelling to the continent to study with Wohler, Liebig, or Dumas, if any of them would have me. That never came to pass, though, as I was required to leave school early to take over the family grocery when my father's severe headaches caused him to retire. I have maintained my personal interest in chemistry, however, and love nothing more than to recreate the experiments of men brilliant enough to have discovered new thoughts and new substances. And it amuses me to work on ideas of my own, none of which have rocked the foundations of chemistry, but have been a constant source of satisfaction to me. I would enjoy very much sharing this hobby of mine with you, Master Sherlock, if you should so desire."

The lad could not take his eyes off the glassware. "I do so desire, Mr. Hathoway. I've heard of chemistry, and it fascinates me."

"Excellent. Most excellent," the man said. "All right, first off, we shall have to get you reading German; you already know French, and those countries have been and still are the leading producers of chemists in the world. Aside from us English, of course, and a Swede or Belgian here and there. I shall start your education by telling you what I understand of the science of chemistry, and then, when through your readings you are more learned than I—probably in a month or so—you can begin teaching me. For, to be honest, many of the concepts of the science I struggle to comprehend. You, no doubt, shall grasp them as a sailor does his anchor. I shall also introduce you to all the equipment of chemical analysis and the rules of running a laboratory, even our small one, safely. Then I'll show you many basic yet varied reactions until we feel confident you will surpass me in creating other more insightful experiments. In this way we may both benefit from each other."

"Your confidence in my progression in this field is flattering, though probably inaccurate," the lad stated, examining a jar of white powder. It was clear as could be that Master Sherlock was terribly interested in learning chemistry; his eyes darted back and forth taking in all the equipment, all the powders, he lifted up one book after another, going through its pages.

"However," the lad continued, "learning German is agreeable to me, for there are philosophers as well as, now, chemists whom I wish to read in their own language. I shall request from Mr. Wharton that he begin such instruction."

"Yes, and Mr. Goff may be of service, as well," Mr. Hathoway responded. Then, upon seeing the look of distaste on the lad's face, he added, "Or…maybe not. Well, I know some German myself; we'll muddle through together."

Mr. Hathoway took a deep breath. "Well, let's just begin with the basics." He rummaged through a box and brought out several volumes. "Here, read these books: *Histoire de la Chimie* by Hoefer; and Scheel's *Chemical Essays in English.* The former will give you a brief history of chemistry, and the latter will introduce you to one of the most eminent, observant, and brilliant chemists of the last century, who discovered oxygen, chlorine, glycerin, uric acid, the pigment Scheel's green, and who looked at innumerable other aspects of chemistry. Although the theory of phlogiston, in which Scheel was a devout believer, has been deposed, you shall see how one goes about proper chemical experimentation and analysis. Also, read this list of "Twenty Rules to Follow in the Laboratory" I wrote for myself some years ago and have followed to the letter ever since. They are self-explanatory and contain mostly common sense, but I shall firmly insist that at all times you work under their guidelines."

He handed them to the lad. "I have as good a library on chemical studies as a hobbyist may acquire. You are welcome to read any and all of my books. I shall put them on the bookshelves over there for your ease of access."

"Thank you," the lad said, "I appreciate that very much." I saw a touch of colour come to his face in his eagerness to begin studying, and my heart swelled at the sight.

Mr. Hathoway turned to me. "Perhaps, also, Mr. Brewster would be kind enough to have Denkins build us some more shelves for the chemicals, for I should like them organized and stored correctly."

"That should be no problem, Mr. Hathoway," I said.

"Excellent. I will help you with the details later." Mr. Hathoway picked up what looked like a thin metal candleholder. "Master Sherlock, is this tiring you out? If so, I can explain the equipment after a nap."

"No," the lad shook his head strongly side to side. "I'm not tired at all. Please tell me now."

I dared to hope the lad's energy was returning in response to this new interest, and that his long seclusion in his bedroom might indeed be ending.

Mr. Hathoway nodded his head. "Very well, then, let's continue. Let me go over with you the equipment one uses in chemistry. This is called a Bunsen burner, after Robert Wilhelm Bunsen, the German chemist who recently developed it. It is one of my prized possessions. He is still alive, by the way, working with just one eye as a professor in Heidelberg. This burner is capable of creating an extremely hot, almost nonluminous flame; air enters here at the base and mixes with gas, which is connected to the burner by this tube. Bunsen also created the spectroscope, which I have a picture of somewhere in one of my journals. He used that to discover the elements rubidium and cesium. He has also created the Bunsen valve, and other amazing inventions." He stopped and took a deep breath. "Excuse me for digressing so, Master Sherlock, but I must admit that I am rather excited to have someone with whom to share my chemical interests."

"Of course. Please continue, Mr. Hathoway," the lad said, eagerly. Mr. Hathoway took another moment to compose himself, and when he resumed his voice was steady and calm.

"These other burners on the table are only, as you no doubt perceive, small alcohol and oil lamps, which suffice quite well for me though they take more time in heating liquids than the Bunsen burner. Of course, since we have no gas in your home, they are what we shall have to use." He handed the burner to the lad, who studied it thoroughly.

"Now, let me review for you the glassware. This flat-bottomed cylindrical vessel is called a beaker, and is used for mixing, and then for pouring, as the pointed lip obviously shows. With these glass rods we can stir mixtures without having metal contaminate the experiment."

The lesson went on for quite a while, and I left, like Master Sherlock, feeling better than I had in months.

No cows sprouted wings, and no explosions occurred, but noxious fumes arose on occasion. We servants learned to dread the use of any chemical that contained sulphur or a few other noxious compounds, and as a general rule the windows in the study were left open day and night. Mrs. Birchall, who proved to be particularly susceptible to developing devastating headaches from sulphuric fumes, was granted a dispensation to avoid cleaning the study if she could detect any such odor in the air. She garnered the courage to enter the room only once or twice a month. As a result, the room fell into complete disarray, but neither Master Sherlock or Mr. Hathoway seemed to mind.

Books on chemistry, what there was available on the subject, were frequently sent for, the lad having written a number of booksellers in London with an open request that all books on chemistry in English, French, or German should be sent to him. Since I was in charge of Mr. Goff, I allowed Master Sherlock an allowance for purchasing books and chemicals. A growing category of chemicals were also, therefore, procured, and Denkins built three sets of sturdy shelves to put the bottles upon in the study—one set for solid chemicals, and one each for inorganic and organic acids, all of them away from the others, because, as Mr. Hathoway told me, they were dangerous when mixed together and needed to be left alone by all the household staff. Jars of water were kept full for using in experiments and cleaning the apparatus, and a system for dealing with the waste products was created by Mr. Hathoway.

After that first day, Master Sherlock walked daily down the hall himself, still in nightgown, slippers, and dressing gown, and spent hours reading from books, reading from Mr. Hathoway's notes, and playing with the chemicals with the precise directions Mr. Hathoway detailed for him. He had become enamoured with chemistry, and it was plain to see that whenever he was engaged in serious experimentation, his depression lifted more so than at any other time. He did not seem to mind the stuffy and occasionally odoriferous atmosphere that sent all of us, even at times Daisy and Mr. Hathoway, running from the room; to him it was just one more observation to note and docket. Often, by the time we servants felt the study's air had diluted itself into a breathable composition again, we would re-enter and find Master Sherlock diligently at work scribbling in his notebook.

"Goodness, Master Sherlock, does not the foul atmosphere of the room drive you to distraction?" I would ask, covering my mouth with my handkerchief.

The lad looked up from his writing, slightly perturbed at my discomfort. "On the contrary, Brewster. I find that the concentrated conditions seem to enhance my ability to think, and to abnegate all distractions." Only once or twice did he quietly request from Mrs. Winters her headache medicine, which now and then made the rounds among the staff.

Mr. Holmes must have been aware at times of his son's chemical activities. Once Master Sherlock enlarged an experiment and made a beaker full of "Mr. Hathoway's Special Wake-up Gas" instead of just a teaspoonful—the study air wafted down into the drawing room and even reached the morning room and library, where Mr. Holmes sat brooding. When Mr. Holmes inquired as to the source of the odor, and I told him, he surprisingly did not seem to mind beyond a grunt and an expletive. Now that the lad left his bedchamber, however, Mr. Holmes avoided the first floor assiduously, going into the drawing room only after 11:00 P.M., when Master Sherlock was in bed. When either Mr. Routh or Father Metcalfe visited— still, for each man, once a week—they were brought to the library.

I cannot relate to you how uncomfortable it was for the entire staff to have Mr. Holmes still so resolute in the avoidance of seeing his son, and how Hillcroft seemed split into two separate households: that of Mr. Holmes, and that of his son. The tension revolving around Mr. Holmes, his constant drinking, his increasing irritability, and his refusal to readmit his son into his life was dreadful. To make matters worse, it seemed that the longer Mr. Holmes affected such an attitude, the more firmly he became ensconced in it. He believed more and more that Mr. Hathoway was the answer for the lad, and that he was relieved of all need even to attempt to be a father to Master Sherlock. How Master Sherlock felt can only be guessed, as the subject of his father was never discussed in his presence after Master Mycroft left. However, his continued melancholia when not in his study persisted, and I have no doubt the rejection by his father became a more acute pain to him than his aunt's death.

For a lad who used to cause havoc through the entire house and surrounding countryside, his living life in the space of two rooms was disheartening. How I longed to see him throw a stick to Daisy as he walked home from his village friends again, or play classical music on his violin in the morning room. The lad never went to his father, for he knew his father would not receive him.

Master Sherlock still did not feel up to resuming his full studies with Mr. Wharton, but had his former tutor send him primers on German. With his own intellect and Mr. Hathoway's help, he was able to begin an apt study of the language.

Mornings were the worst for Master Sherlock's moods. He awoke to another day with his mother and aunt still and eternally dead. Then, upon my bringing his breakfast, no matter how stiff and formal or friendly and relaxed I endeavoured to be, he immediately observed in me that his father still drank. He suffered much after that, and even the tender ministrations of Mr. Hathoway, and his puzzles and reading, afforded no reaction from the lad for some hours. By late morning, though, his interest in his books on chemistry began to overtake his despair, and he would sit reading abstruse texts. By the afternoon, he would generally come out of his depression, and go to the laboratory in his study and learn from Mr. Hathoway about famous chemists and their works, and then do some experiments himself. Less and less were his days lost to mourning now. Once as I walked past his bedroom door, I heard the single pluck of a violin string; I stopped to listen, my heart aflutter, but heard nothing more. Still, we were all greatly encouraged.

In June, after the second month of studying chemistry, Mrs. Winters crossed herself three times and insisted that if Master Sherlock were to spend time cooped up in the study with the vapors and the fumes, he must be taken outside for some fresh air.

"He'll have bad lungs in a year or two, and will wind up spitting up blood by the time he's twelve," she predicted.

I agreed with her concerns, but did not quite see how to implement her idea of getting him outside. It had turned into a rainy June, but Mrs. Winters would be appeased even if he sat in the stables for a bit, with the stable doors open wide.

I approached Mr. Hathoway with the idea, and he offered to discuss it with Master Sherlock; to my joy the lad acquiesced. So several times a week, after hours in his study, he desultorily dressed, and on my signal indicating his father was out of sight, he descended the stairs with Mr. Hathoway. On sunny days, he sat on the back lawn or walked a little with his caretaker; on rainy days, they did indeed sit in the wide stable entrance, protected from the downpour but still enjoying the fresh air, as he read a book. They would return carefully, watching for me to either encourage their proceeding or wave them off until the coast was clear of Mr. Holmes. Never once did the lad and his father encounter one another, to the sadness of the former and the desire of the latter. This was the situation of the household when Master Mycroft returned home at the beginning of July.

Chapter Twenty-Two

Mr. Holmes' Grief

I had kept Master Mycroft apprised of the situation in weekly notes to him, and he knew of the laboratory, the time spent sitting outside, and Mr. Holmes' relentless shunning of Master Sherlock. However, actually to be in the house and see the separation of his father and brother still occurring, to the great detriment of his younger brother, quite agitated and, I daresay, outraged Master Mycroft.

Immediately upon arriving that night, a day earlier than expected, the lad conferred with Mr. Hathoway, who met him at the door. They spent half an hour discussing Master Sherlock and where he stood in terms of the full recovery of his spirits. After a grateful clap on the arm of Mr. Hathoway, Master Mycroft went to greet his brother, asking me to join him. Master Sherlock was sitting in his chair by the window petting Daisy. Master Mycroft knocked once we entered the dimly lit room. "Sherlock, I'm back," he said, standing by the door.

Master Sherlock swung his head around so quickly, the motion was a blur. He looked at his brother, his countenance awash with emotions, then turned away, his teeth biting his lower lip, his hands resting on the dog sitting between his legs. Master Mycroft glanced at me, but I was no help to him in understanding Master Sherlock's behavior. The elder brother then entered the room and sat in the chair adjacent to the young lad.

"I can understand the absence of cake and decorations, since I have arrived home a day earlier than planned; however, your lack of *joie de vivre* at my appearance is somewhat baffling. I should have thought, Sherlock, you would have been glad to see me, as I am to see you."

The lad slowly faced his brother again, tears moistening his eyes. "But I haven't done very well at using my intellect to overcome my depression."

Ah, the lad's reaction at seeing his brother became clear to me, so it must have with Master Mycroft as well. The lad was afraid his brother would find fault with his continued struggle with melancholia, and such a reprimand by his one remaining affectionate relative would be a crushing blow.

Master Mycroft sat back calmly in his chair. "Oh? I have it on good information that you are quite avidly studying the science of chemistry, and too frequently smelling up the study, and occasionally the house, with all sorts of noxious fumes as a result."

"But otherwise, I often fail," the lad said honestly, anxiety gaining in his voice.

"Quite so, quite so," Master Mycroft said. "Still, I am proud of what you have achieved. Perhaps tomorrow you will show me one of your most minimally offensive endeavours."

Master Sherlock searched his brother's face for any sign of insincerity and found none. He threw himself around his brother's neck, holding tightly; Master Mycroft awkwardly embraced his brother's thin body.

"I'll show you how to test for iron with ammonium hydroxide," Master Sherlock said, all trace of anxiety gone. "And the various types of precipitating reactions. I'm very glad you're home, Mycroft. Papa..." He let the sentence die, and Master Mycroft did not comment on it.

I have often thought about that visit of Master Mycroft, how our hopes and desires for a family reconciliation were so high with him finally home. I had never thought a man could change so drastically in so short a time as did Mr. Holmes from the moment of learning of his sister's death in February to the end of July. Of course, his personality had begun altering upon his wife's death almost two years previously, but so magnified was the transformation now that it seemed an entirely new man had been created out of the drunken depths of Mr. Holmes' mind. An angry, suspicious, and unreasonable man now stood where once a man of gentleness and affection had epitomized responsible fatherhood.

Tired from his journeying and in no mood to meet his father that night, Master Mycroft spent the rest of the evening with Master Sherlock. He chatted with the lad about certain political events and a few other topics before he and the lad settled into an air of silent comfort.The next morning was overcast and gloomy, and by midmorning a light drizzle began that would not cease for the rest of the day. Master Mycroft arose late and breakfasted with his brother and Mr. Hathoway. The always present informality that had been part and parcel of the Holmeses' household had reached a zenith since the deaths, and meals were regularly eaten anywhere, in any attire, at any time, due to the capricious nature of Master Sherlock. The lad would not be hungry for half a day, and refuse to eat at all, and then at three o'clock he would want a full-course meal. Oftentimes, it developed that his working on his chemical inquiries would greatly stimulate his appetite, and some time during the afternoon he would request something to eat; unless, of course, he became so involved in his experiments he forgot to eat altogether. Mr. Hathoway, that kind soul, ate as many of his meals as possible with the lad; unless his own hunger grew too loud for him to further ignore, and then he would himself ask for some food. Of course, this meant that meals for the servants could be off schedule as well, as they were called to work during normal meal times and granted rest at other odd intervals. This caused some little aggravation for Mrs. Winters and the rest of us at first, but the good Cook was able to become quite adaptable. For their part, neither Master Sherlock nor Mr. Hathoway ever complained of food too cool or slightly wilted, nor chastised the hurried and perhaps unkempt arrival of a servant who had been eating when called, for they were aware of the inconvenience they created in the staff by their whims. Master Mycroft, as well, was always more interested in the quantity of food prepared than in its quality or exact moment of serving. Only the impeccably dressed Mr. Goff was adamant in an ordered and punctual appearance of meals three times daily in the dining room, which we provided for his solitary comfort.

That morning, after the late breakfast, Master Mycroft gave his younger brother a new puzzle book and a volume on the biographies of varied highwaymen and murderers of last century.

"Well," he said, "I had better see that things are all in order at Hillcroft."

Master Sherlock held the two books, opening them and looking at various pages. "Will you be seeing Papa?" he asked in an offhand way.

"Yes."

The lad glanced up at his brother but then quickly reimmersed himself in his page turning. Nothing more was spoken between them as Master Mycroft left the room.

He descended the stairs for a conference with Mr. Goff on estate and business matters. To his benefit, I must state that Mr. Goff ran the affairs of the Holmeses with a much more polished flair and with much more success than he conducted his own personal affairs. In the four months of his stewardship, no problems had developed and all proceeded smoothly, both in Huddersfield and with the farmers—noteworthy facts which did lessen the staffs' dislike of him. Master Mycroft conversed with Mr. Goff in the library for just a few minutes, to be assured of the man's trustworthiness and competency, and was, I'm sure, repelled by Mr. Goff's curt manner of speaking and irritating character. The lad then said hello to the rest of the servants, and thanked them for their continued patience with and service to his brother. After viewing the horses with Wilcox, Master Mycroft returned to the house, damp from the rain, and, his face a mask of hidden meanings, proceeded with me down the hall to his father's study.

He knocked several times, and announced, "Father, it's me, Mycroft. May I come in?"

He had the master key, which I had held ever since his departure for Eton. I hoped he would not be reduced to using it.

After an interminable wait, I heard a short muffled reply from in the room. I could not discern the words from where I stood observing the lad, but I saw Master Mycroft bristle at their utterance.

"Look here, Father," the lad said with asperity. "I have the master key and shall use it if you do not grant me entrance under your own power. I wish to talk with you this afternoon about certain matters of importance to both of us. Please let me in."

It took some time, but the door finally opened. Mr. Holmes appeared, completely disheveled, and already well into the bottle of wine he held in his hand. "Ah, Mycroft, my genius son. How happy I am to see you back from your studies far from home. Have you glad tidings to share with your father, dear Mycroft?" Mr. Holmes' tone dripped with sarcasm. Master Mycroft did not respond, but when his father waved him into the study, using the hand that held the bottle of wine, in a grand though insincere gesture, he went in, Daniel in the lion's den.

After fifteen minutes of quiet exchange the meeting suddenly took on an intensity on the part of Mr. Holmes, to the extent that I could clearly hear his vitriolic exclamations through the study door. Master Mycroft's voice rose slightly as well, though never neared the volume of his father's.

"How dare you attempt to command me!" Mr. Holmes yelled. "I shall do whatever I please, and as your father, I forbid you to comment on my actions."

"I command you to do nothing, Father," Master Mycroft responded. "You misinterpret my words. I merely request that you visit Sherlock. It is tragic that for five months you have not seen him. His recovery is considerably yet understandably slower due to your absence."

Mr. Holmes growled, "That Hathoway chap is doing fine. Sherlock doesn't need me, now, just like you never did. You have finished what the fairies began." After a pause, he added, "We are all cursed."

Master Mycroft seemed to be speechless for a moment, and then chose to ignore that last absurd comment. "Actually, for all our intellectual similarities, Sherlock does need you, now, as in the past. While I encourage him to use his mental powers to overcome his depression, I never endeavour to break him of his affectionate regard for you, which is still profound, and wanting of your once reciprocal love. You must know this; why do you continue to avoid him so?"

The depth of Mr. Holmes' imbalance was made clear in his next statement. Was this what he had pondered all those solitary hours wandering the house, riding alone through the countryside, or just sitting for days in his study? Were these the thoughts the drink had fostered and fed?

"The fairies have cursed us," Mr. Holmes declared. "They made you two, and now they weave their unnatural spells into forces which kill those who surround you. I'll have no part of either of you. My wine protects me."

Master Mycroft betrayed his exasperation and impatience at his father. "What utter balderdash! Have you gone fully insane?"

"Nothing will happen to you two," Mr. Holmes continued to ramble. "Oh no, just the rest of us. It is the only thing that makes sense."

Master Mycroft tried again. "Father, please, listen to yourself. There is no rational component to your thoughts, as there used to be. What has brought about such a ridiculous belief?"

"Death has. Whomever Sherlock loves, dies. It's unnatural, and so are both of you. It's not me, for I knew Robert and Maggie for years before you both were born and no harm came to them. Maybe it's not you either, for love is foreign to you; but you feed off the same plate as does Sherlock. I'll have no part of either of you," he repeated, spitting his words out viciously. "You and Mr. Goff rule the estate, and Mr. Hathoway can work with Sherlock. I have my wine." His voice then lowered and I had to strain to listen. "The fairies have won; they want you two for themselves. If there are no such beings, then the fates themselves are to blame. I have no love left to offer Sherlock. Neither have I love left for you, though you live at peace without it. I see the lad and anger swells in me, hatred for the world, hatred of the dreams I had of wife and children, and hatred of the reality of death and geniuses. My geniuses. One a stranger to emotions, one drowning in them, both a strain on me I cannot bare." He took a very long drink from the bottle of wine. "This is my gift to you both, your salvation. My love has emptied from me like I empty these bottles. Sherlock will live, and will learn to be strong like you as well. He cannot cry his way through life forever."

Master Mycroft offered numerous protestations to those utterly nonsensical words for some minutes; however, nothing was accomplished but to rouse his father's ire further.

"Get out! Get the hell out!" his father finally demanded of his eldest son.

I dashed down the hall and was twenty feet from the door when Master Mycroft came out into the hallway. He saw me, and my slightly winded appearance no doubt ruined any subterfuge I had meant to maintain regarding not eavesdropping upon his conversation with his father.

"Close the damn door!" erupted from the study, and Master Mycroft obeyed his father without any undue force. Unless I imagined it, I thought I heard something hard land against the door moments after it was shut. Master Mycroft did not react, but strode down the hallway passing me without a glance. He secluded himself in his own bedroom, where he stayed most of the afternoon.

Around four o'clock he went into the study, probably remembering that he had asked Master Sherlock to show him a chemical reaction the night before.

"Well, Sherlock," he began, upon entering the room where Master Sherlock and Mr. Hathoway sat among vials of coloured reagents, "show me the skills you have acquired in your initial studies of chemistry. I believe you said you would illustrate a test for iron or show me various types of precipitating reactions."

Master Sherlock had been watching his brother quite intensely as soon as he had entered the room. Master Mycroft pulled a chair close to the table for an excellent view of the bubbling liquids and intricate glassware, studiously ignoring his brother's fervent perusal of his person.

"Well, Sherlock, show me your new hobby," he said, still avoiding his younger brother's questioning countenance.

Master Sherlock fully understood. His jaw clenched and he lowered his head against his chest, his eyes closed. Mr. Hathoway stood beside him and raised a hand to comfort the lad. Master Mycroft gave a sharp shake of his head to firmly dissuade the man from doing so.

"Brother, tell me, what occurs with this simmering blue liquid?" Master Mycroft asked. There was no answer. He asked another question, "Shall I add some of this white powder into this heated liquid?" At that, the lad looked up and saw Master Mycroft pulling a cork from a jar. Master Mycroft raised his eyebrows at his younger brother. "Shall I?"

Master Sherlock offered a quick smile, his lips then resuming a thin evenness. "Not unless, as I understand it, you wish to organize an immediate evacuation of the entire North Riding." At a quizzical look from his elder brother, Master Sherlock added, "Smelly!" his face scrunching up and his fingers pinching his nostrils together.

Master Mycroft studied the bottle he held. "Dear me, that would never do." He put the cork back in the bottle and placed it once more on the table. "Will you not show me how one tests for iron, then?" he asked again, his gentle persistence finally winning over the lad. Master Sherlock took a deep breath and turned to the apparatus on the table.

"It is a simple set of steps, utilizing ferric ammonium sulfate, sodium bisulphate, and ammonium chloride," Master Sherlock began, focusing his attention upon the equipment and chemicals before him. "However, one hopes Mr. Hathoway will prevent me from heating the final mixture and then ignorantly adding sodium carbonate to the liquid, which, we now know, causes a markedly uncontrollable spilling over of liquid onto the table and any nearby clothes. Brewster, I'm sure you recollect that was the one where we had to discard a total of five pieces of apparel."

"I remember it well, sir," I said ruefully.

That afternoon a number of experiments went satisfactorily for both the lads. They dined late, and out of respect for his brother's request, Master Sherlock dressed and ate in the dining room. Mr. Goff was just leaving the table as the lads and Mr. Hathoway entered.

"Highly irregular dining habits," he scoffed as he left.

"Mr. Goff," Master Mycroft rejoined, somewhat miffed, causing the gentleman to stop in his steps, "I am paying you to look after the business of Hillcroft House, not to offer unwarranted opinions on the behavior of me or my family. Is that quite clear, sir?"

It galled him to respond. "Yes, sir. It is." At a wave of Master Mycroft's hand, he left the room. Dinner was somewhat enlivened after that.

Chapter Twenty-Three
The Confrontation

J wish I could say that the entire summer passed in such a manner, and that once more, Master Mycroft's presence was the Maypole about which everything danced at Hillcroft House. I wish I could say that Master Sherlock improved dramatically with the reserved yet caring mindfulness his brother offered him. I wish everything could have been different, but it wasn't; and now, in this hotel room, I can do nothing but unhappily relate the true events that rapidly coalesced that week.

Blame cannot be laid at the feet of Master Mycroft, for he did the best he could, even if things did worsen as a result of his tireless yet completely ineffectual efforts to change his father's attitude toward him and Master Sherlock. For the next two days, the lad once again was admitted to the study, though each day Mr. Holmes lost his temper more quickly and fiercely. As Master Mycroft left the study on the third day, I clearly heard "And don't come back!" follow him out the door.

Master Mycroft did not attempt a communication with his father on the fourth day, but instead met with Father Metcalfe when that gentleman arrived as usual to see Mr. Holmes; Mr. Routh had finally ceased his visitations as Mr. Holmes' temper flared even at him. Master Mycroft relayed to Father Metcalfe what his father had told him in their first conversation, and how their relations had deteriorated since. He then asked for advice as to how he should continue to proceed with his father.

Father Metcalfe leaned back heavily in the chair. "I have seen this before, you know, this perversion in people that grief and intemperance create, changing and ruining a good gentleman, or even at times a good woman. It always sickens me and draws upon all my religious strength to ward off despair at the misery of mankind." The man shifted in his chair. "Oh, my, such is not what you need to hear for your own peace of mind. Forgive me, Mycroft."

"Have you advice to offer me?" the lad simply asked.

"This is a delicate area, young sir. However, letting him remain in inebriated solitude will not foster a reconciliation, as these past five months have proven, and your pleading for his behavior to change on behalf of your brother suffices for naught, as well. Perhaps something drastic needs to be done." Father Metcalfe rubbed his clean-shaven chin in thought.

"Such as?" Master Mycroft asked, leaning forward with interest.

"Well, I wonder what would happen if you just brought your brother to him. It may crack through these sadly absurd walls he has built around himself. Of course, it may also do nothing but excite his anger, and a blatant rejection of Sherlock with the lad in his presence will hurt the lad greatly. Then again, it is obvious your brother is emotionally distraught now. It seems young Sherlock can lose nothing that he has not lost already, and may gain from his father if God wills it to be."

"I have little faith in God, rector," Master Mycroft admitted.

Father Metcalfe took no offense. "I understand. However, the result of such a course of action is unknown to us all; a few prayers of aid will not be unfounded."

"I will think on your advice," the lad said. Father Metcalfe then attempted to see Mr. Holmes, but was not admitted, and soon gave up trying.

"I say, he is in a mood today," the kind, patient man said, as I gave him his hat, gloves, and walking stick. He shook Master Mycroft's hand and said, "Good luck, lad, and notify me if you need to. I should be quite willing to be present if you choose to bring young Sherlock to him."

"Thank you, rector," the lad replied. "However, I should prefer it remain a private family matter at that time."

Father Metcalfe left, and the lad spent that day and the next in solemn contemplation of Father Metcalfe's idea.

He asked Mr. Hathoway and me to join him in the drawing room after dinner on the fifth night, after Master Sherlock had returned to his bedchamber.

"I wish to hear what you both think of Father Metcalfe's idea," he said after the three of us had been seated in a circle of chairs. "Of bringing Sherlock forthright into my father's presence."

Mr. Hathoway leapt in. "What can be lost? Mr. Holmes may reject the lad? He has done that every day for five months. True, for Master Sherlock to be in the actual presence of his father and be told by his father that he does not care to see him could be injurious to the lad's spirits for a while. But, I wonder if such a final statement may also be a stepping stone to recovery, as all Master Sherlock's nervous energy in regards to his father could then be completely rechanneled into avenues of healing, not wasted uselessly on anticipating that which shall evidently not be forthcoming. And, of course, he will still have you for guidance and support, Master Mycroft, and me, and the rest of the servants, who are all so fond of the lad."

"It appears you have been doing some thinking on the matter, Mr. Hathoway," Master Mycroft noted.

"I have, sir."

"And you, Brewster? What is your view on the subject?"

"I fear I lack the judgment to offer a valuable opinion, sir. On the one hand, I see the lad slowly improving, thanks to Mr. Hathoway and his chemistry laboratory.

And I do agree that Master Sherlock must spend a good deal of thought cogitating upon the rift his father has created between them. However, I am loath fully to recommend bringing the lad to his father, for Mr. Holmes' thoughts and actions remain incomprehensible to me. He has grown unpredictable to me, to us all, I daresay. I shouldn't want anything worse to develop in the house as a result of such a bold plan, and although I do not know what more unpleasant situation could occur, perhaps remaining in this state in which we find ourselves is better than risking a more deleterious one."

Master Mycroft listened to my words with more respect than I felt they should receive. He arose and paced back and forth across the room, his tall, fleshy body not nearly as imposing as his two small, grey, yet brilliant irises.

Finally he sat down again. "You have both offered me important insights. I thank you for that. I find that my decision-making abilities fare more competently in the impersonal affairs of politics and world events, where ideas and interpretations come clear to me without effort. However, such a decision as this rests more upon intuition, and the hope that the outcome shall by chance be favorable to my wishes. I have no factual data or historical information to aid my choice of action. Both of you have pointed out facets of this situation I was already aware of; however, your similar thoughts on the matter were reassuring to me. I may regret this decision, but, if Sherlock agrees, I should like to take him to Father tomorrow. It may be a horrible mistake, or it may bring my father once more into his parental role. As I have told Sherlock a number of times, it is a capital mistake to theorize without any data; however, personal relations are one area where only theory exists."

He took a deep breath. "We shall see what we shall see. And if either of you are praying men, I should welcome and be grateful for your heavenly supplications in regarding whatever may occur tomorrow." We stood, and Master Mycroft left the drawing room.

Mr. Hathoway murmured to me, "May God be with them tomorrow."

I fervently agreed.

In the morning, after breakfast in Master Sherlock's chamber, Master Mycroft asked Mr. Hathoway and me to stay whilst he brought his plan to his brother's attention. We anxiously acquiesced, and Master Sherlock, sitting in his bed, observed us with worried eyes himself. Master Mycroft sat in the chair next to his bed, and the caretaker and I stood at the foot. Master Mycroft took a moment to compose his thoughts before speaking.

"Sherlock, Mr. Hathoway, Brewster, and I have an idea we should appreciate your opinion on. I have spoken to Father Metcalfe about Father, who grows more belligerent each time I seek his company to inquire if he might once again initiate contact with you. I have not told you of the specifics of those meetings; however, let me just relate that the alcohol poisons his mind with ridiculous concerns and convictions that my words cannot transform into rationality. Father Metcalfe suggests that we should simply take you to see Father, and hope that upon seeing you, Father is struck into lucidity and welcomes you back into his life. We have no facts to ensure that such a reaction will occur, Sherlock; and indeed, we must face the dreadful possibility that Father will not react thusly, but instead will order you to begone, or something of the like. What we want to know is whether you will cooperate with our plan, or if you should prefer not to meet with him. We shall in no way be disappointed with whatever decision you make, for your happiness is the center around which our idea revolves. If your choice for yourself is not to confront Father personally, no man could judge you wrong. Pray, tell me what you think."

Master Sherlock had listened to each word of his brother's speech as if they were the only things existing in the universe. When Master Mycroft finished, the room grew deathly silent as we waited for the lad to speak.

"I should like to see Papa," he said after a minute. "I need to know."

Master Mycroft gave Mr. Hathoway and me a curt nod. "Very well, then. We shall go to him in an hour. Sherlock, I feel that it would be better for you to be dressed when we appear before Father."

"I'll get dressed, Mycroft."

"Good. Shall we gather ourselves at the bottom of the stairs in an hour?"

If it had been two hours, I think my stomach would have hardened into stone. As it was, I regretted that we had decided to discuss seeing Mr. Holmes after break-fast, as the eggs and toast sat uncomfortably undigested. I spent the time inform-ing the rest of the staff what was soon to occur, and then took a small quaff of the brandy Mrs. Winters hid in the pantry and offered as a gentle stomachic. I felt bet-ter after that, and busied myself aimlessly cleaning throughout the house until the hour had passed.

Master Sherlock was washed, sharply dressed, his hair was brushed into per-fect order. He was four feet and a half tall, well on the way to the six-foot height his brother had already attained by age sixteen. Both also shared thin black hair and the intensity of their grey eyes. However, so singularly lean was the lad, that I doubt he weighed a pound over seventy-five, a weight his brother had surpassed by age four and now easily weighed more than twice that. It seemed to me that their bodies, far from being simply the genetic expression of the Holmes lines in Master Mycroft and the Lecomtes in Master Sherlock, perhaps were also the phys-ical presentation of their unique individualities; Master Mycroft so firmly and immovably planted in the solid and stolid confidence of his mind, and Master Sher-lock so fragile as a result of his constant struggle with his inherent sensibilities.

Once we were in a circle together, nodding our heads in response to Master Mycroft's "Ready?" we progressed down the hallway to the door of Mr. Holmes' study. Master Mycroft did not knock, but just took out the master key and in a swift move, unlocked the door and opened it. I do not believe that Master Sherlock's heart was beating at all then, his face was so pale. As one we stepped into the room, which was messy beyond description, and stood just inside the door. Master Mycroft was in front, with Master Sherlock to his right side; Mr. Hathoway and I followed behind. I was aware by some sense that the other servants stood nearby in the corridor to enhance their eavesdropping—I fear I had not been a very good role model for them.

At the sound of our entrance, Mr. Holmes, leaning forward onto his desk across the room with his forehead resting on his arms, turned his face towards us and opened his eyes. It took Mr. Holmes' benumbed brain a second to interpret what our presence meant, and then he stood up as if his chair had suddenly burst into flames, knocking over his seat in the process.

Mycroft rushed to speak first. "Father, we thought that since you did not feel up to visiting Sherlock, we would have the courtesy to bring him to you."

I came around to stand by Master Sherlock on his right; the lad's eyes flitted back and forth between his father and the floor by his feet. He stood stock still and mute. We awaited Mr. Holmes' reply, not daring to breathe. In an instant all our fervent hopes came crashing to the ground. I felt nauseous with dismay.

"How dare you. How dare you! I told you I did not wish to see him. I told you to stay out." I'm sure that each word that Mr. Holmes said tore apart the young lad's heart. "How dare you disobey me so blatantly, and in the company of servants."

"Father, can you not even say hello to your youngest son, whom such a short while ago you loved so much?" Master Mycroft spoke with a combination of hopelessness and anger in his voice. He placed his right hand on the shoulder of his younger brother.

Mr Holmes' face grew livid. "You arrogant, wretched lad!" he spat at Master Mycroft. He stomped towards us, and I saw Master Mycroft's body stiffen, as if he was preparing to defend himself or his brother. Mr. Holmes seemed insane in his ire, his words punctuated with spittle and violent gesturing. "Can you never once in your life follow an order from me? Am I a servant for you to command as you will, or do you consider me just an ignorant fool to be disregarded as unimportant? I am your father, damn it! I have had enough of your insolence! Daily I am buffeted by the winds of your insistent clamoring for me to do what you want me to. Daily I tell you to go and leave me be. Now, I will be assured of the end of your meddling from this moment on. I have ever been too lenient with you and your unnatural intelligence—that ends now. You have driven me to the limit of my tolerance, Mycroft, and shall suffer the consequences. What I say from now on will be the law, and that is that."

Master Mycroft hastened to appease his father's mood. In a second everything had gone so horribly wrong. "Father, I'm sorry—"

"Shut up!" Mr. Holmes yelled. I feared he should suffer apoplexy then and there; in retrospect, all would have been better if he had. Instead, he continued his unreasonable and uncontrollable diatribe. We all stood frozen by his terrible temper.

"I will grant you one favor, Mycroft, before I order you to follow my decree as your father. You wish me to say hello to Sherlock?" He stood face to face with his eldest son. "Do you? Do you?" Master Mycroft returned his father's penetrating gaze through narrowed eyes; his jaw clenched, though he said nothing.

Mr. Holmes knelt down in front of Master Sherlock, who had closed his eyes once his father had begun screaming. Tears fell down his face. "Hello, Sherlock," he said, with a cruel smirk. The lad did not respond. "How are you today? Have you taken anyone else out for a walk? I didn't want to see you, but here you are. Crying, as usual."

Master Mycroft could take no more. He reached down and grabbed his father by his shirt and wrenched him back to standing. "Leave Sherlock alone! What on earth has happened to you? What have you become?" Mr. Holmes struggled to free himself from his son's grip, but the lad held on tenaciously, pushing Mr. Holmes back until their movement was stopped by the side of the desk. Then Master Mycroft released his father roughly. "What *has* happened to you, you poor, sick man," he said, shaking his head from side to side. "Your grieving was one thing, but this, this is unforgivable."

Mr. Holmes' rage was fearful to behold, his entire body trembling with the passion of his fury. "Get out! Get out! Get out!" he screamed, pointing to the door. "Get out of my house and never come back. Never! You are banished from here forever. I am your father; I have the power and the right. You have one day to leave this house, and I order you never to come back again. If you do not leave by that time, I will throw you out, have you arrested for trespassing, or shoot you myself." His breathing came in harsh gasps. He lowered his tone to a growl. "Get out of this house."

Master Mycroft was shocked by those words, but when he spoke, his voice did not betray the whirl of emotions he must have been feeling. "I shall take Sherlock with me."

"Sherlock stays here," his father answered, out of sheer perversity, I believe.

"Why?"

"Because I decree it. Go alone and you will receive money for school and to support yourself; take your brother with you and all monies will be cut off now and forever. Now pack your bags and go. Anywhere, just go. Let the fairies direct your travels," he scoffed. Master Mycroft stood straight again, and then turned and strode back to us. "Let us leave," he said. Mr. Hathoway and I made to depart, and when it became apparent that Master Sherlock was unable to move, Master Mycroft gently urged him into movement by grabbing hold of his hand and leading him out.

"Brewster," Mr. Holmes called to me. I stopped in terror; would I be ordered to leave as well? I turned as coolly as I could.

"Sir?"

"Have Mr. Goff give Mycroft two hundred pounds. Then fire the man. I shall take over the running of this estate again. I will have the say."

"As you wish, sir." I exited and closed the door behind me. I found the others waiting for me down the hallway and told them what Mr. Holmes had said. Master Mycroft's countenance continued to maintain a dark frown, though he did say, "Perhaps some good might come of all this. If his drinking ceases." Still leading a silent and weeping Master Sherlock, he added, "Let us go upstairs."

The rest of the day passed in appalling perplexity for the household. None of us had ever imagined the result of the meeting might be a final severance of Master Mycroft from Hillcroft House. Master Mycroft brought his brother to his bedchamber and laid him on the bed, removing his shoes. He then sat in the chair and said nothing until the lad's tears stopped falling. Master Mycroft then began assuring his brother that he would be in constant contact through the post and would let him know where he was at all times. He implored his brother to continue his experimentation with chemistry, and to renew his studies and violin playing. It was the only way, he repeated over and over, that he would escape from the pain and despair of his melancholia.

"Listen to me, Sherlock," he reiterated. "Do you wish to feel this way forever? You have promised never to take your life, and I know you will honor that promise; do you wish to go through life in this terrible state of depression? Only your mind can overshadow your emotions; use it to make life worth living. I have said this over and over, and each time I avow it with more fervour. I only hope that one day you will see it is your only chance. Promise me you will at least try— Mr. Hathoway will help you; Brewster will help you; the rest of the servants give their hearts to you and will aid you in any way they are able. You are not alone. Fight this lethargy. Use your mind; you will reap the benefits in elevated spirits."

Master Sherlock said nothing. Master Mycroft sat back in the chair, closing his eyes and rubbing his forehead. A soft voice floated from the bed. "I'll try, Mycroft, I'll really, really try this time. I cannot stand to live this way."

Master Mycroft observed his brother, and I thought I saw his eyes moisten slightly, but when I looked again after he blinked several times, they were dry. "It will work, I promise you. Write me of your progress."

"Will you be all right?" the lad asked.

"Yes, I shall be fine. Probably better than you. Father has granted me a largesse that surpasses in generosity anything I might have expected, considering that he will also pay for my schooling and lodgings. Perhaps all is not lost with him—I should not have been surprised if he had bestowed a sustenance of much less. I shall spend some time in London, and then return to school and find lodgings. I have few needs and wants, food and books are all. Two hundred pounds will easily last me a year or two." He smiled. "I am glad to be able to discuss this with you." I translated for myself: I am glad you are not catatonic with grief. "It bodes well, I think."

"I shall try," the lad repeated. "I shall strive not to weep again."

"Crying, as usual"—a crueler remark I have never heard uttered from one human being to another. But I was surprised at the lad's swift recovery from the shock in his father's study. His ability to speak did bode well, I thought. Of course, we had known his father might not welcome him with a hug and kisses; the lad had had five months to realise his father was possibly fully estranged from him. Perhaps Mr. Hathoway was right, and now that he knew of his father's unquestioning disregard of him, Master Sherlock understood he could proceed to live his life around that fact, with the help of the rest of us, and through his own gifts.

"Father's termination of Mr. Goff will at least enliven the spirits of the servants," Master Mycroft said. "We shall have to see how Father manages the estate and the business in Huddersfield on his own. It could be disastrous if he does not decrease his drinking, or it may be the responsibility he needs to reclaim himself from his breakdown. If that is the case, everything could change for the better." Master Mycroft scowled. "However, I think it has just been proven painfully obvious that I have no ability to deduce correctly the responses of others in such situations as these. We shall just have to wait and see. In the meantime, I must solely confine myself to areas where data can be gathered and logically ascertained—I recommend you do similarly, Sherlock. Our brains require measurable data to function properly; conjecture and guesswork are anathema to the precision of our minds."

The lad wiped his watery eyes with an arm. "Mycroft," he whispered, "I have one more question to ask."

"What is it, Sherlock?"

"Do you hold me to blame for mother's death?"

Master Mycroft blinked several times and then stood and sat on the edge of the bed by his younger brother. He lifted a hand to place it on the lad's leg, paused briefly in his action, and then awkwardly did so. "Sherlock, dear brother…of course

I don't. You are as guiltless of her death as are the drops of rain that nature sent to nourish the land and fell on her as well. It never has, and never will, enter my mind to lay fault for her passage on you. Father's implication was spoken by a broken man with a brain awash in alcohol. Cast it out of your head."

"I would," the lad murmured, "if I did not somewhat believe it myself."

"You might very well believe the earth is flat, or that vampires exist. You loved her deeply. You never wished her harm. You are guiltless of her death."

"I wish I could believe that. God, Mycroft, I miss her so much—both of them. How did everything go so wrong?" The lad covered his eyes with his hands, then removed them and cast his anxious face upon his brother. "Using my mind will help cleanse me of this awful guilt and wretched depression?"

"I do not know of cleansing, Sherlock. But use your powers and less and less will the guilt and depression lay claim to your soul. Do it; it will work."

"I vow to use them as best I can."

Master Mycroft patted his brother's leg several times, a slight smile softening his face. "Good," he said. "That's good."

The rest of the day passed with Master Mycroft bidding farewell to all the servants, as well as Denkins and Wilcox. He joined me in terminating Mr. Goff after receiving a promissory note for two hundred pounds; the manager was given his six months' wages as promised. Master Mycroft then packed his belongings for his departure the next day, and spent all of his remaining time in the presence of his younger brother, whom he compelled to enter the study and engage in chemical experimentation.

I marvelled at Master Mycroft's poise and apparent equanimity on the eve of his banishment from his home and kin. What he felt about his situation was hidden by his practical analysis of the circumstances, and so effortlessly did he succeed in his stoic demeanor that one would have thought his father had merely ordered him to go to a store to purchase a new pen. At times during the afternoon, a wave of emotion seemed to sweep over his younger brother, paralyzing him— "But we didn't even have a birthday celebration for you"—but with just a few words of encouragement, Master Mycroft was able to re-establish his younger sibling's mental concentration. So the afternoon passed; little was eaten by anyone at supper, which was held in the dining room with all the servants present, and only Mr. Holmes absent. Conversation was minimal, but comfort was drawn by our having joined together as a household. After dinner, Mr. Hathoway, the lads, and I went back to Master Sherlock's bedroom, where Master Mycroft read puzzles to his brother until it was time for us all to retire. In our separate rooms, I am sure that none of us slept a wink, except for, perhaps, the exiled son himself.

Chapter Twenty-four
An Oppressed Household

$\mathcal{M}$aster Mycroft left the next morning, and Master Sherlock did not weep, though the female servants all did, and I came very close.

During the days that followed, the lad became frenzied with activity and did not wish to sit still in quiet contemplation at all. He re-engaged Mr. Wharton as his tutor in the mornings and continued his focus on German, as well as French, Greek, Latin, mathematics, philosophy, and literature. He read his books and was delighted when two obscure volumes by Scheele—*Chemical Essays* and *Air and Fire*—arrived from the booksellers, though he confessed that those books on chemistry, like the others he was steadily borrowing from Mr. Hathoway's collection, were very difficult, and occasionally impossible, for him to understand. Master Sherlock also worked puzzles, played chess, and even began to play the violin again—random notes, haunting sonatas, repetitive scales—which sometimes filled the house more disagreeably than had the odoriferous chemical effluvia. Occasionally, instead of exhibiting the constant lethargy we had grown accustomed to, we now found Master Sherlock bleary-eyed in the morning after having spent the entire night on a particularly difficult geometric conundrum. All this activity was of great benefit to the lad, and only when he sat still doing nothing did his mood plummet into woeful *angst*. Thus was he driven to maintain a constant exertion of mental performance, reactivating his latent yet ever magnificent cerebration, and operating at the height of his ability. This worried us as well, as, in a pattern he developed, he would every several days drain his physical body of so much nervous energy with his never-ending activities that he would fairly collapse at night to sleep for half the following day.

"It does you no harm to take a little rest, Master Sherlock," I said to him one day, as he put down his violin and immediately requested I join him in a game of chess because Mr. Hathoway was out for a walk.

"Actually," the lad said, "it does."

"But surely, Master Mycroft meant for you to develop a balance in your life, not to run yourself ragged reaching for continual mental solace only then to suffer from temporary physical ruin."

"Both extremes suit me presently, Brewster. Will you deny me my solace, achieved through any means possible?"

I realised that in both activity and sleep the lad was free of his grief. That was truly all that was important now. "Certainly not, Master Sherlock."

The lad arranged the pieces on the board. "Will you be white or black?" he asked.

The lad's progress was dampened only by his father's continued drinking. With Mr. Goff gone, Mr. Holmes was once more in charge of the estate and the business in Huddersfield. At first, his attention to those areas was satisfactory, but as soon as he finished with the farm expenses or other household accountings, and answered whatever correspondence was required of him, he took to the bottle and became irritable and unpleasant. After Master Mycroft left, one thing did change with Mr. Holmes; he moved back into the master bedroom on the first floor several weeks later.

"I'll not be chased from my own chamber," he told me. It seemed that his banishment of Master Mycroft and his taking back the running of the estate had returned a certain power to him, though it was at the price of all that had been good and decent in the man. Now it was inevitable that the father and Master Sherlock would cross paths, although both had been assiduous in attempting not to do so.

One Saturday afternoon, about a fortnight after he reclaimed his original bedroom, I espied Mr. Holmes in the first floor hallway heading for the stairway, having just changed his clothes after a long horseback ride. Master Sherlock coincidentally left his room and, turning to the right to head for the study and his waiting caretaker, he encountered his father. The lad was still wearing his dressing gown.

Master Sherlock inhaled in surprise, his head sharply rising to view his father, then averting his gaze. His wide eyes were unable to make contact with his father's face a second time, and he stood stock still. What did I see transpire across the visage of Mr. Holmes as his son came to a halt before him? A hint of pity? A trace of compassion? A sense of hidden love? Perhaps, perhaps not—I am not too sure, for he soon glared and his tongue leapt to flail his son.

"From now on, Sherlock, you'll dress every morning, by God," he said. "No more of this wandering around in nightgowns, do you hear me?" I drew no peace from the fact that Mr. Holmes had acknowledged and spoken to Master Sherlock. Neither did the lad, I'm sure.

"Yes, Papa," he managed to reply softly.

The man stepped around his son and then stopped after a few paces, turning once again to speak brusquely to the lad, who stood without moving. "And I prefer you address me as Father, not Papa. It is time to release our ties to the past, time for you to grow up."

"Yes,"—a pause—"Father." Mr. Holmes might as well have put a stake through the lad's heart.

Without another word, Mr. Holmes continued down the stairs. Master Sherlock was the main victim of his mercurial and critical directives; we servants had been in service to Mr. Holmes for so long, it was indeed difficult for him to find errors in the carrying out of our respected duties. We knew how to run Hillcroft House flawlessly, how he liked his clothes to be laid out, his food to be served, his study to be cleaned, his brandy to be warmed. We knew what to have for him to eat when he returned home from riding, what letters he needed to see immediately upon arrival and which ones could wait for attention at another time, and so on. We did not require his orders to function correctly. Although his tone with us was oftentimes abrupt and almost all his words to us were directives, he was not overtly abusive and no servants were mishandled. Things still ran smoothly at Hillcroft, and since we still received the generous salaries Master Mycroft had instituted, we stayed.

The lad dressed from then on whether he felt up to doing so or not, although he had been doing so regularly now during the weekdays, anyway, wishing to be clean and presentable for his teachers.

After a while, due to the frequency of his addressing Master Sherlock, Mr. Hathoway began calling him simply M.S., showing a delicate, slightly humorous casualness that the lad allowed, after raising his eyebrows in consideration of the initials upon their first use. Master Sherlock, for his part, still used the appellation "Mr. Hathoway" for his caretaker, even though the man had said "Hathoway" was acceptable. It seemed evident to me that the lad was unwilling to be informal with Mr. Hathoway for fear of developing an overt attachment to him.

Once as I brought up lunch for Master Sherlock and Mr. Hathoway, I met the caretaker in the hallway also walking to the lad's bedroom. Master Sherlock sat on his bed scratching Daisy's ears.

"I thought you were reading about Paracelsus," Mr. Hathoway said to the lad. "I was."

"You won't learn quickly if you stop to scratch your dog's ears all the time. That reading should take you another two hours."

"I'm done with it."

"Done? You're done with it?" the caretaker asked.

"Yes. I've learned quite a lot about the steps of alchemical knowledge: distillation, resolution, putrefaction, extraction, calcination, reverberation—I have questions about that one—sublimation, fixation, separation, reduction, coagulation, tincture, and the like. Is that rabbit and potatoes for lunch, Brewster? Do extend to Mrs. Winters," he said, crossing himself and then crossing Daisy's paw in front of her heart, "my gratitude for the preparation of such a delectable meal." I would do anything for the lad when he was in such a salutary mood. I don't believe Mr. Hathoway took his astounded eyes off the lad the entire meal.

Master Sherlock pondered greatly the idea of the philosopher's stone that the medieval scientists hoped to create.

"They believed," he explained to me, as I placed clean underclothes and shirts in his dresser, "that by the process of purification, especially by fire, they would be able to remove all contaminants from living things and be left with only the pure essence—the *materia prima*—which apparently was identical with the philosopher's stone. Such a stone or essence would have the singular properties, Brewster, of changing any base metal to gold, of healing all diseases, and of regenerating the character of the fortunate discoverer." I paused before closing the drawer as a thought sullied my mind. The lad shared my opinion in a weary voice. "Too bad my father is not an alchemist." I said nothing but slowly pushed the drawer in.

"Too bad fire does not always purify, but often just wholly consumes," Master Sherlock added, then sat in his chair looking out the window. His silent cogitation for the next week showed his continued focus on the personal aspects of the subject.

He also enjoyed reading the French chemists. "Maybe I shall return to my mother's country and study chemistry among the vineyards." N. Lemery, Etienne Geoffrey, and Antoine Lavoisier particularly fascinated him, though not always for scientific reasons.

"Look, Mr. Hathoway," the lad exclaimed one day, pointing to a page of a book. "Lavoisier was beheaded in the French Revolution—as was my grandfather's sister, by the way. She was executed for being married to an architect who knew a prince. Lavoisier was brought before the Revolutionary Tribunal on a charge of watering down soldiers' tobacco, and a guilty verdict was assured by the blind injustice of the proceedings. Two more examples of the potentially false distinctions of criminal, accuser, and judge when 'justice' is a shield used to cover a most unjust authority."

Once I was in the first-floor corridor when I heard glass shatter and a terrifying scream. I rushed into the study with my heart in my throat, and to my horror, found Master Sherlock kneeling on the floor, holding his left arm tightly with his right hand. I could see blood oozing from a dreadful wound, and Master Sherlock's face grimacing with the pain.

"Dear God in heaven!" I said, as I ran to the lad's side, pulling out my handkerchief to tie around his arm. "Stay still, Master Sherlock. I'll send Denkins for Mr. Irwin. Was it a dangerous chemical? Where's Mr. Hathoway?" I fumbled with the linen.

"Oh, he went off on a walk to the village," the lad said calmly, standing up just as I had begun laying the cloth on his reddened arm. He held his arm up for me to see. "Realistic blood colour, isn't it?" He then clearly showed me that his arm was uninjured. "Though the liquid isn't quite thick enough; don't you agree?"

I would have strangled the lad if I hadn't been really quite delighted that he had uncovered a touch of his old wanton playfulness, albeit in a manner I found shockingly inappropriate and unfair to me. "You'll give me an ulcer some day, Master Sherlock. I must protest this untoward misuse of my regard for you."

"I'm sorry, Brewster. It was just a whim, to test whether the solution could actually pass for blood. A touch overdramatic, I agree. Please forgive me." And he gave me a rare smile, one that even touched his eyes, bringing a brief sparkle to his grey pupils.

I forgave him.

Another time he caused some little consternation in Mrs. Birchall and Eliza when he secretly treated some wood and coal with certain chemicals that caused multicoloured flames to appear as they burned. To my surprise, Mr. Hathoway had been a silent accomplice in that endeavour, and it was the first time I heard him overtly snicker in amusement. The caretaker also enthralled the young lad with the many ways he knew to make invisible ink, and then have it reappear. Master Sherlock took meat, flour, cheese, milk, and other things from Mrs. Winters to test them for sulphur content. He learned how to discern whether fibers of clothes were cotton, wool, or silk by their appearance during burning, the smell created, and the nature of the ash left over. He had also gotten to a point in his studies where he was able to be given an unknown substance by Mr. Hathoway and through various chemical experiments determine exactly what chemical or mixture of chemicals it was. Such investigations were among his favorite pastimes now. Truly, chemistry seemed to be an avenue back to happiness, and the lad came to depend on it more and more to eradicate his melancholic moods.

Chapter Twenty-five
Mr. Holmes' Absences

After a business trip to Huddersfield in August, Mr. Holmes took to travelling somewhat frequently; exactly where he went and what he did I do not know. Was he spying then? How doubtful, given his unstable state of mind, now that I look back upon it free from well-dressed men with false government documents. From August until the end of the year, Mr. Holmes was gone from Hillcroft House as much as he was there. This was not any easier for the lad, mind you, even though all his father offered him were gruff words and orders. When Mr. Holmes was gone, Master Sherlock was the only one of his family still at Hillcroft, and that played heavily on his mind. I was charged with running things during Mr. Holmes' travels, and here my months of supervising Mr. Goff had given me good insight into the proper functioning of the estate. I am proud to say my work on behalf of the Holmeses was industrious and valuable. On many of Mr. Holmes' trips, I was sure, he was often inebriated, for very often when he arrived home he either was intoxicated, or due to his appearance and the appearance of his clothes and items in his luggage, he no doubt had been. I found many train tickets in his pockets from Huddersfield, and York, one from Whitby, and a few returning from London. He never spoke of those trips and no one ever asked. We had no idea where he stayed or what he did when he was gone, although he did mention gambling a few times, but otherwise his lips were sealed. He travelled a good deal locally as well, no doubt just to get out of the house. I heard from the innkeeper in Askrigg that sometimes when he took a horse out for a ride, he would go to that village and sit in the pub for hours, drinking alone or with others, sometimes playing darts. This made the villagers a little uneasy, unaccustomed as they were to having the gentry in their presence, but there was nothing any of us could do about it. Even Father Metcalfe was not able to convince Mr. Holmes to act as a proper gentleman, and the good man was no longer granted entrance to Hillcroft.

Master Mycroft was as good as his word and wrote to his brother once a week, letting his younger brother know his whereabouts. Master Sherlock was able to return correspondence only once or twice a month. Writing missives to his missing brother was painful for the lad, though he did manage short notes explaining what experiments had been run, what lessons he was learning, what books he had read, what criminals or trials he thought were interesting, and what pieces he was practicing on his violin. It perhaps sounds very dry, but it was exactly the information Master Mycroft would have desired to hear.

In September Master Mycroft wrote to the lad concerned that for all his excellent progress in his studies, Master Sherlock was not practicing that gift of observation for which their brains were so uniquely designed. He implored his brother to begin to leave the house again and travel through the villages, observing what he could of the tradesmen and people he saw. Also, he strongly recommended that Master Sherlock should frequently peruse books detailing the appearance of military men, illnesses, tradesmen, various professions, various native people, not just from England, but also Scotland, Wales, European countries, Africa, India, and the Americas. He requested his younger brother have Mr. Hathoway or myself move things about in his rooms to hone his observations in noting all changes as quickly as possible.

The lad was not averse to any of Master Mycroft's suggestions. Mr. Hathoway mixed up the standard storage of chemicals Master Sherlock had arranged; I disarranged books on his study's bookshelf, moved the furniture—usually just inches—and rearranged his few personal belongings for which he had a fixed position. Mrs. Birchall wore her ring on another finger, and so forth with all of us. It was quite amusing to engage in such surreptitious yet playful attempts to trip the lad up on his ability to observe changes quickly, although it was remarkably difficult to do so, such were his amazing powers. Mrs. Winters even joined in by once not crossing herself in the lad's presence; as he automatically raised his arm to cross himself, he then realised she had not.

"Bravo, Mrs. Winters," he said.

Although Master Sherlock had grown content with his little world of a few rooms in the house, he began to leave Hillcroft for the villages, often on horseback with Mr. Hathoway, who was adept at riding. He first went to the farms, again studying the shepherds, the farmers, their wives and children. Then he travelled to Askrigg and Aysgarth, avoiding Carperby and his old friends as much as he could, although once he was out and about again he did ask me to begin sending the Cotters their weekly food parcels. He did not venture out daily, for he still had all his activities in the house to spend time on, but he did travel as his brother requested several times a week. On one of those trips he took Mr. Hathoway to the Aysgarth Falls, and the caretaker reported to me that the lad spent a number of hours in silent contemplation.

Thus did the time pass at Hillcroft House, and the lad turned ten, his father gone travelling somewhere. A note arrived at the house late in the afternoon of that 6 January, carried by William Grant, the son of the blacksmith in Carperby. "Is father there? MH" I scribbled out a "No. Gone travelling. PB" and handed it to the waiting lad with shaking hands. I paced the whole downstairs, darting my eyes to the window to check for the arrival of Master Mycroft, much as I had dreaded the arrival of his younger brother almost a year ago. Now, as I desired time to fly on eagle's wings, it crept like a snail. Finally I espied Master Mycroft arriving in the blacksmith's cart. My heart leapt into my throat as I rushed to open the front door and usher him inside.

"Praise God above, Master Mycroft. How wonderful it is to see you. Master Sherlock shall be joyous beyond description. How did you know Mr. Holmes would not be at home?" It was difficult to maintain my formal carriage in my excitement at seeing Master Mycroft, and I found myself as agitated as a puppy, moving from foot to foot, my arms open and waving slightly as they waited to receive his outerwear.

The lad handed me his heavy outer clothing, maintaining his hold on several wrapped packages. "I knew nothing, Brewster. I merely hoped, and perhaps somewhat assumed, it would be likely for him to be gone at this time."

"I shall have Mrs. Winters bring you some tea."

"Thank you. Where is my brother?" At that moment the strident tones of the violin came crashing down the stairs. Master Mycroft and I exchanged looks as I smiled apologetically.

"Indeed," the lad said. "Brewster, has a cake been made?"

"Of course, sir," I replied, a little put off by the question.

"Forgive me, Brewster. Of course one has." We winced together as a particularly unpleasant set of chords pained our eardrums.

"I must put a stop to that or run back to the blacksmith's," the lad said, and began to climb the stairs.

"If your kind sir will remember, it was your idea he take up the instrument," I called after him.

"Genius is not faultless, Brewster. I am sure you have realised that by now," he rejoined, not looking back.

While I wanted to be there to see Master Sherlock's reaction to the sudden appearance of his brother, I felt it was my duty to inform the rest of the estate staff of Master Mycroft's arrival, and place his luggage in his bedroom. A general alert was initiated that the first servant to notice the return of Mr. Holmes would alarm the entire household posthaste. I then went upstairs to see to the lads and bring Master Mycroft his tea.

They were sitting in Master Sherlock's bedroom in the chairs by the windows, the young lad beaming so brightly at his elder brother that he shone like a little sun. In his hands he held three gifts wrapped in blue paper and tied with gold ribbon. Master Mycroft behaved as if he had never left the house at all. He was busy setting up the pieces for a game of chess.

"Well, Sherlock, are you going to sit there for hours gripping your presents in frozen, foolish glee, or will you open up the gifts and then set them aside so that I may test your chess skills?" He spoke in a matter-of-fact manner, but his gentle tone betrayed his affection for his brother. Except for their striking grey eyes, I was once again struck by the physical differences between the two lads—the elder a little over six feet tall and probably thirteen stone; the younger perhaps just five feet tall, and not quite seven stone.

"Very well, Mycroft," Master Sherlock said, still dazed at his brother's appearance. He opened up the first present and was rewarded with several books: the predictable puzzle book, a book detailing the most horrible and fantastic crimes that had been reported in Europe since the turn of the century, and a new edition of Shakespearean plays. The second box contained the chemicals Master Sherlock had written to his brother that he and Mr. Hathoway had had some problems in obtaining. The third box contained a full-sized violin and bow.

The lad flushed with pleasure at his treasure trove, but he did not cry. He had not done that since his brother's banishment. "Thank you, Mycroft. Really, and truly, thank you." He held up the violin, caressing the wood. "It's lovely."

His brother adjusted the positions of several chess pieces that were already perfectly in place. "Yes, well, you're welcome. Try to make better music than that which greeted me upon my arrival, won't you? Now, as you are white, it is your move, Sherlock. I hope you have been reading up on effective opening movements."

Master Sherlock lost that game very quickly, his eyes having fallen on his brother as often as they fell on the pieces. Master Mycroft expressed his exasperation at his brother's being so distracted.

"Do try to concentrate, Sherlock," he admonished, though very gently. "I haven't come all this way to see you shame yourself in desultory chess playing. Surely you must have seen my pawn was a danger to your knight." He began setting up the pieces for another game.

The young lad could not stop smiling, even after the minor admonitions of his brother. "Sorry, Mycroft. I'll try harder."

"'Try' nothing, Sherlock. Apply yourself fully to the game. Observe my actions and deduce my intentions; staring at my developing whiskers will afford you no true perception of the subtleties of my strategy."

"Uh-huh," the lad said, as if in a daze.

At that Master Mycroft looked up and saw in his brother's face the love and admiration that poured forth from it unbidden and unstoppable. He went back to arranging the pieces in silence.

"Well," he said when the board was ready. "Enough chess for a while. While there is still some light out, and not too much snow on the ground, perhaps our time would be better spent enjoying the crisp winter air. Are you up for a walk, Sherlock?"

The young lad nodded eagerly.

The elder lad stood; Master Sherlock rose right after him. "Well, then, let's go."

They were gone for an hour, talking and strolling, and when they returned Master Sherlock was still smiling.

He smiled for the whole three days his brother was at Hillcroft House. Each day all of us had grown more apprehensive and fearful that Mr. Holmes would show up.

"I have tested the fates enough, Sherlock," he said to his brother the night before he left. "If Father were to return and find me here, the consequences would be severe for us all, I fear."

"I'll miss you, Mycroft," the lad said.

"We shall continue our correspondence. I am quite satisfied with your progress, and your discovery that your mind has the power to overcome your melancholy. I will endeavour to surreptitiously return home after the school year ends." That was a long time yet, but no more could be expected. Master Sherlock hugged his brother. The next morning Master Mycroft left.

Mr. Holmes arrived a full week later, Master Sherlock greeting him at the door, as Mr. Holmes had, inexplicably, ordered the lad to do whenever he arrived. Mr. Holmes was not drunk, but was irritable and unkempt enough for us all to know he had been the day before.

"Good day, Father," the lad said. "Glad to see you safely home again."

His father said nothing as he took off his coat, scarf, hat, and gloves, and began to walk down the hallway to his study. About halfway down the corridor, he stopped and turned back to the lad, who still stood in the entranceway.

"What's today?" he asked.

"The thirteenth of January, Father. Thursday," the boy answered.

Mr. Holmes' visage was a picture of deep consternation. Suddenly comprehension dawned on his features. "Your birthday," he said gruffly.

Master Sherlock did not say anything. I spoke, "Yes, it was last week, sir. Master Sherlock turned ten."

Mr. Holmes stood still for a moment, eyes squinting as Master Sherlock studied the floor. After a minute, Mr. Holmes patted down his pockets until he felt something in his jacket. "Come over here, Sherlock," he said.

Master Sherlock moved down the hall to stand before his father. "Here," Mr. Holmes said, handing him an object. Then Mr. Holmes turned and went into his study. "I shall take my meals in the study today, Brewster."

The lad wandered back to Mr. Hathoway and myself, holding a fine jackknife in his hands.

"A lovely knife, M.S.," Mr. Hathoway said.

"Yes, quite a lovely knife," I affirmed.

The lad opened and closed the knife, and then put it in his pocket. "Mr. Hathoway, fancy a game of chess?"

"I'd be delighted," the man said.

After chess was chemistry, the violin, his mathematics, and German homework, and then he stayed up the night working the puzzles in the book Master Mycroft had given him.

Another two years passed. Master Sherlock maintained the regular mornings and irregular afternoons he had established, and continued all his studies with increasing aptitude, especially in his understanding and application of chemical analyses. With his new, full-sized violin, his interest in the instrument grew as much as it had in chemistry. He sent for the books Mrs. Willoughby recommended— all in French—on violin method by Geminiani, Mozart, Abbe le fils, and Baillot; Locatelli's *L'arte del violino;* and *Methode de violin* put out by the Conservatoire de Musique. He read voraciously on the history of famous violinists, and especially enjoyed reading about Tartini, Locatelli, Nardini, and Paganini, and loved reviewing Louis-Gabriel Guillemain's life, not necessarily for its artistic merit, but because the man had had the singular determination to commit suicide by stabbing himself fourteen times.

"I should have thought that two or three strikes at most would be enough to guarantee success, and ensure unconsciousness from shock and loss of blood. Unless, of course, the man used a very small knife, or had incredibly poor aim and managed to only cause flesh wounds the first eleven or twelve times," the lad commented to Mr. Hathoway and myself after relating the story of the poor man's demise.

"Or," Mr. Hathoway chimed in, taking his pipe from his mouth, "maybe he hated his wife intensely, for her nagging fastidiousness, and had the firm resolve, fed by his suicidal mania, to leave as large a mess as possible, in spite."

"Maybe it wasn't poor aim, but instead he had become senile," the lad continued happily, "and stabbed himself thirteen times in the shins, before realizing he needed to hit a more vital part for the suicide attempt to work."

"Good thing he didn't use a shotgun. With his fervour they'd have found bits of him from the study to the garden," Mr. Hathoway added.

"Or, maybe," the lad finished, eyes widening and gleaming somewhat manically, "maybe he was killed, and it was just made to look like suicide. Maybe the murderer got away with it. Homicide made to look like an absurd suicide; what a fascinating idea." The lad's eyes remained glazed over for a moment or two, and I only hoped he wasn't getting any ideas he would be wanting to personally test out on others. From Mr. Hathoway's suddenly concerned mien, I could tell he thought similarly.

But, otherwise, the lad loved the musicians for their music. He dreamed of going to hear the masterful performers of the time: Ernst, Wieniawski, Vieuxtemps, or Ole Bull. He practiced daily, usually, for half an hour to two hours, as the mood struck him. He favored Bach's unaccompanied sonatas, Beethoven's Kreutzer sonata, Kreutzer's and Gavinies' etudes, Viotti's concertos, and his own dabbling with musical construction. He progressed slowly on the violin, and whether he knew it or not, the chords and sounds that came from the strings correlated exactly with his mood. Although his proficiency for chemical analysis was more innate and remarkable, by and by the household was less inclined to burn the violin with the morning coal, and more subject to stop whatever activity was being done to listen to the ever-changing, heartfelt notes.

We learned in a letter from Horace Vernet's second wife—Marie Theresa Vernet—that Vernet had passed away in 1863. Master Sherlock spent a day in silence in respect for the man's passing, sitting and reading by the Vernet paintings "A Capuchin Monk Meditating" and "Portrait of a Lady with Her Child," which hung in the library. In the same letter we learned that Master Sherlock's uncle, Charles Lecomte-Vernet, was receiving great and consistent accolades for his artwork, and his showings at the Universal Exhibition were extremely well received.

Mr. Holmes continued travelling a great deal and began writing letters at home that he posted himself, and receiving letters with no return address and written in a scribbled hand. Master Sherlock visited Noah a few times that spring, and I believe he discovered that mental activities were more successful than physical activities in keeping his mood elevated. After all that had happened to him, and was still occurring in his life, I feel Master Sherlock found he had outgrown the light-hearted cavorting and explorations with his uneducated playmates, even though he himself was not yet eleven. He was now uncomfortable around his previous friends; he felt very different from them. I heard him tell Mr. Hathoway, "They exist in a space I see but can no longer set foot in." Thus, after a few attempts at playing with them, he bid them farewell for good and returned to his observant walks and rides with Daisy and Mr. Hathoway. He requested, however, that I still send the Cotters their weekly food, for Noah had welcomed him back with open arms and a frog down his shirt, and that offering of simple and nonjudgmental friendship, after so long an absence on Master Sherlock's part, had touched the lad deeply. Occasionally, just the two of them got together for a countryside jaunt, and whenever they met there was amiable companionship. Master Mycroft visited once in the summer for another three days without discovery, and again the visit was joyful for us all.

For the most part, though, the lad was alone with his tutors, Mr. Hathoway, and the servants. Mr. Holmes completely ignored the lad, snubbing him whenever they accidentally met in the house and showing absolutely no interest in his activities.

Mr. Holmes gave no more gifts at Christmas or for Master Sherlock's birthdays. Yet the lad did well at Hillcroft, and was well looked after, as much as he would allow himself to be; he suffered from few devastating depressions that year, and his violin playing was sweet to behold, though not always his chemistry experiments.

At the lad's eleventh and twelfth birthdays, his father's presence in the home unfortunately necessitated his brother's absence. Master Mycroft nevertheless returned home a couple of times a year to see his brother. Unlike his spontaneous trips, Mr. Holmes' business journeys to Huddersfield were planned in advance, and even if they fell during the school year, somehow Master Mycroft arranged to be allowed to return home. In spite of Mr. Holmes, life settled into a rather pleasant and healthy routine.

In 1864 we received another letter from France, from the elderly Mr. Leon Lecomte, informing us that Charles Lecomte-Vernet had been awarded the Cross of the Légion de Honneur for his contribution to the country over the years with his excellent artwork. Master Sherlock was immensely impressed by that award.

"Perhaps one day I will also bring such honor to my beloved mother's side of the family by somehow earning the right to wear that noble cross."

"I should think that there are innumerable ways you could earn the Legion of Honor, M.S.," Mr. Hathoway responded. "Perhaps through some amazing discoveries in chemistry while you live and work in that fine country. Or by offering violin performances on a tour of France that bring tears to the eyes of each member of the audience."

Master Sherlock said nothing, but leveled his eyes at Mr. Hathoway.

"Of course," the caretaker continued, deliberately avoiding his young charge's stare, "if the tears are created not by beauty, but by…um…a more piercing application of your musical talent, you might wind up in the Bastille, instead. No, no, I think chemistry is really your best chance for recognition."

The lad was quiet for a few seconds. "Thank you for your questionable opinion," he finally said, "but perhaps there will be still another way, for I have not yet fully committed myself to a career of chemical analysis. Time will tell."

So we lived at Hillcroft House until April 1866, when once more everything changed.

Chapter Twenty-Six
A New Development

Mr. Holmes had sent a note from Huddersfield that he would be returning home on the late train, and required of me to see that the house was in immaculate shape and that all the servants were gathered in the entrance hall to greet him at his homecoming. My bristling at his note overshadowed momentarily the unusual nature of it, for, in my opinion, Hillcroft House was always in immaculate condition, except perhaps for the studies of Mr. Holmes and Master Sherlock. Then it dawned on me that for Mr. Holmes to be concerned at the appearance of the house, he must be returning from Huddersfield with someone whom it was important that the estate should impress. I wondered who this person might be. Mr. Holmes had gone to Huddersfield on business, I hoped able to maintain sobriety with his business partners, and then had stayed for an extra week before this note came in the post. Mr. Holmes had never mentioned anyone he saw on his trips, and he also had never explained with whom he kept up a continuous exchange of letters. I was nervous in my anticipation, as was the household and Master Sherlock, though only his violin betrayed his feelings.

The day came quickly. At three o'clock of a terribly rainy spring day, the servants, Mr. Hathoway, and Master Sherlock stood around the entrance hallway awaiting Mr. Holmes' arrival with his mysterious guest. Mr. Wilcox had gone to meet his train. I feared it might be one or more of his drinking partners, and that the house would be invaded by a whole company of intoxicated, irritable, and unruly men, gambling and creating havoc. The drapes were drawn to keep out the spring chill, so when we heard the carriage arrive, we could not see the persons it contained. As I heard Mr. Holmes' steps approach the door, I opened it.

Mr. Holmes entered, his arm entwined with the arm of a woman twenty years his junior, a dark brunette of average height, with a weathered though pretty complexion, and very shapely though slightly plump in appearance. Her clothes were expensive and new, and fringed with lace; her gloves, handbag, and shoes were also the finest quality and newest fashion. I doubt a mouth was closed at the sight of her.

They entered the house, her movements expressing a haughtiness and assurance that unbalanced me somewhat. She began tossing her outer garments to me in an offhand manner I can only describe as arrogant, considering no formal introductions had been made as yet. I held her things as Mr. Holmes surveyed all of us, enjoying the tension he was creating.

"Sir," I said, "good to see you back."

"Brewster, I have an introduction to make."

He lifted and kissed the woman's hand, and turning back to the servants and his son, still holding her hand, said, "I should like to introduce everyone to Gloria Holmes, my new wife."

The silence was as complete as if all sound had disappeared off the face of the earth. Who was this woman? Where was she from? How did they meet? What did her people do? A thousand questions ran through my mind. I wanted to look behind me at the lad, but I couldn't tear my eyes from the sight of the lady lightly kissing Mr. Holmes on the cheek.

Uneasy congratulations trickled out from everyone. People milled about for a few minutes and when the servants moved to one side, all attention focused on Master Sherlock, who had not joined in the celebratory comments.

Mr. Holmes beckoned his son to him. "Greet your stepmother, lad. Don't be rude."

Master Sherlock walked toward the couple, his face unreadable, and bowed before them. "Congratulations, Father, and you, Mrs. Holmes. I must admit to my surprise at such...unexpected news. Forgive my lack of effusive display; it is merely my shock at Father's pronouncement. I wish you both all the happiness in the world."

The lad had changed a lot in these last two years.

Mr. Holmes frowned at his son, but Mrs. Holmes squeaked with glee. "Oh, David, he is just like you said. How adorable." She stood up straight and addressed the lad, mimicking his stiffness and tone. "Thank you very much for your welcoming speech, young genius Sherlock. I very much appreciate your regards for our future happiness." She broke from her artificial posing and giggled. "I think we shall get along just fine; don't you, David?"

"Yes, we'll all get along fine; won't we, Sherlock?"

"It is all our hopes, Father."

"Then let it be our realities," his father responded, narrowing his eyes. In a second he turned to his wife and his face opened into gaiety. "Well, my dear, shall I take you on a tour of the house?"

"Oh, that would be wonderful."

He led her off, heading towards the morning room. "Brewster, take care of our luggage—remove the bags to the master bedroom. Servants, back to work. Sherlock, walk with us."

Thus was a wife and stepmother brought home to Hillcroft House. Certainly you can understand how shocking that was for us—marriage was then, and still is now, often a complicated affair involving a good deal of financial and family arrangements. Simply to come home with a wife, of no obvious connexions or wealth—and of obviously lower-class origins—was patently unheard of. For all her fine costuming, there was a…coarseness about Mrs. Holmes that disclosed a certain lack of breeding. Their marriage was a scandalous affair that all of Mr. Holmes' society would frown upon. I was utterly taken aback, even after all the unusual actions of Mr. Holmes over the last few years. It must have been she to whom he had been writing, and spending so much time with in his frequent travels. If she had a family of distinction, Mr. Holmes certainly would have announced so during his introductions. I was frankly aghast and felt an infinite pity for Master Sherlock; however, upon reflection, perhaps she would bring a stability to the household and to Mr. Holmes. She was, I estimated, about thirty-five years old to Mr. Holmes' fifty-four years. Had she been married before? If so, to whom? If not, what had so postponed previous wedlock? I dreaded to think how they had met. I engaged in avid cleaning to wipe from my mind any thoughts of illicit assignations. My anxieties about the woman were shared by the rest of the staff and Mr. Hathoway. I was intrigued by what Master Sherlock might observe about her, but that disclosure would have to wait until privacy of discourse could be fully assured.

I must say that the lad's ability to cover his emotions and engage in cool, distant interaction was quite commendable. If one were to look at this event as a test of all that the lad had worked so hard to incorporate into himself, he would have passed with the highest marks, and his brother would have been quite proud of him, as were we all.

He walked with his father and stepmother through the house, quiet yet not timid, reserved though not demure. He asked no questions, and displayed no needs. When Mrs. Holmes stopped to study a painting, or a piece of furniture, or to finger the drapes, chatting incessantly all the while, Master Sherlock stood to the side, hands behind his back. In the drawing room she clapped her hands together, and then gave Mr. Holmes a kiss.

"Oh, David, it's all so perfect. Sherlock, how do you say 'What a beautiful home' in French?" she asked the lad.

"*Quelle belle maison.*"

"And in Latin?

"*Quam pulcha domus est.*"

"And in German?"

"*Wie schönes Haus.*"

"And in Italian?"

"I do not know Italian, madam," he said.

"Really? It is such a lovely language. Luigi and his brother Guillano, you remember them, don't you, David? In that restaurant in London? They spoke such lovely Italian. Are you planning to study the language, Sherlock?"

"I had no plans to do so, madam. I am rather busy with my present subjects," he answered.

"Pity. Well, what's in those rooms?" She strolled rapidly down the hallway, leaving father and son together.

"I can read your thoughts, young man, your disapproval. This cold facade you put up, by its very nature, shows me the emotions you try to hide." That was astute of Mr. Holmes. "Well, I have emotions too! You have your studies; now I have her. The genius son has his books, and the drunkard father his whore; isn't that what you think?"

"Certainly not, Father," Master Sherlock said, raising his eyes from the floor to stare at his father.

"I have a right to be happy, dammit," his father said.

"Father, I really do wish nothing more for you than for you to be happy," the lad said, sincerity in his voice and softness in his eyes. "I hope you have made the right decision."

Before Mr. Holmes could angrily respond, Mrs. Holmes dashed back into the room. "Oh, David, the laboratory is great! Do have Sherlock show me an experiment. Have him find me a mixture to keep me young forever. I shall drink it every night, to the envy of all the aging women around me."

Mr. Holmes smiled. "And aging men, my dear."

"Oh, no, you shall drink it with me, and we shall live forever together."

Mr. Holmes took her arm in his. "Come, let me show you the rest of the house."

Supper that night only superficially resembled that first supper with Mrs. Fairburn, that sincerely sweet woman, all those years ago. Mrs. Holmes mood was talkative, but in a forced manner, lacking the natural flair, modesty, and caring of Mrs. Fairburn. Mr. Hathoway was present at the meal, though I am quite sure that he would rather not have been. Mrs. Holmes ate as if she had not a care in the world, while Master Sherlock hardly ingested a morsel of food.

"Goodness, Sherlock," Mrs. Holmes said. "You must eat something. Don't you like the stew?"

"Usually, yes, madam, I do. However, tonight I feel a little indisposed to indigestion—I'm sure it will pass soon."

"You don't have to call me madam, you know," she said.

"I'm sorry?" the lad asked. For the first time since her arrival, his face betrayed a taint of worry.

"I said, you don't have to call me madam. It's so formal, and I hate formality, except with servants, of course. I want you to address me as either 'Gloria' or 'Mother.'"

Considering the lad had begun addressing his caretaker of two years as simply 'Hathoway' only four months ago, this outrageous request on the part of Mrs.

Holmes was certainly a shock to the lad. He paled drastically and it seemed that the rational barriers around his emotions came tumbling down like an avalanche.

"I can't," he whispered frantically. "I just can't." He looked to his father for support.

There was none to be found. "Do as your stepmother asks, Sherlock. Don't be impertinent."

"I can't!" The lad got up and strode from the table.

"Sherlock!" His father's voice sliced through the air like a scythe.

The boy came to an immediate standstill.

"Come back over here. I gave you no permission to leave the table." The lad slowly turned to face his father, his jaws clenched together and breathing short, quick breaths. Mr. Holmes continued, "Now tell my wife how you shall address her."

The lad was trembling slightly. "By your leave, madam, 'madam' is how I shall address you."

Mrs. Holmes drank the whole glass of wine in front of her.

Mr. Holmes stood and opened his mouth in unmitigated ire. "Now you look here, you—"

"Oh, David, let it go," Mrs. Holmes said. "It's not important. Let him call me whatever he wants. Now this wine, that's important. May I have some more, Brewster?" I poured another glass, as Mrs. Holmes pulled Mr. Holmes back down into his chair. Master Sherlock stood by the doorway. "Begone with you," his father said, and the lad vanished.

Mr. Hathoway later found him in his chair by the window, leaning his head against the pane with his eyes shut, a book of German literature open and unheeded on his lap, Daisy nestled against his legs.

"A game of chess, M.S.?" he asked the lad.

The lad did not respond. Mr. Hathoway sat down in the opposite chair. After a few minutes, Master Sherlock began to speak, glumly and dispassionately.

"What is this aura of inconceivable and merciless fate that surrounds human life, Hathoway? To what purpose do we trample our way through the dirt of our lives and others, disturbing any blooming flowers in our path, barely aware of the sun that shines overhead? Who escapes from the chaos of human existence? The minister whose flock seeks refuge from the horrors of their lives in his sermon's words, which he knows to be inadequate for the task? The lowly criminal constantly seeking material comfort through stealth who winds up calling a prison cell home? The city waif crying out that her bruised apples are not tarnished? The businessman who loves his money more than his God? The compassionate doctor sadly watching all the sick and injured waste away and die on a daily basis? The average man who works tenaciously to eke out a living and yet dreams blissfully of the mercy of heaven? The loose women who sell their souls for a morsel of food? For whose benefit are we here on earth? Who is truly the victor? Who truly escapes?"

Mr. Hathoway said nothing. Master Sherlock resumed speaking after a long pause. "She's from the poverty-stricken south end of Huddersfield, Hathoway. I recognize her accent from my visits down there. She once was a respectable seamstress and had some good education, but lately her vocation has not been as honorable as that. She is as much a drunkard as my father, and has a temper to match. I fancy she has been my father's mistress for some time, and has finally convinced him to make her his wife."

"You must write your brother about this, M.S.," Hathoway reported that he told his charge.

"Yes, I must." But he just sat with his eyes closed.

"He shall be pleased with your observations, if nothing else."

At that the lad opened one eye and Mr. Hathoway grinned; then the lad closed it again. "They are elementary," the lad said. He sighed heavily and sank down low in the chair.

"M.S., do not let this little triviality destroy the great gains you have made in this past year."

"If my father's impetuous marriage to a woman of loose morals who wishes me to address her as 'mother' is a little triviality, Hathoway, pray tell, what would you consider of momentous import?"

"The queen visiting; a war breaking out between France, Germany, and Great Britain; Jesus descending from the clouds; an earthquake swallowing up all of China; the plague reappearing as the scourge of Europe; your violin playing for the next month or so."

The lad lifted up his head and gave a little laugh, then opened his eyes and turned to his caretaker. "Point taken," he said, languidly reaching for the chess board. "I'll be white."

The next weeks were spent in a whirlwind of transitions for everyone. Master Sherlock wrote his brother at Cambridge University the next day, and then showed me Master Mycroft's reply. His elder sibling, in a mastery of understatement, had written back, "Quite interesting. Keep using your intellect and keep me informed." Keep using your intellect simply translated into "Don't fall into despondency."

Mr. Holmes ordered Master Sherlock to join him and Mrs. Holmes for lunch and supper every day; otherwise, Master Sherlock was free to continue with his daily routine in much the same manner as before. Mr. and Mrs. Holmes busied themselves in walks, rides in the carriage—Mrs. Holmes was terrified of sitting on a horse—and, yes, sad but true, drinking. They imbibed together as much as Mr. Holmes had done by himself before, not solely in Mr. Holmes' study, but throughout all the house, sometimes with a growing absence of inhibitions. Whilst a good amount of the time their inebriation was noticeable but did not engender offensive behavior, occasionally they would begin to dance together or kiss and hug in a manner most unbecoming to a gentleman and his "lady." At those times we servants avoided the room they occupied until called for.

They still travelled a good deal, and Mrs. Holmes exhibited a flair for purchasing the most expensive items of clothing; however, in my opinion, her choices for room decorations were tasteless and gaudy.

Master Sherlock avoided the both of them as much as was possible away from mealtimes, though once a week he was summoned to play the violin for them after supper, and this he did with great ability. When he was done, Mrs. Holmes would applaud too loudly whilst he stood stoically upright. His neutrality in regards to his stepmother upset her, for it was her way, I think, to twist men to her wiles, and although Master Sherlock was only twelve, she was fully aware that he was old beyond his years.

As I dusted the picture frames, once Mrs. Holmes came upon the lad reading his book of Shakespearean plays in the library and she asked him to read it to her.

"I should really rather not," he said.

"But why?" she asked, pouting.

"It has connexions to the past which I prefer to avoid," he said, rising.

"Then show me an experiment."

"Forgive my blunt manner, madam, but I wish to be left alone to read my plays. I am sure my father is around the house somewhere and can offer you better company than I can."

"Well, he's a piece of work, isn't he?" she asked me, as Master Sherlock left the room.

"He is most remarkable, indeed, madam," I responded.

"You're a little nosy, aren't you, always hanging around like you do?" she accused me with narrowed eyes.

"Does madam request my services at the moment?" I asked, climbing down from the small stool I had used to reach the top of one frame. "If not, I had better check on the cleaning of the ballroom floor."

"I'm going to keep my eye on you, Brewster," she said, wagging a finger at me. "You're a cunning one."

I stood, awaiting her permission to depart. "Oh, begone with you," she said, granting me my leave. I gladly took it.

Chapter Twenty-Seven
Awkwardness and Contention

aster Sherlock wanted nothing to do with his new stepmother; he neither liked nor disliked her, nor wanted to like or dislike her. I'm sure he did not trust her, for he told me once to keep my eye on the silver. One cannot fault the lad for not giving her a chance, for alone she had revealed to me the snake lurking under all those fashionable dresses. Mr. Holmes did not compel his son to call her "mother," nor did he force him to spend time with her. Mr. Holmes had no desire to spend time with Master Sherlock, and he wanted his wife for himself. His desire that the lad join them for meals was, I think, a demonstration of his authority over his brilliant son meant to impress his new wife. Mrs. Holmes' one true benefit to the house was her immediate attention to the flowers in the greenhouse that Denkins had heretofore continued to nurture on his own, but that no one had brought into the house proper. Within a month of Mrs. Holmes' arrival, flower arrangements once more brightly decorated each room of the house. On this account Master Sherlock paid her her due one night at supper a month after her arrival.

"Madam, I must say that your interest in the greenhouse and flowers is commendable and most welcome. Your lovely bouquets contain a mixture of elegance and originality, and have done much to enliven this previously dreary home." I'll give him this: the lad knew how to have a golden tongue if he wished.

Mrs. Holmes was quite shocked by this unwarranted compliment. She patted her hair and blinked a number of times. "Why, thank you, Sherlock. What a dear, sweet thing to say. Did you hear that, David?"

Mr. Holmes stopped eating, wiped his mouth, and leaned over to kiss his wife on the forehead. "The flowers are lovely, Gloria. You don't have to be a genius to see that."

Master Sherlock said nothing, but his appetite suddenly disappeared.

Mr. and Mrs. Holmes' first fight came one week later. I was in Master Sherlock's bedroom, watching Mr. Hathoway and the lad play chess late one night, when we heard this frightful yelling from the ground floor. We three went to the stairs, leaned over the railing, and could clearly perceive Mr. and Mrs. Holmes having a terrible row. "Hmm, forty-two hours later than I had supposed," the lad murmured.

They screamed in anger one after the other; back and forth it went for well nigh an hour, a few crashes punctuating the intensity of the fracas. Then it was over, and Mrs. Holmes stormed out of Mr. Holmes' study and leaned shaking against the wall of the hallway, weeping. "You bastard!" she yelled back to the study. At that Master Sherlock ran down the hallway to the drawing room and returned immediately to his room bearing a single flower. Mrs. Holmes moved awkwardly to the stairs and began climbing them, holding onto a railing for balance as she did so. Mr. Hathoway, myself, and Master Sherlock watched the scene through a crack in the bedroom door. I really was an awful model for the servants. Suddenly, the lad moved out into the hallway. Tears ran down the face of Mrs. Holmes as she neared the second floor landing, mumbling "Bastard." Then her reddened eyes noticed the lad's presence.

"What are you looking at?" she cried out, in a voice slurred from overindulgence in wine, wiping her face with the back of her hands.

"A grief-stricken woman," he said. "I have no comfort for you but this." He took the carnation from behind his back and held it out to her.

She wobbled to a stop in her intoxication. "Why are you giving me this?"

Master Sherlock shrugged. "Because chess will not work for you."

"What?"

He opened his mouth to speak again, but then just held out the flower to her.

She reached for the flower, sniffed it, and then staggered down the hall to the master bedroom, weeping and muttering all the way, holding the flower tightly to her chest.

The lad returned to his bedroom and sat in his chair to resume the chess match.

"M.S.?" Mr. Hathoway asked.

"Masking emotions is one thing, Hathoway; having none is another. I can work with my nature, but cannot disavow it totally." He studied the board with a pensive mien. "You face checkmate in five moves."

"If I lose, will you give me a carnation, too?" Mr. Hathoway asked wryly.

Their arguments became a regular occurrence. After the altercations, Mrs. Holmes would invariably wobble to the master bedchamber or morning room sofa. She stayed there, often by herself for several hours, until Mr. Holmes joined her in the room, either to continue yelling at her or to tender an apology for his words and his actions. She locked the bedroom door after that first quarrel, but Mr. Holmes opened the door with the master key. After that she realised the futility of further lockings, for with a master key no privacy was possible. As a result she began to retreat in her distress to the morning room, for she delighted in its bright airiness and could lie on the sofa for hours moping and fuming. Do not, however, make the erroneous assumption that Mrs. Holmes was constantly the victim of Mr. Holmes' maddened ire. Mrs. Holmes was the perpetrator of the rows as often as Mr. Holmes. And, if you will allow me to say so, what ridiculous rows they were.

The topics of most of their fights were petty and only made important by the amount of alcohol they had consumed. Arguments began over too much travelling or not enough; spending too much money or not enough; jealousy in regards to previous paramours—Mr. Holmes' complaint—or a previous wife—Mrs. Holmes' complaint; whether supper last night was too salty; which wine was best with kidney pies; did that coiffure flatter or not; who was gaining more weight; there was nothing to do in Carperby; and the like. Those were the types of fights initiated when intoxication was a large cause of their unstable temperaments; other fights began without the aid of spirits and those were the nastiest, actually, when the anger of both would swell to tidal-wave heights and something might be broken. However, they generally abstained from violence directed at each other.

Occasionally they even had confrontations in the morning when either Mr. Wharton or Mrs. Willoughby was in the house tutoring Master Sherlock in his study. That was extremely embarrassing to the lad and to the instructors, so it was silently agreed that the lessons would end early and the tutors would take their leave. Those days were very hard for Master Sherlock, and finding him in his chair by the window, an unopened book of philosophy by his side, would be expected, although such depressions did not last longer than that one day.

One afternoon in September, a sober Mr. and Mrs. Holmes had a terrible quarrel in the library when Master Sherlock had gone for a walk with Daisy and Mr. Hathoway. Mrs. Holmes fled in red-faced anger to the morning room and spent thirty minutes pacing back and forth, her verbal outbursts so dreadfully uncouth that I had Eliza sequestered down in the kitchen to spare her the awful verbiage. Meanwhile, Mr. Holmes sat fuming in the drawing room, reading the paper.

When Master Sherlock and Mr. Hathoway came into the house, she was still noticeably upset, though her running stream of caustic oaths had thankfully ceased. As the lad took off his jacket, he espied her kick the leg of the grand piano and then sit down on a chair, holding her foot in clear pain at her impulsive move. The lad motioned for Mr. Hathoway to go upstairs and then entered the morning room and stood with his hands behind his back.

"Madam, deliberately thrusting one's foot rapidly against the stout leg of a grand piano is seldom a good idea."

"Go to hell," she said.

"Is there no other way I may be of service?"

She looked up then at the lad, who had made an occasional habit of coming to her after these fights when he was able to do so without attracting the attention of his father, and who offered his listening presence, or a favor, or sometimes a flower, in an emotionally distant yet sincere manner. It was obviously difficult for the lad to avoid her when she was so upset, and she would welcome his visits. He never endeavoured such contact with his father, who would have rejected his offers outright.

"Some ice, perhaps, for your foot?" he asked.

"I could use a drink," she rejoined.

They looked at each other without speaking until the lad broke the silence. "Perhaps, instead, you would enjoy seeing me perform a chemical experiment. Your elixir of youth still eludes me. I have, however, perfected a few other reactions."

"How about you read me a play?" she requested, her foot pain suddenly seeming to disappear as she stopped rubbing her foot and sat up straight, crossing one leg over the other. This she asked with some little frequency.

The lad bristled. "I'm sorry, but you know I cannot do that."

She leaned back in the chair, her hands on the arms of it. "Then bring me a drink, if you wish to be of service." She smiled. "Please."

The lad strode to the water container on the sideboard and poured her a glass of water. He brought it to her.

She glanced at the water, "tsk, tsk'd," and then took the glass and drank it all down. When she was done, she nodded to the sofa across from herself and said, "Have a seat."

The lad did so.

"Have you never kicked a piano, then?" she asked.

"No, madam. Though I did once ride a serving tray incorrectly down the stairs, with awkward consequences."

They were silent for a moment. "Although, my descent was not induced by anger," he added, "being merely a whim."

"So what does a genius do when he gets angry?"

Master Sherlock shifted uneasily in place. "It is not an emotion I am prone to," he finally admitted.

"Ah, yes. You are prone to depressions; are you not?"

The lad stood up. "This conversation is pointless. It is apparent your foot is already affording you less pain, and your mood seems to have recovered from the sour reaction of your argument with my father. If you will excuse me, I shall return to my chemicals upstairs."

"Sherlock," she quickly responded, "don't take things so seriously. I didn't mean to offend you. Thank you for the water, and the concern. It's really quite sweet of you."

The lad said nothing as he left the room, and nothing as he worked on his experiments all night long, not even bothering to stop for sleep. Mr. Hathoway found him the next morning, pacing back and forth in his study impatiently waiting for a reaction to occur in a beaker filled with blue liquid. Mr. Hathoway was barely able to prepare the lad for Mr. Wharton, and had to swear he would watch the experiment as Master Sherlock sat at the other desk in the study to work with his tutor. As soon as Mr. Wharton left, Master Sherlock changed seats to sit by the apparatus again, and we had almost to drag the lad downstairs to join his father and Mrs. Holmes for lunch. Afterwards, he was right back in the study with the chemicals throughout the rest of the day and night, refusing to go outside at all, and sitting distractedly at the supper table unaware of the food in front of him. Mr. Hathoway found him the next morning asleep in his study chair, his arms and head on the table.

His frenetic activities continued for several more days, until one afternoon we heard another argument developing between Mr. and Mrs. Holmes. The lad had been reading about Morel's *Traite des Degenerescences Physiques, Intellectuelles, et Morales de L'espece Humaine* and *Traite des Maladies Mentales*— I knew he was concerned about the hereditary tendencies of mental imbalances—in the drawing room, when the screaming began invading every corner of every room in the house. I had been polishing the wood of the furniture in the drawing room, and I saw Master Sherlock's unsuccessful endeavours to stay focused on his readings. As the yelling grew in intensity, he closed the book and put it on the table beside his chair. He affected his common pose of leaning back in the chair and closing his eyes.

"Is it the devil that prowls this house, Brewster, or merely that much more potent agitator, the unhappy human heart?" he murmured sadly to me.

"I do not believe in the devil, sir," I answered.

"Really? Nor do I, Brewster, nor do I. And of God?"

"Oh, of course I believe in God, sir."

The lad appeared to be sleeping, only the rise of his thin chest signifying he lived. I was curious now. "Don't you, sir?"

Only his lips moved, his visage a perfect blankness. "Yes, yes, I do. But, still, I wonder."

"YOU GO TO FUCKING HELL!" we heard Mrs. Holmes shriek, as she began her climb up the stairs.

I blushed to the top of my head at those words and Master Sherlock was no less discomforted by that horrible outburst. The lad stood and went to the entrance of the drawing room, watching Mrs. Holmes. At the top of the stairs, her eyes swept back and forth along the corridor of the first floor and they came to rest on the lad.

"Your father's a bloody arsehole!" she yelled, striding to Master Sherlock. Her steady gait indicated she was only minimally intoxicated. I do not believe I had ever seen a woman so enraged; nor did I ever imagine one could be. The dainty, weaker sex, indeed! Mrs. Birchall came out from the master bedroom, and Mr. Hathoway appeared from the study.

"Madam," the lad said, standing, "your words are unsuitable for public discourse. If you wish to discuss your views of my father, let us seek privacy for matters of that sort."

"Why should I want privacy? Everyone knows he's an arsehole. You more than anyone should declare it to the whole countryside."

The lad clenched his jaw then released it. My admiration of his composure was immense. "Madam, pray, have a seat and tell me what your argument was about." He swept his hand to usher her to the sofa in the room. "Brewster, please bring Mrs. Holmes a cup of tea."

I left for the kitchen. Mr. Holmes was still in his study, and I instructed the staff, who were always disturbed by the arguments, to continue with their duties. I returned to the drawing room with tea for both of them, and poured it.

"That will be all, Brewster, thank you," the lad said, dismissing me. They sat there for an hour, and then Mrs. Holmes took a bath. Master Sherlock returned to his bedroom, immersing himself in a book, and he stayed up the night to finish it.

Mr. Hathoway was the one who asked the lad the next day what he had discussed with Mrs. Holmes.

"I discussed nothing, Hathoway. Mrs. Holmes spoke almost incessantly on her own."

"About what, M.S.?"

"About how my father is a difficult man. About how she can be a difficult woman. About the poverty and sin in her past. And especially about how she both loves and hates my father."

"Interesting."

"Unfortunate. It occurs to me that deep melancholy is not the worst situation one may find himself in. I should be loath ever to have love and hate bound together like the hands of a man condemned to hang," the lad said.

"It is not always so, M.S. You have seen true love in the love your parents shared," Mr. Hathoway said. I had spent some time with Mr. Hathoway, telling him of the wonderful life of Hillcroft House before the first Mrs. Holmes' death. "The beauty of such love cannot be denied."

Master Sherlock reached for his violin and plucked a few strings. "And I have seen utter devastation as the result of that love. Can one so blithely risk all for a few years of passionate devotion?"

"It may last a lifetime, if the fates so decree," said Mr. Hathoway. "And I say yes, one can."

"Yet you have never married."

"I have never found a woman I loved."

"Perhaps you are the luckier for it," Master Sherlock murmured. Before Mr. Hathoway could rebut, the lad changed the subject. "If you will excuse me, now,

I should like to dabble with some Beethoven. Mrs. Willoughby arrives in an hour, and I have been careless with my practicing."

For the first time, I wondered whether Master Mycroft's influence on him was truly for good or ill.

Chapter Twenty-Eight
Master Sherlock and Mrs. Holmes

Mrs. Holmes took to coming to Master Sherlock after most fights, when he was home, and when she felt assured that Mr. Holmes would not notice. As winter was soon to set in, the lad visited the waterfalls with Mr. Hathoway regularly, perhaps to avoid his father and Mrs. Holmes, perhaps for his contemplative exercises. For although he allowed Mrs. Holmes to converse with him—or more correctly, to him—after arguments, he was uncomfortable with it. Handing her a flower as she walked by was much different than being the recipient of her sober or drunken complaints and lamentations. He never spoke about what she said, but his constant activity and invariable late nights after her talking to him proved to Mr. Hathoway and myself that the lad was greatly upset by his interactions with her. But why, I wondered. Did he resent her, and only allow her presence out of inbred politeness and a gentle nature? Or did he find himself having affection for her, and feared the consequences of becoming attached to another woman who might die on him as well? Or did he still feel quite neutral about her, but viewed her repeated episodes of confrontation and anger, under the guise of love and marriage, as symptomatic of an incomprehensible world that he, with all his vast intellect, could not explain or even understand? I am not sure, but outside of those times that they sat together after her heated exchanges with his father, Master Sherlock avoided her, and she did not seek him out for companionship.

Once Master Sherlock and I watched her stumbling upstairs after yet another altercation with Mr. Holmes. "Dear me, Master Sherlock, what a pity," I said.

"If I could help her, Brewster, I would," was all he said. "When I inadvertently helped Aunt Margaret's son, I...it pleased me. It is a feeling I would welcome again. Yet, I can do nothing here. I sit, and listen, and do nothing." He sat down on the floor of the library and petted his dog.

By September of that year, Master Sherlock was no longer ordered to dine with his father and Mrs. Holmes, who became erratic in their eating schedule due to their irregular alcohol consumption. The lad was relieved not to be forced to spend time with them in such a tense atmosphere. The lad also stopped playing the violin for them. Mr. Holmes did not seek to impose new edicts upon the lad, as he showed no inclination to share company with his son, content to pass time with his new wife alone. Although I believe Mr. Holmes had expressly ordered Mrs. Holmes not to spend time with Master Sherlock, I know for certain he did not suspect that his wife sought refuge from their rows with his son. For one day he found them together.

It was January third, only three days from Master Sherlock's thirteenth birthday. He had not seen Master Mycroft for a year, for the Holmes travelled so inconsistently and spontaneously it had proven too dangerous for Master Mycroft to return home with the certainty he would not be caught doing so. Even Mr. Holmes' trips to Huddersfield were not regularly scheduled as in the past. We thought perhaps Master Mycroft might return to Carperby and stay at the blacksmith's, and then Master Sherlock would visit him there daily during the Christmas vacation; however, Mr. Holmes still went for frequent rides about the town, and drank with the men at the pub. Eyes might see something and tongues might easily wag, and then Master Mycroft would probably be disowned. It was not worth the risk. So the lads kept up a steady stream of correspondence, but still it was not quite the same.

The Holmeses had been drunk or stuporous from tbe 23rd of December through the 27th, and in fact, when they awoke from their relentless indulgence, they were not even aware that Christmas was over. Gifts were sparse; Master Sherlock gave monetary bonuses to all the staff and to Mr. Hathoway from his personal savings, as he surmised, and was correct in his assumption that Mr. Holmes gave nothing himself. To Mrs. Holmes he gave a bottle of French perfume he had ordered from a store in London. I knew he had also sent for a package of his father's favorite tobacco, but the lad never gave it. Master Sherlock was given small presents from everyone but his father, who cruelly took the box addressed to Master Sherlock that had arrived a week before Christmas from Master Mycroft and tossed it unopened into the morning room fireplace. "Banished sons, banished gifts," was his only comment. Master Sherlock came as close to tears as I had seen in years and spent the rest of that day alone in his room. The package of tobacco was split between Denkins and Wilcox.

The one bright spot of that awful holiday time was Mrs. Holmes' surreptitiously leaving on Master Sherlock's study chair a gift-wrapped book by Mayhew called *London's Underworld.* "Criminals I have known. Read their stories. Some deserve gaol, some pity," the card said, ending with, "Burn this card," which the lad did with what I would describe as pensive hesitation. He opened up the card and reread it a number of times, and the lad's memory was almost purely photographic when he wanted it to be, before bending and carefully placing the card in the middle of the peat fire; he stood there watching it crackle and burn. The lad was enamoured of the book, which he read cover to cover several times, and which initiated hours of thoughtful contemplation.

What drew him to the world of criminals and crimes? How can one ever really know? Even Mr. Hathoway's queries were mainly answered with noncommittal shrugs. It seemed an interest he was born with. Was it simply the gruesomeness of the crimes that horrified and fascinated him so like boys forever before and after him? Perhaps he enjoyed a vicarious thrill through reading of their dangerous and illicit exploits. Perhaps it was the fact that criminals lived outside the laws of society with solid disregard for all the forms and manners which he had been taught exemplified civilization. Or did he compare himself to them, and wonder what it would take to turn himself into a criminal as well; what course of events might lead him to choose a life of crime? Or was he more interested in the capture of the criminals and the punishments meted out to them, as he struggled to understand the judgments of the just on the apparently unjust and the whole concept of justice in a world he seemed to find unaccountably inequitable? Maybe it was a combination of the above, or something else entirely. I do not know, but that book did become one of his most valued possessions.

Mr. and Mrs. Holmes had a very awful fight on 3 January, as Mrs. Holmes complained quite relentlessly about not going to social affairs that holiday season, and how she should have stayed in the city where there was some fun to be had. That completely raised the ire of Mr. Holmes, and the two of them took to screaming like banshees in the morning room. This went on for far longer than any of us servants could bear without feeling compelled to take a nip or two of the brandy ourselves to settle our nerves. Mr. Hathoway took some herbs for a headache, for he had of late developed a bit of a tendency for migraines. Master Sherlock sat in the drawing room, Daisy's head on his lap, petting the animal gently.

Finally, following a foul expletive, Mrs. Holmes began her climb up the stairs, and Mr. Holmes slammed shut the door of his study. Once on the first floor, Mrs. Holmes searched for the lad, and found him unmoved on the drawing room floor. He glanced at her as she entered and then returned his attention to Daisy. She sat down heavily on a chair opposite him, shaking a little and breathing deeply as she fumed, her appearance one of only moderate intoxication. She stared at me though said nothing. She knew the lad often drew comfort from my being in the room, or nearby, and so over the year she had gradually come to treat me with, if not respect, then at least tolerance. Mrs. Holmes sat in silence for a while until her respiration settled into a normal rhythm and her tremors ended.

"I have not had the opportunity to thank you for the book," the lad said finally. "Thank you."

"I've read the book myself," she answered, uselessly attempting to pat her hair into place. "I know someone in most all the categories he describes. It is a whole world unto itself—criminals and victims of all types and shades, from all walks of life, and for all sorts of reasons. In his descriptions of a…particular career of woman, Mr. Mayhew touches upon stories very similar to my own. It is an indescribable feeling, you know, to have your life summed up in one page in a book such as that."

The lad's interest would not have been more piqued if her head had just transformed into a goat's. He stopped petting his dog and blinked several times.

She continued, "Mr. Mayhew shows some compassion in his writing of the poor wretches he discovered. You know, reading of the trials of others doesn't comfort, yet misery does love company. Still," she laughed, "it's not the sort of company you'd like to spend much time with." She smiled thinly. The lad was silent and directed his attention again to Daisy. "It's not easy being a woman, you know. Not easy at all," she said. She looked at Master Sherlock stroking his dog. "Of course, being a genius isn't that easy either, is it?"

Master Sherlock scratched Daisy's ears and the dog licked his chin in gratitude. "My brother is the genius. I am merely unusually quick-witted."

"Ha!" she laughed again. "That's like saying the Pacific is an ocean, but the Atlantic merely a large collection of water."

The lad grinned briefly at her words.

"It isn't easy, is it?" she asked again.

"Science is easy, and languages, and observations."

"And otherwise?"

He shrugged. "Otherwise, it is what it is."

"Dear me, you are the silent sort." She smiled and then changed the subject entirely. This manner of open discourse was unusual for them, for most often at these times Mrs. Holmes focused her conversation with the lad on venting her rage against Mr. Holmes. "My, you've grown this last year. It seems you are constantly going to the tailor's. How tall are you now?"

"Five foot five."

"So!" Mr. Holmes' inebriated voice reverberated through the room, taking us totally by surprise. "You choose solace with the genius." This was very unexpected and undesired. Mr. Holmes had never followed after his wife so quickly; usually, Master Sherlock and Mrs. Holmes would talk for up to a half hour before she sought seclusion. Always before, Mr. Holmes had waited at least an hour before seeking out his wife. The air of the room grew cold to me, and my stomach shrunk to the size of a pebble. Master Sherlock arose from the floor and sat in a chair, his legs together and his hands on his lap. Only Mrs. Holmes did not appear disconcerted by Mr. Holmes' presence in the drawing room.

"He's not a genius," she said, calmly looking at the nails of one of her hands. "He's merely unusually quick-witted."

"Shut up!" he yelled at Mrs. Holmes. "Get out of here, now!" He pointed his thumb behind him into the corridor.

She affected disinterest in his words. "I like it here."

Mr. Holmes spoke slowly, and with as much malice as a tone is possible of garnishing. "You will go to the bedroom right this instant, or I will put you back on the streets of Huddersfield where I found you."

She paled into a wraith, and shivered this time from fear, not rage. "You wouldn't dare! We're married!"

"Watch me," he said. The tension was so alive in the room it felt as if electrical currents were darting through the air. Mrs. Holmes, eyes wide with anxiety, darted directly in front of Mr. Holmes.

"He asked me to join him," she lied, her utterance pouring out of her in a tumultuous rush. "We've spoken only a few times together, and always at his urging. I won't do it again; I promise." She placed her hand on his chest.

"Get out," he reiterated, ignoring her touch, each word pronounced individually and punctuated with precise firmness. She left the room hurriedly without looking back.

Master Sherlock stood with his hands clasped behind his back. Mr. Holmes rubbed his stomach as he abruptly eructed.

"Perhaps I should send you to school, as well," Mr. Holmes said.

"I would, I fear, be a dreadful failure at public school," the lad countered. "I have not the personality for its defined structure, nor do I have the desire to form connexions with others to promote my placement in government service."

"So what are your aspirations? For what do I pay good money to tutors and caretakers?"

"At present, I do not have a definite idea of my future occupation. However, devoting myself to the study of chemistry is not an unpleasant thought."

Mr. Holmes walked to the fireplace, took a cigar from his waistcoat, and lit it. "I've a mind to discharge Mr. Hathoway." Mr. Holmes calmly puffed on the cigar, twisting it in his fingers as he did so.

The lad spun around to face his father. "Why?"

"To punish you for speaking to Mrs. Holmes against my will."

Master Sherlock's head shook back and forth. "What have you let yourself become?" the lad whispered. "If there is a heaven, surely Mama and Aunt Margaret look down from it in horror at who you are now."

What happened next occurred so quickly that I doubted my own eyes. But my ears, they could not prevent the sharp sound of a slap from burrowing into my brain, where it nestles like a parasite to this day. The lad lay half on the sofa, half on the floor, his left hand covering his cheek, his eyes so wide they seemed to occupy almost the entirety of his thin face. Mr. Holmes stood above the lad, looking at his palm as if it did not belong to his body, then around the room as if he did not know where he was. I quickly retrieved the cigar from where he had thrown it onto the carpet prior to hitting his son.

"You hit me," Master Sherlock gasped, allowing his body to slide to the floor. "You hit me." The lad began speaking flatly, as if in a daze. "That's...that's assault...you're a criminal. From good to bad, just to unjust; you're a father, you're a criminal, just like that. Just like that!" He snapped his fingers. I feared the lad was having some sort of breakdown again. Mr. Holmes did not look much better; his mixed reaction to hitting his son caused his face to register innumerable emotions, one after the other—horror, disbelief, confusion, worry, irritation, and then, his comfort and his burden, anger. He took a hip flask from his trouser pocket and drank deeply of its contents.

"It's your fault," he said to the lad, weakly, attempting to convince himself as much as anyone, I felt. "You made me do it. Your impertinence enraged me. It's not my fault, damn it. Any man would treat such disrespect similarly."

The lad pulled his knees up to his chin and wrapped his arms around them. The left side of his face glowed red, and I noticed a think trickle of blood from his mouth. He said nothing but just looked fixedly into the air as if images were dancing in front of his vision, invisible to all but him.

His father went on. "You stay totally away from me and your stepmother. You stay away. No more private talks with her. She is to be left to me. Hathoway can stay if you obey those orders; otherwise, he will be let go. And no more speaking of your mother or aunt." He had been pointing his right index finger at the lad as he gave his directives; of a sudden, he noticed it and put his hand in his pocket. "Do you understand?"

"No, no, I don't. I really don't understand, Father," he said, tears dripping from his eyes. He wiped them away quickly. He raised his head to see his father. "Do you really hate me so?"

His father jerked his head at the question, then ignored it. The added alcohol seemed to thicken his resolve. "Do you understand?" he asked again. "Or shall I fire Hathoway this moment?"

"Do not, I beg you. I shall follow your commands."

"Do not beg; it is unmanly. Stand when I speak to you, lad."

Master Sherlock rose to his feet.

"Leave us in our world, and you will have yours." And with that, he left the room and returned to his study, which he did not leave for two weeks.

Chapter Twenty-Nine
Master Sherlock's Departure

lthough on the surface everything remained as before, and Master Sherlock still had his caretaker, his tutors, his chemical experiments, chess matches, and violin playing, after a few letter exchanges with his brother, the lad began spending an inordinate amount of time outside in solitary wanderings, even though it was still winter. This was surprising to Mr. Hathoway and myself, for we thought the lad would have followed the opposite course of rarely leaving his bedroom. Very often the lad would slip outside as soon as Mr. Wharton left, and Mrs. Winters and I were back to putting food in all his coats and rucksacks, so he could stop for some sustenance during his lonely walks. Sometimes the lad would be gone all day, and as night fell and darkness settled outside, Mr. Hathoway and we servants would be affixed to the windows, watching for the return of the tall, thin lad and his dog. Mr. Hathoway did go with the lad as well at times. They travelled to the frozen waterfalls together and they walked for miles along the roads to towns a noticeable distance away: Hawes, Feetham, Walden, Carlton, and others, enabling Mr. Hathoway to lose his slight paunch. When home, Master Sherlock made a singular point of avoiding all contact with his father and stepmother. Mrs. Holmes had slipped me a note to give to the lad, which I did. He read it, and then crumbled it and threw it to the floor of his study, which was a common place for him to discard unwanted papers and store wanted ones. No one was allowed to touch his papers, although I did not think Mrs. Holmes' note qualified, so motioning with my eyes to the ever-present Mr. Hathoway, I was assured by his eye contact that he would retrieve the note for our future reading.

"Sherlock, I'm sorry. I can't go back. Anything is better than that. I hope you understand," the note said.

One day, as he dressed to go outside after lunch, Mr. Hathoway said, "Perhaps you should visit Noah. It has been a considerable time since last you had his companionship."

"I have no desire to speak of frogs, or to gossip of the village folk, or to imagine myself a knight of the Crusades. I have no desire to run, and skip, and hop, and climb. If he could discourse on the polemics of Socrates, I would find his company of worth. Otherwise, I grow weary of the humdrum interests of minor intellects. It fails to stimulate me."

"Would you care for the company of my minor intellect, M.S.? I shall not speak of frogs, I promise you."

The lad tied his scarf tightly around his neck. "You are welcome to come with me."

"Good. The chill air and a long walk would be refreshing." As he put on his outer garments, he said, "I have been meaning, however, to bring up a philosophical debate on the curative effect of toads on warts. Plato states specifically in one of his writings that Socrates believed only toads with more than seventy-three bumps on them would cause a wart to disappear, if the toad touched the wart during a full moon and then hopped around an oak tree three times." I opened the door for them, and they exited, Mr. Hathoway continuing his outrageous talk, which, though he wouldn't admit it, we knew the lad enjoyed to a certain point. Mr. Hathoway was masterful at attaining and yet never surpassing that threshold. "Socrates, however, did not specify the age the oak needed to be to guarantee the cure would occur, or if other species of tree would suffice."

Mr. Hathoway held up his thumb for the lad to see the wart thereon.

"So what do I do?" he asked, eyebrows raised in mock anxiety.

"I suggest you confer with Mrs. Winters," the lad said drolly. "She is an expert on the subject of trees and wart removal."

And off they went in congenial silence, not returning until suppertime.

Moments such as those balanced the oppressiveness in the household, for Mr. Hathoway was a gentle and humorous man with us all, and he considerably lightened the weight that more than once threatened to sink the hearts of the household staff. His playful verbosity was much appreciated by everyone, and he never teased or made fun of anyone. His complete and utter admiration and affection for Master Sherlock was obvious, though never smothering or otherwise extremely overt.

Mr. Holmes was now disagreeable as a general rule, and Mrs. Holmes was not much better, although her floral displays were maintained, for which we were thankful. For all of his days of drink, though, Mr. Holmes was still able to deal with the business of the estate, and successfully travel to Huddersfield, looking like a corpulent though respectable gentleman with a somewhat decorous wife at his side. At home, he assiduously avoided any contact with his son, and ordered his wife to do likewise. She continued to pass notes to me every so often, usually after a row. The lad, after the third or fourth, requested that I ask her to desist from such subterfuge, and then asked me to burn unopened any notes from then on. What could the lad do? She was not to be trusted. If he confronted her directly, even when Mr. Holmes was out drinking at the pub, and angered or upset her, she might tattle on the lad to his father that Master Sherlock had approached her; if he wrote her, she might hand it to his father. If he approached his father with Mrs. Holmes' letter, there was a chance Mr. Holmes would, in his revengeful ire, make good his continual threats and burn their marriage certificate, have the registry

ruled a forgery, and deposit Mrs. Holmes back on the squalid streets of Huddersfield. Mr. Holmes fairly danced with glee whenever he related to Mrs. Holmes that
the ailing magistrate who had performed their ceremony was already dead, so Mrs.
Holmes would have no one to defend her claim of matrimony. Master Sherlock's
conscience would not allow him to be responsible for the possibility of such a dire
outcome. He was in an impossible position, and so he did what he could—he
burned the notes, did not write back, and continued his long days of walking. In
July, Mrs. Holmes finally stopped handing me letters for the lad; however, Master Sherlock did not cease his walks.

I believe those long jaunts by the lad were the impetus for his thoughts of
leaving hearth and home, of escaping from a house that was endurable only through
the efforts of those who were not relatives to him. In the spring, he was known to
cover twenty to twenty-five miles on some days, walking all the way to waterfalls
he had only previously ridden to, even going so far as to reach the Butter Tubs of
the Pennines on more than one occasion, and to explore all the empty mines of
Swaledale. Daisy was a fellow traveller. He reduced his tutoring with Mr. Wharton to only four days a week, to afford himself one more day for such long treks.
I asked him one day why he walked, not rode, and he enigmatically answered,
"My feet are my own." The horses were his father's, hence, I think, he was training himself for the possibility of leaving Hillcroft. He continued to correspond
with his brother, who turned twenty-one that year and would be graduating from
University to enter government service "at some low clerk level. It is a necessary
first step, but I have no doubt my rise shall be rapid."

"I imagine he will be running the government soon," Master Sherlock said,
evidently quite proud of the career of his brother, which had not yet even begun.
"From the back office, of course. For all his public school education, Mycroft has
turned out even more asocial than I. He calls no man friend, disdains any form of
society, and views the world solely from how it should best be managed to guarantee the safety and productivity of Great Britain."

"Does he have any female acquaintances?" I asked innocently.

Master Sherlock flushed at my query, and I censored myself for speaking without thought. "He has never mentioned such, and I have never asked." We gratefully let that topic die.

The years passed much the same, and once more it was March, though now
of 1868, and the lad was fourteen, five foot eight but only nine stone. And here I
near the end of my sad tale of the lad. One afternoon, a very drunk Mr. Holmes
found a year-and-a-half-old note written from Mrs. Holmes to Master Sherlock
hidden in the desk of the morning room. It was a letter she had never given the
lad, and it detailed how unendurable her life was with Mr. Holmes, and how she

wished she had been born in some faraway land where she might have been a
countess or met and married a man she had actually loved. They had one of their
worst fights yet over that letter, with Mrs. Holmes eventually saying Master Sherlock was responsible in some convoluted manner. Mr. Holmes flew upstairs to
confront his son in his study, waving the letter like it was a flag on a masthead.
Master Sherlock and Mr. Hathoway both rose from the desk, where they had been
working at the laboratory.

"So, you correspond behind my back, do you? It is over a year old, but I have
no doubt there have been more recent exchanges," Mr. Holmes spat.

"No, Father, there have been no exchanges. I do not know what it is you have
in your possession, but I have never corresponded with your wife," the lad said.
"I know not what that says, and I had no hand in it. She acted independently."

"That is not what she says."

"Whom do you believe: your son who you know does not lie, or the woman
who you know does?"

Here, I must state that I can only describe the following scene by prefacing it
with the declaration that I think Mr. Holmes had some sort of mad fit, induced by
an addiction to alcohol, and a heart devastated by loss. Nothing else can explain
to me his brutal actions.

Mr. Holmes picked up a chair and threw it at the chemical apparatus on the
table, causing an explosion of tubes and beakers; the pieces that survived the chair
broke upon hitting the floor. "Damn you!" he yelled.

Master Sherlock would have sprung forward if not for Mr. Hathoway's grabbing him about the chest and struggling to hold him back.

"No!" the lad yelled.

Mr. Holmes picked up a second chair and took to pounding it on the table,
shattering any remaining glassware and scattering tubes and metal clamps and
rods all across the room. Then he approached the shelves against the wall that contained jars of chemicals, but Mr. Hathoway released Master Sherlock and ran to
Mr. Holmes, and in a feat of desperate strength, wrestled the chair from him.

"You can't break the jars; you could kill us all!" he shouted, placing the chair
back on the floor, frantic with alarm. "The chemicals can't be indiscriminantly
mixed!"

Mr. Holmes seemed swollen with ire. He upturned the table the apparatus had
been on, and then spent some time tearing notebooks and papers apart, tossing
them into the air. Mr. Hathoway returned to the lad, once more holding him by his
thin shoulders. Mr. Holmes was breathing heavily as he finished, and once more
glared at Master Sherlock.

"I told you to have no contact with her!" he yelled, pointing at his son.

The lad broke free of his caretaker, and took a few steps until he stood distraught in the middle of the wreckage.

"I had no contact with her!" He looked about the room at the awful damage. "You've ruined everything," he moaned, and who would swear he was referring only to his chemical studies? His raised his face to his father, and for the first time ever, I saw anger suffuse his face. "You despicable drunk. Look at what you've done. This room mirrors your life, and in it everything lies destroyed by your hand. No fairies, no rainstorms, no kicking mares; only you are to blame."

"How dare you speak to me this way! You who are good for nothing but bookwork and self-absorption. I have been tolerant of you and your depressive sensibilities for six long years, and what have I to show for it but this letter in my hand."

"I had nothing to do with that letter, I tell you!"

"You stole my wife and sister from me, and then they died. Now you wish to steal Gloria from me as well." It was at that exact moment that we all knew Mr. Holmes was not quite in his right mind and that argument with him was futile. Master Sherlock understood this and his temper dissipated completely.

"My God, do you really believe that?" he asked.

"Yes! Do not deny it! You know it is true!"

The lad looked back helplessly at me and Mr. Hathoway, and we all dreaded to hear what else Mr. Holmes would say.

"So, I will take someone from you. You should know how to punish criminals, Sherlock, an eye for an eye." Mr. Holmes strode to Mr. Hathoway. "Mr. Hathoway, you are discharged from your duties as my son's caretaker. I want you out of the house tomorrow. I will pay you your wages for six months and will also recompense you for the damage to your chemical equipment."

"Sir, I respectfully request to stay on in my capacity as caretaker. I'm sure this misunderstanding can be fully worked out if we sit down and rationally discuss it."

"Request denied." He turned to his son. "And no more violin lessons either." The lad had taken to going to Mrs. Willoughby's house since last year to avoid her experiencing any discord between Mr. and Mrs. Holmes during the lesson.

"Don't do this," he pleaded with his father.

"It is already done," Mr. Holmes answered.

He left the room. We stood still in shock, the three of us. Then the lad bent down and began sorting through the papers on the floor, picking up any that were salvageable. After a minute of that he stood, put them on a desk, and without a word left the study, going to his bedroom. We followed and found him in the chair by the window. Mr. Hathoway sat in the adjacent chair and I sat on the bed, and although there was the clean-up of the study to attend to and all of Mr. Hathoway's packing, we sat there for some time, saying a word here or there. Mr. Hathoway assured the lad he would write several times a week. When I eventually left them, they still sat as they were, and I felt I had to physically push myself out of the heavy silence of the room. Mr. Hathoway stayed there all the night, leaving only to pack his things as quickly as possible, returning to the lad's side where their good-byes to each other brought tears to my eyes; the lad could barely speak.

Mr. Hathoway left the next day. It was awful for us all, that is all I have to say; the lad did not leave his room for a week. I cleaned the study with Mrs. Birchall and Eliza, and on Master Sherlock's request, sent the chemicals to Mr. Hathoway. I took the liberty of informing Master Mycroft of all that had occurred. After that, Master Sherlock met with Mr. Wharton as usual, though he took his books with him on his walks and did his studies in the countryside, oftentimes coming home terribly late, and a few harrowing times on the weekends not at all. When he would arrive home the next morning he would simply say, "Slept outside." Mr. Hathoway wrote to the lad twice a week for a month, until Mr. Holmes wrote back, ordering the man never to write again. Mr. Hathoway was forced to comply for fear of repercussions on Master Sherlock. Thus the severance was total.

The study looked empty without the laboratory and the chemicals; the only evidence of its previous existence was in the numerous stains upon the wooden table and floor from the reagents spilt over the years. The lad's violin playing was painfully angst-ridden.

Mr. and Mrs. Holmes had many arguments about the lad now, with Mr. Holmes relentlessly suspicious of any communication she might be covertly having with him. Mr. Holmes was under the terrible impression that Mrs. Holmes was transferring her affection and attention from him to Master Sherlock. Their altercations grew so acrimonious that once she ordered Mr. Holmes to take her back to Huddersfield and just be done with it. He choose a different option. In April, after they returned from a trip to Huddersfield, Mr. Holmes entered the lad's bedroom late one night as we played chess. I was not so worthy an opponent as Mr. Hathoway, but there was no one else for him to play. I immediately rose at Mr. Holmes' entrance. The lad stood up listlessly at his father's appearance and did not look at him.

"I have been thinking of what career you should follow as second son. I disapprove of the study of chemistry, and no longer choose to have you succeed as squire of the estate. You cannot live in this room forever, so I have arranged for a career for you," he said, the whiskey on his breath detectable up to ten feet away. "I feel certain you would excel as an officer in the army. Your vaunted chess strategies applied in battle would surely bring disaster to our enemies. I have decided you shall attend the Royal Military College at Sandhurst in Surrey. I think a turn in the military will be perfect for you. First, though, I shall send you to Eton for two years to get you used to the company of other people. When you are sixteen you will be of age to enter the Military College. Such a future will get you out of the house, put some meat on your bones, give you some experience of the world, and generally do you nothing but good."

"As you wish, Father," the lad responded, as I stood stunned and nauseous.

"I've arranged it already. You'll be at school in the autumn, and things will be set in motion for you," he said and left.

"Master Sherlock?" I managed, through a throat dry as a desert.

"Don't worry, Brewster," the lad said. "I won't be here when the autumn comes. And I'll never set foot in an army barracks."

"What do you mean?" I asked, my suspicions raising the hairs on my neck.

"I am leaving Hillcroft to seek my fortune elsewhere. I certainly can do no worse."

I knew it was to happen, but I was still frightened at the idea. "But, what will you do? Where will you go? Master Mycroft—"

"No, I won't go to him, else he will be cut off from all funds, and from any inheritance as well. Although he graduates from Cambridge in two months, he will need my father's financial support for at least another year, and maybe more, if he truly does begin his career at the bottom of the rung and wishes to read and eat in the manner he has grown used to. There is a chance my father shall initiate a search for me, for whatever reason, and Mycroft and Mr. Hathoway are two obvious persons he will think to investigate. I wish to bring no trouble on either of them, and so shall stay quite clear of both. I think I shall just wander for a while. Wander and observe. I shall take Daisy with me."

"Have you any money? You cannot rely on your father's benevolence if you run away from home."

"I have some. I can work for more."

"Work? I have savings; let me offer them to you."

The lad stared at me, unable to speak for a moment. "That is very kind, but I have enough, and Mycroft has sent me some. He is aware of my plans." I made to interject, but Master Sherlock held up his hand to forestall it. "Besides, my father was right about one thing. I have been good so far in life only with my books and my thoughts. This house is now stagnant to me, and I deeply feel that stagnancy is as much my innate enemy as are my sensibilities. It is time I went out and saw a little of the world. You are most kind to offer me your money, but I wish to go out on my own, and manage as I can. Adventures do not frighten me, but rather excite me. My walking treks have prepared me some for hunger, fatigue, and hard beds. My little needs can be easily satisfied once my money runs out. You may have noticed I am a quick learner, and have worked with blacksmiths, farmers, tailors, tinsmiths, and the like. A little work will not defeat me, and will provide me with food and shelter."

"I don't care how much of a genius you are, Master Sherlock. You are still only fourteen. To be out on your own like that, wandering about…"

"Fourteen is old enough. If the children in Mayhew's book are self-sufficient at such an age, so can I be." Silence hung in the room as we sat with our own thoughts.

"You have been an excellent butler, Brewster, and an even better friend. To my dying day I shall never forget you nor your caring heart that delivered compassion to me through all the terrible times we shared. It is only due to the constant ministrations of you and Mr. Hathoway that I feel capable to undertake again such adventures as I was wont to do years ago when I was young and all was right with life. Thank you very much, my dear friend."

I was weeping openly. "You know I have always regarded you as a most remarkable child, and now I see you are the same as a man. It has been an honor and blessing to have been with you these fourteen years, Master Sherlock. Your heavenly mother has never had a reason for shame because of you, and I doubt she ever shall. If only—" I bit back my unnecessary words, and again we sat speechless for a time.

"I wish you the best of luck, and take good care of yourself," I said. "Do not forget to eat regularly, I beg you."

"I shall eat as regularly as possible, Brewster, I promise."

"Will there be enough out there to keep your mind busy?"

"On my walks so far, I have filled my thoughts with observations and ruminations—those will suffice, I think. I shall also take my violin and some books."

"Where do you plan to go?"

"I have no plans to start with. I look forward to travelling incognito. I may eventually aim myself towards one of the chemical laboratories in Germany or France, or pay a first visit to my French relatives. I have defined myself so far, Brewster, solely through moods and intellect. Surely there is more to me than those traits. On my wanderings this last year, I have pondered who I am and what is to be my lot in life. I have come to understand that whatever I am destined for falls outside the regulated constraints of society, for I am not of the temperament to live by the rules and laws of others. I will never put up with the dictates of others again. As I break from my father, I acknowledge a further break from the expectations and standards of my class."

I had to ask the question. "You'll not become a criminal, will you?"

The lad smiled briefly. "That class greatly intrigues me; I do admit. I have considered studying them in some capacity, though how I would do so evades me. However, I have no plans to formally join their ranks." He closed his eyes for a moment. "I shall never bring disgrace upon Mama's memory."

I reached out and grabbed his arm. He opened his eyes. "Promise me," I pleaded, "promise me you'll keep in contact with us."

"You will be staying here in the household?"

"Yes."

"I thought so," he said, nodding his head. "My father does not deserve you, nor the rest of the servants."

"I too have memories of your dear mother."

"Thank you," he whispered. He took a deep breath. "I will send letters to Noah, and he will bring them to Wilcox or Denkins, who will pass them to you. I spoke to Noah several weeks ago about such an eventuality, after I extracted myself from the mud puddle he pushed me into with the aid of his brother Willie, who crouched down behind my legs. Noah has agreed to the arrangement, and bid me a touching good-bye. I will speak with Wilcox and Denkins tomorrow. If they should leave, he has instructions to place the letters among the rocks in the well. Please, do please keep up the Cotter's food parcels until my father orders otherwise."

"I should be delighted to. When will you leave?" I asked.

"The day after tomorrow. You will have to notify Mr. Wharton. Please offer him my eternal gratitude for his tutoring."

"I will." Then his words hit home. "Good God, you're leaving so soon?"

"Yes, I shall bid my secretive good-byes tomorrow to the staff, and arise early the next morning. I'll pack two bags with a few clothes, toiletries, books, food and water, take my violin, set out for a walk with my dog, and then...never come back."

And on 22 April 1868, that is exactly what he did.

Chapter Thirty
A Return to the Present

It had taken two weeks for Mr. Brewster to dictate his recollections to me, using his numerous notebooks as chronological and detailed reference guides. He finished one night, weeping for the youthful Holmes as if what he had related had occurred but yesterday, not almost thirty years ago. His public grief made me uncomfortable, as I have never been an overly expressive man, and I put my pen down and shook my writing hand of its cramps, and then drank some water to hide my unease. His nephew Harry patted his arm compassionately. The aged man composed himself after a few minutes.

"Please excuse my tears, Mr. Cobbett. I was very fond of the lad."

"What an utterly remarkable story, Mr. Brewster. I never imagined such a childhood as that. How extraordinary…and tragic."

"Yes, yes, it was both of those."

"And you were there for it all."

"Yes, until the very end."

We disbanded for the night, and even though it was late, I decided to go for a stroll. I must confess that the history I had uncovered of Sherlock Holmes' childhood had enlivened me with the probability of upcoming fame for me as a reporter. It had never been important to me before, but now I felt a rising excitement at the possibility.

Mr. Brewster's recollections were a singular account of a childhood, a childhood unusual in every aspect, and tragic beyond measure. The change in Sherlock Holmes' personality as a result of those dreadful years after his mother's death was shocking, yet understandable. What a wonderful lad he had been originally! What Sherlock Holmes might have been like as a man if only his mother had lived! I was extremely impressed with Mycroft Holmes in his role of elder brother as well—the biography would do nothing but bring honor to him as an obedient son, and caring, compassionate brother. For a half hour I strode along, brimming with self-satisfaction at the story I had uncovered.

Then, standing down the street on a corner under a gaslight, I seemed to see a wavering form of Wiggins watching me approach. My heart began racing. I shook my head roughly a few times and the vision was gone. I stood disbelieving my eyes, as perspiration dotted my forehead and my hands whirled in frustration that my waistcoat was hidden by the thickness of my coat. Don't worry, lad, it will honor Sherlock Holmes as well, I thought, and at that silent declaration my heart settled down into a calm rhythm.

I began defending the knowledge I had uncovered as I stood still—what others might have wondered about a solitary man lost in thought on a sidewalk near midnight I have no idea. I had no awareness of anyone else around me as I silently explained my biography to a fifteen-year-old lad living hours away. The information brings no shame upon Sherlock Holmes at all, I stated firmly; in fact, he was cast in a most favorable light. All of his depressions are quite understandable, given the nature of his innate sensibilities combined with the unhappiness that descended so completely into Hillcroft House. Mr. Brewster's sympathetic portrait of the young Sherlock shows an honest, sensitive, brilliant, playful boy. No shame or dishonor will be brought upon the memory of so noble a man by the words I will publish. Besides, I finished to myself, Sherlock Holmes is dead, and will not mind the airing of his remarkable childhood years as he lays forever below the Reichenbach Falls.

I was heartened again by my thoughts, and renewed my walking with fresh vigor. The wind was chilly but not uncomfortable, and there were still a few people out on the streets with me. It felt invigorating to be stretching my legs, victorious in the first stage of my investigation. I looked forward to sending a telegram to my editors first thing in the morning, elaborating for them my success. Then I would spend another day or two mired in reporter's shorthand, writing Mr. Brewster's recollections of Hillcroft House after Sherlock Holmes had left. I returned to the hotel, enjoyed a few sherries in solitary celebration, and then fell into a deep and rejuvenating sleep with no Wiggins to torment me.

EXCELLENT SUCCESS WITH BUTLER BREWSTER, JUST A LITTLE MORE TO GO. STOP. REMARKABLE TALE OF CHILDHOOD YEARS. STOP. WILL RETURN IN A FEW DAYS. STOP.

The return telegram from London congratulated me quite effusively and authorized me to continue as I had planned. Mr. Percy Brewster was amenable to proceeding immediately with the history of Hillcroft House. It was evident that the man was enjoying relating his anecdotes, however painful they were to relive, and now that he had begun his storytelling, he was avidly encouraging me to transcribe nonstop. I was willing to do that to the extent my writing hand would allow me.

We sat down the very next day at 10:00 A.M., and Mr. Brewster opened a new journal to use as his reference guide. He then began the most terrible part of the whole history.

Chapter Thirty-One
A Home Without Master Sherlock

The second part of this history will not be such an involved affair, Mr. Cobbett. There is much less to tell, as the players in it are only Mr. and Mrs. Holmes, really, and the story is that of their complete embrace of irreparable decline.

It took four days for Mr. Holmes to notice his son had disappeared, and no doubt if Mrs. Birchall hadn't been caught teary eyed and sniffling as she rehung the cleaned curtains in the master bedroom, he might not have realised it for another few days—or weeks, even. If Mrs. Holmes had discerned the lad's absence before that, she had said nothing to me nor anyone else. They had been drinking regularly, almost stuporous for several days, with only altercations punctuating their insensibility.

"What ails you, woman, that you weep so?" Mr. Holmes demanded of Mrs. Birchall, as he entered the room to change his jacket and trousers. He had spilt wine upon them whilst drinking with Mrs. Holmes in the library. I had followed him to his chambers to aid him in changing clothes.

"Nothing, sir," she said, using her handkerchief to wipe her nose and dab her eyes. "A touch of sadness, that's all."

"Sadness about what?" he persisted. He felt a need to know everything about the servants.

"Why, Master Sherlock, sir," she said, stating what she thought would be obvious.

Mr. Holmes squinted his eyes at her, his arms akimbo. "What of him?"

Mrs. Birchall looked helplessly at me. She was astonished that Mr. Holmes did not know his son had left, and therefore was not very anxious to be the one to relate the news to him. I was not sure myself up until that moment whether or not he had been aware of his son's total absence, and I certainly hadn't had any inclination to ask him. I supposed now was as good a time as any to inform him of Master Sherlock's disappearance, and I was the one to bear such awful tidings.

Mr. Holmes noticed Mrs. Birchall's eyes upon me and turned to face me. "Brewster? What about Sherlock?"

Upon his leave-taking, the lad had given me a letter addressed to his father and requested I hand it to him whenever the time came that his father asked about him. I fingered that letter as it sat folded in my jacket pocket.

I would never disobey Master Sherlock's wishes. "He ran away from home four days ago, sir," I said. And took a good part of our hearts with him, I added silently. We servants missed the lad dreadfully, and were fearful for his safety.

Mr. Holmes blinked a few times, then his shock was made manifest. "He did what?"

"Ran away. Sir." I took out the letter and held it out to Mr. Holmes. He ignored my outstretched hand as his anger grew.

"Where to, damn it?" he demanded to know. "I bet he went to Mycroft. Or to Hathoway. Which one, Brewster? Which one did he fly to?"

"Neither, sir. This letter is from Master Sherlock to you." Mr. Holmes still refused to grasp it, so I decided to narrate its contents; the lad had read the letter to me before sealing it in an envelope. "You may check for yourself at the domiciles of each—the lad took off for parts unknown with his dog. Neither his brother nor his previous caretaker is his point of refuge. He suspected you would bring trouble upon them if he visited either, so he will not be found anywhere around them. He said he would just wander England first, and then perhaps eventually call a foreign land his home. He had saved some money, is travelling simply, and will work if his funds run out." I waved the letter and strode up to him. "It is all here in this letter." He grabbed it from my hand and thrust it deeply into his trouser pocket.

"Work? How dare he?" he exclaimed. "How dare he disregard my plans for him? How dare he...I gave him no right to do so...I...I did not say he could...I...I..."

Mr. Holmes suddenly paled and tottered, and before I could come to his aid, he stumbled for the chamber pot, fell to his knees, and vomited fiercely into it. When he was done he left the pot on the floor, wiped his mouth with his hand, and stood shaking. He waved away my approach to help. Using the walls for balance, he made his way down the first-floor corridor, descended the stairs, using both hands on the railing, and lurched into his study. He did not leave it for a month, accepting only myself to care for his needs; even Mrs. Holmes was turned away, so she drank by herself in the morning room, her coarse descriptions of her husband flying nonstop from her mouth.

I feel I must relate to you the situation at the house with the servants. We were all still there, doing our work, mostly on our own initiative, although we had impetus to do so, for when Mr. Holmes was sober he wanted the house to be in excellent presentation. And, of course, habit and a certain pride attend most reputable servants, and those of us at Hillcroft House had a goodly share of both. Thus we were constant in our energies and our duties. Perhaps the servant most impacted by the house empty of everyone but the Holmeses was Mrs. Winters, who now had only the servants to cook for regularly, and the Holmeses irregularly. This was a woman, I may boast, who had made Hillcroft a very popular place for socializing when Mr. and Mrs. Holmes had, before her death, followed the leisured life of their class. No one had ever left a supper table prepared by Mrs. Winters with either dissatisfaction or an empty stomach. She was loath to be slothful, so we were, no doubt, the best fed servants in northern England. Denkins, Wilcox, Mrs. Birchall, and Eliza all were self-sufficient in their duties, as was I, although I found myself needing to take over the running of the estate and the farms, even the business in Huddersfield, as Mr. Holmes became more and more dependent on the drink and less able to manage his financial affairs.

"You do it," were Mr. Holmes slurred words when I informed him that bills from tradesmen were overdue. As he languished in his study, he scribbled a note allowing me to write checks and pay bills, and that is simply how I fell into being steward of everything.

One other change occurred; after Master Sherlock left, Mrs. Winters no longer left food out for the little people.

When Mr. Holmes finally left his study, he and Mrs. Holmes packed a number of suitcases and departed from Hillcroft House. That was not too upsetting to me, for I was glad not to have to look upon his bloated visage, and I will admit that my compassion for the man was entirely gone, leaving a sourness in my stomach and a bitter taste in my mouth. He did not tell me where he and Mrs. Holmes were going.

One week after they were gone, about six weeks after Master Sherlock had left, Denkins brought me a letter, his face beaming with anticipation and joy. I gathered all the servants into the library and opened up the missive to read aloud. I confess my hands trembled as I removed the letter from the envelope. I have the letter here; it is the only one of all he sent that I still possess.

My Dear Brewster, and all my dear servants,

Forgive me my lapse in correspondence. All is well with me as I grow accustomed to this life of wandering. I shan't say where I am or plan to go, for fear of my father discovering this note, but be assured that I am still in England. I am one week from the postmark's locale, as a very accommodating innkeeper promised to post my letter for me seven days after I left his spartan although pleasant establishment. I do not stay in any one place too long. I enjoy the travelling and observing. Daisy keeps me company, and my books stimulate me. I sleep in fields, barns, and inns. Mrs. Winters, I get enough to eat, though no food as magnificent as yours.

I remain sincerely and gratefully yours,
Sherlock Holmes

It was not much, but the lad had never been one for effusive and lengthy correspondence, even with his brother. Yet just to know that he was alive and well
and adapting to his solitary journeying brought joy to each of us. I handed the letter around for everyone to read, and then hid it upstairs in my bedchamber in one
of my notebooks. All other letters I then locked in the trunk in my quarters; that
first missive, though, so dear to me, I wanted to be able to hold and cherish frequently, so I placed it in an early notebook. My notebooks I kept in an unlocked
drawer in my desk, and the ease of access to my frequent writing in the notebooks
was more convenient to me than a locked trunk. Mr. Holmes never entered the
rooms of his servants, so there was no risk of discovery.

Master Sherlock continued to write, though infrequently. A good many months
after, towards the end of the year, we received news from the lad that he had gained
employment as an actor with a travelling troupe. He did not at that time mention the
name of the troupe, and while he said he was using an alias in place of his true name,
he did not reveal that name to me. He still feared his father's discovery of him.

I was naturally surprised at his joining an acting troupe. Upon reflection, though,
I remembered one time when the famous Sam Wild's acting troupe had been in
Huddersfield—July of 1860, I see here in my notebook—and coincidentally Master Sherlock and his parents had been there for his father's business. Master Sherlock dragged his poor mother to the troupe's show, which was delightful for him,
but somewhat discomfitting for Mrs. Holmes, as those shows were usually popu-
lated by the lower classes, most often those of a disorderly nature. Master Sherlock
had no compunction about being in such company, given his friendships with the
village lads, but Mrs. Holmes, outside her charity work, was not normally found
in the association of somewhat rowdy masses. Nevertheless, her happiness at her
son's happiness, plus the fact that Mr. Wild gave them the best seats in the house,
away from the rabble a bit, ensured her enjoyment of the acting. Master Sherlock
acted out scenes from the plays for months afterwards, interspersed with his Shakespearean reading with his mother. After his quickly passing phase of wanting to be
an actor years and years ago, I never suspected he harbored a true desire to become
a thespian. Acting and chemistry, one must admit, are not exactly bed mates, yet I
recalled with a new insight his ruse of a bloody arm.

My life rotated around caring for the estate and waiting for the next letter from
Master Sherlock. Thus did the rest of the year pass and half the next. I noticed a
disturbing trend developing with the estate: an increasing number of bills due to
certain individuals, jewelry shops, clothing establishments, expensive hotels in
London—the Langham!—and other assorted establishments of what type I did
not know. When Mr. Holmes was home once, I asked him about such bills.

"Mrs. Holmes requires finery when we travel," he said. "I, too, have an image to uphold. It would not do for us to be seen in less than perfect attire or to be staying at hotels that lack a noteworthy reputation for service and wealthy clientele."

"Of course, sir," I replied. "But these other bills, one to a certain Mr. Cummins' establishment in London, one to a Mr. Fitzpatrick, one to a Mr. Bigelow, they are disturbingly large, sir, and I wonder how they should be listed in the account book."

Mr. Holmes gave me an even stare. "As poor investments."

I bowed to him. "As you say, sir." It was immediately clear to me; he was gambling, at disreputable gambling houses in London, perhaps at a club, and no doubt at the turf, for I had found tickets to several racetracks—York, Rippon, and even Ascot, way down in Berkshire—in his trousers after he returned home. I was greatly concerned at these expenditures, for his income could not keep up with bills such as these.

"Brewster," Mr. Holmes called to me once, as I passed the library one day in September of 1868. Mrs. Holmes was napping upstairs in the master bedroom.

"Sir?"

Corpulent and balding, yet wearing a fine Tweed suit, he stood at the unlit fireplace. "Have you heard anything from Sherlock?"

I was surprised by the blunt and unexpected question, and I felt a twinge of compassion for the man for his asking. Master Sherlock did not want me to mention his letters to his father, and had suggested that I claim ignorance about him if his father approached me for information. Yet this was not the spiteful anger of a man about to track down his son for punishment; this was the pitiful heartache of a father who had lost his whole family due to death and his own sinful excesses. Still, I was wary, for this concern could turn to ugliness in less sober moods. I would never do anything to put the lad in peril. I often wondered if I should just burn the letters he sent, but I delighted in removing them from the trunk every so often and rereading them. I formulated in my mind the best answer.

"I received a note last month, a few words, that is all. He is well. He wishes everyone well. He doubted he would write again." Some truths, some lies.

"Have you still the letter?"

"No, sir. I burned it as per Master Sherlock's request. I'm sorry, I did not realise you would be interested in seeing it, sir."

"Show me any other letters that arrive from Sherlock, Brewster. My orders rate higher than his." I could not discern clearly his motivation for wanting to see Master Sherlock's communications, and that made me fearful for the lad's sake.

"Of course, sir," I blatantly dissembled.

"Please leave me now," he said.

Mr. Holmes rarely asked about Master Sherlock after that—maybe three or four times a year—but each time he did, I told him I had no further news, and he became appallingly inebriated. As far as I know, Mr. Holmes never attempted to contact Master Mycroft or Mr. Hathoway about Master Sherlock. Noah and Denkins were perfect in their subterfuge; Mr. Holmes, examining all the letters that arrived at Hillcroft House, never caught them in their role as covert postmen. I began to include a shilling into the Cotter's weekly food sack.

Chapter Thirty-Two
The Fall of Hillcroft House

ometime towards the end of 1870, the finances of Mr. Holmes began taking a dreadful turn. He had been gambling away large amounts of money and continued the luxurious living that was clearly beyond his means. The bills continued to escalate, reaching a point where drastic action was needed to stave off impending financial ruin. A day after Mr. and Mrs. Holmes' return from another trip, I approached them in the drawing room after supper.

"Mr. Holmes, sir, I must speak to you about the financial situation of the estate," I began. "It is reaching a precarious state."

He laid aside his newspaper. Mrs. Holmes kept sipping her wine.

I had the account books with me and opened them up, bending over him to show him the drain on his savings that his travelling and expenditures were creating.

"Sir, if you will be so kind as to observe," I said, pointing to the entry columns in which I had carefully detailed all financial transactions, except for the money I had surreptitiously sent to Master Mycroft each Christmas under "farm repairs," who then relayed a portion of it to his younger brother. "You have, in the last two years, sir, spent upwards of 4,500 pounds annually on travelling and miscellaneous expenses, while the farms and estate have required another 900 pounds. With a yearly income from the farms and the firm in Huddersfield at 3,000 pounds, I have had to use your lessening savings to pay the bills, a debit of approximately 2,400 pounds each year. Your savings are now at only 6,000 pounds and cannot long withstand such continued excessive spending, sir, especially if the miscellaneous expenses increase."

"Is that true, David?" Mrs. Holmes asked. "And I so love our little trips. It is the only time I find you tolerable."

"Quiet, woman," he growled. I held in the shudder to which my contempt for the woman gave rise. For her and for drink, Mr. Holmes had driven his son away—it was substituting mud for milk and honey. I was dizzied by the confounding nature of human weakness.

He gave a cursory glance at the books, and turned a page or two without any true interest. "Very well, Brewster. That is all." He waved me away.

I took my leave, troubled by his dismissal and his apparent lack of interest over the accounting books and what they represented about the estate. I wrote to Master Mycroft for advice, and even though I burned his return letter, I remember his words: "Prepare for the worst. It appears inevitable. Do not worry yourself for my future inheritance; I have come to realise there shall be no such transference to myself or my brother. Take care of the servants; be generous towards them. Set aside monies for yourself and the rest; my father will soon begin letting them go, I believe. Place five hundred pounds in a London bank under my brother's stage name for him to claim upon his re-entrance into society." He then told me his brother's pseudonym.

I did as he wrote, putting aside £200 for us servants in a bank account under a false name, and placing £500 in Master Sherlock's alias account. I imagine that using the stage name on the account was designed to prevent any future creditors from tracking down the sons for monies owed to the creditors by Mr. Holmes. I also sent some money to Master Mycroft. At first I was apprehensive of being found out, but Mr. Holmes never even mentioned the books, let alone glanced through them, and I was able to hide those withdrawals in his travelling expenses, which he kept no track of, and in imaginary expenses of running the estate and the farms. It seemed to me, anyway, a far better thing to have the money go towards helping decent people than have it all wasted on despicable vices.

When the monies had been transferred, we all simply waited for the inevitable to occur.

We did not wait long, for Mr. Holmes' temper worsened noticeably with his continued drinking. His wife was no longer the sole outlet for his mercurial temperament. Finding an absurd and trivial mishap in the morning room one day in January 1871—the pillows on the sofa were not correctly placed—he fired Eliza on the spot, though he gave her a two-week notice. She was upset, but the fortnight's allowance was fortuitous, as I was able to calm her by writing Master Mycroft, who found a suitable situation for her in London through an acquaintance. I wrote her an excellent letter of recommendation, and had Mr. Holmes sign it unknowingly whilst he was intoxicated, which was shockingly devious of me. I gave Eliza her quarterly wages, plus an extra £10 to aid her relocation and to assuage her grief at leaving Mrs. Birchall, whom she looked upon as a second mother. Thus did we bid her a sad farewell. I felt compelled to dismiss Mrs. Winters' helper, Marianne, as such was the minimal nature of the cook's work, that I did not feel the extra cost of her helper was warranted any longer. Since she was a local girl who did not stay the night, I merely gave her wages for the month and a £5 bonus when I released her.

Denkins and the other outside workers were next, in February 1871, as Mr. Holmes dismissed him for not catching enough rabbits with his traps. "Wilcox can plant the garden," was his only additional comment, and that was that. I gave Denkins a letter of recommendation, too, signed in the same manner as Eliza's. He received double wages upon his leaving, as I gave him a very generous extra £40, for Master Mycroft was not able to secure him another position. His local helpers were each released with £5.

I questioned Master Mycroft about taking out a loan, with the estate as collateral, but he instructed me not to do so. "Investigate the selling of our shares in Vickerson's Mill. Proceed without my father's knowledge; I shall take responsibility for the sale." I wrote Mr. Vickerson as estate manager; he was pleased to hear from me, as Mr. Holmes had not been in contact with him for eight months. I explained the situation as delicately as possible, wanting to cast no aspersions on Mr. Holmes in my inquiries into the sale of his portion of the business. Mr. Vickerson was quite amenable to finding a buyer, or perhaps even buying the shares himself. He was very decent in writing about "Mr. Holmes' sad illness" and how he rued that events had taken "such an unfortunate turn." My respect for the man's delicacy was high, and I could only imagine that he had been aware of Mr. Holmes' drinking for quite a long time.

In May of 1871, unbeknownst to Mr. Holmes, Mr. Vickerson bought the shares himself for a nice sum. Mr. Holmes signed the contract to sell without knowing it. You may think it reprehensible to have repeatedly acted so deceptively, especially in regards to such an important matter, Mr. Cobbett, but there was no other way to stave off impending bankruptcy, for the Holmeses had continued to travel and spend money in an unbelievable manner. Besides, I had Master Mycroft's permission to proceed with such a justified action. I and Master Mycroft signed the contract as well, in case Mr. Holmes decided to contest the sale after I told him what we had done.

First, though, with that money, I sent more to Master Sherlock's incognito account, enough to see him through University and beyond if he lived frugally, and some more to Master Mycroft, who transferred his money also to his brother's account. Then I paid off the bills that had accumulated. Finally, I approached Mr. Holmes in the library, where he and his wife sat, drinking wine and singing rather opprobrious tavern songs. I cannot say whether I preferred that dubious entertainment to their arguments.

"Sir," I interrupted, as they finished one particularly offensive tune, "if I may have a moment." Mrs. Birchall and Mrs. Winters stood nearby in the hallway, fearful of Mr. Holmes' reaction to what I had to tell him. They had no need to worry; I had no intention of telling the truth.

"God, Brewster, what is it now?" he grumbled.

I entered the room and stood straight in front of him. "Sir, to pay off your accumulating bills, I was instructed by you to sell your share of Vickerson's Mill. This I did two weeks ago to Mr. Vickerson himself. You signed the contract; however, due to your…slight incapacity at the time, I just wanted to ensure you were cognizant of the fact of the sale. We were in great need of the funds, sir."

Mr. Holmes' brow knit together, and he put his whiskey glass down. "I told you to sell the business? I signed the contract? What are you talking about?"

I produced a copy of the contract—without either Master Mycroft's signature or my own—and showed him. "Dear me," I said, "I feared, sir, that you might not have remembered, given the fact that you and Mrs. Holmes spent a number of days incapacitated after the signing of the contract. Certainly, sir, I never would have proceeded in such a course of action without your full agreement. I went over the entire transaction with you at the time. However, as I was doing the accounts today, I did wonder if you had a recollection of it all, which is why I felt the need to bring it up now." What a ridiculous pack of lies it all was, and it was only Mr. Holmes' deteriorated condition that made the story believable.

"So we got more money to spend?" Mrs. Holmes asked, pouring whiskey into her already half-full glass.

My stomach contracted painfully. I did not favor her with a reply, but stood facing Mr. Holmes.

Upon my silence, he asked, "So, we have more money to spend?"

"Yes, sir. And as I stated, we will need the money to pay off bills, if they continue to arise as they have these last years."

His anger flared. "Damn the bills."

"Sir, it was imperative we pay a few bills, which I have already done. The rest of the funds have already been placed into your account." Mr. Vickerson had allowed us to put a smaller amount than he truly paid on the contract, so Mr. Holmes would not, if he checked the books, wonder where the amounts I had sent off to his sons had gone to. He never did check, but one could not be too cautious; which was why Master Mycroft had told me to talk to his father. Although Mr. Holmes had not been to Vickerson's for eight months, there was a chance he might return there; hence we needed for him to be aware that he was no longer a part of the mill.

Mr. Holmes swallowed a large amount of whiskey. Then he paused for a while. "Better to get out now before the market erodes, anyway," he stated somewhat glumly.

"Of course, sir."

"Let's go to London, David," Mrs. Holmes interjected. "Your luck is bound to turn around at your club. One can't lose at whist forever. And the racetrack, I do so love appearing there. And we rarely argue among the elite."

Mr. Holmes drank another glass, his face dark. Don't do it, I silently pleaded. "Brewster," he said, "you and Mrs. Birchall prepare our bags. We leave tomorrow for London." I left the library, and pains pierced my stomach as if I had swallowed shards of glass. They left the next day.

Oh, dear God, how they spent money! I have to assume that Mr. Holmes knew what he was doing to himself and the estate, that he was aware of the imminent ruin that quickly approached. I have to think that he wanted it to happen in some way, for how else to explain such financially destructive behavior? Was it some type of personal penance he had initiated, to punish himself by total ruination? Was it to punish his sons by assuring that no inheritance was left for them? Or had the alcohol so destroyed his rational mind that he had completely embraced a life of utter debauchery and irresponsibility, truly not caring about anything, his sons, his estate, his dignity? No one will ever know for sure.

It was a lonely house, as you can imagine, with just Mrs. Birchall, Mrs. Winters, and I, and Wilcox still living in his cottage. They kept as busy as they could, but I was driven to despair by my responsibilities. I began to dread the mail, for the bills never ceased, and I found myself falling into a rare melancholy that detracted greatly from my duties. Only another letter from Master Sherlock in October of 1871, relating his recent return to England from a travelling tour in America, and thanking me for my continued efforts on behalf of the estate, lifted my spirits and renewed my commitment to managing the remains of Hillcroft House. I showed the letter to the others, and saw smiles grace the faces where dourness had lately laid claim. To celebrate, we had mutton that night, and plum duff.

However, my bill-paying efforts were to no avail. The Holmeses maintained their expenditures, and by March of 1872 so many bills had fallen into arrears— one bill alone sent by Mr. Fitzpatrick's establishment was for £2,200 pounds— that there was just no money to pay them, and creditors had written, and then come to Hillcroft several times. With hopeful sincerity, I was able to acquire a few more months of time before legal proceedings would begin, and the house and furniture, the horses, the farms, everything would be sold. At this time the Holmeses arrived home for an increasingly rare visit.

I approached Mr. Holmes early the next morning in the library; Mrs. Holmes was still asleep upstairs. He looked frightful—unshaven, reddened eyes, wearing disheveled and dirty clothes, his collar and cravat undone. I believed he had stayed up all night, but it did not seem as if he had partaken of alcohol, for he was sober and without signs of suffering from the ill effects of previous overindulgence. He sat in a chair by the fireplace, doing nothing but staring into the flames. When he heard my footsteps, he glanced at me, and then turned back to the blaze.

"For God's sake, go away, Brewster," he said hoarsely.

"I cannot do that, sir. I must speak to you. In your absence, several creditors have appeared, demanding money that we do not have to give. I fear that they will take Hillcroft House from you, sir, and that there is nothing we can do."

Mr. Holmes sat like a statue and said nothing for a while. Then, as I prepared to exit the room he said something absolutely astonishing.

"Have a seat, Brewster, won't you? Pull up a chair next to me."

Once I felt that I had my legs under control again, I did so. For a moment, nostalgia threatened to overwhelm me as I fought back tears, remembering how in the not so distant past Mr. Holmes and I had shared many a casual conversation by a congenial fire in a warm and loving home.

We dwelt in silence for some time, the crackling of the flames the only noise. He sat without moving, his hands gripping the sides of the chair. He did not look at me, and what I saw of him I cannot say, his face wooden and neutral, his eyes directed at the flames, but with a blankness that made me doubt he was actually viewing it. I felt compelled at times to speak, but held my tongue, realizing the uselessness of any words.

Perhaps half an hour passed thusly, though it seemed much longer to me. He then spoke softly, a mere whisper, "Thank you, Brewster. For everything. You're a good man. I'm sorry..." He paused, and then simply repeated, "Thank you."

That's it, then, I thought, my stomach rebelling at the finality of his utterance. I said nothing, but arose and left, my eyes moistening at the sense of utter defeat that hung over Mr. Holmes, and for a moment, in his words, the touch of regret and remorse that seemed to permeate his words. Unlike Master Sherlock, I had never been able to conquer my tears.

Later that evening, they began arguing so loudly we heard it from the servants' quarters next to the kitchen, where Mrs. Winters, Mrs. Birchall, Wilcox, and I had been grimly sitting. I had shared with them my early morning experience with Mr. Holmes, and we had fallen to talking about the years when Master Sherlock had been a young lad, and all of life had been good and promising.

The yelling began right away at a fevered pitch. You might think, Mr. Cobbett, we should have become inured to it after so many altercations after so many years, but simple, gentle folk are always bothered by violence, whether by tongue or fist. However, with this row, there was a sense of terrible dread that clutched at our souls, and we were compelled to proceed into the morning room the better to hear the quarrel as it raged across the hallway in the library.

It was an appalling display of temper from both of them; crashes of china and knicknacks added to the hideous screaming. They cast blame, aspersions, and hatred upon each other, using grotesque vernacular and abhorrent curses. And then Mr. Holmes ended it in the way he had attempted to after Mrs. Fairburn died—he threw a lamp against the wall, then another against the opposite one, and flames broke out at once, spreading immediately to the curtains.

We four stood aghast at the scene, disbelieving what we saw. I am ashamed to admit that both Wilcox and Mrs. Winters were quicker to react than I, running into the library in a futile attempt to douse the flames with jacket and shawl. The sight they met with was incredible—Mr. and Mrs. Holmes still engaged in fervent acrimony, as flames grew in intensity and heat around them. One glimpse was enough to realise the house was lost, for it was a clear night of no rain, and it was all Wilcox and I could do to drag Mr. and Mrs. Holmes from the room.

I do not know if you have ever witnessed a fire attack a home, Mr. Cobbett, but let me tell you that nothing travels as fast as a fire in a house which contains rooms of old wood. The smoke and heat, combined with fear, were enough to drive Mrs. Birchall and Mrs. Winters quickly outside, for which I was grateful, as Wilcox and I continued our struggles with the Holmeses. After some minutes of futile pushing and pulling, during which, to my horror, Mr. Holmes deliberately broke another two lit lamps from the morning room, spreading the fire further, I decided I had better save what I could. I ran for the account books and other essential papers, and then darted around the house trying to collect anything of monetary or sentimental value: a few daguerreotypes, the cameo brooch of Mrs. Holmes, the last remaining pieces of silver, when suddenly my own possessions came to mind. My notebooks! The letters!

I ran up the main staircase to the second floor, with the fire spreading dangerously. By the time I made the second floor, there was smoke even up there. I ran first to Mrs. Winters' room and ripped her pillow from the pillowcase, putting what I had carried upstairs into the pillowcase. I threw in whatever I could ascertain were important and meaningful items from her room. I then went into Mrs. Birchall's bedroom and did the same, praying that the items I had chosen from both were what would best soothe their losses. By the time I entered my own chambers, the smoke was terrible, and I was finding it hard to see and breathe. I was quite terrified, I do not mind telling you, and swiftly opened my desk drawers and procured my notebooks, which I have used as constant reference in my telling of this long, involved, and sordid tale. I then knelt by the locked trunk. With shaking hands, I endeavoured to fit my key into the lock, but was unable to do so correctly. I drew back, and on a second, more forceful attempt, the key missed the lock again and sprang from my hand, landing under my bedside table. I began to hack deeply from the bad air, but went after the key. When I could not simply espy it under the table, and a rapid jumping of my hand all over the the floor did not discern the key, I had had enough. Panicking, yet tinged with deep regret, I left the room with the sack, consigning my trunk and the letters to their fiery fate. It was quite lucky, I suppose, that out of the habit of writing in my notebooks so frequently, I had felt it too much of a bother to lock them in the trunk, or they might very well also have been lost forever.

I ran down the servant's staircase, where the air was not yet quite so bad, and left the house through the greenhouse door. I ran around to the front of the house, and by that time I was quite gasping for air, with hacking coughs further debilitating me. The flames were now visible in all of the windows of the ground floor and a few of the first floor. Thick, dark smoke wafted upwards, darker than the night sky. I pushed myself to reach Mrs. Winters and Mrs. Birchall, who stood well back from the house, holding on to each other in shock and misery. Wilcox stood near them, breathing and coughing as I was, though covered with more grime.

When they saw me approach, the women began crying, and all three praised God. I dropped the sack, and we held each other for a moment, until I realised we were the only ones on the front lawn.

"Dear God," I implored Wilcox, grabbing his arms. "Where are Mr. and Mrs. Holmes?"

"I couldn't get them out," he cried, his words rushing out in a frenzy. "I dragged her out, but she followed me back in when I returned for Mr. Holmes. I tried again; I tried so hard, but they wouldn't come, they wouldn't come! They were still arguing, still fighting, with flames licking their clothes! It got so bad, Brewster, I had to leave them! I had to! They never did come out. God in Heaven, they never did come out."

I let go of him, and an all-encompassing numbness settled over my immobile body and my despairing mind. I stood watching the fire consume the house as Mr. Holmes had watched the coal fire earlier that very morning, my face wooden and neutral.

There is just a little bit more to finish up, Mr. Cobbett, and then my tale will have been fully told. I'm sure you can imagine the sight the burning house made, visible all the way to the village in its last flair of brightness. The village folk came in droves to assist, and when they saw they couldn't help, they stayed and watched, murmuring among themselves. I cannot say that any were glad for the tragedy, because for all his private miseries, Mr. Holmes had not caused problems in the village, outside of his lack of interaction with it in his old role of proper gentleman. The times he drank in the pubs were all the local folk saw of his darkened personality; in fact, the gifts to the Cotters were well known, even though Master Sherlock was no longer a playmate of the poor lads, and that was looked upon well by the villagers. Mrs. Winters' village helper, being confined in the kitchen all day and a very nice, simple girl, was not a font of gossip, and the £5 she and Denkins' helpers had received upon being let go was viewed very well by the village folk. Thus, the mood that claimed the gathering was a mixture of sympathy and solemnity, sadness and respect. For all humanity, I think, it strikes a lonesome chord when the end of an era appears, whether in an empire, or in a gentry family.

By morning the fire had burned itself out. The house was destroyed to its stone foundations. Wilcox had removed the terrified horses and the carriage and cart from the stables, well before the wind took the fire to that building as well. Somewhere along the way, coffee and blankets were brought, and Wilcox and I stood all night observing the conflagration. The women were taken to the Metcalfes' home, gratefully clutching their belongings I had saved. They were given a libation or two to settle them down, a prayer or two to comfort and strengthen them, and then put to bed.

In the early morning, I hired the wheelwright's eldest son to take the train north into Dunham and then rent a horse and ride for Bishop Auckland, the nearest telegram station to Carperby. I gave him a message to send to Master Mycroft at his office, notifying him of the tragedy. I then spent some time stepping carefully through the rubble, looking for any items that had escaped being consumed. I found a few small statuettes, several glasses, and some books, but my stomach began aching so badly I had to stop. Later that day I learned the constable had uncovered the bones of Mr. and Mrs. Holmes and had had them taken to the carpenter's for placement in coffins. I cannot tell you how thankful I am to God on high that I did not see the remains among the wreckage, that I was not there when the dreadful discovery was made.

Many people, including the Metcalfes, Mr. Routh, Mr. and Mrs. Cornelius Brown, the aged Mr. Irwin, and a score of village folk, offered food and drink, a bath, clean clothes, and a place to rest. I must have been a disturbing sight—wandering around aimlessly, filthy, weeping, pressing my notebooks to my chest tightly as if I wanted to absorb them into my body. Wilcox took Mr. Routh up on his generous offer to shelter the three horses temporarily, and then the poor man, guilt writ on his face, retired to his cottage for solitary grieving and sleep. Certainly no one blamed the man but he himself. How could they? In my explanation of events, I said that we had all been asleep when the fire had begun, perhaps in the library flue which was due for a cleaning. By the time we on the second floor were awakened by the black smoke and hurriedly dressed, grabbed a few personal items, and dashed down the servants' staircase, the ground and first floors were engulfed by fire. I sent Mrs. Winters for Wilcox, and we endeavoured to enter the house to aid Mr. and Mrs. Holmes, but the smoke and heat were too intense; we were driven back outside. We could only assume that the smoke had quickly suffocated the Holmeses and prevented their escape. It was all taken as the grim truth. How easily lies now fell from my once pure lips!

Very late that evening, the exhausted lad returned back from Dunham with a telegram from Master Mycroft, delivering it to me in the Fox and Hound in Carperby, where I had chosen to spend the night, graciously refusing the numerous kind offers of a bed from village and gentry folk alike. The telegram informed me that Masters Mycroft and Sherlock would be arriving the next evening. My stomach fluttered at the thought of seeing them again, especially Master Sherlock. Master Mycroft requested that I find them lodging in the inn at Askrigg; they were loath to socialize with any good-hearted neighbours at this black time. They also asked me to arrange for the burial of their father next to their dear departed mother in Aysgarth, and for Mrs. Holmes to be buried far from their parents' graves, and in her maiden name of Smythe. Upon reading the letter, I retired for the evening in my room. To my surprise, even with the excitement of seeing the lads, the appalling event of last night, and my chronic insomnia, I slept a number of hours. The next morning I arranged all of Master Mycroft's specifications at the church.

I met the lads at the Askrigg station that night. What a pair they made! Both very tall, over six feet, with fine black hair, and grey eyes that cut like a knife. The elder lad, only twenty-four, was already two stone overweight. Master Sherlock, not quite eighteen, flashing me a quick smile and proffering me his hand—while Master Mycroft stood still with his hands clasped behind his back—was probably almost two stone underweight, and he moved easily, with a quickness and grace Master Mycroft would never exhibit. Master Sherlock had a surprisingly powerful grip, and I realised that for all his thinness he had developed an athletic build and strength. I was deeply affected by their appearance, and I fear my emotions got the best of me.

"Master Mycroft, Master Sherlock, I'm so glad to see you," I remarked, fighting back tears. "I'm awfully sorry about what happened."

"As are we all, Brewster," Master Sherlock replied.

Master Mycroft "Hmmff'd," and then turned his attention to perusing the few people who were at the station.

"I have arranged rooms for you at the George and Dragon, as you desired, although that was quite unsatisfactory to a number of your parents' old friends, who were more than willing to put you up."

"The inn shall suffice very well, Brewster," Master Sherlock said. "We are not of a mood for company."

Master Mycroft looked bored at those words, while Master Sherlock's eyes betrayed a hint of softness. It made me light with joy. The lads were of a much more similar mold now, I could perceive, though I knew the younger lad had not lost all his sensibilities.

We began to walk to the inn. I continued to speak. "The church arrangements are also made. Father Metcalf thought of having the funeral the day after tomorrow."

Master Sherlock answered. "We do not want a funeral. A private gathering at the grave will do, with us, Father Metcalfe, and the servants, if you all wish to attend."

"Of course we wish to attend, sir. The others are wholly anticipating seeing you again. Your letters were the one thing that made the house bearable these long years."

There was a pause. "I look forward to seeing them again, too, Brewster."

For some reason, I needed to fill the night air with discourse. "Do you still act, Master Sherlock?" I asked.

"No. I am to go to University in the autumn."

"It is a regret of mine that I never saw you perform. What shall you study at University? Chemistry?"

Master Sherlock took in a deep breath. "I have not really made up my mind yet."

"Well, I know you will excel at any subject matter. And you, Master Mycroft, how goes your government work?"

"It progresses adequately along the line I had planned for my advancement," the elder lad said.

"Oh." I imagined he had figured out to the hour, minute, and second when he would attain the position he strove for, whatever it was; who he would be with when he was awarded it; what the weather would be like that day; and what he would have had for breakfast.

I gathered my courage to speak again. "The story I related to the villagers and your old family friends, which they may make reference to, of how the fire began, was entirely false. If you would like, I shall tell you the facts, although you will not be happier for them."

Master Mycroft "Hmmf'd" again. "No doubt father burnt the house down himself, and refused to leave it as it was consumed by flames. Probably his odious wife was too busy screaming at him to save herself."

I could not resist the temptation. "Is that a guess, Master Mycroft?"

I saw a brief grin raise Master Sherlock's lips, then they returned to even level.

"Certainly not," Master Mycroft said curtly. "It is a valid conjecture given the vices and personalities of my father and his wife, and extrapolating from their behavior of the last several years."

"Well, it is correct," I admitted softly, once again stunned at his callous recital of his thoughts. "Mr. and Mrs. Holmes were engaged in a vile quarrel when he threw lighted lamps, at first in irrational anger, and then for purely destructive purposes. Wilcox, who endeavoured to drag them to safety, says they were arguing as he fled the house, and no doubt until their deaths."

The lads said nothing. I went on as we neared the inn. "I was able to save the account books, some other papers, some daguerreotypes, and assorted household items." I looked up into the night sky and hoped the plenitude of stars foretold a better life for Mr. and Mrs. Holmes. "I really am extremely sorry," I said, again.

"There is no need to be," Master Mycroft replied.

The lads met with the other servants; they saw Father Metcalfe and his wife, Mr. Routh, the Browns, and Mr. Irwin; they stood silently together at the graveside ceremony; and they met with creditors about signing over the estate lands and the farms. They visited the burnt ruin of Hillcroft House, to which Master Mycroft gave all of ten minutes of his attention before taking the carriage back to town, while Master Sherlock spent half a day there, wandering through the house and across the grounds, before walking back to Askrigg.

I think he briefly stopped in at Noah Cotter's hovel in Carperby, for he mentioned to me that his old friend had already married a girl from Aysgarth and she was with child.

"Thus doors to the past shut one by one, Brewster, until the last one is closed and locked forever," he said, as we sat in his room at the inn talking after supper. We had spoken of Mr. Hathoway, who was caretaker for an elderly woman in Bristol, and a little of Master Sherlock's acting career.

"Yes, but it must be exciting for you to have new doors opening up in your future, Master Sherlock," I said.

His eyes drifted off into deep thought and his lips moved into a pensive smile. "Indeed," he said softly, leaning back in his chair and glancing out the window into the dark night. Only then did I realise the poor lad had not expurgated his depressive tendencies in his vagabond years of acting. Mr. Irwin was right, I knew now—the lad would struggle with his melancholia for life. I only prayed that somehow his life would become so fulfilling to him, and so stimulating to his mind, that he would find himself too busy and cerebral to languish for long in his neurasthenic moods.

He realised he had betrayed himself to me, so pulled himself away from the window and changed the subject. "So, Brewster, you are a free man now. Will you seek gainful employment again, or retire?"

"I will retire, Master Sherlock. After all, I am almost sixty. I have saved a good portion of my wages over the years, and the hundred pounds you and your brother have given me is beyond generous." They had also given Mrs. Winters, Mrs. Birchall, and Mr. Wilcox £50 each, which meant that they had taken from their own funds for some of it, as I had only set aside £200 for us. "I will settle here in Carperby, I think, for it is a pleasing community to me, and I am comfortable here. There is a house available at the edge of town which I shall probably purchase."

"If you ever need anything..." the lad said, his pupils fixed upon me, "you have but to call."

I felt tears once more well in my eyes. "I've said it before, and I'll say it again, sir. It was my honor to butler to you and your brother. What happened in your home was terrible, and I tender my supplications nightly, asking that you and Master Mycroft may live long, fruitful lives."

Master Sherlock turned his head to the window again, and the room was silent for a moment.

"Good-bye, Brewster. I wish you well," he said, and I left, not insulted by his short words, but understanding that his apparent offhand and curt manner masked emotions he kept in tight rein.

"Good night, sir, and God bless you both," I said at the door.

"And you, my dear friend," he responded.

By the end of the week the lads were gone, Wilcox had gone to another position that Master Mycroft had found for him in Cornwall, Mrs. Birchall and Mrs. Winters left together for Selby to live in Mrs. Birchall's spinster sister's house, and I bought the house you found me in, where I have lived ever since in the shadow of the ruin once known at Hillcroft House.

And now my tale is done.

Chapter Thirty-Three
Brewster's Recital Ends

ou see," Mr. Brewster said, his eyes burning in the vividness of his recollection, his face wrinkled and thoughtful, "I told you the finale would be short."

"Short, and utterly dreadful," I said.

"You may think me cold-hearted, but I feel it was all for the better. What would have happened otherwise? Mr. Holmes would have lost the house and estate, and wound up where? Perhaps the fire was for the best. At least it was all over for the lads, and their lives were now fully their own."

"So, are you of the opinion that Mr. Holmes caused the fire premeditatively? To save face in the looming threat of bankruptcy? Do you also believe he therefore committed suicide rather than face the disgrace of poverty?"

Mr. Brewster observed his clasped hands as he spoke in a whisper. "Yes, I believe so."

I sat back and ran my hand through my hair, then took a very deep breath, and let all the words I had written over the past weeks settle in my mind as I exhaled.

"Incredible," I said, aware that nothing I could say would capture fully my feelings. "Your interesting tale certainly explains some of the mysterious and inexplicable aspects of Sherlock Holmes that we encountered in the stories told by Dr. Watson. His complete reticence in mentioning his origins, for one. His aversion to women another. His love of chemistry and the violin. His history of theatrics. Good God, the public will stand in lines to buy this biography."

Mr. Brewster grew concerned. "You must swear to me that you will not change or modify my words in any way, not at all. For only then shall I rest knowing that Sherlock Holmes will be presented in the manner in which I have attempted to portray him."

I laid my hand upon the arm of the butler. "You have my sworn assurance, sir, that no tampering with your words will occur. They stand firmly upon your excellent presentation, and I strongly feel there is no improving upon them. I promise you that my newspaper will release them de facto in serial form, preserving Sherlock Holmes' image for the best."

Then this most commendable and noble man's eyes misted. "I never did get my emotions under control," he stated, as he reached for his handkerchief.

"Did you ever see the lads again?" I asked.

"Master Mycroft, never. Master Sherlock, just once. That last visit for their father's funeral was our complete break. Oh, it was not for the fact that the lads were uncaring; I think they just needed to sever themselves totally from their past and from Carperby. I do not begrudge them that need, for actually, I relished a calm, new life with no piercing grey eyes that set my hair on edge. Carperby and the northern dales were and still are lovely to me, especially without the pressures of living with Mr. Holmes. Living among the simple folk in the country has enabled my poor stomach to be pain free ever since. It's a wonder I never died of an ulcer all those years! My affection for the lads never dimmed, mind you, but I realised that with the burning of Hillcroft House, I could shed my old life and become a new person.

You may think that it is hard for a butler to give up his routine of running a household, especially after a lifetime of committed service, but after all I had been through at Hillcroft, it was not so difficult for me. Through the post, I stayed in touch with Mrs. Winters and Mrs. Birchall in Selby, for we had developed a deep friendship over the years; like soldiers developing comradeship during a war, I imagine. I also maintained contact with Mr. Hathoway by letter. He was shocked, naturally, at learning of the demise of Hillcroft. And I had my acquaintances in Bridlington to whom I paid visits. But really, it was wonderful for me to have only myself to care for, and a simple life to live. One by one, however, all the players in this drama I've told have passed away. I last saw Master Sherlock at Mr. Hathoway's funeral. Then strange men came to my door, and poor Noah Cotter became an embittered man. About the time that the allure of my solitary life began to falter and I felt loneliness increase, Harry appeared, and once more I was happy and content. I delighted in learning that Master Sherlock was developing fame for his work against crime, and avidly followed the stories his friend Dr. Watson wrote. I never sought to contact him; I felt he would wish to let sleeping dogs lie. But as the years passed, I began to question my continued reticence in revealing his child-hood years. You know the rest of my life since then."

"Indeed, and what a life you have lived," I marvelled. "I must say, Mr. Brewster, my admiration and respect for your committed, tolerant, and loyal service to the Holmes family overwhelms me. I believe that if the world had more such men as you, certainly we would be a thousand steps closer to achieving a paradise on earth. In all ways your character shines above the darkness you have related these last weeks, and I can honestly say I feel uncommonly lucky to have made your acquaintance, not just for my biography, but for meeting such a unique and commendable man as yourself."

I prayed he could hear the sincerity in my tone, and see it on my countenance, for my feelings were real, and I needed this man to know that I sang his praises solely to acknowledge him, and not for what he had done for me. I believe he fully understood, for he reached for his handkerchief again.

We were done, the Brewsters and I. Percy Brewster's story had been told, and it remained for me to fill in the missing years of acting to complete my biography of Sherlock Holmes, but that would take a whole new investigation to uncover. We had finished in the late morning of the third day with his recollections of life at Hillcroft after Sherlock Holmes left—the aged man could only speak for a couple of hours at a time without needing a rest. Harry and I left the room to enable Mr. Brewster to sleep, and we planned a grand supper that night at a well known local restaurant to celebrate our success. The Brewsters would be returning to Carperby the next day. I assured Harry that before any publication occurred, a contract would be written, detailing the percentage of sales his uncle would receive. We shook hands on it and with that I excused myself, for I felt the need for solitude.

I went back to my room and decided to telegraph my editors again. I left my notebooks at first on my bed, but then some nagging intuition had me hand them to the desk clerk on the ground floor to place in the hotel safe. After all, lightning could strike the building and start a fire, or someone could throw a lighted lamp; I wanted those notebooks protected from acts of God and thieves. I doubted Mr. Brewster would have the strength to repeat all his recollections, nor did I wish to transcribe them once more.

I strode about town for a while, stopping at a telegraph office a good way from the hotel.

BUTLER'S STORY NOW COMPLETE. STOP. WILL SELL LIKE HOT-CAKES. STOP. NO NEED FOR REPLY. STOP.

I had my luncheon at a French restaurant, perhaps overindulged in the claret, and spent another two hours walking in the cold air, a gaiety suffusing my carriage so that it seemed I fairly bounced along the street. I knew I had struck literary gold with these memoirs, and I imagined the queues of people lining up to buy the special newspaper installments of the biography stretching for a whole block wherever a newstand stood, my name forming on everyone's lips. Perhaps I would give speeches to students, or to the general public, on how I attacked the problem of finding Holmes' past. No doubt, I realised, having his father become so famous could only aide my son's advancement in his accounting firm. My two daughters would weep from their high regard of me; all the grandchildren would be swelled with pride. With the money I earned I would pay for Wiggins to be formally educated, and I would deliver weekly sacks of food to his family in Aldgate. And Eleanor, dear Eleanor, would I see her face awash with love and approval, hanging over the edge of a cloud in the sky? At that one moment in Richmond no doubts about Holmes and my decision to proceed as planned ate my conscience like acid, no worries sent me into a frenzy of waistcoat pulling, no doubts of morals and ethics agitated my soul. Everything was right—the investigation was right, the biography was right, my imagined rewards were right. I floated down the street.

I returned to the hotel and spent the afternoon reading, slumbering a little, and fantasizing further about the pleasant consequences destined to occur after the publication of Holmes' biography.

Supper that night with the Brewsters added to my alcohol intake for the day but was fully enjoyable nonetheless. The three of us were quite tired and ready to leave Richmond. We lifted many a glass of wine in numerous toasts, thanked each other profusely, and wished each other well. Then we were riding back to the hotel, laughing with joy at the near future, shaking hands in the hallway by our bed-chambers, and saying good night.

I spent some little time looking out my hotel window before preparing myself for sleep. The night sky was clear, and I could see a few stars even over the lights of the gas lamps in the city. It was a peaceful sky, heavenly in its reflection of serenity, and it tendered a soothing respite to us worldly denizens below still struggling to live day by day. My life had been one of steady work, a dreamless life, with ancient goals long since met and none ever created to replace them. Yet in two weeks everything had changed. My life had a purpose now, to share this child-hood history of Holmes with a world still grieving his death, showing them the truly pure heart he contained, and that would only enhance his image in the eyes of his mourners. And I, who had lived in agreeable obscurity, now looked forward to living in agreeable fame.

I undressed and slid under the covers of my bed. I dreamed of a chemistry lab-oratory that had a waterfall dripping down the back wall, where Holmes and I boiled innumerable beakers of coloured fluids while we discussed the meaning of life.

Epilogue

here is very little more to tell as I write this last entry, except to explain how all my dreams of fame have been crushed by the man who has been behind all the intrigue in this tale—Mycroft Holmes. I am not surprised that a man so high up in the government of our country, so valuable to its operation, so respected by all our officials, would be able to dictate the terms he has to me with the utter confidence that his orders will be followed. After all, it has been made very clear to me that Mycroft Holmes *is* the government.

It is a short narrative; I have not the heart to belabor the events that occurred when I returned to London from Richmond. I was met leaving the train by two large men, perfectly attired as gentleman, with fine overcoats, top hats, and gloves, yet both upheld a menacing quality about them that made me wary, and, I admit, a little afraid. They requested I follow them, assuring me my luggage would be kept in storage until I returned to claim the bags. Before I could even begin a protest, one of my arms was grabbed, forcefully but not painfully, and I was led out of the station by the taller of the two; the other man, to my utter dismay, grabbed from my clutches my briefcase which contained Percy Brewster's transcribed remembrances.

I was about to cry for help, when the one holding my arm whispered in my ear, "Come along quietly; you won't be harmed. If you make a scene it will just go worse for you."

What could I do? The man with my case was a few steps in front, heading toward a cab. I decided to stay with that case, even if meant I must be kidnapped by these mysterious men. Thus I allowed myself to be pushed inside the four-wheeler, one man beside me, one facing me. Quiet as clams, they both sat stiff and formal during our drive through the city; the blinds were up, so I was able to watch our progression from street to street, until we wound up in Pall Mall stopping at the Diogenes Club, second home to Mycroft Holmes. A premonition of doom ran tingling down my body, and my breath suddenly seemed remiss in bringing enough air into my lungs.

"Come on, don't dally," I was told, as the men waited outside the cab for me to descend.

I didn't want to go. I was desperate not to go. But, hiding my dismay, I climbed down onto the pavement and, garnering all the dignity I was able to muster, I strode to the entrance following a nod toward the door from one of the men. I knew where we were going, so once inside I climbed the stairs to the floor containing Mycroft's roomy, bookshelf-lined office, with a large window behind his desk that looked out onto the street.

One of the men opened the door and waved me inside. The other, with the case, came in after me, depositing the case on Mycroft's desk, as the elder Holmes stood behind it. After Mycroft said, "Well done," while still maintaining his view out the window, both of the men took their silent leave. A brief thought of grabbing my case and running out the door, down into the street, then hopping a cab to my office, flitted through my head. I was not, in general, an active, adventurous man; but this—this was my life, my dreams. Mycroft, obese and slow, could never stop me. I inched a foot toward the desk.

"Don't try it," Mycroft said, not even glancing at me. "Those two men are standing outside the door in the hallway. I could never stop you, but they surely would."

I froze, all thought evaporating from my head. It was uncanny. He was uncanny.

Mycroft pointed out the window. "Look at that man over there," he said, pointing down to the street. I could not see him from where I stood, in the middle of the room, so, having no reason not to go to him other than juvenile petulance, I exhaled deeply to calm myself and strode behind the desk. There was a man, thin, walking hunched over against the slightly windy day, his arms wrapped in front of his chest, a thick scarf around his neck. "He has tuberculosis," Mycroft added.

I narrowed my eye and saw the man coughing into his hand, which held a handkerchief.

"Notice the extra handkerchief protruding from his coat pocket," Mycroft said, and I did. "Do you observe the other signs? It's a fairly easy illness to deduce."

I stared at Mycroft as he stood there, his thick hands hanging by his sides, his watery grey eyes darting back and forth, up and down the street in avid concentration, observing, analyzing everyone and everything he espied. His jowls and his fine, thinning hair aged him, belying the fact that he was not even fifty years old. I suddenly sensed how this game was to be played and I spoke as I imagined I had been led to do.

"You diagnosed Robert Sherlock with tuberculosis when you were but a child," I said.

He turned then, and looked at me, his eyes drifting off into memory and contemplation. "Yes, yes, I did, didn't I?"

"You didn't want to, but your father ordered you to."

A small smile came to his lips and he pushed off from the window. "Shall we sit down by the fire? It's cold by the window." He crossed to the sofa and chairs positioned by the roaring flames of the fireplace and plopped heavily into a thickly padded chair. I followed slowly after him.

"Take off your coat. It's warm over here," he said, motioning to the fire.

It was warm, and I took off my outer garments, placing them on the sofa. Then I decided to put him on the spot as best I could.

"Why did you bring me here? You had no right to," I accused, sitting down gently on the matching chair facing him.

"I had some right. After all, it is my family's history that you wish to publish," Mycroft stated, leaning his corpulent form back in the chair.

"How did you know that?" I asked.

"I've had you followed since you spoke to me," he said, plainly, reaching for a cigar from a box by his side. "I know everything." He held one out to me. "Cigar?"

My body seemed transformed into bronze, immobile, cast into a statue of myself there on the chair. I couldn't move and my thoughts struggled for expression. "You had me followed? You know everything?" I repeated lamely.

"Yes. You see, Mr. Cobbett, I am not a public man. I dislike people, to tell you the truth; they bore me terribly. I don't like to mingle with them, or have them show any interest in me. I have my life set into a firm routine of work, club, and home, and I enjoy being left alone to follow it. I thrive on a hermit's life lived in the largest city in the world. It is enough I have to put up with some of the dim-witted state officials I am obliged to mix with regularly; to be put in front of the unobserving public's eye is complete anathema to me. My brother shares many of those similar attributes, although his little consulting practice has thrived on Dr. Watson's printed recreations of some of his cases. Therefore—"

Suddenly I comprehended exactly what he had just said. "*Shares* many of the same attributes? Your brother *shares* them? Not *shared*, but *shares*?"

Mr. Holmes took a few puffs from his lit cigar. "Very good, Mr. Cobbett, very good. Yes, *shares.*" He nodded his head once for emphasis.

"But what about the events at the Reichenbach Falls? What about Professor Moriarty? What about 'The Final Problem'? Didn't he die as Dr. Watson wrote? As he believes?"

"No, he did not."

My voice rose loudly. "How can you keep that a secret?"

"The truth will out some day, I'm sure, Mr. Cobbett, but for now let me just say that my brother is indeed alive. I know him well enough to state that he does not wish to return to London to face the publication of his childhood years."

I was stunned speechless and slouched back on my chair, too weak to maintain my posture. Mycroft Holmes smoked his cigar and waited for me to recover.

"He will return to London?" I whispered.

"At some point in the future."

"I don't believe it," I mumbled.

"It's quite true. Neither of us ever welcomed any search into, or discovery of, our past, for the obvious reasons of which you are now aware. That is why I had all mention of us removed from the student lists of the schools we attended, and why I even had the pages noting our births removed from the birth registry in

Askrigg. And that is why I instituted the pact with the village folk, to keep them from ever gossiping about our family to others who might attempt to publish that sought-after information."

My mind raced with all this information. "You had Noah Cotter put in gaol!" I said, pointing my finger at him in recrimination.

"Yes, he was placed in gaol just long enough for the village folk to be notified of his imprisonment. Then I told him he had two choices: he could be sent to Canada, where he would be given a good job and, if he never mentioned my family again, he would stay a free man; or he could continue to languish in gaol where his silence would be forcefully guaranteed and where everyone would believe him to be, anyway. I assured him that his family would be cared for no matter which path he followed, and indeed they have been. He opted for Canada and self-imposed silence."

"Does your brother Sherlock know what you did to Noah? That you tore him apart from his family?"

Mycroft narrowed his eyes at me, until they were small beads in his fleshy face. "No." And then he added, quietly, "Noah had become a drunken brute himself, you know."

I had a thousand and one questions to ask him, but foremost was, of course, my own fate. "And me, what do you plan to do with me? Put me in gaol, too?"

"Certainly not. I'm merely going to prevent you from publishing Brewster's story."

Anger swelled in me, a rare emotion, and I sat up straight in my chair. "What gives you the right to do that?"

"I have claimed the right."

"You can't just do what you wish to at any given time. That story is a valid biography and the laws of this nation allow me to publish it."

"Mr. Cobbett, surely you must know by now. *I* am this country."

A chill filled my bones. I saw the hopelessness of my situation as if it were painted on the walls.

"Neither I nor Sherlock want anyone to know of our problematic past and our alcoholic father. Nor does Sherlock want his daily life as a child paraded around for all to read and discuss. I am impressed that you tracked down Percy Brewster; it does you much credit as a reporter. However, the tale goes no further than that case in which it sits."

A lingering flame of ire enabled me to shoot one more spark into the air between us. "My editor knows about the story, as do others on the newspaper staff. You can't keep them all quiet."

"Of course I can. I have already handled them; they are committed to silence. No one wishes to have trouble enter his life, Mr. Cobbett. At least not the sort of trouble I am capable of providing."

In my head I watched my dreams of fame dissolve away like a small puddle in a desert. Innumerable questions about their childhood, about how Mycroft had followed me, how he had erased the Holmes brothers from their school rolls, how he had arranged everything, seemed unnecessary now. I felt a great lethargy overcome me, and I barely had the energy to ask the most important question of all. "So, what happens next? What happens to me?"

Mycroft put out his cigar in the glass ashtray on the table beside him. "Simply, you lock up the story in a trunk and go about living your life as if this episode never happened. You never mention it to anyone. You forget everything you heard in our little meeting today. If you attempt to publish the story or speak about our past, you will—disappear, as did Noah Cotter, and you won't be seen again. Your children and grandchildren would not like that, I daresay."

I grew confused, and skipped over the threat of gaol or deportation. "Lock up the story in a trunk? You mean, you aren't going to take it away from me? Burn it up?"

Mycroft clasped his hands together over his bulbous stomach. "No. When Sherlock and I have died, do what you will with the story. Neither of us will care if others know our past then." He smiled. "Just please don't try to kill us prematurely."

I could think of nothing to say.

"You see, I am not as odious a man as you first thought. I have my morals, as Sherlock does. My brother helps people, in his own, trivial way; meanwhile, I am helping the country. That story would seriously impair both our abilities to do our jobs. I simply won't allow it."

I risked a comment. "It would also seriously impair your brother's mood, and you won't allow that, either, will you?"

I wondered what he would answer; would he say anything, or plainly ignore my pointed inquiry? Mycroft stared at me until I felt the hairs in back of my neck stand on end, and I pulled down my waistcoat as I broke eye contact first. Then a few words reached my ears.

"No," Mycroft said, "I won't." He stood up then, as suddenly as he could move his mass, grunting as he pushed himself out of the chair using his arms and legs. "So, we understand each other, Mr. Cobbett?"

He wasn't holding out his hand to shake. I stood up as tall and proud as I could and replied, "Yes."

"Good. Then please take your case and go. I have work to do."

My future was over that curtly. I left, returned to the train station for my luggage, went home and unpacked, putting the whole case in a trunk in my attic. I then went to my office, not believing that the impossible had happened, that the ideals of the freedom of the press had been waylaid by one obese man unknown to the country, who indeed *was* the country. I spent very little time in the office;

no one would look me in the eye, including my editor. Seeing the truth of Mycroft's statement, I considered resigning there on the spot, but held myself back from that rash action. I could see myself sitting at home without a job, staring out the window for days at a time, a book lying ignored on my lap. It was a haunting image, and I held my tongue as I turned and left the office.

The next day, I went to my solicitor and added a codicil to my will saying that the case in the trunk was not to be opened until both Mycroft and Sherlock Holmes had passed away. I then wrote a letter to Harry and Percy Brewster, stating that due to unavoidable difficulties, the story could not be published for some time to come, adding that it would be a very good idea to maintain their silence regarding what they knew of Sherlock Holmes and his family. I felt like a despicable traitor sending that letter off, and it took a week for my appetite to return. Imagine my surprise when a missive came from Percy Brewster not long after, telling me he understood, that they would comply, that he was not really much surprised at the outcome. Then he wished me well. I do not believe I have ever met a more saintly man than he.

I have reached a certain little peace with this whole series of adventures. I am empty of anger and of disappointment, though when it occasionally comes to mind that those years of Sherlock Holmes travelling with an acting troupe will probably never be uncovered, I grow a bit saddened, for I am sure it is as amazing a tale as this one told by Percy Brewster. Searching out that story of Holmes' adolescence is something that I would have done with relish, but I realize the futility of such an investigation if its fruits wind up merely sitting in a trunk in my attic. I maintain my crime reporting in London, though work a bit less, spending more time with my own children and grandchildren, committed to leaving them with a wholly different tale of me to share among themselves and my family's future generations than what Mr. David Holmes left for his progeny to record. And, in some way, I am relieved that Wiggins will never have cause to regret trusting me with his fond memories of Sherlock Holmes, which led me to discovering the roots of the man. Though publishing that biography would have brought me fame, I now can admit it would have shamed that masterful detective, who in his lifetime deserved better than to see his childhood dragged through the mud in front of all of London and the world.

I took the time to write out the whole story in clear English, as Mycroft Holmes did not say that doing so was forbidden. I will now wrap this little epilogue and the completed version in protective paper and then in a cover of leather before putting it back in the case, and replacing the case in the trunk. I do hope that one day this remarkable tale becomes known to the public, even if I, like the genius Holmes brothers, am not around when that occurs.